PETROCELLI

by John Rachel

Published by
Literary Vagabond Books
Los Angeles • Osaka
literaryvagabond.com

LITERARY   VAGABOND

Petrocelli
Copyright © 2015
by John D Rachel

Print Book ISBN #978-0-692-56684-8

Cover Art by Timothy Rankin

Table of Contents

Acknowledgements

Special appreciation goes out to Justin Beardsell for helping me bridge enormous generation gaps and connecting me with contemporary youth culture. Also to Ryan Paul Burke and Max Coldham Brewer for bringing me up to speed on currently popular traditional and designer recreational drugs.

As has become my heartfelt custom, I want to thank my best friend and wife, Masumi Nishida, for her encouragement and faith in me, and her magnificent ongoing role as my teacher and guide in discovering the wonders of Japan and Japanese culture, despite my resistance to achieving even a rudimentary grasp of the Japanese language.

Lastly, for their belief in me and their unwavering enthusiasm, thanks and butterfly kisses go out to my unapologetic publisher Literary Vagabond Books, specifically the svelte and droll head of that organization, Sybil Fairbanks, and my new editor there, Patrice Morgenthaal. Both of you are studies in and witness to the irrepressible power of the human imagination.

Note from the Author

Various authoritative articles and news stories, and the widely reported protests against the use of child and forced labor by prominent American corporations or their direct suppliers — the Gap, Nike, Levi-Strauss, Wal-Mart, Phillips-Van Heusen, Hanes, J.C. Penney, Firestone, to name a few — had years ago piqued my awareness and concern about widespread practices related to trafficking. But it was the time I spent during 2007 living in Africa, Thailand, Laos, and Cambodia which really codified my understanding of the flesh trade for both sweatshops and the sex service industry. It is currently estimated that human trafficking is annually a 36 billion dollar business worldwide. I have also read there are more than 25 million people in the world kept in bondage as slaves. I fear this is a low figure.

A non-fiction book I read while in Thailand called *Sex Slaves* by Louise Brown (© Copyright June 1, 2001: Vurago UK) became the central inspiration for this novel. It elucidates in excruciating detail what countless young girls (and boys) must endure as they are bought and sold in the ever-expanding global market for young prostitutes. This relatively brief but powerful book prompted the extensive research on my part into human trafficking, which became the factual underpinning for my story.

Though *Petrocelli* is entirely fictional, shortly after I finished writing it, I started to see more and more articles appear on credible online news services (e.g. mainstream sites such as bbc.co.uk and cnn.com) which paralleled my story line. These reports both confirmed the accuracy of much of what I describe in the book and illustrate the expanding scope of these criminal and abusive enterprises.

While there is no shortage of crises these days, human trafficking is emblematic of a sickness that is spreading throughout the world. It is a horrible and heartbreaking indictment of our lack of progress in many areas of human rights and one that goes to the core of pandemic contemporary amorality. Many thought we'd be doing better by now. Of course, that's just me talking and I am interested in what you have to say. Please feel free to email me your comments … john@jdrachel.com … though I am not accepting death threats or proposals of marriage at this time. You can be brutally frank, though understandably I would prefer you to be brutally kind.

Also feel free to visit my personal web and blog site: http://jdrachel.com.

Chapter 1

BROOKLYN, 2005 ... Not A Nice Place To Visit
And I Wouldn't Want To Live There

Sutter Avenue

"Wudja look at that! She can't be twelve years old."

"She's a little fucking gook. Who can tell?"

Hot turquoise micro-mini. Black top with a silver playbunny logo. Long straight black hair sweeping provocatively over half of her face and caressing her back. Purple lipstick and silver-glitter eye-shadow. Shiny ribbon necklaces, bracelets, hoop earrings, and a tiny white vinyl purse. A glitzy little china doll. Ninety-five pounds soaking wet. Getting into a stretch Hummer limo.

"What I'd like to know is ... what kinda man wants to fuck that?"

Shawna, a plus-size black who was a regular fixture here on Sutter Avenue, jumped off the curb, turned her backside to the limo pulling away, and theatrically grabbed her big ass. "Here some cushion for the pushin' when you're done with the scarecrow, mothafucka!"

Lilly, her best friend and nightly co-worker here on Brooklyn's unofficial but regularly patronized meat street, burst out laughing.

"Sistah Shawnee ... you ... you are insanious!!"

"This is shit. Monday night. What the fuck are we doin' out here? One hoonie and he goes for that sushi shit. Man, this ain't worth it. I'm goin' home."

"I hear ya. Believe me, I hear ya. But I ain't got a choice. Either I bring something home or there's one severe ass-kickin' with my name on it."

"Lilly, Lilly. How I love ya, girl! You my favorite sis. Tomorrow witcha. Same ole same ole!"

Tony's Place

The alley seemed unusually quiet. Walking up to Tony's, he noticed the neon sign was not lit. But the door was open and there was Tony behind the bar, business as usual. Nirvana's *Lithium* was mid-song but the volume was so low it sounded like a gramophone.

"Hey. Your sign is out. You know? "

"What can I say? I'm energy conscious."

"Where is everybody? Any lookers tonight?"

"It's still early, Lenny. Give it some time."

"What? Like ten years?"

Leonis Petrocelli aka "Lucky Lenny" was born and raised in Brooklyn and spent all but one of his 34 years there. That one year was the worst of his life. His parents had split up and as a misguided attempt to keep him in a stable home environment, they sent him as a young man of 15-years to live with his grandparents in Des Moines, Iowa. Ambitious and bright but averse to any real effort, he had always gotten by on his good looks and audacious street smarts. That was basic equipment in Brooklyn. In Iowa it made him an emperor.

He still hated it. The kids in Iowa made the worst dorks in New York look like Johnny Depp.

"The usual?"

"Tony, my man, tonight I say the hell with the usual. Like Winston Churchill once said, change is the master key. Tonight we're taking the road less traveled."

"You're the boss."

"So tell me, what's fizzy but daring?"

"A Shirley Temple, no sugar, extra twist of lime, stick of licorice and three shots of Sterno."

"You read my mind. You are a genius. The Albert Einstein of mixology."

Tony popped the cap off of a Mickey's Malt Liquor, then poured a shot of Cutty Sark. Without fail, the dialogue was the same every time. Winston Churchill. The road less traveled. Some absurd concoction. Then the Mickey's and the scotch. Some things in life have to be predictable. The anchor against all of the intervening chaos.

They sat in silence. No one came in. Mondays and Tuesdays, always quiet. But tonight? Like a morgue. Fortunately, Tony was a paradigm Stoic. He just adjusted his pace and went with the flow. Or lack of it.

They just sat and let the time slip. A Zen vacuum. The shot of scotch was long gone. Eventually, the Mickey's down to one final swig.

"Another round, Lenny?"

He shook his head, swallowed the last sip of the malt liquor, gave a thumb's up, got up off the stool to leave.

Lenny theatrically looked around at the empty bar. "Just pace yourself, Tony. I think you can handle this."

"Thanks for the gracious words of encouragement."

"No problem. If I see anybody out there, I'll send 'em in. Dead or alive."

"The Mother Theresa of Brooklyn. They're gonna name a church after you."

"Bite me, you ungrateful tub of spaghetti. With friends like me ..."

"I'll have to *rent* pallbearers. See ya tomorrow."

"Not if I see you first."

Winks. Grins. He started to leave, then hesitated as he heard the toilet flush. He glanced at Tony. Tony didn't look up but kept polishing a glass.

Lenny rolled down the sleeves of his shirt as he headed out the door. The day had finally cooled off a bit. Welcome relief. No breeze but at least bearable. This summer had been hell on earth.

As Lenny turned the corner, he almost ran into her.

He wished he had. Oh yes. What an eye-popper! Tall and thin, nice tits. And the face. Full curvy lips painted wet dream red. Eyes like flying saucers. Cameron Diaz with black hair. He wanted to lick her neck.

"Hi, Lenny."

"Have we met?"

"Come on. Has it been that long? You know who I am."

"No. I don't think so. Lot of people know me. Doesn't mean I know them."

"You kill me. So you're gonna play MIA with me."

"Sure. I could do that. Let's get a drink and talk about it."

"Better yet. Let's have a drink at my place."

"Your place. Close by?"

"I'll make it worth the walk."

Lenny knew this type too well. What did she want? She definitely wanted something. Careful. You don't have time for this. Well … yes. Maybe I do, Lenny thought. This one looks like she could be an excellent toss.

"Do you have a name?"

"You seriously don't remember me?"

"Let's say — just theoretically, of course — that I'm at present in the throes of massive amnesia. And you, my little mannequin dream doll, can save me. Bring it all back in a flood. By just giving me a *little* something to go on."

"P. S. 131 … does that jar anything loose?"

"Yeah. My gag reflex. If you really went there, you know I wasn't around very much."

"But I was. You couldn't have missed me the four days you stopped by for your cameos. Now they call it stalking."

Lenny tried to get a good look at her. They had moved onto the street but the light wasn't good. Who was this chick? Was she playing him?

He took her arm and they stopped walking. He studied her face.

"Alicia Krysynski!"

"Alicia Peters. Married. Divorced. At least people can spell Peters. Well, maybe not your friends." An easy mocking laugh. Then a seductive smile.

"My god, you have changed just a bit, I'd say. Just look at you! Where are the pigtails? And the bottle lenses? Straight-A René. Miss goody two shoes."

"Still such a charmer. Come on, my place is not far."

"You can't be doing very well if you still live in this dump of a neighborhood."

"I have my summer villa here."

Lenny laughed but without conviction. "A summer villa. That's rich."

"Keeps me in touch. It's always good to remember where you came from."

The Date

A studio apartment. He looked around. Something didn't click. Where were the dishes?

After closing the door, Alicia turned toward Lenny. Unbuttoning her blouse, she walked up to him and kissed him deep and hard. A tongue that could swim the Atlantic.

The sleeper sofa was already pulled out into a bed. She pulled him down on top of her. Her hand in his pants. Waves of pleasure rippled through his whole body. Before he knew what happened, his clothes were off and she had her skirt up around her stomach. Her blouse disappeared. No bra. He could spend eternity with those tits. Eternity!

With the finesse, prowess and bedroom manners of a stud bull, he entered her quickly.

Oh god. Oh god! This is so good! Oh yes. OH YES!!

He collapsed, swallowed by the hard-fucking carnal ecstasy. His breathing slowed.

"Alicia … Alicia. That was so amazing!!"

A male voice. "I thought it was pretty amazing. How about you?"

Another male voice. "I've seen better. But it wasn't bad. It was up there. Maybe a seven or eight. Lenny's got an ugly ass, though."

Lenny froze. Finally he slowly turned. Sitting at the table were two familiar faces.

"Rule number one. Never trust a chick." This was Frankie, who insisted on being called Franklin. The organization's south side chitman.

"Rule number two. Heat always within reach." Martin was fondling Lenny's Storm 45 Beretta. "You taught us well. You should know better."

"What's going on? Who told you to—?"

Frankie. "You did, Leonis. You did."

Martin. "Get dressed. We got an appointment."

So they had turned. Someone must have gotten to them. Money? That's loyalty for you. Thugs for sale to the highest bidder.

Lenny got up slowly, staring directly at Frankie. "Franklin. You really don't want to do this. Don't mess things up for yourself. I'll forget this ever—"

"Get dressed." Martin was pointing Lenny's gun directly at him. "And shut the fuck up!"

Alicia had already put herself back together and looked at Lenny amused. With mocking melodrama and sarcasm. Soap opera chagrin. "I always loved you, Lenny. I wished things had worked out." She laughed a little too loud and was out the door.

"Alicia … what did I ever do to you?"

"I said, shut the fuck up, Lenny! Get dressed or we take you like that."

Dante's Dungeon

Frankie drove. Martin sat in the back seat, gun pointed at Lenny's neck.

No one said anything. What was there to say?

What was *this*? They were pulling up to the rectory of St. Francis of Assisi — the diocese office where a Bishop Mulcahey held court. Chief of the New York Catholic gestapo. The Teflon priest. Accused of fondling little boys in Minneapolis. Promoted beyond the reach of the law. In fact, here he was the law.

As the car pulled up, the Bishop greeted them with a broad smile. His hands cupped for prayer. Or prey.

"It went smoothly I see. Welcome, Lenny. It's been a while."

"Been a little busy." Lenny trying to feign cool while he figured out what was going on.

"It's never too late. The Lord has infinite patience. Even for scumbags like you."

The Bishop went on into the rectory office but by the time they got Lenny inside, he was no where to be seen. They sat Lenny down in front of the big maple desk, clearly an antique of great value. The large desktop had only a few folders, a telephone, and a gold penholder. Martin and Frankie stood behind him.

Lenny looked around. The walls were covered with framed dignitary photographs and certificates honoring the Bishop. There was his Doctorate in Theology, an inscribed photo of the new Pope Benedict, and a large ornately framed portrait of John Paul II.

Barely audible was an exchange of words from behind the Bishop's private chamber door. When it opened, Bishop Mulcahey came through looking directly at Lenny. A smile was fixed on his weathered face, his bushy eyebrows adding a comic counterpoint to the formality of his cassock and sanctity of his skullcap. He sat down and looked at Lenny.

Before the Bishop could speak, Lenny piped in. "I have been admiring your walls. You hang with some heavyweights. A real admiration society."

"What's your point? Be careful, Lenny."

"My point is there is something missing in your collection."

"And what's that, Lenny?"

"Pictures of all the young boys you diddled."

"You know, you're always a little behind the curve. You have no idea where you're going. And you just don't know when to stop. Look around you. Try to grasp your situation, Lenny. Maybe try thinking before you flap your jaw."

"Thanks for the advice. I guess I should just be grateful I'm not twelve years old and in here alone with you."

The Bishop took a deep breath. "Do you have any idea why you're here? Lenny … it seems you've upset some people."

"Bless me father, for I have sinned. And who exactly are these people?"

"*Me.*"

"From the bottom of my heart, Bishop, I'm sorry. It won't happen again. Can I go now?"

"I know who you work for, Lenny."

"What are you talking about?"

"It's a dead end. Franklin and Martin have seen the light. They're helping. But you're the key."

"What exactly are you saying? What do you want from me?"

"Work with me. I'm going to take this apart. You're going to be out of a job anyway."

"So, you're saying my new role models should be these two vermin you have added to your distinguished staff?"

The bishop stood, then stared down at the empty surface of his desk at a spot right in front of him. A weariness seemed to settle into his body as he balled both hands into tight fists and leaned heavily into his knuckles. He looked at Lenny, eyes leaden with exasperation. He shook his head.

"Just take him down, gentlemen. Maybe he'll be more inclined to cooperate in a few days."

They escorted Lenny out of the rectory and across the courtyard. In the very back of the gothic cathedral, in the shadows of a wing which housed a wedding chapel, was a steel trap door, apparently the entrance to a storage cellar. They removed the padlocks and when the doors were open, dirty cement stairs descended into a dark, cavernous space. Piled everywhere were garden implements and other groundskeeping equipment. It all looked to be in serious disrepair, rusty and caked with dried mud. At the very back was a cage-like structure, securely strapped to the cement walls.

The bottom of the cage was covered in moldy straw. There was a cot, dirty and discolored with time, a wool blanket, and a small pillow, incongruously covered with a brand new pillowcase. Next to a stool was a large chamber pot and a pitcher. An old garden hose draped in the corner of the cage, maybe a foot off the ground, leaked a miser's share of water.

"Make yourself at home. I'll have the butler bring you some tea and crumpets." Martin thought he was such a comedian. He always tried too hard. No one ever laughed. Except for him.

The cage was chained and locked. They left him there in the dark. When the outside storm cellar doors slammed — loud, heavy, metallic — Lenny could see he would have a lot of time on his hands the next few days.

The Neighborhood

"He's dead, I tell ya. That's all. He's dead. Deal with it."

Keary, a light-skinned AfricAm whose bout of pessimism was no more than a passing moment of theater, was on a neighborhood walkabout with Markham, Lenny's sys-ad guru. Self-taught geek Markham always kept things running for everyone around him, was as even-tempered as an operating system, but also had a keen and sportive eye for the glitches in his fellow human beings. His mouth was always breaking into a satirical grin. A real Irish laddie minus the bottle of stout.

"You, Keary, are a drama queen."

"Hey, don't get me wrong. It doesn't change anything. At least not for now."

"Just do your job and stop worrying. It'll all shake out. What are your options, homey? Work at McDonalds?"

"He's dead. That's it."

"Two weeks is a blink. How long we been with him? Three years? He's probably shacked up with some Shakira. If she's got pierced nipples, we may never see him again."

They passed Mama's Phat Boy Body Shop. The sign said ...

Delusional advertising. The lot looked like a auto salvage depot that had been bombed. All high-speed chase catastrophes. Phat Boy pulling on a tire iron the size of a city hall flagpole.

"Hey Phat Boy! Lookin' good." Keary's diplomatic sensibilities. He bought friends with a salvo of flattery. Pointing at a demolished '96 Olds. "Nice tint job. You do that?"

"Fuck you!!" Massive man, massive voice. Words rumbled out of him like an earthquake. "Still bleachin' the leather, I see. Ever win that date with Michael Jackson?"

"Ha ha ha. Phat Boy, *you* are alright! It's all good." Keary's rapper mode. Hip hop hands.

Markham shaking his head. Cheshire cart smile. "Hey, my man! When did you become a gangbanger? Nice hand work."

"No gang stuff there, my friend. That was the real thing. Standard American sign language."

"Sign language. You're kidding, right?"

"Nope. I just told Phat Boy he looked like a pregnant walrus."

"Keary, my man. You never cease to amaze me." Markham stopped in his tracks and feigned surprise. "What a coincidence! Here we are! I'm thinkin' it's as good time as any to check in to ground control."

"Yo, bro'! A recommendation which is both tactically and strategically sound."

They turned off the main street into an alley. Another sharp angle into a small lot, a short stroll to a door in the corner. Steel with three locked deadbolts.

This was computer central, the cyber headquarters for everything. The lists. The skin ads. Email connections. Where they took Visa and Mastercard. And you got stroked. Yes ... at the very least you got stroked. Everything was negotiable.

Once inside, they secured the door and activated the videocams. Two small surveillance monitors came to life, one with a view of the lot and the other an alley feed.

"Damn Sam. Looks like Fantasy Knights is offline again. What's with that server? Or I guess it could be the station." Markham tapped the reboot button. "Mark my words. No more OEMs ever! I'll build 'em myself from now on."

Keary only monitored the auto-spreadsheets. But that itself was a big job. Up to $30,000 a day at $300-1000 a pop. Check maybe every eight or nine hours. Look for anomalies. Sudden drops in activity. Gaps in booking. One thing about sex. It was 24-7. So the lights were never off.

Markham was responsible for everything else. The usual geek stuff of keeping 17 networked computers working and failsafe. Mainly it was security. Both cyber and real world security.

The cyber end was easy. Domains registered in Russia, business addresses phantomed in the Philippines, sites hosted in Tuvalu and mirrored in Australia.

Sixteen websites spread in cyberspace like a thin fog. It would take years for anyone to sort it out.

Real world security was another matter. They had to have a physical presence to keep things operating and current. The girls were here in New York. But they came and went. Constant data updates. Photos, video bios, calendars. The input geeks worked at night, 12 midnight till 4 am. Mostly college students. Good pay for basic computer skills.

They had to keep things securely under wraps. It skirted the edges of the law. Actually, it was on the wrong side of the law. Prostitution is prostitution.

They had been raided twice. But this is where Markham's genius really showed. What did the blues find? Hmm. Just 17 computers hosting catalog sales for camping supplies, health products, office equipment, and sports accessories. Astrological and Tarot Card readings. And oh yes, don't forget the weight loss program for busy executives and new moms. Lastly, a cute little Cyber Camp for the kids.

All the real stuff, meaning the escort services, were in secure hidden folders, behind the desktop facades of legitimate businesses. All they had to do to look proper and upstanding, was reboot the master server, holding down the shift key. Welcome to our family cyber mall.

Today everything looked fine. Money was a little off. But this was the end of summer. Vacations always hurt business. The local boys at the beach with the wife and kids. Charming.

They locked up and headed out.

"Hey homey. Have you talked to Martin lately? We were supposed to do a Mets game." Markham was a diehard fan. Ergo the twenty plus Mets t-shirts. Everyone speculated he would even wear one at his own wedding.

"Yeah, I saw him. But it's been a while. He was very abrupt. Said he was in a hurry."

"Maybe he's with Lenny."

"With the body? Or do you mean he's dead too?"

"Keary, the incorrigible drama queen."

"You're just jealous of the royal jewels. See if I invite you to the Winter Lingerie Ball. You'd look like shit in a whalebone bodice anyway. And you'd probably choke on your wig. If you didn't fall down the steps. Gerry Adams in high heels? I don't think so!"

"Is that supposed to make sense? Are you high?"

"High on life, mama!" He broke into a song. Then started dancing.

> *"Ooh, I'm too sexy for my love ...*
> *too sexy for my love ... "*

Cage Etiquette

Lenny's peristaltic reflex finally calmed. Détente between him and the chamber pot. Which was now overflowing with shit, piss and vomit. Would they ever empty this thing?

He had confined his puking to the pot and the far corner of the cage. But the stench was relentless. The cage was small. Too small to even stand up. His joints ached. And his whole body was caked with his personally generated filth.

And what were they feeding him? It was dark down here but he doubted the food would be recognizable under any conditions. It certainly didn't taste like anything he had ever eaten before. Textures of an autopsy.

The girls came in twice a day with bowls of this food slop. They were petite and silent. Little geishas. Maybe very young. He couldn't really tell. They all had black hair.

They put the bowl by the cage door. He fed himself with his hands, through openings just large enough for them to fit through. The girls only came back to take the last bowl away and replace it with the new one. There was just enough light to sense the revulsion on their small faces. What did they do to pull this duty? All of them were extremely cautious. No possibility of his grabbing them.

Lenny lost all concept of time. There were few clues. He saw a little light on the stairs when the cellar door was open. Both meals were during daylight hours. What difference did it make anyway? He was weak. He was sick. Admittedly very frightened. Would this ever end?

He heard the locks coming off the cellar door. Down the stairs came a frail body. Very short black hair. A boy this time? No ... another young girl. She carried a small penlight. Lighting the path through the equipment rubble.

The switching of the bowls.

"Please ... please help me."

She hesitated. Kept her eyes averted. Shoe gazing.

"Please."

She ran. And stumbled. Got up and kept running.

Lenny finally lost it. He started to sob. "Please ... please ..." It felt like he cried forever. Cried at the base of an infinite staircase. Cried at the altar of lost worlds, dissolving dreams. "Please ... please ..." Pleading before the gatekeeper of memories. Reaching for the deliquescing images of a faint and fading reality becoming even more remote and impossible. Distant shimmering mirages. "Please ... please ..." he cried, creating eddies of nothingness with his outstretched arms. Eventually his world closed over him like a sepulchral shroud and banished every trace of light. All he could see and feel was darkness. All he heard was perfect silence.

He awoke with a start. She had come back.

"The Bishop says God wants you punished."

For the first time in his life, Lenny had nothing to say. He just stared silently into the eyes of an angel. Big beautiful eyes. Asian eyes.

Eyes avoiding his. "I can't help you," she whispered almost apologetically.

How old? She couldn't have been more than 13 or 14. These Asians always look so young anyway.

Then she glowered at him accusingly.

"Are you the Devil?"

Lenny wanted to reply. To form some words. Nothing came. His mouth would not move. His mind produced nothing. He so desperately wanted to say something. But there was nothing there. Empty. His mind a complete blank.

"I will pray for you. I have to go now."

She was on her feet and gone almost instantly.

Lenny ... Lenny ... Lenny. You asshole! You blew it. You fucking blew it.

His face was frozen between pain and insane. He glared into the emptiness of the dark, cavernous space for what must have been hours.

Now think. Think you numbskull. She'll come back. She'll come back and you have to be ready. You've *got* to be ready. What the fuck are you gonna say? She's gonna come back. Do you think maybe you can handle this little girl next time? Maybe not freeze up like a helpless moron. Get it together, Lenny. And think, goddammit. Think! Know what your gonna say and be ready to say it.

Hours passed. The sound of the locks. Light on the stairs. It must be mealtime.

Long hair.

A different one.

Switching of the bowls.

"She wanted me to give you this." The new girl laid a tiny piece of paper next to the bowl.

Lenny picked it up. It was the size of a business card but on paper stock. It was printed in red ink and said ...

I'm Djin Djin
I'm from Thailand
Do you want to fuck me?

Chapter 2

PASSPORT PLEASE!

In Bed with the King

Luxury hotel room. The Mandarin Oriental in Bangkok. Breathtaking view of the Chao Phraya River.

Christine is beautiful, blonde, smart and wholesome. Inviolably virtuous. The crucifix on her necklace is not a fashion statement. She is the real thing. She even saved it for marriage. God bless her.

"Christine?"

The phone rang and her anticipation was evident.

"Ohmigod. Tom, it's you! Oh sweetheart, it's so good to hear your voice. Things here are going great. They couldn't be better."

"Have they given you the grand tour? What's it like?"

"Wonderful. Wonderful. The kids are so beautiful. Their faces. Their eyes. It's all I can do to keep from crying."

"And they seem to have it together?"

"Oh yes. Very organized. We spent three days on the trip. Two whole days in Nong Khai. It's right on the border of Laos. They have like a school, or monastery, some kind of big ancient building. That's where the children live. For now."

"Boys or girls?"

"Both. Maybe more girls than boys."

"How old are they?"

"I'd say 10 years to maybe 14. It's hard to tell. But they are so adorable. The way they hug you. They're so full of love. Just craving some affection. They're a little shy but then they really warm up."

"Just so you know, everything here is fine. Megan might spend a night or two at her friend's house. Danny's his usual invisible self. I think maybe I hear some stirrings from upstairs. We're just getting our day started."

"So what time is it there?"

"A little after seven. It's early morning."

"Right right. Twelve hours. Oh goodness! I have to go. I really have to go. The banquet. Give my love to Megan. Tell her mommy misses her. And Danny too. Love you. I'll be back in just a couple more days. Love you. Love you so. God bless."

She looked in the mirror and frantically started to fool with her makeup but then looked at her watch. Better not. Can't be late for the big night.

The banquet hall was full, everyone in formal dress. She was escorted to her seat at one of the VIP guest tables by a short but very proper young man. A speaker was well into his oration.

"... one of the real rewards of my job, being part of something which is of inestimable value to everyone involved. Everyone here knows that this program has set a new standard for humanitarian assistance. And it provides an irreplaceable bridge between our two great nations …"

"I'm sorry. But what is his name?" she whispered. Christine loved people but was so bad with names.

"Nitya Pibulsonggram. He's the Minister of Foreign Affairs. Here, let me write it down for you. It's a difficult spelling."

"Thank you so much," she pantomimed. She took the piece of paper and entered his name in her PDA.

Speaker after speaker came and went. Their English was surprisingly good but as the evening rolled on the speeches started to sound all the same. Even so, Christine's energy was unflagging and she took care to catalog each and every one, name and title. You never know. Might need a favor down the line.

The banquet climaxed with a brief but ceremonious appearance by His Majesty King Bhumibol Adulyadej himself. With the first lady no less, Queen Sirikit! Short speech. Miracles do happen. Unctuous applause. Kodak moments. Then to Christine's astonishment at the close of his remarks …

"Finally, I wish at this time to give special recognition to our American counterparts, three individuals who have demonstrated special commitment and extraordinary initiative in this effort. Mr. William Parker. Please stand. Mrs. Geraldine Freed. Thank you. Thank you. And last but not least, Mrs. Christine Lindholm. Mrs. Lindholm, stand so we can see you. Everyone, please show your appreciation for the hard work and dedication of these individuals. Thank you. Thank you. And now please enjoy the rest of your evening and the splendors and charm of my beautiful country."

Their names read off of prompter cards. But it still felt good. Christine was reeling as she mixed with the guests and other dignitaries, now that the formal banquet program had ended.

Whew! What an evening! What an adventure this has been! God bless this amazing country and these fine people.

Children of Nong Khai

It was business. These pathetic women should be grateful for small favors. And now they think they can change their minds. Just like that. Sentimental old fools. They can't afford to feed themselves, much less their children. So be it. At least the little fuckers won't starve to death. Their husbands know the real deal. You don't see them bellowing like swamp buffalos over this. It was business. Pure and simple.

Once the real money came in, Dok Phnom could claim clean hands and walk away from all of this misery. Unfortunately for now, he had to just sit tight. He sure hoped the Americans would come through soon. They promised. These children would be leaving early next week. The money better be here by then. He had to be back in Nakhom Phanom very soon. Had some handwringing Hungarian delegation coming. Some bleeding heart Belgians right after them. This was almost too good to be true. He would retire within two years. Move back to America.

The Siddartha Schools were a stroke of genius. Certainly he had no problem filling the schools with beautiful little starving faces. Poster kids for all of the relief organizations and their fundraising campaigns. Sad eyes and skinny limbs meant big bucks. From America and the EU countries. And he had them all coming to him! Beating down his teakwood doors. Save The Children. Children International. TEAR Fund. Compassion International. Christian Children's Fund.

It started way back. Maybe the toilets didn't flush but they had internet access at Vientiane High School in Laos, and that paved the way for his B. S. degree at Syracuse University in the States. Then on to the graduate program in NGO Management and Development at Rutgers University in New Brunswick, New Jersey. That was where he really got wind of the goldmine there was out there. NGOs funded by all of the corporate foundations. CEOs trying to gussy up the image of the corporate plunderers with high-visibility philanthropy, squeezing every bit of public relations juice out of what amounted to pocket change donations. But all that petty cash coming in from a lot of different places added up. Some of these save-the-world institutions were awash in money. All you had to do was say the right things and on went the spigots. Make them look good. They write the checks. That was the name of the game right down the line. Everyone winked and slept well.

Dok Phnom chose his squalor with the eye of a saint and the heart of a pillager. It was ironic that these cesspools of poverty were to be his fountains of affluence. Chiang Rai was doing well. And Nakhon Phanom definitely held its own. But Nong Khai had been his first setup and remained the flagship in the fleet. Everything had fallen into place from the get go. The abandoned monastery was huge. Ready made for over two hundred kids, if you packed them in just so. And Nong Khai itself never ran dry of the on-the-brink-of-starving families ready to offload one or two offspring, just to ease the burden of survival. Both from the city and the surrounding countryside. The hill tribes were especially easy prey. Too dumb to breathe.

Dok took an almost sick delight in seeing the expression on a mother or father's face when they found out that not only would their child receive food and shelter but were being enrolled in a special school for spiritual development. Based on newly discovered secret teachings of the Buddha himself no less.

The child sponsorship groups loved it. Even if they weren't, the kids were billed as orphans. Poor little dears. No where to turn. But you can help. Put your bloated wallet to work and get a picture for your marble mantel, your own little sad-faced abandoned boy or girl from Bangladesh. Or Malaysia. The Philippines. Or Thailand. It didn't matter where. This was better than Prozac and a martini to wash away the white-guilt of the master race.

Everything went so smoothly until it was time to ship them out. Then the mothers started bawling. Oh how they wailed and whined. "I'll never see my baby again." Boo hoo. You'd never see them again if they had starved to death. You made your deal. This is business.

Dok never asked where they ended up. But it didn't take a Rhodes Scholar to figure out where the market was for this kind of trafficking. Bodies were bodies and did what bodies did. They ended up either in a factory or on the streets in some big city. Boston. New York, London, San Francisco, Houston, Frankfort. Even Bangkok itself. He was just filling billets. Nothing personal. And as far as he could tell, they ended up better off than they would have here in northern Thailand. In this disease-ridden filth and blight. If starvation didn't take you down, then yellow fever or tuberculosis would. Or maybe H5N1 Avian or H1N1 Swine. That was the latest off the runway of human misery. Count your blessings, you little fucks.

One Night in Bangkok

After the formal banquet and especially after being personally singled out by the King of Thailand, Christine was beside herself with excitement. She wanted to call her husband Tom right away and tell him everything, but he would be at his office. It would have to wait. She tried to relax but couldn't sleep. Finally the adrenaline dissipated and she managed to sleep a couple hours.

Next morning, she headed out early for a day of splurge shopping. Bangkok had everything. From junk and trinkets to high fashion. At the end of the day, most of the time being spent at the MBK Mall and Siam Discovery Center, respectively huge and exquisite, she had filled a newly bought suitcase with the day's plunder. Clothes to die for, souvenirs for friends, shirts and silk ties for Tom, and a few gifts for her two kids.

When she returned she had a message waiting for her from Roger. He was an old friend from college who had kept in touch over the years and was now based in Bangkok. Finally, they would get together again, catch up, and certainly reminisce about their days together in Campus Youth for Christ, the organization where they had met. It was there, she was introduced to and charmed by her husband-to-be. Those were heady days. How much they all craved the chance to truly get involved and change the world. Spread the blessed teachings of the New Testament, try to eliminate some of the horrible suffering in the world, and in general just build on the good works of the Lord Savior Himself.

Christine got in the back seat of the bright pink taxi.

"Thongchai, thank you for coming so late at night. Good to see you again."

"No problem. Good see you."

"You have been so good to me. Taking me everywhere in this crazy city. You are the best driver in Thailand!"

Face beaming. "Tank you. Tank you. Where we go tonight?"

"I am meeting my friend Roger. It's somewhere off Sukhumvit. I have it written down."

"Long street. But not far way."

Christine pulled her PDA out of her purse and started tapping on the keyboard.

"Here it is. I am supposed to meet an old friend at Nana Entertainment Plaza. Is that some sort of shopping mall?"

The look of mild shock registered on Thongchai's face in the glow of the dashboard lights. "Sure that right? Sure you want go to Nana Plaza?"

"Yes yes. That's the place. Nana Entertainment Plaza."

Thongchai headed down Sukhumvit Road, one of the busiest streets in Bangkok, where businessmen and tourists came from all over the world to enjoy the unique attractions of the city and spend copious amounts of foreign cash.

Christine was transfixed by the lights, the intensity of activity, the seemingly endless streams of people. They came to a very congested intersection and waited for the light to change.

Thongchai pointing. "Right there. Very close"

Beautiful young ladies, dressed immodestly to the teeth teemed the sidewalks.

"All of these girls. They are beautiful. But ... what are they all doing here?" Noticing one whose microscopic skirt showcased her exquisitely slim legs and whose D-cup breasts burst from her delicately provocative tank top. "My goodness, look at that girl in the white top and yellow miniskirt. She's a young thing."

Thongchai started to laugh but then respectfully stopped and smiled at Christine. "That no girl. That a boy. A ladyboy."

"That's not a girl? I am so confused."

The light changed and they edged around the corner, splitting the throngs of jaywalkers. Thongchai pulled to the side and Christine looked into what looked like a scaled-down but no less dazzling version of Las Vegas.

"There he is! That's him in the blue shirt. Can I get out here?"

"No problem. Me wait?"

"No no. My friend said he would get me back to the hotel. Thongchai, my friend, thank you so much. Kòp koon. Kòp koon. I go to the airport tomorrow. I guess I will see you then. Okay?"

"Have good time, Miss Christine."

She crossed the busy street, nearly getting hit by a motor scooter. Normally someone totally in charge, she felt uncharacteristically overwhelmed. The noise, the glare, the crowd, the frenzy, all came at her from every possible direction. She felt extremely vulnerable and struggled to get her bearings, when the strong reassuring arms of a still familiar thirty-something male, engulfed her in a big bear hug.

"Christine! My goodness, look at you. More beautiful than ever. Marriage is good for you!"

"Roger. This is crazy. What are we doing here? I'm sorry. I don't mean to be rude. It's so good to see you again. Really. I sincerely mean it. But frankly I am a bit dumfounded by your choice of meeting places. Where are we?"

"Don't worry. I'll explain. It will all become very clear. Let's walk."

Christine was tentative but Roger confidently led the way. They walked a short lane into a three-story mall. But a mall unlike anything Christine had ever seen, or could have even imagined. Bars fronted both sides of the lane. Each had indescribably sexy young girls seated on barstools, giggling and waving. Some held drink special signs, others just smiled and yelled out invitations to come in. Several paid special attention to Roger, coming up to him, trying to lead him by the hand or arm into their respective establishments. One very pretty girl in a bikini held a sign to Roger's face that read …

Glass Beer All Night 60 B
Pussy Mirror

"These girls all seem to know you, Roger. I see you … you've changed."

"No. Yes. But no. Them? I've never seen them before. They are just doing business."

"What kind of business, Roger? Or do I need to ask?"

They moved into the huge courtyard area, itself holding several cabana bars, also populated by young Asian ladies. There were scores of middle-aged white men scattered among them, luxuriating in the attention of the girls.

"I think I have seen enough, Roger. Can we leave?"

"Actually you haven't. Trust me. This is important."

He guided her forward. She couldn't help but stare at the huge fluorescent and neon signs advertising the names of the clubs … Pretty Lady, Cathouse, Rainbow, Obsession, Voodoo, Fantasia, G-Spot, Lollipop, Spanky's, Playskool, Hollywood Rock. They all had very skimpily dressed girls, posing provocatively, seductively flirting with potential customers.

Christine shuddered, closed her eyes and shook her head. Roger took her by the arm and pointed to a door, above which chaser lights over a garish flashing background spelled out *Obsession*.

They walked in and Christine was immediately subjected to suspicious looks by the several girls standing by the door. But a waitress glided over and guided them to a bleacher-style seat close to the stage.

Embarrassed and growing increasingly angry, Christine hesitatingly glanced up at the raised catwalk in front of her. Eight stunningly beautiful young Asian girls dressed in miniscule silver lamé bikini tops and black fine mesh miniskirts, through which the shadow of their pubic hair could be seen, danced and swayed. Each had a spot marked by a pole and when a song ended, they would rotate to the next position, allowing the customers throughout the room the opportunity to see each girl. At the end of a rotation, the last girl would come off and circulate the club, usually going up to some man she had made eye contact with from the catwalk. A new girl would come onstage to replace her. In the club were perhaps twenty five or thirty equally bewitching girls, providing a breathtaking visual parade of young flesh that Christine could never have imagined possible. Astoundingly, this was just one club of dozens in the complex. Her face betrayed both her bewilderment and disapproval.

Finally, she could not look anymore. She had seen enough for an eternity. This was a corruption of God's design and a debasement of the human soul which filled her with a rage she had never had to brook. She turned to Roger, placing her hands directly on his cheeks, turning his head toward her. She held his face resolutely and stared directly into his eyes.

"Roger, yes or no. Do you still accept Jesus Christ as your personal savior?"

"Yes, of course I do. But ..."

"Then why did you drag me here? This is disgusting. What exactly are we doing in this child brothel? "

"Christine. Please, just listen. You're working for that child sponsorship organization, right?"

"Yes. What's that got to do with it?"

"I ... I ... I don't want to be the one to have to break it to you. But ..."

"But nothing. I am very offended. And I want to leave here immediately." She started to get out of her seat.

"Wait." He gently took her arm. "It's very simple, Christine. I just thought you should see where some of your young girls end up."

If incredulity were ice, then Christine instantly turned into a mountain-size glacier. Her mouth dropped open as if she had been shot full of animal tranquilizer. Her eyes were as big as saucers, as her thoughts tossed about in the blizzard of disbelief and shock Roger's last statement had unleashed in her head.

"You're crazy, Roger. I'm leaving."

"They toured you through a monastery in Nong Khai, right?"

"Roger, I'm leaving. With or without you, I'm leaving. Right now!"

"Wait." Pointing to a waifish little girl, perhaps the youngest one there, who was leaning against a table next to the stage. "See her. The one with the blue things in her hair. She came from Nong Khai. I'll go get her. You can ask her yourself."

Christine glanced over at the girl. She had to fight back the tears. This was an especially delicate looking one she had noticed right after they sat down. So young. She barely had breasts and still had the sweet face of a child. Twelve? Thirteen? Was that legal? Was Roger telling her the truth? She had been to the monastery. It had been one of the most special days of her life.

No! No! There was no way what he said was true. Something had happened to him. Maybe Thailand had driven him over the edge. Or he had embraced the dark side. If the Beast lived anywhere, it was here in Bangkok. In any case, this wasn't the time or place to analyze or judge any of it. For the moment, she only knew she had to get out of here. Immediately! Before she started screaming.

"Roger, I don't know why you're doing this. But you are making this up. This is some sick fantasy. Or maybe I should give you the benefit of the doubt. Perhaps you have just lost your mind. Whatever is going on with you, I don't know and I don't care. I do know I am leaving this playground of filth. Right now! Don't try to stop me. You will be in my prayers, Roger. Good night."

Christine was out the door before Roger even got to his feet.

"Please, Christine. Listen!"

The courtyard area was even more crowded that it was twenty minutes ago when they had arrived, but Christine pushed through like a Big 10 fullback.

Roger couldn't begin to keep up, girls still blocking his way and grabbing at him as he tried to catch up with her. He made it to the sidewalk in front of the plaza just in time to see Christine close the door of a taxi, which quickly joined the line of cars turning onto Sukhumvit Road. He was devastated by his sense of failure. With her credibility and connections, she was his best hope. And now he doubted she would ever speak to him again. But she had to. Too much was at stake. He had to do something. As he headed back to his apartment, a single thought kept running through his head: You will be in my prayers, as well, Christine.

Siddartha Schools

The open-bed truck pulled into a small space next to the market. Driving over scattered piles of garbage. It was shortly before noon. And the market was teaming like a huge Petri dish. The air hot and thick with humidity and the vapors of desperation. Even the faces of the young looked weathered. The old mummified.

Rice, flour, oilseeds, fresh vegetables, fruits were portioned. A few measly bahts tendered. Hopeful tinges of gratitude softened the eyes of the vendors, at least for the moment granted another few hours reprieve from total hopelessness.

The monk and his assistant got out of the truck leaving the driver behind the wheel smoking a cigarette.

They circled through the stalls. The monk would point at a child crouching behind the bags of rice and cassava. The assistant would then talk to the mother or father, preferably the father, then gently lead the child back to the truck. Pat on the head. Maybe hold his or her hand for assurance. Then into the flat bed of the vehicle he or she went.

There were a number of markets in Nong Khai, each serving its area of the city. Today had gone well. They had over twenty children, all under fourteen or fifteen, more girls than boys, as had been instructed. The Master would be pleased. The school term was filling up fast. More young souls to surrender to the egolessness of Buddha's wisdom.

At the monastery, every day started the same. Up at 4:30 am, into the great hall by five. Each child brought a prayer mat and assumed the humility position, kneeling but curled forward in a little ball. Eyes closed and forehead on the mat. They stayed like that for only an hour but it seemed like an eternity. No sleeping allowed. The master had a sixth sense about that and dealt a cruel blow to the back of anyone who drifted off.

There was a gong struck at the beginning and end of the hour. Three severe looking monks off to the side provided the shrill mantra of backnoise music. More drone than melody, and not enough rhythm or dynamics to break the hypnotic, dumbing shroud weaved by the relentless inculcations of the Master.

What he said was of little consequence. It was the way he said it. Alternating between low, authoritative repetitions and a high singsong which almost sounded maternal, the words either drubbed their ears until they wobbled punch-drunk and defenseless, or the syllables danced a blissful but sedative ballet, rendering their inchoate little minds docile and contrite.

The Master's mesmeric evangelism trained on two parallel tracks: Obedience and discipline. Obedience to the random senseless demands of others who wielded the power. Discipline to immediately retreat into the void of comatose surrender whenever reality required it. Obedience. Blind. Unquestioning. Complete submission to the iron shackles of rolled dice tyranny. Discipline. Instantaneous and resolute. The inversion of consciousness when life became intolerable. Too painful. Too humiliating. Or just too inexplicably cruel.

Obedience.

Discipline.

One hour every morning. One hour every evening. Sunrise and sunset for little minds.

If the meditative brainwashing which opened and closed each official day of "schooling" was the theory, the long and exhausting twelve hours between them was the practice. Each and every day, the children saw the daylight hours come and go, working at a wide range of exhausting, arbitrary, and transparently meaningless tasks. Scrubbing to no visible effect the stone floors and walls. Digging and hoeing but never planting huge tracts of barren soil. Carting water from the wells to huge cisterns that seemed to feed no irrigation system or laundry or household room. Parading the grounds in "orbits of the sun and moon" to honor the spiritual quest and earthly mission of the greatest teacher of them all, the Buddha himself.

In the summer, this took place in a hot dank cauldron. In the winter, the cold air penetrated to the marrow of their shivering bodies. Which was worse? More children died of exposure in the winter. In the purgatory of summer they just collapsed.

The latest fresh batch was coming in at the perfect time. Probably won't lose any of them. Just need to make sure and move them out before the New Year and the onset of lethally severe cold.

Four months was usually enough training. The children arrived already weak in both body and spirit. Poverty delivers the perfect body blow to human tenacity. A void in the stomach creates a vacuum in the soul. And the Master was there to fill it.

The only relief from the tortuous schedule for the children took two forms: the tri-annual photo portrait sessions, and a rare visit by a group of well-meaning benefactors from one of the child sponsorship agencies. Just a couple weeks ago, a large delegation from New York came here to Nong Khai. The Chiang Rai facility had a delegation visit the previous spring — five hyperventilating round-eyes from Indiana and Illinois who smiled and cried and thanked the Lord for all the wonderful things everyone there was doing to give hope and make life more bearable for these beautiful little creatures.

Round-eye: "And what's your name?"

Little boy: "I'm hungry. Are you my new mommy?"

Translator: "He says he is Kongbej Mee. And he loves Jesus."

No one at the Siddartha Schools had the entire picture. The young monks did as they were told and didn't question the severity or hardships, since the treatment of the children paralleled their own preparation for the holy life. Even the Master willingly adopted to a see-no-evil myopia. He merely focused on preparing the children for their new lives in the cradles of affluence, and so doing reaped the generous financial rewards for keeping his normally perceptive gaze blissfully averted.

Young monk: "The children are tired and hungry."

The Master: "And we are grateful for the strength these sufferings will engender."

Young monk: "The little one we called Yen Ying Pim passed away this morning."

The Master: "And joined the egoless Oneness that is All. We should envy this little flower."

After enduring four months of the spiritual boot camp, each new batch of Buddha's dutiful little soldiers were treated to a devotional rite-of-passage party. The monastery's main hall was filled with music, food, desserts, games, balloons and festive flags. Most of the children had not smiled from the day they had arrived. But the monumental contrast of this final lavish event with their prior spartan living conditions and with the Master's obsessive attention and smothering pedagogy, coupled with the realization that they were finally getting out of this dreadful place, brought laughter and cries of playful abandon to all two hundred plus innocent little faces. Which, of course, were photographed and videotaped from every possible angle and in every euphoric light. These were the photographs shown to inquiring dignitaries and prospective donors. These were the photos and video clips posted on the web, for the world to see and marvel at what the Siddartha School was accomplishing in this blighted area of northern Thailand. The curious and concerned were awed and pleased. King Bhumibol Adulyadej was especially proud of the fine example set before the international community.

The children ate and played and sang and laughed. No getting up at 4:30 am tomorrow. Tomorrow began the next phase, their lives in the real world. So let them party themselves silly tonight. Because by this time tomorrow, they would all be gone. Making room for the next little orphan army. Buddha's little photo ops.

And that Dok Phnom. What an amazing and efficient administrator he turned out to be! Educated in America. Connected with every world-class child sponsorship organization in the world. He ran a tight ship. You could tell he really loved his work. He was as tireless as he was timely. At exactly 12 noon tomorrow, the buses would arrive. Thirty minutes later, off they would go.

Thus the children came and went. Photos landed in the mailboxes of their foster parents in America or Denmark or the United Kingdom. $25 per month per sad face. The money was divided up. The Master's cut was deposited directly by Dok Phnom in the Siddartha School Enlightenment Trust. Praise the infinite wisdom of the Buddha. And the generosity of the round eyes.

And the children? Yes the children. Into the slipstream of fate. Fate and fortunes. Fortunes made and paradise lost. Little souls overwhelmed by the raw power of Original Sin. Little souls who would never get close to the Garden. Or be able to ask the round-eye God …'Why?'

The Saint and the Sinner

Christine could barely open her eyes? She was so groggy. What time was it? After 11. The morning was almost gone. How long had she slept? 12 hours. Jet lag was like major anesthesia.

She put on a robe and wandered down the stairs and into to the family room. There was her 12-year-old daughter consumed in a book. She looked over her shoulder and saw that it was the second in the Harry Potter series.

As she wandered into the kitchen to make some coffee, Tom swept by her and pecked her on the cheek with a kiss.

"Look who rose from the dead. I'll be right back. Gotta get something from the storage locker."

She made the coffee, strong but with lots of sugar and milk, then went back to sit in the family room. On her way to the sofa she bent down and wrapping her arms around her daughter, gave her a big hug and kiss. Her daughter was still engrossed in the book.

"Hi, mommy. Did you have a nice trip?"

"It was amazing, Megan, simply amazing. I am so tired, though. Still half asleep. Did you stay overnight with Heather?"

"No, she went with her parents to Connecticut for the week."

Christine sipped on her coffee and made the slow journey back to full consciousness. It was a very beautiful day. The late morning sun streamed in through the white voile curtains. The fragrance of jasmine and yew lightly tinged the warm breeze.

Suddenly, Christine was jolted out of her reverie. The image of the girls at the Obsessions girly bar in Bangkok with Roger sitting there, assaulted her like a mugger. Here was her beautiful daughter, just a few years younger, so innocent, so unaware of the ugliness and dangers of the world. She wanted to protect her from all of it but was possessed by a feeling of helplessness. What a sick world! Those poor young girls. Tears started streaming down her cheeks.

"Christine! Are you okay?" Tom was back and had his big loving arms around her. "What's upsetting you?"

It took a moment for Christine to get her composure back. She wiped her eyes on the sleeve of her robe and held on to Tom for dear life.

"Something happened my last night. Something so weird, so disturbing. It's hard to talk about … I met with Roger."

"You saw Roger! How is he doing?"

"We should go in the other room. This is not for young ears."

They went into the kitchen. Christine talked as Tom made himself a sandwich.

"I … I don't know what to say about Roger. He looked the same. At first it felt like old times and it was great to see him. But …"

"But?"

"Well, he met me at this … this bar for prostitutes. I mean these were really young girls, say fourteen to eighteen. Twenty at tops. Incredibly beautiful girls. All Thai or at least from somewhere in Asia."

"He took you to a pick-up bar? Full of prostitutes? I don't get it. What was he thinking?"

"I didn't get it either. It was horrible. I mean we are supposed to be open-minded and forgiving of others who have fallen into sin. And frankly, I don't think these girls had a choice. But there were so many of them. On display. All for sale. It was overwhelming. I tried to leave as soon as I got there but Roger kept insisting."

"Roger? *Our* Roger? I'm not getting it. What was his role in all of this?"

"Well … he seemed to be saying that some of the orphans, these little girls that go through the child sponsorship program, end up like that. You know, working in a girly bar, selling their bodies. I didn't stay around to argue with him about it. It was repulsive. I was so upset I couldn't see or think."

"Roger is a good man. He is devoted to Christ and spreading Christian values. I can't …"

"Is or was? I mean, I have given the whole thing a lot of thought. Truth is, I couldn't stop thinking about it. I was there, right there in the monastery, with the monks and the kids. And it just doesn't seem possible that somehow they end up the way Roger seems to think."

"Christine, I'm sure you're right. I hope you're right. All of your good work. There is too much negativity in the world. You are *doing* something about it. Something amazing and beautiful. Do you want me to talk to him? We still have his number, right?"

"No, love. Just hold off for now. After what I saw, I don't want Roger in our lives right now, no matter how far away he lives. I still shake when I think about it. That's why I was crying."

"I understand. But Roger has always been solid. He's a great friend. Hey, he introduced us! I can't put that all aside. Not yet. If nothing else, say he has flipped out or something, it's our responsibility to pray for him, reach out to him, and do what we can to help. That's our Christian duty."

"I just need some time. And I need to get my head on straight. I feel like I've been drugged. You never have this much trouble with jetlag, do you? I mean, you always seem to just snap back the next day."

"Well, I put on a good show. Just rest. Everything here is good. I'm taking Megan to soccer later. I'll pick up Danny from school. We'll have dinner when we get back, maybe rent a movie. We'll get you back on schedule."

"We had better! I have that fund-raising thing on Tuesday and don't want to make a complete fool of myself. Especially after this trip. I feel more on top of it, more motivated than ever. I really know how this can work, why this is so important. It just takes money. As always. Money."

"Tuesday? Yeah, right right. I remember now. Where is it at? Some school auditorium?"

"Yes, over in Brooklyn. They said that there will be a decent number of people there. They're bringing in organizations from all the boroughs. So I need to figure out exactly what I'm going to say. The old speeches won't do the job anymore."

Christine spent two days working on her address. This meeting was more about getting other service groups involved with her work, than directly raising money. If she could make them aware of the incredible things the child sponsorship organizations were doing, show them the real impact their efforts were having on the lives of real children in the world, share with them her own personal experiences in Thailand, then these people would go out and rally their own troops, bringing in more money and volunteers to fundraise for the cause.

And while the confrontation with Roger still nagged at Christine, it didn't lessen her commitment. Roger had to be wrong. She totally believed in what she was doing and was certain it did a lot of good in the world. Certainly far more good than harm.

The auditorium was packed. They had done a good job getting the word out.

A few minutes into her presentation, Christine realized this was a genuinely receptive and friendly audience. Abandoning her tightly crafted speech, she just loosened up and just started to talk. Talk from her heart about her visit to Thailand, the kids, the orphan school, living conditions in Asia, and so on.

By the end, practically everyone there was in tears. They rose and with enthusiastic and heartfelt applause gave her a standing ovation. At the informal coffee and cookie reception afterwards, she was bombarded by greetings, handshakes, compliments, promises to help, and specific inquiries as to what else individuals might do to reach out to these helpless children.

"Have you ever thought about adopting one?"

Christine had never heard that one. Caught slightly off guard, she looked up and took in the person asking the question.

Very interesting persona.

The girl had on a billowing burgundy headdress shaped like a pirate's hat. Black velour choker set with a huge green stone. Creamy white organdy halter top, immodestly showing her ample breasts. Plaid demi-cape. Elbow-length brown suede gloves accessorized with a multitude of gold jewel bracelets. Definitely not your typical urban or suburban do-gooder, who tended to be either completely fashion-myopic or dressed like they were applying for a bank loan.

"Actually adopting a child? Not just sponsoring."

"Yes. Legal adoption."

"That's an intriguing thought. I know some celebrities do that. But I hadn't considered it myself. I have two children."

"No room at the inn, eh?"

"And you?"

"Yes. I have been trying to adopt a ten-year old. Well, actually he's eleven now. It's been over a year. He's from Indonesia."

"And how is it going? The adoption I mean."

"It's a buncha shit."

Okay, thought Christine. Mouth of a truck driver.

"So much bureaucracy. You'd think I was asking to test a fucking nuclear bomb in their country. It's driving me crazy."

"I'm sorry. I'm Christine. And you are?"

"Alicia. Alicia Peters."

Well, Alicia Peters. You look great but you are certainly a little rough around the edges.

"And what do you do for a living, Alicia?"

"A lot of things. I'm a freelance journalist. I'm getting some of my stuff published but not quite enough, if I want to both eat and have a place to live. So I temp, pick up the odd job here and there. Which is a big factor in the adoption. I'm not what they consider …" Making quotation marks with her fingers. "… the model career woman."

"I see. I assume you're not married."

"Exactly. So there are lifestyle issues. No one man in my life. In fact the men come and go. More often than I care to admit. But I don't think that's the entire story. Something else is going on. And I can't put my finger on it."

Christine liked her. And despite the differences on the surface, she decided to take a chance.

"Alicia. I'd like to talk more with you more about all of this. Would you like to meet for lunch sometime?"

"Absolutely. That's what I was thinking."

"That's what you were thinking? When?"

"When I heard about this meeting from my friend over there." Points in the direction of a group of people talking away on the other side of the room. "When they said you had recently actually *been* there, in southeast Asia I mean, I was sure I had to meet you. So voilà! Here I am."

Christine pulled out a business card and a pen. She wrote her personal cell and home numbers on the back.

"Here. Give me a call toward the end of the week. We'll make a date."

"Good. In fact, great! You're not as stuffy as I thought you'd be. I think we'll make good friends. Ciao."

Christine followed her as Alicia headed for the exit. Stuffy? Did she say stuffy? Christine burst out laughing. Sometimes it's good to see yourself from the outside.

Chapter 3

CITY STREETS: Turf Wars

The Fire Within

How quickly the human body disintegrates. Only three weeks and Lenny had lost 17 pounds. His high metabolism deprived of its normal steady diet of malt liquor, scotch and fast food turned on itself. His immune system had broken ranks and joined the enemy. Running sores appeared on his face and back. This morning he woke up shivering and greeted the day by dry heaving on himself. He only cared about dying. The sooner the better.

Through the white noise in his head, he could hear the metallic clunk of the door being opened. A few moments later, a gasp.

"Oh my God! I am sorry. So sorry."

He forced himself to look. She was back! The boy cut. Was her name Djin Djin?

"I'll get help. Please don't die."

He lost consciousness.

When he came to, he was blinded by a handheld electric lamp. Male voices.

"This is disgusting. What are you trying to do here?" Apparently a doctor. He was reaching in his fake leather briefcase for something. Two vials and a hypodermic needle.

"I don't make the decisions here. This comes from high up." That was his dear friend Martin. Apparently still in the service of the Bishop. Holy orders.

"How high up? Divinely ordained torture? God must be a malicious fucker." Bedside manners of Joseph Stalin. He vacated the air from the hypo chamber and put on latex gloves.

"You know who I'm talking about. Just do it. We can't let this shitfuck die."

He was rolled onto his side. He could now see the Asian girl standing back against the damp cellar wall. Her fingers in her ears. Eyes cast down. Tears streaked her innocent young face. Lenny felt a sharp pain in his rear. Antibiotics? He would have preferred a lethal injection.

"He'll live. Clean him up, for Christ's sake. Or he'll just get worse. Here's some ointment for those sores." Martin passed it to the girl.

The medicine man hastily packed up and bolted for the stairs. He looked like he was gagging. A few of Martin's bull strides and he was gone as well. It was just Lenny and the little girl.

Hesitantly, she stooped and picked up a basin of water near her feet and approached him. The cage door had been left open. Lenny noticed that he was laying on a large wool blanket.

"Are you Djin Djin? Is that your name?"

"We are all Djin Djin. I am called Kimnai."

She dipped a sponge in the water and gently began to wipe Lenny's face. The warmth of the water and her delicate touch soothed him. Waves of pleasure at a human touch were mixed with sharp spasms of shivering. And sharp pain as she patted the sores.

"Sorry. I try to be gentle."

Lenny tried to relax. But then the fever took over. As he started to shake uncontrollably, he struggled into fetal position. She quickly covered him with the blanket.

Lenny fought hard to keep his chattering teeth from biting his lips and tongue. Just before he lost consciousness was when he saw it. The girl was wearing sandals and the second toe on her left foot was missing. Gone. Severed at the base.

Then blackness.

Djin Djin Girls

Everyone knew the routine. And the rules. The local girls had their territories staked out, knew each other, and let camaraderie trump competitiveness. There was a steady flow of business. Enough to go around. The johns knew where to look, and the regulars pretty well could tell you who would be working and where they were on a given night.

As long as there was no trouble, and there rarely was, the cops turned a blind eye. Sometimes they'd accept a small donation for the Policemen's Field Day Fund. Or take some gratitude in trade for their fine job of community policing.

Everybody seemed content with the way things were. No one saw any reason to fix what wasn't broken.

Then one night it all changed.

They descended like locusts. At least that was the perception of the locals. The regular girls.

At first no one paid much attention to the Lincoln Navigators, one black and one silver. Loosely in tandem, they crossed the intersection of Caster and Utica, then parked around the corner and across from Sammy's Deli & Liquor. Not a hot spot for curbside soliciting. Too much moving traffic for the johns to stop and negotiate.

The girls got out of the far side of the oversized SUVs. Fifteen or sixteen someone counted. And what a sight they were. Young and hot. Thin little things who looked more like a high school cheerleading squad than a battalion of hookers. Except for the way they dressed.

They had pulled out all of the stops. Skirts so short they would have a dead man in heat. Dazzlingly bright colors. A DayGlo parade. Tight skimpy tops that showed as much cleavage as their waifish bodies could produce. Most had long black hair that swept across their bare backs or lay provocatively on their young breasts. Small shiny vinyl handbags hung down against their slender hips. Large sparkly earrings and armfuls of either shiny plastic or high-gloss silver bracelets completed the flashdance of their allure.

And could they strut their stuff! Perched either on impossibly high platform shoes, clear or a shiny plastic, or sporting knee-high boots — white vinyl or black patent leather — with long thin spike heals, they walked a moist lubricated walk, a slippery seductive sashay. They knew exactly what you wanted and how to get you there. Knew what you were thinking before you did.

Word spread fast. The johns flocked like vultures to fresh kill.

The little Asian girls even offered business cards which left nothing to the imagination. Basic white paper stock with red printing. Every school day morning, children would walk over the hundreds of simple calling cards which littered the sidewalks …

> I'm Djin Djin
> I'm from Thailand
> Do you want to fuck me?

The young school kids were too embarrassed to even dare look at them, averting their eyes to anywhere but the ground. But the high school boys had a field day. Holding one out to a female classmate, "Hey Samantha, this fell out of your purse."

No. Nothing would be the same. Not as long as the Djin Djin girls were around.

Peaceful coexistence was out of the question. The "regulars" watched their fortunes go down down down, as cars would drive right by them, then stop for a little Asian doll. Annoyance turned to desperation, which turned to resentment. Which was one short hop to rage.

With a lot of time on their hands, and their anger building to volcanic levels, the locals needed to hatch a plan. It was slow going at first, a lot of whining and swagger. Night after night went by with no shortage of crazy ideas and fantastic schemes which had more payback than promise of improving the situation.

"I say we chop them up and take them in a rickshaw down to C-town and dump them. Those chinks will eat anything. I can see the menu now. 'Fried rice $3. With beef, pork, chicken or Djin Djin just add 75 cents.' Works for me."

"How about a slow boat to China?"

"Not China, you dumb 'ho. These little bitches are from Thailand."

"Thailand. Where the fuck is Thailand?"

"Just take the N train to Coney Island and turn left. Keep going 'til you see a lot of bamboo."

So they had some good laughs and vented a lot of frustration but basically nothing was really getting done. And something needed to get done. Soon!

Lilly probably logged more street time than any of the other girls. She listened to the bad mouthing and outrageous schemes night after night, and took it all in, while her mind walked the avenues inside her own head, looking for the right doors to open. She was an organizer and knew they had to form some sort of committee to give some focus to their energies or else nothing would happen. At least get the girls all in a room at the same time so that they could brainstorm until they arrived at some real world plan. Then take coordinated action.

She came up with a possible approach on her own that she planned on running by the others. While it was a little risky, at least it offered some hope. She called it the Ad Hoc Committee To Save Our Neighborhood, an organization which hopefully would rally the more respectable members of the community to help clear the prostitutes off the streets. This of course put themselves directly in the crosshairs. But Lilly figured the regular girls could lay low until the Asians were gone, then they gradually and without attracting a lot of attention, come back to reclaim their territory. Certainly at this point they had nothing to lose. None of them were making much money, so laying low would just be an unpaid vacation from all of their unpaid working.

The first meeting was scheduled for the following Tuesday.

The hitch came on Saturday night. Saturday was a money day. Even if the rest of the week was slow, usually on Saturday from noon on late into the evening, there was a steady flow of johns. Around midnight was when it all peaked, the streets were lined with cruisers, and the action was fast and furious. In the past the girls had always seen some serious paper.

It was about 11 pm and Lilly and Shawna were in their favorite spot about a block downwind from a Popeyes Fried Chicken. Lilly actually had pulled a couple of tricks that day but while Shawna had a lot of lookie-loos, she had yet to get any takers.

They heard the subsonic rumble of some Spanish hip hop and then spotted the familiar low slung tricked-out ride of Hector, one of Shawna's regulars from way back. They hadn't seen him in a while and both of them smiled as the car glided toward them. Hector was a real character and always had some crazy and cool things to lay on them. He smoked so much reefer, the girls could get high just standing next to the car talking to him. And he was good pay. Always rounded up to the nearest hundred and called Shawna his special loca chica.

The running joke was his unfailing promise to bring her an 50-carat diamond engagement ring. And then saying with big sad chihuahua eyes, how he forgot and left it in the safe back at his Upper East Side condo.

The car approached and Shawna stepped off the curb and opened her arms like she was going to give him a big hug. She could see he had two buddies with him.

But as the car approached, Shawna saw the driver's side window rolling up. When Hector pulled even with her, he didn't even give her a glance but instead flipped her off. Then he pulled the car over to the curb about fifty yards further, where three Djin Djin girls were standing under a street lamp.

Lilly was the first to say anything. "What was that all about?"

Shawna looked like she just found out her whole family had been killed in a car crash.

"Lilly, I truly respect you and what you're trying to do and I'll try to be there on Tuesday. But for now, I can't take this shit no more. Sometimes a niggah gotta take things into her own hands."

"Shawna, wait! Don't. Please don't …"

But Shawna was already crossing the busy street, cars screeching to a halt, honking at her. "Hey, you fat 'ho, what the fuck do you think you're doin'?"

There was a Djin Djin girl directly across from her, standing next to a news stand, freshening her lipstick.

"Come here you little cunt. You and me gotta talk."

"Uh … no … no. Must go now."

Walking up to her and grabbing her hair and twisting it around her hand, Shawna forced the girl to her knees. She tightened her grip and yanked the girl's head side to side.

"Ow! Please. No! Don't hurt. Please don't hurt."

"Just who do you think you are, you little shit? Huh? Just who?"

"I just like you. Try to make money."

"You are stealing *my* money, you bitch. You are taking food off *my* table."

"Ow! Please. You hurting me."

"Oh gee! So velly solly. Don't mean to hurt the poor little girl. I no hurt you. Actually I'm what I'm gonna do is *kill* you!"

Shawna dragged the girl by her hair, forcing her to her feet, then bent her over the hood of a parked car. She then started punching, slapping, kicking, scratching, and gouging, all the while screaming at the top of her lungs.

"Fuck you, you little motherfucker. You skinny little wasted piece of sushi. Get the fuck out of my territory and stay out. You have fucked me long enough. Slanty-eyed slut whore. You are history! Go back to where you came from, you fucking whore gook motherfucker. You …"

Cars stopped, people came running from up and down the street and in less than 60 seconds a sizeable crowd surrounded the them. It took two stocky, rather muscular guys to pull Shawna off the girl, who then curled into a tight ball, whimpering and still covering her face with her blood-streaked arms. Two other Djin Djin girls came over to her and convinced her it was safe to make a retreat, then quickly escorted her away from the scene.

The two young men continued to tightly grip Shawna, and gradually talked her down. Soon she collapsed, exhausted by the enormous amount of energy expended in her paroxysm of violence. She started to sob.

"I just wanna go home. Can I go home?"

"We definitely need to get you outta here. Before the police arrive. Come with us."

Shawna got up and glanced at them as they led her away. The both wore characteristic red berets which were familiar symbols in other parts of Brooklyn.

"You Guardian Angels?"

"Yeah, we are. Our van is right around the corner. You can't go home. They'll be looking for you."

"Who? Those little whores?"

"The blues. They'll definitely take you downtown"

They got in the van and pulled away heading north, where the Guardian Angels precinct office was located. The driver spoke evenly as he made his way through traffic.

"We think the local cops are in on this. Everyone is up in arms about this whole Djin Djin situation. The whole community. Especially the parent-teacher groups. They came to us first because they knew that unless something serious came down, you know, a riot or something, the police would keep their distance. The idea was for us to talk to the blues and try to get them to do something. But when we met with Fiori, the Precinct Captain, he told us to back off."

His partner riding shotgun piped in. "I was right there. He made it very clear. Fiori looked right at us and said something like, 'You don't want to touch this. This is a time bomb ticking. Forget you ever heard of the Djin Djin girls.' There was no room for discussion."

Shawna was trying to process all of this. What did this mean? The cops were on the take. What's new? She had had to pay her dues along the way, just like all the other girls. But had their loyalties shifted?

After spending two days in a safe house belonging to the sister of one of the Angels, Shawna made her way back home. It was Tuesday and she arrived in time to attend the first meeting Lilly had organized.

It certainly was a hot and heavy affair, though hardly very productive. She heard the same self-pitying whining, wild-eyed threats, yelling and cursing, that she had been hearing every night on the streets. Finally, Lilly shared her idea about an Ad Hoc Committee To Save Our Neighborhood. There was a lot of moaning and confusion.

"Who the hell is Ad Hoc, some friend of yours?"

"How about a Fuck You Committee To Kick Some Asian Ass?"

"Whatcha thinkin' girl? You gone crazy on us? That's like lining up in front of a firing squad hoping they gonna miss. They'll shoot us and then go look for some Djin Djin booty to hump."

Everyone left discouraged but agreed to meet the following Tuesday.

They were all back on the street later that night and for the next couple days, things seemed to be pretty normal, or as normal as they had been since the Djin Djin girls had invaded.

Then something amazing and baffling happened.

It was Friday, early evening. Gradually the regular girls appeared, slipping into doorways, and strutting their way up and down the main drag. But it was uncharacteristically quiet. Something was very different. By eight o'clock, it was more like a private cemetery than a flesh-for-fantasy hooker haven.

"Lilly girl, am I imagining this? Or are you seein' what I'm seein'?"

"They're gone."

And they were. There was that night and for the coming weeks no sign of the Djin Djin girls.

Christmas in September

The inside of his eyelids were a melting field of light. He opened them to the gradual dissolving of a formless cloud. Then objects appeared. And the shape of a room. The smell of floor wax and disinfectant. And food cooking.

He heard little voices in the background. Giggling. Chattering away.

It took several minutes for his eyes to focus. But the gelatinous blur eventually cleared. He was in a small room. A bedroom? Definitely not a hospital. There were dozens of framed picture prints on the walls, sacred scenes from the Bible. Adam and Eve being evicted. Moses receiving the Ten Commandments. Baby Jesus glowing and swaddling in a barn, adored by the usual manger suspects. Jesus handing loaves of bread to his loyal disciples. Jesus dying on the cross. There was a rosary hanging from a nail.

Lenny tried to move his arm. What the fuck was this? Tied to the bed. Feet as well tethered to the bed frame. Definitely not a hospital.

Kimnai cautiously rounded the doorway. Seeing Lenny awake she stopped abruptly. Surprise and relief on her wide-eyed young face. She backed into the hall.

"Please don't leave. I've forgotten your name."

"Kimnai. I need to let them know. I'll be right back."

She disappeared and Lenny could hear her brisk, light steps receding.

Lenny took a quick survey of himself. Bandages. He could feel several bandages. On his face, his neck and back. There was another taped over a needle inserted in his left arm. The bottle feeding him a clear liquid was jerry rigged over his head to a curtain rod behind him. Nice work. I'm in really good hands.

Sarcasm felt good. Evidence he wasn't dreaming.

Several little round Asian faces appeared at the door. Whispering. Exchanging comments in some Asian language. He recognized two or three of them. They had been down there to feed him. All girls. All wearing the same skirt and blouse combination. Navy blue and white. What was this, a school?

Heavy footsteps approached.

"You are looking much better." The Bishop. Attired this time less formally in black pants, and a black shirt with a cleric collar. Hair not quite combed. Kimnai still in the hall, peering around the Bishop timidly.

"Like you fucking care."

"Oh Lenny, we care. We care a lot. We can't let anything happen to you until we get what we want out of you."

"I don't have anything you want."

"Oh, I think you do. But rest for now. We will talk over the next few days."

The Bishop left as abruptly as he had appeared. Not much on ceremony, except for his public appearances at the altar, Lenny thought. What a phony. What an evil bastard!

Kimnai entered and tentatively approached the side of the bed. "Can I get you anything?" Her lips trembled slightly and her eyes fought against the tears that pressed from within.

"You are a very sweet girl. But I don't think you can help me."

"I'll be right back."

She was gone for three or four minutes and returned with a glass of orange juice in one hand and a book in the other. She put a straw in the glass and tipped it towards Lenny. When the juice touched his tongue, he realized how thirsty he was and emptied the glass quickly. The orange juice burned his parched mouth and filled his stomach with a hot unpleasant sensation. But still tasted good.

Kimnai began to read: "No one knew how high the river went up into the mountains. Many had tried to find its source but to no avail. Everyday the villagers bent beside the waters, to bathe and do their laundry …"

And so it went for the next few days. Kimnai there by his side, ministering to his needs, changing his bandages, bringing food and liquids, reading him stories from her homeland. Thailand.

Sometimes she would stop and stifle a sniffle. But quickly recovering, she would continue. She often laughed at parts in the stories. Lenny had no idea what was funny. But he could not help but be charmed by this fragile little Thai angel.

"How old are you, Kimnai?"

"I am fourteen. Fifteen very soon, in December."

"What are you doing here? In America, I mean."

"I don't know. I just ended up here."

Lenny's appetite was returning. Kimnai fed him. Just like a baby. One spoonful at a time. He could feel his strength returning. Two of the bandages came off. He was a quick healer.

This routine, pleasant enough under the circumstances, was only interrupted each morning by a visit from the doctor. The same one that gave him an injection in the cage. Lenny assumed he was a doctor. He seemed to know something about medicine. But no way could he be a practicing professional. Maybe his licensed had been jerked. Malpractice? Involuntary manslaughter? Not like Lenny had any choice in the matter. He was strapped to a bed and at the mercy of this hack.

The fever had abated and Lenny could feel his health slowly rebuilding. Kimnai took great pains to provide what comfort she could. What an amazing child! And yes, even at fourteen, still a child.

"Kimnai, do you have brothers and sisters?"

Excitedly. "Oh yes! Three sisters. Two brothers. One brother older than me. The rest younger. A lot younger. My parents got very busy." She giggled. "One time I caught them. They were so mad. But I heard them and I thought something was wrong."

"Are they over here?"

"No … just me." Smiling. Puckering her lips and posing like she was on the cover of Cosmopolitan. "I am the world traveler in the family, you see." Laughing at herself.

"Why are you here? With the Bishop, I mean?"

"It's time for a story, Mr. Lenny. What would you like to hear? Maybe a Bible story?"

"Oh no, PLEASE! Please, no Bible stories."

"How can you expect God to forgive you?" She was playfully taunting him, wagging her tiny finger in his face. "He is infinitely good and patient and compassionate. But you might be pushing his limits."

Lenny was charmed. Where did this crazy little girl come from? What a piece of work! Fourteen going on twenty-five. But still so innocent. If I ever have a kid, she better like this one or I'll dump her in the Hudson.

"So where are we? Is this a dormitory?"

"It used to be a convent. Where all the penguins lived before they moved the school." Hands covering a giggle.

They passed the rest of the afternoon like this. Lenny was definitely getting back up to speed. He was feeling pretty decent. Despite being a prisoner. In a convent no less. What would the boys think about this? And his hanging out with a 14-year-old girl. But he realized that his escape from the jaws of death was in no small part due to this sweet, young lady who was taking such pains to nurse him to health and buoy his spirits. Who woulda thunk?

He heard someone coming down the hall. At least two, maybe three of them. Definitely men.

The Bishop entered first. Followed by Lenny's former associates, Martin and Frankie. Lenny's face went hot and his eyes narrowed. Turncoats!

Bishop Mulcahey gently touched Kimnai's cheek and said, "You may go now child. Thank you. Back to your room."

Frankie closed the door behind her. He and Martin then leaned against it. Hands clasped in front of them, staring at him. They looked like a couple of bad dreams in search of a victim.

The Bishop sat in the chair next to the bed Kimnai always used when reading to Lenny.

"So. Do you feel like talking? Maybe things will go better for you if you get some of this off your chest."

Mockingly. "Are you hearing my confession?"

"Yes … yes, you could put it that way. I know who you work for, Lenny. At least I think I do. I'd like to know what you know and how you are involved in all of this."

"All of what?" Lenny was getting pissed.

"I see you've taken a liking to Kimnai. You like the little girls, eh? Not just for business."

"Yeah, just like you like the little boys."

"Lenny, you don't have to believe this. But what I am saying happens to be true. That never happened."

"Right right. And God pitches for the Yankees."

"How are you getting these girls into the country? And who's teaching them the ropes?"

"What are you talking about?"

"You know what I'm talking about! The Djin Djin girls. These adolescents from Thailand that are working the streets. With the fine work of Frankie and Martin here, we just managed to rescue fifteen of them. Every girl you see staying her was out there making your bosses rich selling their young bodies."

"Listen, your royal holiness, the first I ever heard of the Djin Djin girls is when I arrived here at this slumber party you threw for them. The question is, in my view, what is *your* interest in them?"

Bishop points his thumb at Frankie and Martin, still in statue mode. "Your friends tell me you run a very lucrative sex business for some guys out of Chicago."

"So? We have a little online thing happening. You can lease a nice piece from us. Pro stuff. And all our girls are white and over 18."

"No no, uh uh! I hear that you and your sorry compatriots control all of the action out there and this Asian invasion is just the latest entrepreneurial venture."

"You are sadly misinformed."

"Lenny, my malignant miscreant. There is a cancer spreading. And we're going to stop it."

"You should know. It's called the Catholic Church. The cancer is being spread by you and all of the other priests who can't keep their pants zipped."

The Bishop's face reddened, though he tried to masquerade composure. He casually stood up and walked over to Frankie and whispered something. Frankie pulled out his cell phone and stepped into the hall.

Back in the chair, the Bishop cupped his hands in front of him. His eyes burrowed ominously into Lenny's. "I don't know why you are protecting them. But I can assure you, it's not worth it."

"I'm not protecting anyone. I have no idea how it got started … this Asian thing. I don't work the streets. This is 2005. The internet is where it's at. It's clean. No risk."

"You really expect me to believe this. You can swim in the ocean and not get wet?"

"Look. What I do is simple. Just go to www.newyorkpantieraid.com or www.nylickers.tv and you'll get the whole picture. That's what I do. That's all I do."

"You're on the inside of this. You know exactly what's going on with these poor girls. Play dumb and you'll just get yourself in deeper. You must be a very sick man to be part of any organization—"

The door opened and the doctor entered looking agitated.

Lenny couldn't conceal his hatred for this hack. "Dr. Freakenstein."

The Bishop smiled and extended his arms, a gesture of welcome.

"Ah yes. Thanks for coming on short notice. I know you're a busy man." The Bishop a consummate diplomat even with the scum of the earth. "Lenny here is very tense. Very tense. And quite uncooperative. I think he needs a sedative. A very strong sedative."

The doctor quickly opened his cheap briefcase. Impatiently. The Bishop's instructions were obviously being carried out under duress. Out came the syringe and bottle. And again on went the latex gloves.

Lenny glared at him with contempt. What? Does this guy think I have AIDS?

The Bishop stood to leave. "Lenny. You need more time to think. You need to … to work on your priorities. God be with you." Then to the doctor as he left, "Put him out, please."

The needle stung going in. Lenny felt a dull burning knot in his arm as the doctor hastily pushed the plunger. Within seconds, Lenny's consciousness collapsed on itself.

In the timeless void of unconsciousness, dreams come and go. Tumbling, floating, flashing, flying, dissolving one into another. Juxtapositions of random mind stuff. Collages of imagery dance to a music which plays in a separate, cocooned reality. Sounds and smells go in through the normal channels but merely massage the surrealistic theater of the subconscious — until the chemistry and synaptic energy of the human body align and again join us to what we think of as the real world.

Lenny heard Christmas music. Faintly at first. But as in fits and starts he came to, the music overwhelmed the internal hum of his own guttural moaning. Louder and louder it played. Until it was like thunder. A deafening roar.

"God rest ye merry gentlemen
Let nothing you dismay
Remember Christ our Savior
Was born on Christmas Day"

Through his eyelids came bright flashing. On and off. On and off.

Lenny fought the grogginess, the paralyzing numbness which was slowly releasing its grip, and finally managed to raise himself onto one elbow. He forced his eyes open and was nearly blinded as a Christmas tree flashed in a brilliant burst hundreds of bright white bulbs. On and off. On and off. He then spotted the huge speaker cabinets. Rock concert-size behemoths, with massive mid-range horns on top. Blasting out a thunderous chorus of male voices.

"God rest ye merry gentlemen ..."

It was the loudest music he ever remembered hearing.

"Let nothing you dismay ..."

He closed his eyes as tight as he could and clamped his hands over his ears. But nothing kept out the outrageous sensory din.

"Remember Christ our Savior ..."

He shuddered, and then forced himself to look around. Yes, he was back in his cage. But they had done some redecorating to his chamber of horrors.

"Was born on Christmas Day ..."

The entire dungeon was accessorized with holly, tinsel, bulbs, red and green crepe, strings of flashing lights, and sprays of spruce. A tiny sprig of mistletoe hung from the top of his cage.

It was Christmas in September.

A Kidnapping

The human mind protects itself. At least it tries. But its floodgate is more a dike than a dam. And in a tsunami, far more of the torrent breaches the top than is held back by the nervous system's feeble protective levee.

After four days, the razor edge of the sensory juggernaut was perhaps somewhat dulled. But it still continued to cut deeply into Lenny's sensibilities, hacking away at his sanity and control.

The pulsing of the lights seemed embedded in a fiery glare which persisted even when his eyes were closed. His eyes burned like acid had been thrown into them, and random bursts of what felt like electric shocks shot from the top of his head down through his neck and arms. He no longer heard the words and melody of *God Rest Ye Merry Gentlemen*. What he heard and felt was a searing roar, like a screaming nuclear explosion, which pushed its way into his ears like darning needles and hacked mercilessly at his eardrums. The pain was excruciating and the pressure in his head kept building until he would scream like a wounded beast. This paradoxically would produce 30 or 40 seconds of relief. But the self-induced deafness was short-lived and would make a cowering retreat from the cruel and relentless assault of the music.

This Möbius strip of psychological torture would loop over and over again, predictably leading Lenny closer to the fringes and threshold of his own sanity.

He had not slept in almost 100 hours, instead would periodically slip into a momentary stupor, like a fighter reeling from a landed punch, still standing but in some gelatinous bowl of consciousness where everything slogged and limped, lurched and stumbled in a surreal yaw. Then suddenly he would see his own face rush at him, but his face as a roaring belching diesel truck, speeding at him out of control and crushing him, rolling over his mutilated corpse. Instantly he'd be back in the room. Frightened by the hallucination. Frightened to be out of it.

It had just happened again and Lenny was shaking. And crying. Was he crying? He really couldn't tell anymore.

Then suddenly everything stopped!

The room was dark and silent.

Power failure?

Lenny tried to stand up but his legs wouldn't support him. Huge vaporous sheets like the Northern Lights floated before his eyes. He knew the cellar was silent but a hurricane still hummed in his head. Not very loud, but a deep persistent howl. Ebbing sonic aftershocks.

Soon he was just barely able to hear real sounds from outside. Human voices. Loud thuds. Truck or car engines. More voices, this time children. And orders from adults. In hushed tones. Doors slamming.

Suddenly, a loud metallic crack sent a shock through him like a lightning bolt. Someone broke the lock on the cellar and was opening the door. Flashlights at the top pointing down the stairs. Looking for something. Him?

Who were they? Should he try to speak out? Then the lights pulled back and he heard footsteps receding.

Now he could hear vehicles pulling away. Several. There had to be three or four of them.

Then silence.

Lenny sat still for the longest time. He felt punch-drunk. But after a while the phantom lights and sounds he had experienced when the power was cut were almost gone. The numbness in his limbs and face started to dissolve and he sensed his mind was gradually beginning to clear.

Lenny sat there and let the real world slowly bathe him like a warm spring shower.

He glanced toward the stairs. Either the street lights or a full moon dimly filtered in from the outside. The cellar door was open. Exhausted as he was, he could not let this chance get by. He struggled to his feet and fought for his balance. Then took a few cautious steps. He hit his toe on something and stepped over it. As he approached the stairs, he started to feel more confidence. But he still climbed up very slowly and on all fours.

Peering out cautiously, he determined that no one was there out in the yard or parking lot. But the door to the rectory office was open and a light was on.

Unsteadily, Lenny crossed the yard and cautiously approached. When he looked in, he could not conceal his shock. Or his spiteful euphoria. For right before his eyes in the center of the room, looking completely helpless and horribly frightened was Bishop Mulcahey, gagged and bound to his executive office chair.

"Well well. Kind of kinky tonight, are we?"

The Bishop's eyes bulged in his head like hard boiled eggs, as he tried to say something and struggled against the ropes. His face was red with fear and fury and with pig-like grunting apparently was appealing to Lenny for help.

Lenny certainly understood but was still too weak to laugh. He managed a sadistic smile.

"You fucking want *me* to help *you*?" Gesturing to himself. "After this? After what you've done to me?"

Lenny circled the Bishop, who tried to follow Lenny with his terror-filled eyes. Lenny just kept pointing at the Bishop. As he continued his unsteady circling and jabbing his index finger toward the Bishop, Lenny's face contorted and he started breathing hard, each breath pumping with more and more rage. He was filled with more hatred than he thought was humanly possible. He tried to form words, to tell this cruel fuck what he thought of him.

But nothing came out. Nothing but the sound of an animal. A whimpering, crying song of pain and frustration.

Then Lenny stopped directly in front of the Bishop. He unzipped his fly and pulled out his penis. The Bishop looked horrified. Humiliated. Lenny was going to piss on him. And try he did. The Bishop pleaded with his eyes for Lenny to stop. He struggled violently against his binding, tried to form sounds which might make sense through the duct tape over his mouth. And Lenny tried his best to make the yellow Baptism flow.

But to no avail. Words had failed him. Now his piss had failed him.

No justice in the world.

Lenny put it away and zipped up. Suddenly with all of the strength he could muster, he kicked the Bishop square in the chest, sending him over backwards. The Bishop tumbled back, then onto his side, chair still tied to his body and arms.

Lenny could hear the Bishop moan as he made his way out of the room and into the night.

Big John

John Maximilian Harrison was pretty much a regular guy. He grew up in Pulaski, a small town in the western end of Virginia, undistinguished in every respect except for its proximity to Roanoke. John was born on a Tuesday in August, from infancy went to church every Sunday with his mom, dad and older sister. He transitioned from Cub Scouts to Eagle Scouts decked out with a decent number of merit badges, and in his high school years played varsity football and baseball while maintaining a C+ average. He loved shop class and it never crossed his mind to go to college.

John was a bit introverted but notwithstanding that, was the first among his hang buddies to have a steady girlfriend. He met Maggie at an after-game dance in their sophomore year and soon they were inseparable. It was puppy love as big as the sky and adolescent heat magnified by their shyness and prying eyes. This was 1963 and it was a small town. Everyone knew everyone and everything everyone was doing. The sexual revolution still over a decade away, especially for Pulaski. So despite the ferocity of their adolescent urges, they were determined and agreed to save the big moment for marriage. And so they did. It was the Christian thing to do.

After graduating high school, John and Maggie both took steady jobs, he as a lathe operator in a local furniture factory and she as a hospital nurse's aide, pooling and saving their money. They spent Friday and Saturday evenings seeing a movie or roller skating. Then overlooking the levy one county over, they would pant and groan in unfulfilled heavy petting. Late into the night, exhausted but unsatisfied they would lie in one another's arms and breathlessly share their dreams of the house and family they would one day have.

By then, John had a white '58 Chevy convertible with a St. Christopher's statue on the dash, wore his dishwater blond hair in a tight oily jellyroll, kept a pack of cigarettes folded in the left sleeve of his t-shirt, rarely drank or played poker with the boys, but at least a couple times a year attended the drag races in Roanoke. He still never missed Sunday church and every week added his weak and pitchless voice to the congregation's singing of the hymns. John always listened in rapt attention to the stories of Jesus and his disciples wandering the desert and visiting the villages of Galilee.

Pretty ordinary stuff for a pretty regular guy.

Then came Vietnam.

No one seemed to know what exactly was going on over there, at least no one John personally knew. But it appeared to be about stopping the cancerous spread of Communism. And as everyone was saying, either you stepped up to the plate and fulfilled your patriotic duty, or the plate stepped up to you in the form of the draft. Early in 1967 John signed on for three years in the Army. First choice infantry.

John kicked ass in boot camp. It was hard but at the same time very exciting and more fun than he had had in his entire life. He met guys from everywhere: Florida, Montana, Oklahoma, California, Ohio, Texas. They were a fiery bunch, thick with camaraderie, and totally committed to the idea of deep-sixing some commie gooks and making 'Veet-nay-um' safe for democracy and the American way.

When graduation from basic training arrived, everyone was stoked. Enough of the play stuff. Now for the real action. They were on their way to Vietnam! But no way was John going to get stuck in front of a typewriter in Saigon, or unloading trucks at some supply depot behind the lines. They were each given three choices of assignment and for all three John wrote 'COMBAT' big and bold. He wanted action.

Action he got.

Within three days of landing at Tan Son Nhut Airport and fast-track briefing at Camp Alpha, the in-processing base in Saigon, he was deployed to Berin Sac, the operational camp in Binh Dinh Province. Only one of his boot camp buds was part of this new contingent. But again, all the newbies that arrived with him came from everywhere in the States and were as fired up as he was. All enlistees. All there because they wanted to be.

The day after he transported to Berin Sac and reported to the commanding officer, he went out on his first patrol — and got a quick education in what this war was like. How unlike any other war it was. How invisible the enemy was and at the same time how devastatingly lethal. They lost three men in just five hours. And not a shot was fired.

The first one took a land mine up the ass and what was left of him dropped to the ground like a lawn bag full of meat scraps. His name was Eddie. From Georgia — Atlanta, Georgia.

Number two was Tony. From Chicago. Tony noticed some suspicious looking dirt, like it had recently been dug up and then tamped down. He circled around it cautiously and fell into the real trap. A large hole in the ground completely camouflaged by grass and branches. He was impaled on three bamboo spears dipped in human excrement. The shit wasn't really necessary as one of the poles went into the base of his neck right up into his brain.

At that point everyone was badly shaken. And extremely suspicious of everything that moved and everything that didn't. They went to huge extremes to cover for one another, not taking a step or making a move without the concurrence of someone else, especially from the guys that had been here for a while and knew at least some of the guerilla-style tricks the Vietcong typically used. John's nerves were already completely frayed and this was only his first day out. But he and the remaining grunts of the recon company made slow, steady progress, and eventually were within two kilometers and the relative safety of camp.

Then someone shouted, "Heads up. There's someone up there. Over on the right side of the road behind that truck." They all pulled their guns close to their chests and got ready to fire. Then a little girl maybe six or seven years old ran out from behind what looked like an abandoned farm vehicle. She scurried across the path and disappeared into the bushes on the other side. As they all breathed a sigh of relief, one of the new guys who had arrived with John walked over next to where the little girl was sitting and noticed a doll made of straw and burlap laying on the ground. His name was Jessie and he was from North Dakota.

"Hey little girl, you forgot something."

As he bent down to pick up the doll, his squad leader shouted "No! Don't touch that!!"

But it was too late. The explosion was deafening and sent everyone sprawling. Everyone except for Jessie. There was nothing left of the upper half of Jessie's body when the smoke cleared. His legs lay several feet from the mangled truck like large twisted sausages.

Between the gasping and the convulsive sobs, John fought for control.

So this is Vietnam. God help us!

That was one of the worst days. Three men gone. Just like that. Three young men in the vitality and promise of youth vanquished by an unseen enemy.

Yes, it was one of the worst of many other bad days. Some consolation. Hey, today no one got deep-sixed! Only had one guy get his arms blown off. Or maybe only got his eyes cooked in their sockets like escargot. And that guy over there sure lucked out. Granted, he'll spend the rest of his life sitting in a wheelchair like a human rag doll and shitting into a plastic bag. But at least he's alive. A lot of others didn't make it. Like on the *really* bad days.

After weeks and eventually months of this living nightmare, John began to realize that none of them were the wiser for all of this unimaginable, incomprehensible carnage. With all of their collective battlefield experience, none of them were capable of even guessing the answer to the most basic questions of warfare: Where's the enemy? Who am I fighting?

Yes, there were skirmishes. The occasional brief encounters with something resembling a military unit. A squadron of GIs walking through what appeared to be an unoccupied forest. Then gunfire opening up from everywhere. From all sides and every direction. From snipers above in the trees. Even from below. The Cong would be half-buried in the ground or hiding in concealed trenches. The machine guns would unload up into the legs or up through the pelvis and torso of some defenseless grunt.

Ambushes made for much bigger numbers. They would always get at least four of our guys. One time only a single guy from an entire platoon survived.

But mostly this was an enemy that was shy and cunning, preferring the unpredictability and angst of invisibility, to the glamour and prowess of real military engagements. Thus it was the slow attrition that ultimately delivered the real numbers. One GI at a time, capped, poisoned, impaled, incinerated, exploded, skewered, snipered. One GI at a time sent home either in a body bag, or to be fitted for prosthetics. Drip drip. Chinese water torture. Drip drip drip. Vietcong murder torture. They took the American Army apart one GI at a time.

Something had to be done. And eventually something was done. It was a plan that came down from high in the command chain but whose implementation was left in the hands of individual squad leaders, sometimes the individual infantryman himself. For better or worse, high command's response to this cruel and unorthodox enemy was cryptically called the Zippo mission, or more descriptively "search and destroy". For John and the decimated fighting force of 1st Battalion, it was not a minute too soon. Something certainly needed to be done.

Later the following year, this tactic — the search and destroy mission, which was unique to the Vietnam War — would become fodder for the media and self-righteous pundits and politicians back in America. While John's platoon continued to duck bullets and sidestep landmines and other lethal traps, pompous opportunists back on American TV or in their editorial columns, would be carrying on and on about what would infamously be called the Mai Lai Massacre, and a Lt. William Calley would join the prominent ranks of history's most sinister wartime villains.

Lt. Calley just did what any self-respecting commander was doing at the time: Looking out for his men. Before this particular expedition, his Charlie Company had been hit and hit hard. Ambushes, land mines, the whole array of Vietcong tricks and traps. When they entered the village of My Lai, they were beyond edgy. They were desperate to get in, get the job done, and get out. *Without* taking men away in body bags. Or calling in the Medivacs.

There were reports in the news that there was no enemy fire. That Calley and his men went in unopposed and just opened up on the villagers, that the search and destroy mission turned into an orgy of killing, a bloodbath inflicted on innocent civilians. Even women, children, and the elderly. Shot, bayoneted, assassinated, in cold blood. There was one reported rape and killing of a young girl. Of kneeling victims murdered gangland-style with a bullet in the back of the head. Elderly blown away as they offered their last prayers to Buddha. And of one group of villagers ordered by Lt. Calley himself to dig a ditch and climb in, where they were exterminated like animals with multiple bursts of machine gun fire.

Reports.

Well, they could file all the reports they wanted. It's so easy sitting behind a typewriter in some office far-removed from the reality of the war, with a glass of lemonade on your desk, and some nice piece of ass keeping your pencils sharpened and your file folders tidy.

But as John and the guys in his and similar units knew, this My Lai thing was just business as usual in a war zone that was unlike any other war zone in history. In fact, compared to some of the shit he had been through, some of the Zippos he had been part of, My Lai was a fucking tea party. And this Lt. Calley guy should have been decorated with a Congressional Medal of Honor instead of dragged across the television screens and editorial pages of America to be humiliated, condemned, and lynched by the grain-fed media.

Innocent victims? Defenseless civilians? There were no such things in 'Nam. John had seen guys set up and murdered *by* women, children, and the elderly. One time a group of villagers knelt and prayed solemnly just before lobbing hand grenades and instantly killing three of his buddies. Another time, there was one of the finest young things you have ever seen, who wiggled her tight little Asian ass at a horndog infantryman, and when he went to her hut for some afternoon delight, was greeted by a hail of Kalishnikov bullets.

Innocent civilians. Fuck them all! None of them wanted us there. They did what they thought they had to do. And we did what we had to do. It was that simple. Search them out and destroy the motherfuckers before they destroyed you!

There was one time when John's unit attempted a more restrained approach to search and destroy. And it cost them dearly.

It was seven months into the Zippo missions. Apparently some negative feedback had made its way back to some the generals at command headquarters, hearsay about how the initial search and destroy mission ops directives were being misconstrued and how there were some instances of implementation which were in violation of the sacrosanct Geneva conventions. So a new clarification order was issued addressing some of these concerns and delineating a new set of counterinsurgency tactics. Generally it stipulated that there should be as much emphasis on "search", that is, the proper identification of enemy targets, as "destroy", which was their elimination from the field of engagement.

Right. Maybe they should hand out a questionnaire. Or check their family photo albums. Maybe sit around the village for a few days and eavesdrop in on some conversations over green tea.

But this was the military and chain of command was ironclad. After the order officially arrived at John's unit, as senseless and suicidal as it appeared to be, they now had to apply the new criteria and exercise demonstrable restraint in the field.

The first Zippo mission under the new guidelines was in Nam Tu'o'ng, about 30 kilometers from base camp. Even if no one had seen them, everyone knew that the immediate area was teeming with Cong. Evidence of movement of small squads and light equipment had been picked up by air recon for the past three months. And some of the surrounding fields were proving to be heavily mined, not the typical outcome of a decent rice harvest.

With an area presence of at minimum three months, it was highly likely that the guerillas had gotten to the locals, and with their effective combination of bribes, bombast and threats, won over enough of the peasants to create considerable loyalty to their cause, and certainly more of concern to John's unit, lethal levels of anti-government and anti-American sentiment.

It was a time bomb ticking. One that had to be defused and dissembled.

They arrived late in the morning on a Saturday and felt reasonably comfortable that the villagers were not aware of their presence, not yet anyway.

"Alright, everyone knows what the new orders are. So just be cool."

John had been seething at the thought of this senseless, horribly dangerous interference from high command. Usually he never questioned. He was the perfect soldier. But the guys up top couldn't possibly know what was going on here on the ground. Usually they went in blazing. Fuck identifying the enemy. They were all the enemy. It wasn't a matter of 'if' they would turn on you, it was a matter of 'when'. John and his men weren't trigger-happy killers. Certainly they weren't bloodthirsty. It was just about survival. And getting the job done.

"Those new orders are gonna get us killed."

"Orders are orders, John. We can still be sharp. Just keep your eyes open and everybody cover. Fire at anything suspicious. Just like always."

They split into two groups so they could enter the village from opposite sides.

When they met in the middle of town, it was all but empty. One old man sat next to his hut. He had one leg missing and stared into an undefined distance like a blind man. But he spoke some English.

"You come. Finally you come. Other soldiers pass by."

"We need to look around your village, old man."

"I bring everyone. They in huts. Very hot."

With surprising agility, he got to his feet and with primitive crutches constructed out of bamboo and held together with twine, hobbled from one hut to another. One by one, the villagers came out and wandered to an area in front of the soldiers. There were over sixty of them, all ages, children, adults, the elderly. They looked humble, frightened. And harmless.

Nevertheless, no one in John's unit let their guard down even for an instant. They kept their rifles trained on the villagers, and kept an eye for any suspicious movement, bulges in clothing, anything that might signal a potential attack.

"Frankie. Take Hank, Richard and Rondo and make sure the village is clean. Be careful. There may be tunnels."

The inspection team was extremely cautious. But it was a small village. They were done in a little over twenty minutes.

"Tell your people we are done here for now. They can go back to doing whatever they were doing. But we'll be back."

The villagers scurried away, back to their respective huts. Almost too quickly. Even the old man left hastily with two children in tow, and disappeared into the hut furthest from where the unit stood. John and his men were still wary and continued to hold their M16s high on their shoulders in firing ready position.

Slowly and cautiously they started to back out of the village, with the men at the advancing edge doing 360s to make sure they weren't getting caught from the rear.

Suddenly, bursts of flame and smoke issued from the two huts at the back of the village. Before anyone barely registered what was happening, the explosions of two grenades from a Vietcong RPG-7 rocket launcher were taking apart three of the infantrymen. Dropping to the ground, John and his men immediately opened fire but the M16s of the two guys on either side of him jammed. Then a burst of fire from huts on each side of the scattering members of his unit, these from Simonov semi-automatics, caught two more of the Americans.

They were still alive but cried out in pain and terror.

The unit continued to be pinned down for the next ten minutes, but finally their superiority in tactics and firepower quickly reversed what advantage the attackers had by virtue of surprise. Volley after volley of hand-thrown and M-79 delivered grenades silenced the guerillas and reduced every last hut to a smoking pile of reeds. Everything that moved was gunned down, and just to make sure the "destroy" aspect of the mission was thoroughly implemented, the members of John's unit fanned out over the entire village and put a bullet into the head of each and every one of these diabolical motherfuckers. Yes, they had done some damage. But now it was certain that no one from this village would ever again inflict their sinister, commie-inspired cruelty and treachery on a God-fearing American soldier.

It was probably for the best that the reporters and pundits didn't know about this or countless other slaughterfests just like it. By default they glommed onto and had a field day with the My Lai affair. With the war becoming more and more unpopular by the day, this gruesome story was perfect grist for a media mill which would seize on any opportunity to discredit America and the brave men who with every moment spent walking through the fields and jungles of Vietnam, risked everything to keep these very same reporters and pundits safe and comfortable in their air-conditioned offices with their water coolers and fluorescent lights.

John became a walking cauldron of rage. My Lai, my ass!

If they only knew the truth. The reality that he lived. It was survival. One day at a time. One Vietcong corpse at a time.

Fuck these self-important cowards, with their bloated egos who suck on the tits of other people's horror! Who faced no greater danger than a tangled telephone cord or a paper cut. John had been there and knew the truth. He knew that this was an enemy more vicious, more incorrigible, more cunning and ruthless than America had ever faced. An enemy with the face of a child, a mother, even an old man. Every slanty-eyed gook carried a death warrant with your name on it. There was only one solution. Kill them all!

For over two years, John crawled through this jungle of fear and death, somehow surviving, while the men he served with, one by one met their maker. Every time one of his buddies went down, he renewed his vow to avenge their deaths. He cursed the godlessness and treachery of Vietnam. He sobbed as he collected their dog tags and each time whispered a final prayer and farewell to his vanquished comrade. Then he went looking for the monsters who were responsible for the carnage. Anyone with slanty eyes. Anyone.

John could never kill enough of these gooks to slake his thirst for their blood, or cool the volcanic furnace of hatred which each day burned hotter and hotter in his heart. He stopped sleeping and volunteered for extra Zippo duty, living for the rush of entering into a new village and cleansing the planet of the commie vermin who arbitrarily destroyed good decent human beings, cut down without hesitation or remorse, the brave young American soldiers who were the best men John had ever known.

When his tour of duty ended, he even tried to reenlist but was rejected. Psychiatric reasons they said. Right. What did these pencil pushers know? What could they possibly know? John had been there. He knew the truth. He knew what he had to do. And he did it.

After he was decommissioned and returned stateside, he took a bus to Roanoke and figured from there he could hitch a ride back home to Pulaski. The bus arrived late in the evening, so he got a cheap motel room by the bus station to chill out. He would head out in the morning.

After four cans of beer and an hour of late night news on TV, John was still restless. Something was eating at him. It just didn't feel right, going back home after what he had been through. He wanted to see Maggie but did she want to see him? She hadn't written him in over a year. Twenty-six of his letters unanswered. He had even tried calling her during the Christmas holidays but couldn't get hold of her.

What was there in Pulaski? Who could he talk to? No one would understand. None of his friends were around. His parents? What could he say to them? "Yeah, I killed a few thousand gooks. How's grandpa? Hey mom, your hair looks nice." Even Pastor Jim wouldn't understand. His mouth would open wide in a toothy Pepsodent grin and his hand would go on the shoulder. Then they would kneel and solemnly pray for God's mercy and forgiveness. How pathetic. How absurd! Like Pastor Jim had even the slightest clue as to what God might have in mind for a vile and violent place like 'Nam. John had been there. He knew the truth. He knew what he had to do. And he did it.

What now?

He leaned back onto his pillow and stared at the ceiling for what seemed like hours. Then he had to piss. Badly. On his way back from the bathroom, he saw on the corner of the cheap laminated wood table next to his bed a Gideon's Bible. Standard equipment in dive motels across America.

John picked it up and opened it randomly to a page in the New Testament. His eyes immediately went to Matthew 3:10 …

> *And now also the axe is laid unto the root of the trees:*
> *therefore every tree which bringeth not forth good fruit*
> *is hewn down, and cast into the fire.*

The verse entered him like a sweet syrup, coating his tongue and throat, the hollow of his chest, and the linings of the sound chamber in his mind. Like a mantra of milk and honey, it repeated itself, a tape loop which played to his craving psyche like a beautiful and familiar piece of music. John felt a warmth and pleasant ache spread through his body. Then stark images started to explode in his head. Police beating the traitorous anti-war protesters marching in Times Square. The storefront window of a military recruiting center in the Bronx smeared with eggs and vulgar graffiti. Hundreds of Asians with their pathetic pleading eyes at a rally in Battery Park courting public support for political refugee asylum appeals by their relatives in Vietnam. His heart pounded like a jackhammer. He could smell jasmine and the stench of decomposing corpses. His hands clenched like tightly-wound balls of spring steel. Tears formed and pooled in his eyes.

John just stood there. For hours. The sun came up.

Finally, he threw loose items into his duffel bag.

He arrived at the bus station just as the ticket office opened.

"New York City, please."

Chapter 4

MALAYSIA: The New Economics

Outsourcing

It had to be done. Basic economics. Save production costs and improve the bottom line.

Outsourcing.

This was the clarion call, the new mantra which drove the re-organization of corporate supply chains from the 1980s on. God bless you, Ronald Reagan. Maybe you weren't such a great actor, but you sure put the corporations on a fast track to some serious money, when you got rid of all those silly regulations and artificial barriers to the free flow of human labor. And put into place trade agreements which made the stockholders of major manufacturing firms wet their pants with joy.

And hats off to you too, George Sr. and Billy Bob. Looking in the sauce pan of consortiums and associations, it's a delectable alphabet soup bubbling over the edges indeed. It whets the appetite, coats the tongue, and warms the belly of every free-market capitalist across America and Europe. WTO, FTAA, ASEAN, NAFTA, MEFTA, APEC.

Jangle jangle. Come on down. Everyone's a winner.

Especially those poor uneducated, underemployed, underfed creatures in the third world. Until we came along, what were their prospects? More empty bellies. Until we came along, what were their chances of surviving? Infant mortality rates in high double digits. Until we came along, what was the quality of life? Disease and unsanitary food and drinking water making miserable their short and unsatisfying lives. Until we came along ...

And now we have Taco Bell in Beijing, McDonalds in Danang, KFC in Hanoi, Starbucks in Vientiane, Burger King in Bangkok, Pizza Hut in Kuala Lumpur.

Fast food for people on a fast track to happiness. Western style happiness.

Now *that* is progress. Welcome to the new economy.

Work Ethic

Her father named her Dawa, which means 'born on a Monday', because she was. It was a Tibetan name, her grandfather being from there and who having found his way down to Mong Nai, Burma via Dhaka and Chittagong, fathered seven children by a Burmese woman, one of whom was Dawa's father, Sonam.

Sonam, as a young man sought a brighter future, so at sixteen he piled all of his meager possessions on his back, headed east, and eventually settled in Ban Huai Luang, a farming village in the very north of Thailand.

There he met Kama Choi, a quiet but graceful young girl from a hillside tribe. They married and she soon became Dawa's mother.

Dawa was the first of the six children, four girls and two boys, spaced only twelve to fourteen months apart. She was just turning six, when her mother's frail body finally was overwhelmed by the punishing strains of successive birthings, the brutal work laboring in the rice fields, and the constant struggle to keep her family fed and clothed. The relatively young woman died in childbirth, after bringing into the world the newest member of the family, a baby girl born blind and with a cleft palate.

It all proved too much for Sonam. Gripped by grief and despair, his spirit irreparably broken, he sat for days crying and mumbling incantations. If it weren't for the kindness of families in adjacent huts, the children would have starved. The new baby, receiving but the bare minimum of attention and care, soon became very sick and died. Covered with flies, she lay in the corner of the hut on a reed mat. Sonam was too weak and paralyzed to move her.

To mitigate the crisis, Dawa's grandmother, living less than two kilometers away, moved in. And then began to move the children out. The three youngest were sent back to her own village, where they would be cared for by her sister and her sister's three grown children, who all lived and worked on the family farm.

Dawa and her brother Boonchu were put on the first of a series of buses and eventually arrived back in Burma, where their paternal grandparents still lived and struggled to sell their handwoven baskets and floor mats at a local market.

Unfortunately, the grandparents were old beyond their years, always just barely feeding themselves. The additional responsibility and financial burden of two young children taxed their broken bodies beyond their limits. In desperate need of money, only six months after they had arrived, Dawa and her brother were sold to a child labor broker back in Thailand.

Dawa was healthy and strong for her size, certainly capable of doing menial farm work, rice planting and harvesting. So for the next five years, until she was twelve, she worked seven days a week at six different farms around Nong Khai and later Udon Thani. She was given a place to sleep and enough food to keep her alive. Though they often worked on the same farm, she saw her brother only occasionally, and never saw the rest of her family ever again.

Shortly after her twelfth birthday, a boy she worked with was sent out to fetch her from the paddy, where she was spacing rice plants, and removing those which were stunted or diseased. She was told to gather her things, and carrying what little she had in a small bundle, she climbed on the back of a pick-up truck. For two days she bounced around with thirteen other children, all slightly older than her, alternately clutching her possessions or using them as a pillow. The only relief from the blazing hot sun was at night, when it cooled enough for them to breathe. There wasn't enough room for them to lay down. They slept upright, leaning against one another or the side of the truck bed.

Finally, exhausted, hungry, filthy, they arrived in Da Nang City, Vietnam.

It was just before midnight when they pulled up to a large, windowless cinderblock building. They were immediately taken inside to a barracks dorm, nothing more than eighty or more grimy mats on the cement floor of a warehouse in a manufacturing zone on the outskirts of the city. They randomly scattered and collapsed on the provided mats, some already occupied by children their own age, who appeared to have been staying there for some time. Within twenty minutes, Dawa and the other new arrivals were sound asleep.

It felt like she had only been sleeping for a very short time, when she was jarred from the bottomless immersion of a dream about her mother and younger brother, by a loud and cacophonous banging. She bolted upright and saw a short, nearly bald man, fat stomach and bulbous legs stuffed into hemp drawstring pants, wearing a Coke Classic t-shirt, banging on the side of a metal garbage can with a cane. He seemed to take a cruel delight in the raucous exercise.

"Wake up, my pathetic little monkeys! It's time to go to work. No slagging. Get your food and eat quick. No time for delays."

A boy maybe thirteen or fourteen on the mat next to her, spoke softly as he quickly rolled up his bed clothes.

"That's Tinh Huynh. He's the boss here. Do what he says or you'll be in big trouble."

They all herded through a door and then formed a single file. Each was given a small serving of rice and a bowl of watery soup. They were in a cafeteria-style room but there were only three long tables, not enough to seat more than twenty. Dawa stood there looking around, before finally sitting down and leaning against the wall opposite the serving line. Though the rice tasted stale and dirty, and the colorless soup was so salty it burned the throat, all the children ate hungrily. Dawa wondered when their last meal had been.

Someone was reading her mind. "We had some food around 9 pm last night. Same time every night."

It was the boy who slept on mat next to her. He came over and sandwiching himself between a couple of other children, sat at her feet.

"I've been here over a year. It never gets any better. It's a prison. But I think the food is better in prison."

"Do you have a name?"

"Just call me Pretzel."

She timidly smiled, almost giggled. When was the last time she giggled?

"I'm Dawa. I'm from Thailand. What time is it? I am still so tired."

"Maybe 4:30 or 5:00. There are no clocks around here. But they make us start before the sun comes up."

Tinh Huynh entered the room banging on the garbage can again.

"Time to go. Those who have been here know where you're supposed to be. The ones who arrived last night, stay here and I will explain. Let's go now. Hurry! Hurry!"

All but the fourteen new arrivals scurried out of the room, leaving their bowls and plates where they had been sitting. Dawa waved a timid good-bye to Pretzel but he was on his way out and didn't see her.

One girl on the other side of the room was bent over. Her hands covered her mouth but a soft whimpering could be heard coming from her.

"You! What's wrong with you? Are you sick?"

Tinh Huynh walked over to her and putting the cane under her chin, forced her to sit upright. Her face was wet and blotchy.

"The rest of you. See what we have here? This is a good lesson for all of you. You see, this young lady cries because she is so very anxious to get to work. And she thinks my talking, this lecture from the esteemed Tinh Huynh, is a waste of her time."

He whacked her across the head with the cane, delivering a severe blow directly to her ear.

"While your work ethic is very admirable, little mannequin, I cannot let your disrespect for me go unpunished. You will remain here when the others have been dismissed."

The girl slumped back, pain from the blow and fear for the confrontation to come, her face twisting in humiliation and agony.

"The rules are simple here. You work and do what you are told to do. That is why you are here. You'll get a meal at mid-day and another this evening. If you need to piss or shit, you can do that. Since there are only four toilets in the latrine, you will be told when you can go. If you have to go, just wait until your turn. When your time comes, use it. You will not get another for at least six hours. If you have a problem, let your foreman know and if it is a legitimate complaint, he will bring it up with me. I cannot be bothered directly with your problems. Usually it is just whining about nothing. So do not *ever* try to talk to me, unless I address you first. Today will be easy. We will teach you what to do. But tomorrow on, you work and work hard. No talking. Anyone caught talking will be severely punished. Now, all of you, get up and go through that door. My assistant Kuhn is waiting to show you what you need to know."

Pointing at the girl who had been crying.

"You, weeping willow. You stay here with me. The rest of you go. Now. Quickly! Time is wasting!"

Dawa was swept through the door by the panicky group. The collective fear of the man was a thick, shared hysteria.

Waiting on the other side was Kuhn, a frightening sight on his own terms. He was uncommonly tall, concentration-camp thin, with a severe, angular face and pronounced jaw. His eyes were huge and deep-set, hair medium-length but loose and greasy. His teeth were too large for his mouth and were discolored and rotting, though several were conspicuously outlined with gold reinforcements. There was a slight jerkiness to his head as he spoke.

"We make toys. Toys for the spoiled little children in America and Europe to play with for a few minutes, then toss away. These toys are cheap and of little value. They only have to last as long as it takes for these fat, overfed kids to eat the greasy shit they feed them in America and then move on to some other silly diversion. I have seen this with my own eyes, when I attended university in America. Yes, this stickman who stands before you has been to a great university in the Promised Land. Now he is here with you on one important mission. And that is to get you to make as many toys as humanly possible, as quickly as possible. We are not concerned with quality. We are concerned with quantity. You will work fast, not stop to sneeze, not stop to wipe your brow or pick your nose, and especially not to talk to anyone around you. You are here to make toys. Many many toys. Understood?"

He scanned the frightened faces of this latest harvest of human flesh, then walked over to Dawa and gestured for her to come with him.

"I will take you one at a time to your workstations. Do not talk or wander. Wait here until I come back for you."

A security guard armed with a pistol and club stepped into the room and signaled by his demeanor his intent to enforce Kuhn's instructions.

Dawa could barely keep up as she followed Kuhn into a narrow corridor and down a flight of stairs. Then through another hallway which led to a series of large widely-spaced doors.

"Let's see your hands."

Dawa tentatively held out her hands which he roughly took, turning them front and back.

"You'll be good for paints. Looks like you've been doing a lot of work in the fields. Been on a farm?"

"Yes. Planting rice."

"Clean the dirt out of your nails before you touch anything. Come in here."

He opened a door marked *Paints and Stripping*.

As soon as they walked in, Dawa's breath caught in her throat and her eyes started to burn. There was some acrid vapor that seemed to permeate the entire work area.

"Don't worry. You'll get used to it."

As they worked their way across the large underlit room, she wiped her eyes with the backs of her hands and looked around. Too many tables to count were arranged in loose rows, each with a young worker wearing latex gloves bent over whatever it was they were working on. The clear majority were girls, all with their hair either very short or pulled back in a ponytail. They all had either visors or caps, which partially eclipsed their faces. One girl she passed directly in front of briefly looked up. Her lips were swollen and cracked. Dawa was taken back by the ashen hue to her complexion. The girl looked to be about twelve but her skin had the dull inelasticity of an old woman.

Kuhn kept moving and led her finally to an empty table next to a windowless cement wall.

When she sat down as he instructed, she couldn't help but notice that against the entire wall directly in front of her was a series of spray booths. Various colored clouds of spray paint billowed out into the room. There were three large exhaust fans high above them near the ceiling but they were entirely ineffective. The blades of one were not turning at all.

"First, clean your hands with this." He liberally poured a clear solvent from an unmarked white can onto her palms and fingers. "You will be using this solvent to clean the extra paint from the bottom side of the toys, where the labels go. Here is a box of them to be done." Pointing at a large empty container. "Just put them in here when you're done. Someone else will take care of them. It doesn't take a lot of brains, doing this. But if you have any questions, that's your man there." Kuhn nodded towards a man with a frame like a buffalo. He was American or European, with brooding eyes and a stern mouth. "His name is Hogan. But I wouldn't bother him if you don't need to. He's a little testy."

"I don't understand. What do you mean?"

"Never mind. Just do your job."

Dawa reached for the first toy and started cleaning it with the solvent and a cloth. Her eyes started watering again. That was the smell when she first came in. This cleaning solution.

Suddenly an image came into her mind and filled her chest with an aching sensation, a wistful longing. She was sitting with her mother, who was telling her a story. It was only a couple weeks before she was to give birth and her mother's belly was a big balloon containing the new baby girl. Finally her mother smiled and finished the story by saying, "And that is why there are flowers. They are kisses from the earth."

Flowers and kisses.

Dawa, a girl of twelve with a strong sinewy body and pensive eyes, gazed through the paint haze of the cinderblock and cement crypt she found herself in, and feared she would never see a flower again. Or ever know what it felt like to be kissed.

Happy Meals

Hinge Toys was a Hong Kong based firm, established in 1996, which made toys for a number of American corporations for various product promotions. Their biggest customer was McDonald's and Hinge was the primary supplier of the prizes included with Happy Meals across the globe. Hinge was also the target of many workers-rights groups, who demonstrated, sued and organized boycotts to protest their abysmal working conditions and use of child labor.

As Dawa found out, new "employees" were paid an apprenticeship rate of six cents per hour, which was well under Vietnam's minimum wage. When they had accumulated enough expertise and proficiency at their jobs — though the work was menial, requiring no special skills, and the simple, highly repetitive tasks were easily learned in the first couple days — they could eventually make as much as eight cents an hour. Working ten hours a day, seven days a week, this still fell far short of what was needed to subsist anywhere in or around Da Nang.

Dawa and her specially contracted colleagues, of course, did not have to worry about eating or a place to stay. As tasteless and meager as the meals were, they assuaged the hunger pangs and kept the young workers alive. And sleeping in the packhouse dormitory helped to tamp down the haunting sense of isolation and calm the dull ache of homesickness.

But the harsh truth was they only saw a small portion of what meager wage was coming to them. Most of their earnings went back to Hinge as reimbursement for their purchase fee, the money initially laid out to "buy" their services. This was the money received by whoever had sold them to Hinge. Until this contract fee was paid off, the young workers were only occasionally given some negligible pocket money for personal items they might need. Typically it took about two years for a young worker to pay off his or her contract.

Though she missed working outdoors, Dawa easily adapted to physical demands of the work at Hinge. The hours were long but she was quite used to that, after several years working on the farms. She didn't like being restricted to sitting at a table for twelve hours a day, but at least her back and muscles didn't ache from bending to plant, dig and hoe all day as before.

The real problem was her sensitivity to the chemicals used so injudiciously and with very little ventilation. She had reacted that very first day when she walked into *Paints and Stripping*, finding it difficult to breathe or handle the intense burning to her eyes. As time went on, things only got worse.

One day she woke up with boils on her neck and shoulders. She was often dizzy, regularly had severe headaches, and one time passed out and crumbled to the floor at her workstation.

All of this resulted in frequent visits to the company doctor, at what was ceremoniously called the "infirmary", nothing more than an unsanitary glass-enclosed cubicle at the back of the factory near the loading dock. Each time she came in with some variation to her painful reaction to the chemical stew she worked in and breathed all day, the doctor on duty dispensed some generic something, usually the same pills every time, regardless of her specific symptoms.

The pills offered no relief whatsoever. But with each visit, another exorbitant debit was added to her employee ledger, adding even more weeks of misery to the duration of her indenture.

The main culprit was acetone. This powerful solvent, chemically known as 2-propanone, was ubiquitously used worldwide in industrial settings because of its ability to dissolve just about any organic and non-organic compound. It made the removal of paint, oil, tar — just about anything — a simple wipe and a swipe.

Unfortunately, the fumes also dissolve brain cells. And are even suspected to be carcinogenic. Higher concentrations can cause collapse, coma and death. Besides the usual dizziness, nausea, headaches, and occasional unconsciousness, acetone exposure wreaks havoc on women's menstrual cycles, and has been causally linked with damage to developing fetuses.

Watchdog organizations in the U. S. and Europe had been aware for some time that the brutal working conditions at Hinge included exposure at high levels to acetone and other nefarious solvents, notoriously coupled with the use of very young workers, trucked in from all parts of southeast Asia. It was suspected that many, if not all of them, were trafficked slaves.

About a year after Dawa arrived, it all came to a head. The watchdog NGOs put on a PR blitz which coincided with a slight paucity in the non-stop data streaming of human misery in the world media. It resulted in 15 minutes of fame for the cause. Someone secretly shot some video. The eyes of the bleeding hearts in America in particular, gazed over the trays holding their Hungry-Man

TV Dinners, and looked in shocked wonder at news reports of children laboring over plastic toy parts and fainting in toxic clouds of potentially lethal chemicals.

Hinge was in big trouble.

The Board of Directors convened an emergency meeting in Hong Kong, immediately followed by a late night press conference. They emphatically denied any knowledge that this kind of thing was happening on their watch, under their watchful eyes, and in defiance of their principled oversight. But they promised to get to the bottom of the troubling accusations and, if indeed any such unsavory activities were occurring at the Da Nang facility, to identify and correct any and all such problems, and moreover, unforgivingly punish those responsible.

Privately, recognizing that there was no way to clean up the mess, they unanimously agreed that they needed to shut down the plant temporarily, until this all blew over. The collective memory of the public was short. This so-called scandal would easily be buried under the inevitable torrent of newer high-drama images of human cruelty and suffering, from other distant locations around the world. It was just a matter of waiting it out. Hopefully there would be a tsunami or famine or ethnic cleansing to get this thing behind them. The sooner the better.

Director #1: "Fuck those ass-licking busy-bodies! Who do they think they are, interfering with the way we run our company? It's ours to run as we see fit."

Director #2: "Who's in charge there? Is it still Tinh Huynh?"

Chairman: "Yes. He's our man. A very effective manager."

Director #3: "I met him. They call him Attila the Huynh."

Director #2: "Tell him to board the place up tight. Make it look like it's shut down. But it should to be ready to be up and running again within 48 hours. We'll let him know when."

Chairman: "My thoughts, as well. And we should send the workers to the fabric works at Changkat Jering. We certainly can use some more bodies down there."

Director #3: "They can't absorb all of them."

Chairman: "Our American buyer will take the hot and sexy girls. Any that are left over, they can go back to Bangkok or wherever. Thailand is like a big human sponge."

Director #1: "Okay, that's that. Let's adjourn. I need a good meal and a fuck."

The next day Dawa and all of the other young workers were loaded into the boxcar of a train which arrived two days later in Ho Chi Minh City. From there they were taken by a chartered bus to Hai Long, where two small cargo boats would transport them to Malaysia.

While sailing, they were allowed to go topside. Dawa relished the opportunity to breathe fresh air and look out over the vast expanse of the South China Sea.

The second day out, her friend Pretzel came up next to her at the rail.

"I have something for you. A special gift."

"Pretzel, you're a very funny boy."

"I smuggled this out, under my ponytail."

He handed her a plastic Happy Meal toy.

She managed a smile, a look of feigned gratitude.

After he walked away, she dropped it overboard and it instantly disappeared in the gunmetal gray of the sea.

Chop Chop

Dawa crawled onto her sleeping mat. She hurt. She hurt badly. He had been rough before. An epileptic grunting pig. But this time it took him forever. And he thrust so hard it felt like she was going to split in half.

Gregor was Russian. Around 40 years old. Puffy from too much vodka for too many years. But under the flaccid layer of gummy skin was enormous bulk. A gigantic chunk of meat and bones, more of a barrel than a bottle.

He ran the dungarees section of the Hinge Fabric Works apparel factory at Changkat Jering. And he used his position of authority to alleviate the sexual cravings exacerbated by being around so many young girls.

Dawa was put into rotation, one of over forty adolescent female workers, almost the day she arrived. Gregor liked to jump right in and sample the new goods to see which ones he preferred. And he had a real fixation for the youngest ones, assuming correctly that the chances of nailing a virgin were inversely proportional to age. Dawa at only twelve was most certainly virgin material.

The first time he entered her, the pain caused her to pass out. She apparently was carried back to the dorm and left to sleep it off. When she came too, the sharp throbbing in her loins was excruciating. She went into the bathroom and found the inside of her thighs caked with blood and her vaginal area swollen and suffused with red and purple bruises. It took over a week for her to return to normal.

Apparently, Gregor liked what he saw. Dawa was frequently brought to him out of turn, thus subjected to three or four times the number of rapes as any of the other girls. Rape it was, completely and loathsomely against her will, though she was too petrified at the prospect of even more brutal treatment, to show any sign that she objected, or attempt to put up any resistance.

Gregor was rough to the point of being barbarous. When he came close to climaxing, he lost any semblance of control, became a thrashing animal, unaware of the incredible pain Dawa was enduring, certainly incapable of any mercy toward her. Dawa knew better than to reveal her suffering, thus did her best to hide her agony by merely turning her head to the side and biting her lower lip.

But inside she was screaming. Twelve years old. In spite of the frequency of Gregor's assaults, her little body could not stretch nearly enough. She never completely healed and the deep-flesh throbbing and cramping never completely subsided.

Gregor had taken her again last night. Now she hurt so badly she couldn't fall asleep. She was completely exhausted and unable to stop sobbing till just before the sun came up, when she was again herded along to her workstation.

As she sat at the fabric cutting table, she came to a decision. She had to escape. They might catch her and kill her. But that would be better than this.

For the rest of the day, Dawa experienced a calm she had never felt before. She did her work mechanically but efficiently, and there was nothing about her behavior or demeanor which would tip off even the most intent observer as to what she was feeling or the joyful prospect of her newly planned escape. Inside she already felt she had been liberated. The beckoning of new possibilities, away from this drudgery and physical torment, filled her with a hopeful excitement.

After lights out that evening, she lay on her sleeping mat as usual, faking unconsciousness. But behind her closed eyelids, she could see the path she would take through the other sleeping children, to the doorway of the dorm, out the rear entrance of the building, and toward the sliding fence gate where traffic in and out of the factory grounds was monitored by a single guard.

She wasn't quite sure how she would make it beyond this critical threshold but was sure that if she were patient and cautious, she would somehow be able to slip by the guard and be on her way to freedom.

When she could only hear the soft rhythmic breathing of sleep among those right around her, and no one else in the room seemed be stirring, out she went. Ever so quietly, she tip-toed the path she saw in her mind's eye and could just barely discern in the faint scattered light that came from under the door at the end of the room. Out the door. No one in sight. Crouching low but taking brisk steps, she headed straight for the entrance gate.

Much to her astonishment, when she got near the gate no one was in the guard booth. She was certainly surprised but most grateful to whatever set of circumstances blessed her escape with one less difficult obstacle.

Staying close to the fence and low to the ground just to be safe, she quietly swung open the pedestrian gate and slipped through.

Before her now was a long service road, between two deep ditches and bordered by heavily wooded land. Cutting through the forest was not an option. In the dark, she would make very slow progress and probably get lost. So she ducked into the right side ditch, walking, sometimes crawling. Fortunately, there had been very little rain for the past several weeks, so the ditch was dry and afforded easy passage.

For the entire two kilometer length, there was no sign of anyone else. No vehicle lights, no sounds that would indicate she was being followed. As she steadily worked her way down the service road, her confidence grew that she was in the clear. Once she reached the T at the end of the road, she could make her way onto one of the adjacent farms and find a place to hide until daybreak.

She could barely see in the dark pall of the night. But just as she reached the end of the service road, there was a brief break in the clouds, and the gentle, faint light of a quarter moon lit up the countryside enough for her to see that the T in the road was close ahead. She crept quietly forward, came to the edge of the embankment where the ditch made a 90 degree turn, and ever so cautiously started onto the gravely surface of the perpendicular dirt road. She saw some bushes opposite her, the other side of which was a vast rice paddy. She figured she would cross the paddy, then see if she could find either a manmade or natural shelter in the vicinity. There she would rest and cocoon herself for the night.

When she got to the center of the road, two headlights suddenly switched on. Dawa was caught blinded and exposed in their glare. She froze as two soldiers got out, came over, roughly grabbed her arms, then threw her into the cab of their military jeep.

"Kind of late for a young girl like you to be walking around all by herself, wouldn't you say?"

Dawa was too miserable and frightened to cry. She stared straight ahead, resigning herself to whatever fate she might now have to endure. Everyone knew the reputation of the military in this country. Thugs in nicely-pressed khakis. Nevertheless she still hoped that they wouldn't take her back. Anything but that.

To her horror, they immediately drove back down the service road. When they got to the gate, Dawa could see in the vehicle's headlight beams two people standing, waiting for her. One was a young man, rifle in hand, dressed in a guard uniform. The other was the beast himself — Gregor.

The soldiers harshly yanked her from the vehicle, dragged her over to Gregor and threw her at his feet. She couldn't bring herself to look at him and just stared helplessly at the dirt, only inches from her face. She panted like a dog and trembled, her entire body in the grip of a cold sweat and debilitating nausea.

"My little kitten. You have been wandering. Wandering away from home. But this is your lucky day. These fine soldiers found you and kept you from getting lost."

Gregor handed the two soldiers three 100 RM notes each, which they quickly pocketed. They jumped in the jeep and drove away.

Dawa was roughly pulled to her feet by the guard and escorted back into the dorm building. But instead of going to the sleeping area, she was taken to the other end of the building and sequestered in a small supply closet full of chemical solvents, brushes, brooms and rags. She cowered in the corner as they closed and locked the door behind them. She curled up in a tight ball, trembling, using a huge floor mop as a headrest.

The night seemed interminable. Instead of sleeping, she gradually was seized by an unpleasant state where she was irritably semi-conscious, startled by the slightest noise. By the time the door was noisily unlocked, she was a total wreck. Dawa squirmed and flinched warily, then fitfully struggled as they reached in to pull her to her feet.

After they dragged her into the light, Dawa could see that the closet was one of many storage compartments in a long row, all of which opened on the long hallway of a raw industrial structure. Far overhead were I-beams and clusters of opaque square windows. Many of them were broken and there were shards of dirty glass on the cement floor. At the end of the hallway, against the cinderblock wall was a thick workbench and a large wooden throne chair. This is where they took her, dragged by two silent guards and the loquacious Gregor.

"So you think we just let you workers come and go. That we don't have proper security here. You know, my kitten, it goes both ways. We can't let just anyone walk in here and harm our precious workers. Little kittens like you. So what you didn't notice were the very advanced IR motion detectors. Courtesy of our enlightened owners in Hong Kong. We knew the minute you tried to leave."

Dawa suddenly realized she never stood a chance of escaping. She had in her desperation been fooling herself. What now? She was a portrait of fear. Just as nakedly, they made no attempt to hide the utter thrill they were feeling as they leered at their defenseless quarry.

"This is very bad for discipline, you know, little kitten. We can't allow others to think that they can just pick up and leave. All of you have contracts to fulfill. So we will need — as we have had to do occasionally in the past — to make an example of you. As a warning to the others."

They pushed her into the chair, the guards grabbing her arms and pulling them back so there was no way she could get up. Gregor grabbed her left leg at the ankle. Dawa hadn't noticed until he placed her foot on it, but there was an anvil right at the base of the chair. Gregor grabbed some rope and quickly lashed her foot to both the chair and the anvil. Dawa started to scream but there was no one else around to hear.

"You tell your friends, little kitten, this is what happens when you try to escape."

Gregor picked up a chisel and a hammer and in one motion amputated the second toe from Dawa's left foot.

Surprisingly in that moment there was little pain. Dawa looked at the blood running out of her foot as if she were a disembodied observer. She floated out and away from it all, as she fainted and consciousness evaporated into the vapor of oblivion.

"That is what happens, little kitten."

The Fall Collection

"She's a virgin?"

"Oh yeah. She's only thirteen. Wait till you see the end. Lotsa blood. No doubt about it. She's a fuckin' virgin, alright. Fresh as they come."

They were watching a video that had been shot just the night before. The TV monitor was hooked up directly with the VHS camera that had been used to video the rape scene.

"People pay a lot for this. It's the real thing. Which is why we shoot it as a home movie. The amateur vibe. Makes it even more authentic."

"How much?"

"150. 200 dollars a pop. We'll sell 5000 on the internet. The VHS market another 10,000. DVDs and video-CDs, maybe 15 or 20,000. It's pure profit. No crew. No production costs. The little cunts? We just keep an eye out for the really sweet and innocent ones when they ship them in. And run 'em through when we need a new movie. They have no idea they are on camera. Makes it even more real. Look at the kid. She's bawling her eyes out. That's not acting. No way."

"Who's the bull?"

"That's Gregor. Russian guy with a cock like a baseball bat. He likes the young ones."

"Fantastic! Really nice work. You guys are going to make us filthy rich. So when is the fashion show? You know we're flying back tomorrow afternoon."

"Got it covered. First thing tomorrow morning. Just bring your peepers."

After a good night's sleep and a breakfast heavy on fruit and local delicacies, they filed into a large bay of one of the unused warehouse structures adjacent to the main production facility. There were a handful of folding chairs arranged in front of an area which was covered with woven rattan mats. Not exactly New York or Paris chic, but it would do for today's viewing.

The American was not there, however, to look at clothes. He was there to look at faces and bodies. He was looking for the right stuff. The hot stuff.

"We'll bring them out five at a time. They'll be carrying numbers. Here is a clipboard. You see one you like, just write down the number. We'll take it from there."

Out they came, five at a time, looking very perplexed and shy. They first faced forward, then were told to turn sideways, then their backs to the special audience, which consisted of only three men, finally again facing front so the cardboard signs with the number could be seen. That group was marched out and replaced by another five.

All young girls. The youngest twelve, though they claimed she was fourteen, and the oldest sixteen. Having been pre-selected for this particular cattle call meant these were the cream of the crop. Each one quite haunting and beautiful in her own way.

It was hard to decide. So much luscious young flesh to choose from. In the end, the American ended up taking 82 of the nearly hundred girls which had been paraded before him. The few they didn't take were either too flat-chested or so undernourished that they appeared emaciated and sickly.

The 82 may not have been perfect pictures of health and ideal objects of male sexual fantasy at this point in time, but they would clean up and fill out just fine, eventually to become the kind of sexy young things that torque heads and cause traffic jams. They would be hotter than hot when his team got done with them.

"Okay, I guess we're finished here."

67

"We'll have them in Singapore by the end of the week. If all goes well, they'll be on your doorstep within five weeks."

"Perfect. And let me just say that, once again, you've come through with flying colors. Excellent work!"

"It's my pleasure, Mr. Danko. Have a pleasant flight back to Chicago."

Chapter 5

THE WINDY CITY: Smoke Gets In Your Eyes

Family Reunion

Lenny was getting restless. He had maybe stayed home too long. Granted he was still weak and somewhat disoriented, ears ringing and skin itching where the scabs still lingered. But today he decided the best thing he could do is get back into something resembling his usual rhythm. Stop being such a wuss.

He picked up the phone and hit Autodial #1.

"Top of the fuckin' morning to you, blarney boy. You guys both in the control room?"

"Is this who I think it is? Where are you? How are you?!"

"Fine fine. Just had a little unplanned vacation. Tell Keary to do a quick interim spreadsheet. Have him print it so I can take it with. Say, the last five weeks."

"You got it. By the way, we just got a FedEx in from Chicago. Addressed to you personally."

"Chicago? Fine. I'm on my way. See you in a blink."

It was only a ten minute walk. But he was still weak and decided to take a taxi. The dispatcher said he had a guy right in the neighborhood. Be there in two or three minutes.

He felt wobbly just going down the short flight of stairs from his bedroom to street level. Lenny wanted to avoid talking to anyone. He stayed in his doorway until the yellow car pulled up in front.

Another towelhead. They're taking over the whole fucking city. At least the taxi services. And they all love this damn awful Taj Mahal disco music. Grateful that the ride took less than five minutes, Lenny tossed a $5 bill over the seat into the drivers lap.

"This is fine. Drop me here."

He turned the corner into the alley. They must have spotted him on the videocam because Keary opened the steel door just as Lenny approached it.

"Holy shit! What happened to you? You look terrible."

"Thanks. You know how to make a guy feel great."

"So where you been? We thought maybe you got married and settled down in Scarsdale."

"Just got roughed up a little. Don't wanna talk about it. Have either Martin or Frankie been sniffing around here?"

"Nope. Haven't seen or heard peep from either of them for … I don't know how long. From before you vanished."

Markham pried himself away from a computer monitor and started across the room. His expression of shock betrayed his usual geek cool.

"What the fuck!" From a guy who rarely cursed. "Sweet mother of Jesus, have you looked in a mirror lately? You look like the night of the living dead."

"It's just this new California diet plan I been on. The few people who have survived it really swear by it."

"So you don't kiss and tell. Okay. Anyway, everything here is running fine. We're a little down. But it's that time of year. And we had a decent week last week. Isn't that what you said, Keary? With the holidays approaching, things should ramp up again."

"Here are the spreads. I still have to run the end-of-the-quarter next week." Handing over the print-out and a FedEx Overnight. "And this came just yesterday. From Chi-town."

Lenny looked inside and saw immediately the airline ticket, with a hand-written note paper-clipped in back.

Lenny, when you feel up to it, come and see us. Ticket is open ended. You confirm date/time. Let Jessica know. Hope you're okay. — Harold Danko

Lenny slid them back in the envelope.

Keary in his mischievous mode. "Oh … and we just put on two new data entry girls on Tuesday and Wednesday nights. Ugly as a hemorrhoid on a horse. I think they're lezzies. They look at each other with dog-fuck eyes. But I will say, they are fast and accurate."

"Uh … thanks for your Shakespearian characterization of the situation. I feel so good about it, I think I'll take another five weeks off and look for my inner child."

Try as they could, the three veterans of street cool could not suppress a laugh. It was obvious that Keary and Markham were glad to see him. For his part, Lenny felt for the first time in a long time that he was back in control.

But there was Chicago. What did they want? How much did they know about the how and why of what had happened? He had better get on a plane ASAP.

Willis Tower

"Lenny, Lenny. So good to see you."

Danko as always dressed to the teeth and beaming 500 megawatts of charm. Armani suit, top end Rolex, tanning bed glow, choppers whiter than a Crane bathroom fixture, and the top half of his face floating in the pleasant Zen of a recent Botox treatment. He should probably run for Mayor. Or Governor.

"Glad I could make it. Had a rough couple of weeks."

"We know all about it, Lenny. Heads are gonna roll. Nobody fucks with our Lenny and gets to sleep with the fat lady. We've got someone working it."

The office door opened and #2 walked in. Ed Valley. Tiny limp from a vehicular accident which prematurely ended his military service. But still the Renaissance man from Topeka. Ed always dressed more casually than Harold. The good cop and bad cop of couture. Like Harold, Ed was in his mid 40's but looked country club healthy. Lots of fire in the belly and hedonism in his eyes. He loved a good laugh, a strong drink, a Cuban cigar, and an athletic blond to ride like an unbroken mare.

Big handshake and a hug. "We were worried about you, Lenny. Tell us what you know."

"I think it was a case of mistaken identity. It must have been. You know Mulcahey …"

"The infamous Bishop Mulcahey."

"None other. His place was crawling with these little Asian girls. Then someone came and cleaned him out. That's when I got away."

"Did you see who sprung them?"

"Not a chance. I was locked down tight. But someone got in, roughed up Mulcahey, and split with the girls. They call them Djin Djin girls. Hot little teens from Thailand."

Harold's turn. "So why do you think they came for you?"

"I don't know. I really don't know. With the internet thing, we should be under everyone's radar. Our girls only hit the streets to pick up groceries. I don't get it."

Ed leaned back in his chair. Low Midwestern drawl. "It comes and goes. That's what I've seen. Always changing. New people on the scene. Let's face it. Selling pussy has never been a Tupperware party. But sometimes … when the stakes are high … sometimes it's gonna end up being a war zone."

Harold reached over and paged his secretary. "Jessica, can you come in, please? Lenny, are you up for a drink?"

"Does the Pope shit in the woods?"

"I'll take that as a yes." Jessica stuck her head in the door. "Brandy and three snifters. Make it the Remy Martin X.O. Thanks, Jessie."

Harold stood up and walked casually to the side of his office. "Lenny, come here." There were no office furnishings for this span of the floor-to-ceiling windows, an arrangement calculated to provide a completely unobstructed view of the frenzied city below. Cars, buses and other vehicles crawled through the grid. Corpuscles in the capillaries of Chicago.

Lenny joined Harold and Ed followed. The three of them stood side by side gazing over the sprawl. Feeling the hum.

Harold broke the reverie. "Do you know why I like it up here?"

Lenny's silent reaction was instant and knee-jerk. What a stupid question! Who wouldn't love it up here? A person would have to be dead or in a coma. But he maintained his casual quietude and said nothing.

"Perspective. Yes, Lenny … perspective. See, those people down there can't see anything. They get the tiniest little piece of the puzzle. They're microbes. But from up here, Lenny, you see the whole plan. The big picture. That's why gods live on the tops of mountains."

Gods? Mountains? Lenny glanced at Harold. He appeared to be serious.

Jessica came in with a tray. They each took a glass and Harold poured.

"This is to you, Lenny. A new chapter."

71

Lenny really didn't get the whole brandy thing. Harold and Ed cupped their hands around their glasses and savored the aroma of the stuff like it was neck of some hot sexy Shakira. He personally thought it was pungent and had to fight to keep himself from full-on gagging. You were either a scotch man or a brandy man. He was a scotch man.

Danko continued waxing philosophical. "Brooklyn is important to us. We started this whole thing with Brooklyn. Even though Ed here is from Kansas and I'm from Minneapolis … I'll bet you didn't know that, did you, Lenny? That I'm from Minneapolis."

"No, as a matter of fact I didn't."

"But Brooklyn. Yes, Brooklyn is everything to Ed and I. You're our man in Brooklyn, Lenny. And we're gonna take special care of you. Very special care of you from now on. And you're gonna take special care of us."

Ed took his cue.

"Lenny, you got that whole internet thing running like a fine Swiss watch. But apparently things are stirring up out there. In the streets. And we need to be on top of it. Whatever happens, it all starts in the streets. Things are changing and we have to keep up. Sink or swim, they say. Lenny, did you know that sharks don't have lungs?"

"No … I hadn't run across that."

"Well they don't. And the only way they can breathe is to keep swimming. Forcing the oxygenated water through them. By moving, all the time moving. See, that's us. We're moving and we're gonna keep on moving. We're looking for new openings. New situations. We want you to look at new situations."

Harold shook his head. Pain real or imagined on his face. "We're all family here, Lenny. What the Bishop did to you back there, he did to me. And it ain't *ever* gonna happen again. We take care of family. You take care of us. We take care of you. Another important item. Work with the blues. They're on board. You'll figure out how that all works."

As if choreographed, Harold and Ed both took the last pull of their drinks. Enigmatic smiles. They studied Lenny. Searching his face. Like they were waiting for him to say something. Or had something themselves they were leaving unsaid.

He felt rather uncomfortable and avoided looking directly at either of them.

Ed poured himself another shot, then raised his glass and seemed to be looking for something in the reddish-brown liquid in the bottom of his snifter. He then turned to Lenny and held his brandy snifter between them as if to make a toast.

"How does the expression go, Lenny? All ships rise in a rising tide?"

What were they saying? Lenny was lost in the fog of generalities. He just wanted a clue as to what they expected of him. Why they had brought him here. Other than to extend their commiseration over his encounter with the Bishop and paint a fairy tale picture of the future.

"So what exactly do you want me to be doing?" Lenny's question disappeared into an abyss. Harold and Ed now just stared straight ahead, quietly looking out at the skyline.

After what seemed like an eternity, Harold suddenly started slapping him on the back, then put his arm around him, and finally grabbed Lenny's neck firmly in his hand.

"You, my friend, are going to make a lot of money! We all are. The most important thing is to keep a clear head. Don't get sidetracked. Focus. It's all about focus. Plain and simple."

Harold then abruptly changed the subject, though what the subject had been still wasn't clear.

"Lenny, my boy! A little birdie told me you have a birthday coming up. Well, Ed and I have decided to make this a *very* special occasion. Just to show how much we appreciate having you on board. Jessica will be getting ahold of you."

Ed then unceremoniously took Lenny's drink and set it down. He walked him toward the door, as Harold continued to stare out at the panoramic view. The meeting was over.

"By the way, Lenny. Make sure your passport is current. Have a pleasant flight back, my man."

On the plane back home, Lenny tried to sort it out. He was of two minds about his visit. Harold and Ed were nearly impossible to read. This was the first time he had visited them on their home turf. And this was the first "social call" that had ever been arranged. All his previous interactions with them had been nuts-and-bolts — the questions, answers, direct orders and periodic monitoring that goes with running a business.

Of course, he was flattered by the exuberant attention and familial concern of the two men at very top of the organization. And by their enthusiastic predictions of big things to come. But they were so perplexing. He was going to be their point man — their "man in Brooklyn" — but what exactly was he supposed to be doing? They were the odd couple, that's for sure.

He felt excited and at the same time slightly hollow. Nerves? Jetlag? Existential quandary?

Whatever. It looked like interesting times ahead.

St. Lawrence Seaway

It was the long way around. Expensive. But the safest way to get the cargo where it needed to go. And combining the human cargo with several tons of toys, jewelry, household appliance parts, designer athletic shoes, t-shirts, fad clothes, and so on, much of it made by the very same human cargo which was now in the barracks section of the hold, actually made it a cost-effective and low-visibility way to get the young bodies into the States.

The diciest part of the journey was the transfer from the local cargo boats arriving in Singapore from Kampung Sepetang. All of the customs facilitators except for one diehard do-gooder were in bed with Hinge Fabric Works, some of them more than doubling their salaries with the blind-eye bonuses Hinge provided. But Singapore was still an international hub for a sizeable portion of Asia's sea transport, and it didn't need its clean reputation tarnished with human trafficking scandals. So there were bullets sweated the three or four times a year the young bodies came through, and extreme precautions taken to keep the sensitive shipment invisible to anyone who might have a stake in exposing the illegal cargo — government officials, reputation-building politicians, and especially those nosy watchdog groups who were always looking to make trouble.

So far there had not even been any close calls. The one "do-gooder" civil service lifer who was above taking a bribe, was typically sent for an on-site inspection at a local warehouse as far from the shipyard itself as could be arranged, and the transfer of the kids slotted in the busiest part of the day, when the docks were tumultuous and chaotic.

'Kids' was not really accurate. The human cargo in these shipments were all adolescents, and all girls. Youngest maybe thirteen or fourteen, the older ones eighteen, a few at nineteen. All Asian, originally from villages in Burma and Thailand, Laos and Cambodia, sometimes Vietnam, even Malaysia itself, though because it was a Muslim country that was rare. They all had been working on farms and in factories, and some had been tenderized in pseudo-monastic schools. All had been collected and selected on the basis of their physical beauty and erotic appeal. Keeping them out of sight then, was also prompted by safety considerations, meaning the need to keep them away from the virile and often aggressive shipyard workers. It was a long process which brought them to the Singapore docks, and now they needed to be cautiously packaged and sent on the high seas for special customers in the United States.

The girls were secretly herded into custom-fitted steel containers, then all of the steel containers and crates of legitimate cargo were together quickly loaded onto a medium-sized D-class cargo ship, either a one-stop to North America briefly docking in Capetown, South Africa, or one where they would there be offloaded to another vessel completing the journey.

Either way, the human cargo would then sail from the southern tip of Africa northwest into the Atlantic, navigating to a point just south of Newfoundland where it entered the Gulf of St. Lawrence. Sailing up the St. Lawrence River towards Montreal, it would pick up the St. Lawrence Seaway, and in Canadian waters alone traverse nearly 1800 miles of locks, lakes and rivers, ultimately arriving in Duluth, Minnesota.

Duluth was the perfect port of call for this kind of smuggling. As the 20th largest port in America, the sheer amount of tonnage which passed through kept it in a perpetual frenzy, bordering on chaos. In terms of customs oversight, it was so grossly understaffed that locals joked that they could bring in the entire province of Ontario including the city of Toronto, and no one would check the bill of lading.

To date the vessels had been typical utility haulers, converted timber ships, and bulk container transporters, fitting in perfectly with the other vessels which serviced the mining and timber industries of Minnesota, North and South Dakota, Wyoming and Montana. Like most of the others, they sailed to and from foreign countries under the flags of China, Malaysia, Japan, Australia, even Belgium and Holland.

Before the girls were disembarked, they were loaded into two 10 x 20 foot steel containers marked *Assembled Toys (NVA – 2 of 6)* and *Wearing Apparel (USPOA – 3 of 6)* and were quickly sandwiched on the dock loading area between similar containers, which probably actually contained the referenced items. Sometimes even before the ink of the officiating entry approval stamp was dry, these containers were taken to a warehouse about seven miles outside of the Duluth city limits into a new industrial park on the opposite side of town.

It was a miracle that so far none of the girls had died. After living and working under hardly the best of conditions, they were not always in very good health. Besides vulnerability to infectious diseases, the exposure to extreme swings of climate punished their young bodies and pushed them to their limits.

If they arrived in Duluth in the winter, with its sub-zero temperatures and mountains of snow, they found themselves in an environment they had never imagined, much less experienced. They were given sweaters and thick pants, draped with the padding covers usually used to cover cargo, but still huddled together in the shipping containers, a shivering gaggle of young girls, with pleading eyes and gaunt frightened faces.

Things improved slightly at the warehouse, where something resembling a college dorm was set up, with proper beds, a large bathroom facility with a six-person shower room, and lockers which were stuffed with the variety of clothes which comprised their new wardrobe. Here they would also be introduced to the joys and staples of the American diet — pizza, hamburgers, French fries, shakes — and of course American television, in its own banal but dazzling fashion, a complete education for those uneducated in the American way.

In fact, it was here in this remote warehouse in the very north of Minnesota, far from the mainstream of urban life, that they would over the next four weeks be "Americanized", schooled and trained in a very special boot-camp, to be shaped and styled for their new jobs.

This was the vocational training center for the Djin Djin girls.

Charm School

This is how you walk.
This is how you talk.
This is what to say.
This is what they pay.

The perfect job training institute. No frills here. Just the nitty gritty. The nuts and bolts.

The girls didn't need to know the line of succession to the powers and duties of the President. They didn't need to know the Second Law of Thermodynamics. They didn't need poetry. They didn't need mathematics. They only needed to know $300 when they saw it. They didn't need Shakespeare or Hemingway or tearoom propriety. They didn't even need very much English. 'I am Djin Djin. You want blowjob? I give you boom boom.'

Yes, charm school. Very charming indeed.

At the end of the four weeks, they would in their cute broken English be speaking the poetry of sex. It would sound like William Wordsworth to the men licking their lips in anticipation of twenty minutes jumping the bones of these delicious young girls.

Of course, there were the safety issues. Condoms. Always use condoms. The men would always try to talk you out of them. Pretty stupid on their part. How do they know you don't have STDs? But men are stupid. And they would all say the same thing. 'I am clean. Only been with the wife.' Right. The wife and twenty whores in the last six months.

So always, *always* use a condom. For the pussy. In the butt. Even for a blowjob. And if the condom breaks, it's time for immediate action. Even right in front of the guy if necessary. You will be carrying the stuff, so use it. First the spermicidal foam. Then the antiseptic douche. Immediately. It's your life at stake here, girls.

The other safety issue. The occasional freak. Some guy who likes to rough you up a bit. Or a lot. Again, you got what you need. Pepper spray. The attractive and very feminine purse-size bottle of Mace. And if it looks like you have a stalker on your tail, we'll get you a 50,000 volt Taser. You are all very petite. Just about every man in America has physical size over you. A huge advantage in strength. Don't take any chances. Don't take any shit. Take them down and run.

The last three days of the training session were always the favorite for the girls. This was when they got their new outfits. A dazzling selection of amazing clothes, size 2 for the really big girls, sizes 0 and 1 for the rest. Hot pants, miniskirts, halters, sexy tight Ts, blouses, bustiers, tricot camisoles, latex bras and lace bodysuits. For cooler weather, cashmere wraps, fur vests, leather and suede jackets, latex catsuits. Accessories! Earrings and bracelets. Necklaces, toe rings, anklets. Hairclips, pins, tiaras, hair ties, and designer headbands. Rhinestone barrettes. Leather and plastic boots, shoes, sandals, studded platforms, spikes. And the makeup. Yes, the makeup! Their precious young faces would transform before their very eyes, and they now looked like the seductive and glamorous models which graced the covers of the fashion magazines which lay around the school by the hundreds, to acquaint the girls with the current styles and looks they should imitate.

It was at these fitting and glamour make-over sessions that most of their apprehensions and fears almost completely melted away.

If all they had to do was have sex with strangers in order to wear these clothes, look more beautiful than they could have imagined possible, and best of all live in America, that's what they would do. After all, many of them had been forced by some grunting farmer or filthy factory foreman to do this very same thing, just to continue working under miserable conditions in a country that only promised a life of hunger, illness and early death. All anyone had ever talked about back home, even in some of the remotest villages, was going to America, greatest country in the entire world.

So this was their chance. To live in America. To live the American Dream. As Djin Djin girls.

Lenny needed to bring the boys up to speed. So he asked Markham and Keary to meet him at Penny's, a coffee shop a few blocks from computer central. They finished eating and were talking business. Markham had been noticing a number of attempts at breaching his finely wrought wall of cyber security.

"Something is going on, that's for sure. I've detected fifty-three attempted incursions in just the past ten days. It's a coordinated attack."

"Is that a lot?"

"Typically we get one or two a month. We are way under the radar for this kind of thing. The typical geek hackers don't try to take down sex sites. Not unless someone puts them up to it."

"It's not cyber punks?"

"Maybe it's the Christian Right. It's Pat Robertson!" Always helpful Keary.

"No, *way* too professional to be kids. I was right there for three of the attempts and monitored the whole thing. Looked at the command sets, the randomization of passwords, even some of the code. These guys are good! Nothing got through but I am wondering, why now? Why are we all of a sudden such a target?"

Lenny paused to collect his thoughts. He needed to explain but not say too much.

"Remember my last visit to Chicago? Well … it's better if you don't know everything. Actually, I don't know everything. But the big boys are breaking some new ground here. Expanding the range of business activities. And that probably has some people on the warpath. So I'm thinking that somebody is just fucking with us. You know, looking for a way into the system to make life uncomfortable. Put a ghost in the machine. Make us nervous. Now, Markham, be straight with me. You sure you got this handled?"

"Lenny, I'm always straight with you. If I were worried I'd let you know. They're not going to get into the system. And even if they did, they will never get to anything that could make a difference. Remember, I used to be a hacker. I know how they think. And the college boys all come from the same box. They certainly can't shut us down, not any of it. They can try to pull stuff out. All they're gonna get is some nice JPEGs of some very fine ladies. Everything else is so encrypted, they'd be better off reading the Dead Sea Scrolls."

"Good. I know I can count on you. But I just wanted to make sure. See, the other side of this is that you won't see much of me for the next few months."

"Oh no, not that! How can we go on? How will we be able to function?" Keary with his minstrel-show face.

"Granted, I'm not around all that much now, but Chicago has always wanted me to keep tabs on things here. But here's the new deal. Now they seem to want me out covering some other new front for them. There's maybe even international travel involved."

"Oh, so you get to jet-set around with Paris Hilton, while Markham and I have to babysit these retards. Nice. Which by the way brings to mind our latest hire. A girl in from Vermont, with huge tits, who close as I can tell never wears any underwear, top or bottom."

"And has Tourette's syndrome."

"Fuck you, Markham, you don't know that."

"She has Tourette's, really bad. She gets really wound up around 2 am and it sounds like the Gotti Clan with road rage."

"Alright, whatever. But she's quick. And good on the eyes."

"Except for that thing, that twitchy thing she does with her head."

Lenny was by now bent over laughing. He was sure going to miss these two. He held up his hands in a call for a cease-fire.

"Can I get a word in here? I have to say, the entry clerks you have paraded through here, have represented a very strange cross section of humanity. Not to say that the work doesn't get done. You guys always are good about that. But Keary, I am curious to know. Where did you find this latest one?"

"Well um, actually … actually it was at a support group."

"A support group? A support group for what?"

"People with Tourette's Syndrome."

Lenny lost it. Finally he managed enough control to put forth the obvious question.

"So, Keary, do you … I mean it doesn't seem to me that you … "

"No, of course not. *I* don't have Tourette's Syndrome."

"So I guess the next question … "

"Right right right, I know. What was I doing there? You see I have been going to these different support groups. Tourette's is on Monday nights. Sunday nights, it's PWHRLAP."

"The PWH what?"

"People Who Have Recently Lost A Pet. Now there's a bunch of crybabies! Tuesdays it's Denture Wearers Have Feelings Too. A little older crowd but everyone has a great smile."

"You're making this up, right? You have to be making this up."

"Nope. The younger ones either went through a windshield or over the handle bars of their bike. Met a very hot blond there. Then on Wednesday you got two. People With Scoliosis. And Freckled People Are Not Freaks. I fit in perfect there."

"Oh jeez!" Markham laughing and rolling his eyes.

"Friday nights it's the Dyslexics Dance Party. And Saturdays I usually just chill out a bit. But listen to me! I am here to tell you guys, there is absolutely no better way to meet babes. They all sit around these tables talking about the most personal things, and then they need all sorts of reassurance and love. It's like picking apples. I can't tell you how many times I have gotten laid after one of these sob club get-togethers."

"You pick up dyslexic girls with scoliosis?"

"Granted, you meet a few quirky ones. But on the whole, it's been one mighty fine fuckfest. With some serious lookers! And in this case, since right behind the happiness and daydreamy bliss of my love meat, is finding the best talent I can for computer central, we ended up with a very solid employee."

"Who sounds like she needs an exorcism."

"Whatever. You're nitpicking again, Markham. You're obviously jealous at all of the pussy I'm getting, Mr. Cyber Celibate. You're still wishing someone would invent a laptop with a labia."

"I'm doing just fine. And my bedroom doesn't look like the bar scene in Star Wars."

Lenny back to business. "Okay okay. I have to say I really am going to miss you guys. But this works out good for both of you as well."

"When does your sabbatical start?"

"Immediately. And that means the two of you need to take complete charge here."

"So this is a promotion." Keary the eagle-eye opportunist. "Can I still wear sandals?"

"You will be able to buy brand new top-of-the-line sandals. You are getting a 50% raise. Both of you. And will be reporting directly to Chicago. Keary, just put together your spreads as usual. But from now on you will FedEx them direct to Ed Valley, attention Jessica. And Markham, I want you to be the mouthpiece. Once a week, give them a call. Friday. You'll wanna talk to Harold. That's Mr. Danko to you. Or if he's not available, schmooze it up with Jessica. She's the key to getting along with everyone. If she likes you, everything will go smoothly."

"And you? Are you open to hearing from your old buds? Or is this the Last Supper?"

"Hey, both of you. Listen up. I'm always here for you. You got my number. Just remember, I won't always be available to talk. But if there are any serious problems, hit me up. I'll do what I can."

Handshakes and mafia-style hugs. It was *How To Succeed In Business Without Trying* and the *Godfather* rolled in one. Then Lenny was out the door. Markham and Keary went back to bitch slapping each other. The Second Law of Thermodynamics, gravity, and chucking and jiving. Fixed principles and universal constants. The stuff of reality. Real life on the blister of the space-time continuum we call Earth.

Chapter 6

SAVING THE WORLD: God's Holy Work

Safe Sex

It was a Friday night four weeks ago. The Djin Djin girls just disappeared.
Now, as suddenly as they were gone, they had come back.
Back with a vengeance.
And style.

It seemed to Lilly and the other regulars that there were even more of the Asian dolls than before. Who could say? They were like a rash that wouldn't go away. What was again clear was something needed to be done and soon.

Lilly started talking again about the Ad Hoc Committee, a plan which for the most part was misunderstood. She organized another Tuesday night meeting and tried to explain her idea. But this meeting was louder and more chaotic than the last. The prevailing sentiment finally seemed to be, "Whatever. Just do it, girl. And it better work!"

But before she could even get in touch with some of the local gentry who would certainly be interested in "cleaning up" the community, a strange thing happened. In a storefront that had been empty for some time, a service organization called the STD Prevention Center opened up an office staffed with three ungainly young female counselors. The reception desk displayed a variety of literature on safe sex, feminine hygiene and birth control. Represented were organizations which ran the gamut from established and respectable to fringe and edgy: the Family Planning Council, Brooklyn Female Health Services, the Gay/Lesbian Coalition, Women's Abuse Hotline, Ho's 4 Life, the Transgender Support Group.

Front and center on a folding card table next to the front door was a box of free condoms. The flip-up sign on the portable display read ...

No Glove No Love

The center was open from 10 am till 2 am daily. During these hours, whichever of the plain Janes was on duty could be seen sitting in the glare of the extremely bright fluorescent lights, working on a computer or rifling through a stack of paperwork. All three of them seemed to compete for the daily prize awarded for the most unattractive, sexless and ill-fitting attire. There seemed to be no depths of tastelessness which would go unexplored making sure that no one, male or female, would be tempted to flirt with, much less jump the bones of one of these girls.

One glaring anomaly was that, other than being locked and unlocked from the inside, the front door was never touched. No one ever came into the center. No one ever looked at the literature. No one even took any free condoms. Whatever larger body was funding it, their fiduciary generosity could not have been predicated on the success, or even the prospect of success at delivering on the stated mission, that is, preventing STDs in this part of Brooklyn. It appeared to be one of those great ideas on paper, the perfect funding magnet in a grant proposal, a real feel-good-look-we-are-making-a-difference kind of enterprise, which in the real world was a total boondoggle, a Department of Nothing for Nobody.

There were a few occasional visitors, however. Quite occasional but quite conspicuous. But never via the front door.

Inexplicably, one or two NYPD cops would come in through the rear employee entrance off the alley, then be seen talking to the counselor on duty, sitting at the computer workstation, or just kicking back enjoying a cup of java. This was coupled with a significant increase in the number of patrol cars seen in the area now. Significant increase? Relatively speaking. Unless there was an incident response, seeing a squad car more than once a night had meant the blues were lavishing attention on them. But now they were becoming a more common sight. Four, maybe five times each evening, they would cruise by, staying on the scene the short amount of time the idle crawl of their vehicle would accrue — except, that is, when they pulled into the alley behind the STD Prevention Center to stop to say hi to Miss Dressed-Like-A-Sack-Lunch. Then and only then, they might hang around for a half hour or so.

What were they doing in there? What were they yakking about?

It all seemed very strange. And more to the point, it left Lilly and the other girls wondering what their own next move should be. The blues seemed no more interested in what was going on than a blind person sitting in front of a fish tank. If they were around for some reason, they were sure doing a good job of hiding it. They seemed to share the HIV Prevention Center's complete indifference, not seeming to even notice the street girls, Djin Djin or otherwise.

But there they were.

On the other hand, that the opening of the center and the increased presence of the blues coincided with the inexplicable and sudden return of the Djin Djin girls, was not lost on Lilly and company. Still what did it mean? And how should they go about eradicating the Asian Invasion that continued to crimp their style and create all of that empty space in their purses where the money should be?

Ecclesiastes 3: 1-8 …

There is an appointed time for everything.
And there is a time for every event under heaven —

A time to give birth and a time to die; A time to
plant and a time to uproot what is planted.

A time to kill and a time to heal; A time to
tear down and a time to build up.

A time to weep and a time to laugh;
A time to mourn and a time to dance.

A time to throw stones and a time to gather stones;
A time to embrace and a time to shun embracing.

A time to search and a time to give up as lost;
A time to keep and a time to throw away.

A time to tear apart and a time to sew together;
A time to be silent and a time to speak.

A time to love and a time to hate;
A time for war and a time for peace.

There is also a time for the shit to hit the fan.
And that time had arriveth.

St. John the Baptist of Hell's Kitchen

It was late in the evening when John Harrison walked out of the NYC Port Authority Bus Terminal at 8th Avenue and 42nd Street. Early summer 1969. He had no idea where he was or where he was headed. But it felt right. It felt like home. He walked past the pushers, pimps and prostitutes that lined the streets and hovered in the doorways, gaining momentum and certitude. He saw the bums asleep in the doorways, or sometimes right in the middle of the sidewalk. He saw the dirty old men who slipped in and out of the porn theaters and adult bookstores. He saw the glassy-eyed whores, with skirts so short you could see their bare asses and cunts when they bent over, so strung out they hardly knew where they were. He saw the winos with their filthy hands curled around empty Boone's Farm and MD20 bottles, passed out in the alleys.

Without a doubt this city was full of the sordid and the sinful. But at least they were real Americans. At least these pathetic miscreants had within them the hope of salvation. They were but fallen angels, victims of the corruption, the poison that was now coursing through the arteries and veins of the most amazing country in all of history. John could see what had happened. He could see what was going on. He knew the truth. He knew what he had to do.

Matthew 3:10…

And now also the axe is laid unto the root of the trees:
therefore every tree which bringeth not forth good fruit
is hewn down, and cast into the fire.

Yes, *they* were here. Cunning. Stealthy. All but invisible. But John would find them wherever they were. And uproot them from the good earth of this great country, like a surgeon removes a malignant tumor. He'd commit them to the furnace of final damnation. God bless America!

John wandered the better part of two days in a huge circle, going all the way from Times Square to Battery Park where he gazed with reverence at the

Statue of Liberty, back up through Wall Street, across Houston into Greenwich Village.

For several days, he slept in doorways, hidden behind buildings, or in alleys, sandwiched between dumpsters. Then wandering again, he found an abandoned room one floor above a shooting gallery on the Lower Eastside. That lasted a only few days. The smack franchise expanded and needed the floor space.

For two weeks he crashed at a shelter in the West Village. But there was a 14-day limit so he moved on. Then he completed the sweeping distended circle by wandering up through Chelsea and into Hell's Kitchen, along 9th Avenue.

He headed west toward the river and set up in what he thought was an abandoned warehouse near the docks. But the owner showed up a week later to find John asleep on a pile of clothing and newspapers.

He and John hit it right off. A veteran of World War II, he had a keen understanding and sympathetic eye for anyone who had been on active duty and seen real action. After swapping army stories, they came to an agreement amicable to both of them. Now John had a home. In Hell's Kitchen. What perfect name for this hell on Earth path to glory.

John went right to work and within a couple weeks his "room" was exactly how he wanted it. It was a combination of a fortress, command center, and shrine. He replaced the plywood door with a thick industrial monster reinforced with steel on the outside, which he found in a nearby pile of rubbish, then installed four padlocks and a 2x8 crossbar.

One wall was covered with both street and subway maps of Manhattan and each of the surrounding boroughs. Another wall had a full-length mirror with a large chunk missing from one corner, and face cards from a poker deck taped along the edges. On either side of the mirror were shelves and wall hooks. There he kept all of his mission gear and clothing, mainly fatigues and body liners. But also conspicuous on a wooden hanger next to the door was his Galilee robe, which he wore when praying or when he dispensed blessings and baptisms on his walks through Central Park, Times Square and the Village.

The last wall opposite the door hosted the shrine. On the entire wall itself hung camouflage netting which John had picked up at an army surplus store near SoHo. Over that and dominating the field of vision, stretched a huge American flag, secured at the top within inches of the ceiling and hung on end so that it provided the backdrop to two folding tables, which held John's special objects of reverence and contemplation. On one table was a large plaster sculpture depicting the Last Supper. Around the neck of each Apostle was the dog tag of one of his buddies who had been killed in Vietnam. A picture of John in full combat gear taken in Berin Sac leaned against the Last Supper table right in front of Jesus. Also sharing this surface space was a small leather-bound copy of the New Testament open to the Gospel of Matthew, and incongruously, an ashtray overflowing with cigarette butts and two empty soda bottles. On the other table there was a manger scene, John's bayonet, a plastic chalice, an Army-issue axe, a walkie-talkie and two canteens. Several more canteens were piled under the table next to his infantry boots and a pair of shabby leather sandals. Beside the manger leaning against the wall was a cheap unframed print of Raphael's *Madonna and Child with the Infant Baptist*. Several more dog tags were ceremoniously arranged in front of the painting in a flat mottled glass candy dish. A pair of candleholders caked with dusty wax held white candles burned down to the base.

Besides the American flag, the other object of fascination that constantly elicited reverent awe in John was the large wooden crucifix dramatically suspended in mid-air right above and slightly in front of the tables. Held in place with fishing line, it leaned at an angle like a soaring bird or an ascending aircraft.

Around the neck of Jesus was John's dog tag.

This was exactly how the room remained for the next thirty-seven years. The original owner of the building died and was replaced by a management company. The rest of the building was usually vacant, so he by default was the best tenant. He paid his rent and nobody bothered him.

John established a routine that would be the chapter and verse of his daily living, repeated over 13,000 times, as days, weeks, months and years rolled by.

He got up at 5:30 am and spent the early morning doing military calisthenics, isotonics and isometrics, then running 4 miles through the streets of Manhattan carrying a utility belt and a light backpack. He wound down from this by reading the Bible for an hour, concluding with a self-composed prayer for the redemption of the American people and God's personal intervention in delivering them from the clutches of the communist infiltrators, which he knew were now imbedded in the body politic, like intestinal parasites.

Afternoons, he made the rounds as a holy soldier in God's special infantry, preaching the Good Word. Eventually, the high priest in him took precedence over the preacher, and John placed more and more emphasis and gave greater time to performing baptisms. He baptized anyone who accepted his offer to administer the sacrament. The ceremony was performed either at the fountain in Washington Square or the duck pond at the south end of Central Park. He soon became widely known as St. John the Baptist of Hell's Kitchen, another colorful but harmless nutcase among the thousands that populated the city.

Evenings were spent reading the same military manuals he had kept since his tour of duty in Vietnam, and going to the library to look at new unclassified military publications which would keep him sharp and in-the-loop, for his pending assignments.

If he had learned anything in 'Nam, it was that patience is the key to a successful mission. Patience and staying alert. He hadn't gotten specific orders from high command yet, but he knew it was just a matter of time.

The only break in his daily routine was Sundays when John attended services at a midtown Methodist church. He always wore his Galilee robes but over the years had become such a regular fixture there, he was completely accepted and drew no special attention from the regular attendees. Sometimes a young child would come up and ask him if he was a saint. John was very fond of children, and whenever this happened he very gently bestowed a special blessing on the inquisitive child, then offered, "Shouldn't we all live as saints?"

And so it went day after day, week after week.

Thirty-seven years goes by in a flash, when you know who you are, why you're here, and what's gotta be done. In boot camp, they used to tell each other, "Keep your eye on the prize." Exactly. Stay focused. Make every moment count.

In just about every respect, John was probably in the best shape of his life. Mentally. Physically. His hard work, discipline and dedication had paid off generously. He was a model soldier in the service of his country. For inspiration, he drew from the heart-rending and still vivid memories he carried of his fellow soldiers, those men who had died in Vietnam in combat defending the immutable values that made America great. The men whose dog tags were arrayed in the memorial shrine he had constructed in his room.

He was also and equally in the service of his Creator, as a man of the cloth, his ministry fashioned over time in a manner of his own design and making. As a model, he drew on the example of none other than John the Baptist, who in John's mind was right behind Jesus, in terms of the majesty and profound impact of his ministry. After all, even Jesus went to him at one point to be baptized, humbling Himself before John, who He regarded in some respects a mentor. And wasn't baptism the first crucial step in the long and sacred journey to salvation?

John spent a good deal of his time praying and waiting. He knew his orders would be coming soon. In 'Nam he had it constantly drilled into him by his superiors that timing was everything, and that waiting was a key component of successfully engaging the enemy. Waiting for the opportune time and place to take him apart. Waiting for a sign or signal which pointed the way. Waiting for precise orders from high command, who with their privileged position and special access knew exactly when it was best to move forward.

It was a Thursday, late in September, just after midnight. It was starting to get cool at night and John was hunkered down in his army-issue sleeping bag. He heard a crackle from the walkie-talkie and jumped up and grabbed it.

"Private first class Harrison here."

. . .

"Sir. Very quiet, sir. No sign of enemy movement. Should I stay situated?"

. . .

"Sir. I read and will make necessary preparations. Anything further?"

. . .

"Yes, sir. God bless America, sir. We will prevail!"

So he had his assignment. The men at central command post were absolutely brilliant tacticians. He had always been amazed at their ingenuity and extraordinary sensibilities. Here was proof again. In two days he would intercept the enemy on their own turf. A surprise attack. A search and destroy mission from behind enemy lines.

Theater of Operation: Brooklyn.

Despite his excitement, he forced himself to get some rest. He needed to be fresh, have a clear mind and a sharp edge when he went into battle. As an American soldier, he was better equipped and better trained than these monkeys the North Vietnamese called troops, but they were clever and could surprise you. He soon fell into a deep sleep.

John awoke a little after sunrise, did his calisthenics, ate a can of pork and beans, brewed some coffee, and started to work on the mission plan. Less than 48 hours to put this together. No room for error. Lives were at stake, not the least of all his own.

Brooklyn? What did he know about Brooklyn?

He looked over the street maps as he sipped on his coffee. Then he turned, took a couple steps and knelt down on a tarp that had been folded and placed under the suspended crucifix. He knelt in humility, sufferance and gratitude. Silently he began to pray.

John deeply felt that he had so much to be thankful for. Not only did he know exactly why he was here, what he had to do, and why he had to do it, but John was blessed by the Savior, Our Lord Jesus Christ, with a personal hotline to God the Creator Himself. John only had to believe, to pray, to be silent, and wait for the Voice of Infinite Wisdom. He would be told exactly what he needed to know. Everything would become clear. Just like that.

John didn't move for almost three hours.

Then a smile spread across his face. He stood up and glanced at the objects on the tables. He picked up the black and white picture of him in Nam Tu'o'ng. There he was, standing over three dead bodies, fresh kill who lay at his feet. He looked proud, was grinning broadly. His left foot rested on the face of the corpse in the middle. He put the photo back.

"Time to rock."

The two days went by quickly. But now he was ready. Ready as he ever would be.

He waited until sunset to deploy. By the time he got to Brooklyn it was completely dark. John worked his way through the side streets and alleys, constantly checking the map he had sketched on the back of a sandwich bag to make sure he was following his orders to a tee.

He could tell he was close. Prudently staying out of the glare of the streetlights and headlights of passing vehicles, he turned one final corner.

Yes, this was it. He had arrived. Keeping close to the walls, he slipped down the alley and found a good place to hide behind a dumpster. Now it was just a matter of identifying the target, then taking care of business.

He didn't have to wait long. About twenty minutes later, a metallic burgundy Chrysler PT Cruiser pulled up to the entrance of the alley.

Out stepped the slanty-eye. What an eyeful she was! A little waif dressed in lust lure. A real Ho Chi Minh whore. He knew immediately. This was the target. This was the enemy.

Oh yes, he had seen this type before. Wiley and vicious. One of those sweet little Cong chicks who would come over and do their little seductive dance and then pull you against their lithe little commie bodies. And she'd have a razorblade in her mouth and faster than you could spring a boner, slide the blade between her teeth and slice your juggler like a flimsy garden hose.

This one was very slight but he knew from experience was no less dangerous. She backed away from the street and casually looked in both directions. Then she stepped over to the corner of the building adjacent to the alley and leaned against the wall, as she pawed through her vinyl handbag.

John took advantage of her preoccupation and moved quickly. He was right behind her before she noticed him. Before she could react, he had his one arm around her waste and his other hand over her mouth and was dragging her back to his spot behind the dumpster. She was indeed a tiny thing and incapable of any credible resistance. He forced her to the ground and straddled her, keeping her mouth covered.

"If you make one sound, I'll kill ya."

Cautiously he removed his hand. She panted in fear.

"Please. Please no hurt. I give you blowjob. Free blowjob. No hurt."

"A free blowjob, eh? Hmm. How generous." A subtle smile appeared on his face as he hesitated for a moment, almost as if he was considering her offer.

Then suddenly his demeanor changed. His face now burned with rage and glaring at her with poison in his eyes, he slapped her viciously across the face.

"You filthy little commie slut! I'll give you something to suck on."

He pulled out his axe with one hand and grabbing her neck with the other, shoved the handle down the girl's throat. Her eyes were full of terror and pain, and she struggled as much as her petite frame would allow. But there was little she could do against John's strength and relative bulk. He repeatedly jammed the handle into her throat, which gurgled with blood.

"Blow job. You fucking little murdering commie bitch! You insult me. You insult my country. And you insult my God. No more! You are dead commie meat."

Within a minute, the girl stopped struggling and was dead. John gently relaxed his grip but continued to kneel over her. He pulled the ax handle out of her throat.

He continued to straddle the body, staring at the face of the young girl, frozen at the moment of death in pain and terror. Putting the ax handle to his lips, he licked it, seeming to savor each drop of the girl's blood. When the handle was clean, he gripped it firmly in his right hand and raised it over his head.

"You think you can kill my brothers and get away with it. Is that what you think?"

Ax severs her left arm.

"They were Americans. Good American soldiers. Good people."

Ax to the center of her chest.

"They were family. They were more than family. More than you could ever know. All you know is killing innocent people with your clever tricks and your booby traps and sending little children with bombs and grenades."

Ax to the base of her neck.

"So beautiful. You're so beautiful and you use your beauty to get close to us so you can destroy us because you think your way is the right way. The only way."

87

Ax into the center of her face.

"Let's see where it gets you." Picking up her skirt and grabbing his bayonet he cut off her panties. "Well … what have we here? The ultimate weapon. The commie cunt weapon. Commie cunt brainwashing. Commie cunt indoctrination." He pulled out his erect penis and rubbed it against her. "You'd really like some of this, wouldn't you? Some American cock. Some good Christian cock, so you could brag to your fucking commie friends about how you spread your legs and reeled in a good solid American soldier, a God-fearing American soldier, and made him a slave to your sick commie ways." John stood up, tucked his penis back in his pants and zipped up. "No way, little gook girl. I'm on to your little games of deception. You are messing with the wrong man! See, I know what's going on. And I know what's gotta be done."

John reached into his army knapsack and pulled out his canteen, filled earlier with gasoline. He generously doused her body, threw the canteen aside, then pulled out some matches. He lit one and stared at it, eyes wide with fascination, lips puckered, mouth in a tight grin.

"God sees everything."

John flicked the match and the girl burst into flames. He turned and ran out of the alley, disappearing into the night.

Community Policing

The body, or what was left of it, was found by the one they called Nancy. She was working the late shift at the STD Prevention Center and was locking the rear door, when she heard some growling and scuffling noises. They seemed to be coming from beside or behind a dumpster about fifty feet further into the alley. She would have ignored it, assuming it was just some mischievous dogs, either playing or on the verge of a territorial confrontation, except she also noticed the flickering of a small fire, perhaps some rubbish that had somehow gotten ignited. She decided to have a look.

As she approached, she could not help but notice the smell of burnt flesh. Not cuisine burnt. More industrial burnt, an animal but with other chemical things caught in the conflagration.

Then she saw the body. And two dogs tearing at what remained of the flesh. She gagged, tried to hold back, but filled her hands with bile and the partially digested tofu salad she had eaten just an hour ago.

She ran out of the alley into the street screaming for help. An older man cruising by in a new Buick Enclave station wagon, decided she was not crazy, probably not tricking, and actually in serious need of assistance. He dialed 911 on his cell phone and the police were on the scene within minutes.

The alley and connecting streets were cordoned off and there were squad cars everywhere. Nancy sat slumped over in her office sobbing uncontrollably until she was finally given a sedative by medics on the scene. She was a total basket case. Questioning her would have to wait until tomorrow or the next day. She was escorted out, a blotchy-faced, staggering, partial-paralytic, between two men dressed in antiseptic whites, holding her up by her arms.

The Djin Djin girls were huddled together at the scene but back from the yellow police tape. This was a bomb dropped directly in their own living room, mutilating one of their own and ravaging any sense of security they may have developed over the weeks they had worked the area without incident. Despite the accoutrements and posturing and the adult nature of their business, they were just little girls who were now very frightened, who suddenly felt they had nowhere to turn. Certainly, the local girls wouldn't help them. Maybe it was the local girls who did this!

Shawna hated the Djin Djins. But even she would not have wished this on any one of them. This was a working girl's worst nightmare come true. Some totally deranged john, some sick motherfucker who had a bad childhood, or was out of his mind on crank or PCP, chops a girl up and cremates her practically in plain sight. Or at least right here within a few feet of the sidewalks which they all used night after night just to make a few bucks. Shawna had been close by and ran into the alley as soon as she heard the geek girl from the center screaming like she had lost her mind. She saw firsthand what had been done to the little Asian. Her hair had burnt off but it was obvious from what was left of the face that it was a Djin Djin. Who the fuck did this? Is this motherfucker still anywhere around? Who was next?

Shawna half-walked and half-stumbled. Lilly started toward her as soon as she saw her coming. Shock and pain was written all over Shawna's tear-streaked face. It was obvious something very serious had happened. But Lilly shied away from crime scenes as a matter of principle. She had over the years seen too much to need to see any more. And no way was she getting near the local cops.

"It's one of the Asians. Chopped up and burned." Lilly had never seen this side of her normally unflappable friend. Shawna looked completely drained. Vulnerable. Defeated. "I'm going home, Lilly. I can't handle this."

As she watched Shawna walk away, Lilly popped open her cell phone and called.

"This is Lilly. You helped my friend Shawna a while ago. Maybe you should get over here. Some serious shit goin' down. I'll meet you corner of Turner and Maple."

A sizeable crowd had gathered despite efforts by the police to disperse them. No one seemed to notice the Guardian Angels van as it drove by and pulled over to the curb two blocks away from the mob. As she had promised, Lilly was waiting and quickly jumped in the passenger seat. She looked into the back of the van.

"You alone? I thought you guys always traveled in pairs."

"Everyone's got the flu. Just me tonight. What's going on?"

"I didn't get close. But someone got chopped up. A little oriental. That's what they're saying. And burned."

"Burned?"

"Someone said the sick bastard who killed her set her on fire. She's flame-broiled. I don't know everything. Give it about two more minutes. Believe me, it's all anyone is going to be talking about for the next month."

"Why me? I mean the cops are all over the place. They've got it covered. And we have no official jurisdiction ..."

"You can cut the official bullshit talk. You know who you're talkin' to? I know what you told Shawna about the shithead cops. You think they're protecting the Djin Djins."

"Guess they're not doing a very good job, eh?"

"But you know what this means. This means our asses are gonna be headed for the ringer. You know they'll try to pin this on one of us. If they been listening to the tom tom, they know we hate them. So who they gonna come to? Who'll they try to pin this on?"

"Well, maybe one of your sisters *did* do it. How do you know?"

"Billy. Your name is Billy, right? Billy, I been working these streets since I was fifteen. Ain't tellin' you how old I am. But it's been a few years. And 'sisters' is right. These *are* my sisters. My family. And there ain't a single one of them who would do this. Yeah, everyone is pissed off about the little chinks, stealing our business and all. People always talk big. But none of my girls would do this. This is some really sick shit."

"I don't know what I can do. I mean ..."

"Just believe me. That's all. Be there. Be there if we need you. We didn't do this."

"I'll do what I can. I ... I do believe you. But we can't break any laws. If they're looking for someone and they've got a warrant, we can't hide anyone."

"Exactly. Just do what you can. We've got nobody on our side. And I'm expecting some bad shit to come down."

And bad shit did come down, indeed.

For the next two weeks, the whole neighborhood was turned over and turned upside down. Not that they ever got closer to finding out who the killer was. But it wasn't from a lack of putting on a good show. Or a lack of messing with everybody and everything.

Though the legality of it was highly suspect, a limited pedestrian curfew was put into effect. 10 pm every night, the streets and sidewalks were supposed to be clear of foot traffic. Of course, it was selectively enforced. It seemed that the Djin Djin girls came and went as usual.

Every local shop owner was repeatedly questioned, queried and intimidated. As if the very misfortune of running a store in a bad part of town somehow contributed to the murder. Even stores which were not all that close to the scene of the murder came under pressure. Anything resembling normal commerce came to a halt. Most regular customers didn't cotton to the idea of proximity to the ubiquitous army of blues.

All of the non-Asian street girls got pulled in. If someone was chewing gum with their mouth open, they'd find some obscure law against it and downtown she went. Each and every one of the regular girls was repeatedly held overnight on some minor infraction or trumped up charge, then grilled up one side and down the other.

"Where were you the night of the crime?"

"Which crime? There's more crime in my part of town than anyplace else on the fucking planet. And you guys sit uptown in a goddamn doughnut shop talking baseball."

"You know what crime. The murder of the young Asian girl."

"Where do you think I was? I was hosting a dinner party at my condo over on 5th Avenue. Donald Trump was there. You should've come by."

"Just watch yourself. Your attitude is gonna get you another night here."

"Suit yourself, copper. Just tell the chef I prefer vinaigrette and roasted pine nuts. No more fucking ranch dressing for this mama."

The treatment of the Djin Djin girls was entirely another matter. They were respectfully invited into a squad car, some brief conversation would take place, usually involving a lot of laughing and flirtation, then they would be politely placed back on the street to go on about their business. Sometimes to make their preferential treatment look a little less obvious, the car would pull away, maybe go around the block. But they still let every single Djin Djin go with nothing but a pat on the behind and a wink. Certainly none of them got taken downtown.

This, of course, exacerbated the growing hostility between the regulars and the Djin Djin girls, and additionally the regulars and the cops. Shawna grew increasingly incensed and vocal about the sweetheart deal the Djin Djin girls had going. And she became more and more obsessed with finding something incriminating. Something scandalous which would blow the lid on the whole arrangement.

Lilly tried to be the voice of reason.

"Say you find something. So what? Who ya gonna tell? And who's gonna believe a 'ho like you, over the word of the blues?"

"I don't know. I don't fucking care. The mayor? The governor? I'll take it to Oprah!"

"Shawna, you know I love ya. But you are foolin' yourself. Big time. It just ain't gonna happen, girl. You're just askin' for trouble."

But Shawna couldn't be deterred. She kept her eyes peeled for an opportunity to catch the cops in something, even if she didn't know what.

Her opportunity came one evening right around 10 pm. In anticipation of curfew, she had gone down a side street where she hoped she would draw less heat from the patrol cops. The johns had adjusted themselves to the "new rules" and took to cruising the more residential areas and alleys off of the main drag as the night wore on. Shawna was tucked in a doorway, visible but not conspicuous when she saw a police car coming. She pressed back as far out of sight as possible as it passed. They didn't see her. But she saw them. And the two Djin Djin girls in the back seat. They pulled into a short alley only a half a block further. After waiting a few minutes to convince herself and get up the courage, Shawna very cautiously made her way to the entrance of the alley.

It was dark but Shawna could still make out what was going on. One of the officers was in back with a Djin Djin and the other Djin Djin had moved into the passenger seat. Only their shoulders and their bobbing heads could be seen.

But yes, it was obvious what was going on, alright. The two cops were getting some serious head, compliments of the local talent. The local Asian talent.

It didn't take long. The girl in the front switched back to the rear seat, the car started, and they were on their way. Shawna wanted to follow them but couldn't possibly keep up, and in reality thought better of it, because with her luck they would haul her in again on a curfew violation. But as the squad car passed, she got a clear view of the officer in the passenger seat.

"Holy shit!"

She pulled out her cell phone and paced and gesticulated like a crazy person for the four seconds it took for her party to come on the line.

"Lilly! Get the Angels down here to pick us up. Immediately! You won't fucking believe what I just saw."

By the time Shawna hooked up with Lilly, the Guardian Angel van was pulling up.

"You guys are not gonna believe it. I just saw two blues and two Djin Djins having their own little BJ party. One cop I couldn't really see. But the other one, I know like I know sweet Jesus Hisself."

"Who? Who was it, Lilly?"

"None other than the most self-righteous fuck on the planet, the guy that's giving us all of the shit out there. That Fiori guy. The one you were tellin' me about, the one you met with."

"Captain Fiori? From Precinct Headquarters? Are you sure?"

"Of course I'm sure. They had me down there three times already. That ugly motherfucker came in all three times to shake me down, like I knew anything about who killed the chink. Believe me, I *know* what the dude looks like."

"Fiori. It makes sense. I figured his name had to come up eventually."

"So you're all over this."

"Not really. It's just that the Djin Djin thing is everywhere. So just in the normal course of business, we end up investigating this and that, and putting the pieces together. It seems whatever comes up points a finger at the cops. We can't pin anything on them. But it sure looks like some of them are on the take. The Asians get very special treatment. It's like the police here are their very own private protection service."

"The fucking cops would run over a schoolteacher to make it easier for one of those Asian sluts to cross the street."

"Unfortunately, I think we've been ruffling some feathers. Lately it's looking more and more that Fiori has it in for us. Just a feeling we're getting."

"Well, he was getting a feeling hisself tonight."

"Listen, Shawna. I really appreciate your help. I'm not quite sure where to go with this. But we'll figure it out. There's got to be a way clean this up. This shouldn't be going on. Especially with people getting killed."

"Especially with them kicking our asses every night. And treating the Djin Djins like they are a holy treasure to the community. Fuck that shit!"

Billy got on the phone the next morning. This was touchy business. The whole idea of the Guardian Angels was to enhance the service given to the community by the municipal police, working in parallel to provide citizen-based community policing. This meant cooperation at all levels with the local cops. But what were they supposed to do if the cops proved to be corrupt, in bed with the criminal elements they were supposed to be policing? This made them adversaries. Both the charter of the Guardian Angels and basic morality left no doubt as to what they should do. Billy got a hold of the board of directors, the chapter captains, and the founder of the Angels himself, and set up an emergency meeting to map out a strategy for addressing this very serious and controversial breach of the public trust. They would meet in executive session in four days.

The meeting never took place.

Here is how it was described three days after Shawna and Lilly met with them. From page two of the New York Post ...

GUARDIAN ANGELS BUSTED FOR DEALING DRUGS

A Guardian Angels precinct office in Brooklyn was raided and shut down, alleged to be the headquarters for a major regional drug dealing ring. Shortly after midnight yesterday, a special Drug Law Enforcement Unit entered the unoccupied facility and found large quantities of heroin, cocaine, methamphetamine, and marijuana. Numerous guns, suspected to be stolen or unregistered, were also confiscated in the raid. Billy Gresham and Peter Mangione, respectively precinct captain and street team leader, who ran and worked out of the Brooklyn facility, were arrested shortly after the raid at their respective homes. They are now in custody.

A week later, a second Djin Djin girl was found murdered and mutilated beyond possible identification. Her body was found behind a row of hedges at the rear of an apartment, just off of Flatbush Blvd. The girl's face had been eaten away by a concentrated solution of lye. The autopsy and forensic analysis would reveal that a military issue handgun had been inserted in the girl's rectum and fired three times.

Girls Just Wanna Have Fun!

Alicia finally slipped off her black satin-faced Ralph Lauren elevation jacket and continued to speak through man-sized bites of peach cobbler, occasionally sipping on a tumbler of whole milk.

"There's no logical explanation for the way I turned out. I mean, my parents were like Emily Post meets Father Knows Best. But the neighborhood was total crap. Propriety in a pigsty. My high school was a boot camp for losers and creeps. I used to wonder if my teachers had even finished high school themselves. But you do what you can. I read a lot. The classics. And was obsessed with fashion magazines."

Alicia and Christine finally found some common ground on their calendars and were having lunch at a smart restaurant-deli on Amsterdam and 73rd Street.

Alicia's suggestion. Now that the gays had gentrified the neighborhood, it was sinfully chic, wide-eyed and wonderful. The waiters never stopped smiling and always made a huge fuss over her. She loved the male attention without the usual tension of elevated blood-levels of testosterone.

Christine smiled like she had found a treasure trunk in the attic. "You have a very different energy than anyone else I know, that's for sure."

"Tell me about the people you know."

Her smile faded. "Christians. All of my friends are devout Christians. They all have committed their lives to Jesus, go to church at least once a week, read Bible stories to their children, and look forward to the day they will cash in on the perfect lives they lead here on Earth, collecting their reward and spending eternity with God and the angels in Heaven."

"Christine! My my. You actually sound a bit cynical. Where is that coming from?"

"I'm not some ditzy praise-the-Lord blonde bimbo, you know. I see what's going on around me. I've been thinking about this for a long time. Every Sunday for my entire life, I have gone to church. After a while, you know every hymn, every Bible story, every parable and passage by heart. You even know what the pastor is going to say next. So I would look around. I would see how for most people the devotion, the worship, the prayers, the singing, the entire process is just a mechanical exercise. Robotics. Repetition and rote. And I couldn't help but notice how they behaved. Come Monday, all of it was back on the shelf. Tucked away till next Sunday. People revert to doing the same evils they claim to abhor and completely condemn when they are promising at services to dedicate their lives to Christ, respect the Ten Commandments, and the live by the example and teachings of the Savior."

"The very reasons I have always avoided church. The hypocrisy. Doesn't it make you sick? Aren't you pissed off that people are so lame? So horribly disingenuous? Is that why you're cynical?"

"Well, actually I'm not cynical at all. I'm merely realistic. People are people. I just know not to rely on them. Most people will write a check but otherwise won't lift a finger to actually help others."

"Do you ever talk to anyone about this?"

"I'm talking to you right now."

"But you hardly know me."

"There is something about you, Alicia, as potty-mouth and weird as you are, which makes me feel I can trust you. You are so open and … and real! And the answer to your question is 'no'. There is no one else I could possibly talk to about how I feel."

"No one. What about your husband?"

"Not even my husband. Especially my husband, who is my best friend and in every way the perfect man for me."

"How can someone be perfect for you if you can't share everything?"

"He is perfect because we don't share everything. There's nothing in the wedding vows that I recall, about laying everything on the table. We love and respect one another. But he wouldn't understand. And I wouldn't want to burst his bubble. He is a beautiful innocent."

Alicia was stunned. This was not what she expected.

What had she expected?

"Christine. You need to have some fun. Do you ever have any fun?"

"Of course I have fun. But I really don't think we mean the same thing. You are way too wild for me. I mean, I'm not judging you. You should do what you think is right."

"Whatever. Maybe I need to have less fun. Or a different kind of fun. Being an Olympic level sinner, as I admit to being, gets tedious, you know. The parties, the lost weekends, the club hopping, the orgies. Let me just tell you from experience, one that I am sure you haven't personally had, after a while one orgy is just like another. And you just get through them by imagining that the next day you will be walking through Central Park counting gum wrappers and learning to make pigeon sounds."

Christine does her best pigeon warble.

"That was phenomenal! You should go on Stupid Pet Tricks."

"Except it would be the pigeon doing something. Maybe singing like Macy Gray."

"Right right. Good point. But that could come in handy. The pigeon thing."

"It does. People feed me bread crusts all the time. I never go hungry."

"What? No Macadamia nuts? Cheap bastards."

Christine abruptly stops laughing as she looks at her watch.

"Whoa! Where does the time go?"

"Me too. Got an assignment briefing to go to. Something about some Barbie Doll Fan Club in the Bronx. Apparently there is a White Trash Barbie Doll Fan Club in Portland, Oregon. So the Bronx people are going ballistic, considering it the desecration of a sacred symbol of American culture, and are declaring next Monday the official National Ken and Barbie Day. It's all about protecting family values. They got a parade permit and everything. A shit assignment for shit money. But I gotta eat."

They both start to collect their things. Alicia signaled for the waiter, who happened to be looking right at her. He headed over with a conspiratorial grin on his face.

"Now girl." Pointing to her coat. "I really don't think you need to take that along. It's plenty warm out there. Besides, honey, this would look great on me!"

"I am sure it would, Carl. But ya never know about the weather these days. Everything is just so topsy-turvy with the ozone layer and global warming. Could be a furnace out there. Or it might be a blizzard. Ya just never know. Thanks for the offer, though."

Handing her the check. "Here you go. It comes to $34.56. And if you change your mind about the jacket, you know right where to find me. Do you have any aviator goggles?"

Christine reached over and took the check, then handed it back to Carl with two twenties. She winked at Alicia. "My treat this time. I meant to ask you. How is the adoption going? The little boy from Indonesia?"

"Have you got three hours? It's a freakin' mess. Next time, I'll bring you up to speed."

"Yes. Next time. So let's do this again soon."

They hug. In a friendly mocking way, Carl hugs the waiter standing next to him, who then goes behind the bar and hugs the bartender. The three of them silly-smile and pinky-wave at Alicia and Christine as they make their way out onto Amsterdam Avenue.

Love is in the air. Life is wide-eyed and wonderful.

Next Monday is National Ken and Barbie Day in the Bronx.

War Games

It's very early morning. John Harrison is holding the walkie-talkie and speaking with fierce concentration. He's dressed in combat fatigues.

"Second Lieutenant Harrison here, sir. Can't talk at length. Too much counter-intel in the area. But I just wanted to file my regular report."

. . .

"Yes, sir. I have engaged the enemy. But very selectively."

. . .

"That is an affirmative, sir. Behind the recognized line of engagement. Deep penetration. But I am badly outnumbered. They're swarming over the entire area. It is like the 8th Plague of Egypt."

. . .

"Yes, sir. That is correct, sir. I am taking them out one at a time. Same tactics they use on us."

. . .

"Yes, sir. That is an affirmative. I will continue as per your mission ops communiqué of 26 September. Next report will be one week from today at 0600."

. . .

"Thank you, sir. You are very generous. I am just doing my job. God bless America. Out."

Chapter 7

THE ART OF PERSUASION: Poetry and Polemics

Happy Birthday, Mr. Goodbar

It was Saturday. And tomorrow he would turn 35. Lenny never made a big deal out of his birthday. Just another day, if you think about it. But if anyone else wanted to make it some kind of big event, he could go along with that.

A courier came to his house just before noon and handed him an express delivery envelope. Inside was just a simple note from Chicago.

Lenny – We decided to give you a two-part b-day present. Still on for tomorrow. But tonight, go to Tony's around 7. Look for a bald Jap guy Yoshikaze (works for us). He'll take care of you. – Harold

That takes care of the weekend. Or the better part of it. Harold and Ed had promised to do something special. Until now he hadn't heard any more about it. And frankly hadn't given it very much thought.

Lenny walked into Tony's a little after 7 and there were the usual suspects. Working all week long so that starting Friday night and continuing through the weekend, they could dissolve the drudgery of the their meaningless jobs in shots of whiskey and pitchers of flavorless American beer. Almost every booth and table was occupied with the grinning and dazed, the semicool and sodden, the uncouth and ambivalent, the indifferent and unnotable, the overweight and unsexy, the defeated but still optimistic, the 30 and 40 somethings who could temporarily re-animate the corpse of their abandoned dreams with a night of loud conversation and a jukebox stuffed with retros and retreads, the nostalgic oldies which triggered the memories of better days.

Lenny looked around and spotted Yoshikaze sitting alone in a corner booth.

They shook hands, gave each other the once over and Yoshikaze signaled to Tony behind the bar for a round. Within a minute, there was a shot of Cuttysark and a Mickey's Malt Liquor in front of Lenny, a snifter of brandy being held up by Yoshikaze as a toast.

"It is an honor to meet you, Mr. Petrocelli."

"Lenny. Please, just call me Lenny. The last time someone called me 'Mr. Petrocelli', his partner was putting handcuffs on me."

"I seriously doubt that. Don't they call you 'Lucky Lenny'? I hear you are made of steel and coated with Teflon."

"Great for making omelettes. Momma's little helper in the kitchen."

They smiled their guarded smiles in a moment of shared amusement and male bonding, comfortable as they needed to be for what would probably be an hour or two of superficial interaction.

"Yes. Breaking eggs. You can't make an omelette without breaking a few eggs. Is that what you say here in America?"

"Yoshikaze. From your name I'd say you are Japanese. Correct?"

"Yes, but I have lived here for over ten years. Here actually being Chicago. And I have worked for my bosses … our bosses … for almost six years now."

"There are a lot of people I haven't met."

"I travel a lot. Singapore. Taiwan. Thailand. Special assignments. They just wanted me to meet you and … uh. Well, you will see. This should make you happy."

"My birthday gift. Part one."

"Yes, Mr. … I mean, Lenny. Happy birthday!"

Another theatrical toast.

They downed their drinks and stood up. Lenny waved at Tony, then flipped him the bird. Tony laughed and shook his head as Lenny and Yoshikaze disappeared out the door.

Yoshikaze had a driver waiting in a black Infiniti G35. Tinted windows. Black leather interior. Looked like a mafia doomsday weapon. Or maybe Don Corleone's fuckwagon.

It was less than 15 minutes before they arrived at a warehouse on Halleck Street near the docks. Lenny got out and followed Yoshikaze, who popped open the padlocks and led him into the building.

"Just wait here. I'll get the lights."

The thick metallic thud of the circuit breaker reverberated throughout the cavernous room. Bright spotlights illuminated the area in the very center, where in stark relief two men in tailored suits were seated next to one another in pinewood kitchen chairs. There were ropes going around them, holding their lifeless bodies upright. The pool of blood on the floor around the legs of each chair was dark and thick. The room smelled like entrails.

Both men had been decapitated. Their heads rested in their laps, expressionless and leaning back against their stomachs.

Incongruously, about fifteen feet directly in front of them stood a heavy-duty camera tripod. Underneath it was an equipment bag for what was probably professional photographic gear.

Lenny took only a few steps before he realized who they were. Martin and Frankie.

"Did you do this?"

"Yes. I do what needs to be done. Like I said, special assignments. Happy birthday, Lenny. This is good, right?"

"They were my friends. At least, at one time. Then they fucked me. So … it is what it is."

No one said anything on the ride back. They pulled up in front of Lenny's place.

"Have a good one, Lenny. I'll probably be seeing you around."

"Right. You too."

Lenny felt both sick and relieved. Two less thugs to worry about. Fucking traitors no less. But at the same time, he felt nauseous and haunted by the repulsive image of two men who he had spent a decent amount of time with in the past, dead at the hands of a paid executioner. Payback. Gruesome payback.

Even if they had turned on him, each had a story, a life they were living out until this. He knew Frankie's wife. Had seen the two of them with their two kids one day, playing at a neighborhood playground one beautiful Sunday afternoon. What would happen to them now that Frankie was dead? And Martin. Lenny gone to a few ballgames with him. They had knocked down beers at Tony's a couple times. He knew Martin was big on the horses and had a lot of gambling debts.

It is what it is. Lenny told himself he shouldn't be thinking of these things. They got what they deserved. This is the way things are done. We don't work for Citibank or Macy's, for chrissake. These guys knew the rules. And whatever the other side offered them, they should've known better. So that's that. You lose, motherfuckers. Your markers came due.

Still he felt anxious. Maybe it was the but-for-the-grace-of-God-there-go-I factor. More like … but for the grace of Harold Danko and Ed Valley!

Yes, that was a big part of it. The reminder that it could be him in one of those chairs. Certainly, he was making some incredible money at work that was sleazy but relatively easy.

On the other hand, the stakes were high. Very high. You fuck up bad enough and you pay with your life. No margin for error.

Tonight was a wake up call. These guys play for keeps. He always had to be very careful. And that's that.

His phone rang. He looked at the caller ID. It was a Chicago number.

"How is the best looking guy east of Lake Michigan?"

"Jessica." Relieved it wasn't Danko or Valley. "Yes, thank you. I'm fine."

"You have an appointment, a *birthday* appointment at the Plaza Hotel tomorrow. Make sure you arrive by 4 o'clock. You will be treated in grand style from there on. Does that work for you?"

"Okay, 4 pm at the Plaza. Wow! They're pulling out all the stops, eh? Tell them I really appreciate it."

"That's the way they are. Happy Birthday, Lenny."

"Of course. It's not till tomorrow. But thanks! I'll have one on you."

Sunday at one of the finest hotels in the city. His own private birthday party. Awesome!

Then he flashed on Frankie and Martin in the warehouse and anxiety again clawed at the walls of his stomach like a desperate animal. He momentarily felt dizzy. Then it passed. He needed to get beyond that business. It was over. Nothing anyone could do now.

He needed a beer. He popped the cap as he returned from the fridge and plopped down. Very soon, he fell asleep watching some low-budget sci-fi flick on television.

When he opened his eyes Sunday morning, the first thing he saw was a warm, half-empty bottle of Mickey's sitting on the side table. A TV evangelist was in the midst of a high-pitch harangue, beseeching the Good Lord to fill a wheelchair-bound old lady with the healing power of the Holy Spirit. She shook like an epileptic, eyes rolling in her head like a slot machine, then suddenly she jumped up and started doing a jig in front of an awestruck and applauding congregation. Lenny nixed the TV as soon as he could grab the remote.

Usually on Sunday he stopped by computer central and looked over the latest spreads. But that was all being handled directly now. He was still waiting for clear directions on what Chicago had in mind for him to do. He had talked to Danko beginning of last week but not gotten much insight.

"Listen. Just relax for now. Once you get going, you're going to be busier than a one-armed wallpaper hanger. Enjoy the downtime, Lenny."

So for today, all he had on his calendar was to be spoiled rotten for his birthday. Okay!

He splurged and took a taxi all the way from Brooklyn to the Plaza. It dropped him at 5th Avenue and Central Park South, arriving just before 4 pm. His room was ready and it was absolutely incredible! The Rose Suite was larger than his flat and even had a butler's pantry, stocked with wines, whiskeys, imported salamis, fresh-baked French and Italian breads, bottled water from all over the world, chocolates, truffles, you name it. They must have thought he was going to be there a week instead of just one night.

They had the whole thing carefully planned out. His itinerary was printed in elegant cursive on a thick rustic watermark stock:

A valet will direct you to where you need to be and will have your limousine available for transport.

4:30 pm - Massage (Spa at Mandarin Oriental)
6:00 pm - Manicure (Allure Day Spa)
7:30 pm - Dinner in the Oak Room
10:00 pm - Shows (Larry Flynt's Hustler Club)
12:00 pm - Special Visitor

He unpacked the few things he brought for the overnight. His duffel bag looked incongruous in the midst of the stunning splendor of his luxury accommodations. Lenny was shaking his head in awe when there was a knock at the door. It was the valet.

"Good afternoon, sir. I am William and am here to make your birthday stay a pleasant one. May I help you unpack, sir?"

"No no. Thanks, William. Pleased to meet you."

"A car is waiting to take you to the Mandarin Oriental for your massage. I trust you will find it a very pleasurable experience. In the closet is a jacket, shirt and tie for this evening's events, which require dress attire. If you could try them on, sir."

Lenny went to the closet and took out the shirt and jacket.

"If they do not fit correctly, I can have them altered by the time you return."

They fit better than his own clothes. How did they know?

"That won't be necessary. They're perfect."

"Then, when you are ready, sir, I'll have the car pull up to the front lobby."

A glimmering white stretch Lincoln Continental limo. A massage that left him so relaxed he could barely manage to walk out of the spa. A manicure that included herbal wraps and a feather touch rejuvenating skin treatment from an exquisite young blonde hand-aesthetics specialist. He could get used to this kind of life. This was better than sex. Well ... almost.

When he got back to the Plaza, he traded his casuals for the jacket and tie and headed down to the hotel's world-renowned Oak Room for a seven-course meal. Lenny laughed to himself at the thought of ordering his usual Cuttysark and Mickey's combo. He resigned himself to drinking a $450 bottle of French wine with his meal, and a cordial of Charbay Nostalgie Black Walnut Liqueur as a finishing touch.

Back in the limo for a very short ride to the Hustler Club. There he had an open tab and for over two hours took in some great cocktails, some of the most beautiful girls in Manhattan, and several private shows in the VIP champagne suites.

When Lenny got back to the hotel he felt good. Real good. His face just plain hurt from smiling so much. It is pretty amazing how much you can drink when it's the quality stuff. The stuff he couldn't afford. But then again, it's just a matter of ordering your priorities. They did say he was going to be making more money. Apparently a lot more money.

He slid the electronic key and opened the door to his suite.

There was a night lamp near the door but the sitting room was dark. From the bedroom emanated the soft flickering of candlelight. When he approached the doorway, he could see at least a dozen long thin candles in crystal hurricane lamps giving the room a warm romantic glow.

He squinted and she was barely visible in the soft light. In the bed was a girl with her back to him. The covers were pulled up to just under her thin arms and her long black hair lay on the pillow and her shoulder.

"I hope your name is not Alicia Peters."

She turned and indeed it was not Alicia, but a very young Asian girl with a face that was the soft flower of innocence, with eyes that were alluring pools of sadness. She was delicate and beyond beautiful. He felt the hungry grind of lust building in his pants. Lenny could barely breathe and slowly slid onto the bed to get a better look.

He recognized her.

"Mr. Lenny. I your birthday gift. Come. I will love you. All night I will love you."

He felt his throat constrict and his mouth go dry. A single violent shiver shot through him like an electric current. His manhood softened and retreated like a cowering worm.

She pulled away the covers, sat up and reached for him.

"No. No, sweetheart. Please."

He couldn't let her touch him. Apparently she did not recognize him.

But yes, he knew her. At least he had seen her before. She was one of the girls who had fed him when he was in Mulcahey's cellar dungeon. One of the girls who had kept him alive. A Djin Djin girl.

He sat down on the opposite side of the bed.

"How old are you?"

"I am fifteen. But I fuck like a champion. I make you very happy."

"Not tonight, sweetheart. Not tonight. You are very beautiful … and … well normally I would but …"

"It's okay. I stay with you?"

"No. Thank you. Thank you but you had better go."

She looked puzzled but then swung her legs around over the other side of the bed, reached down and picked up her clothes, then started to dress. Still a little confused, she made dressing a seductive affair, perhaps thinking Lenny would change his mind.

Lenny tried not to stare. But she was *so* incredibly beautiful. And the alcohol still lubricated his male curiosity and fascination. Look at her. This should have been a perfect way to cap off a phenomenal evening. But … he couldn't do it.

He just couldn't do it.

When the girl was dressed, she came over behind him and placing her delicate hands on his shoulders, kissed the back of his neck. Her touch was feather-light and Lenny imagined this is what the fingers of an angel felt like.

"Happy birthday, Mr. Lenny. You big hunk of man. Bye-bye."

She slipped out of the room. A moment later, he heard the muted click of the door latch.

And she was gone. A Djin Djin girl. Working for Harold and Ed.

What was happening to him? Had he gone soft? Well … yes. He had. Quite literally. There is no way he couldn't have fucked that little girl no matter what. She was just a child. But beyond that, she was one of the little Asians who took care of him when he was in the dungeon. And one of her friends, little Kimnai, had saved his life. Kimnai was only fourteen years old. And it killed Lenny to think about it. But it all became clear now. Kimnai was probably out there in the streets right now turning tricks. Making money for *his* bosses.

Lenny felt both angry and ashamed. This was definitely the first time in his life he had ever turned away a piece of ass. And an extraordinarily beautiful one at that. But he hated Chicago this! For going this far. Would they stop at nothing to make a buck?

Yeah, he was going soft. Soft in the head? No, soft in the heart.

In some ways it didn't seem possible that he could give a shit. He needed to sort this out. He felt like such a hypocrite. After all, he was a purveyor of sex on the internet. Those were young girls as well. Why should he be fucked up over this Asian thing? It's just the New Economy. Everything is for sale. That's the way it is now.

But maybe there was a limit. There *had* to be a limit. There were things he wouldn't touch, things he wouldn't do, no matter how good the money or how desperate his need. This was one of those lines that shouldn't be crossed.

He thought of Kimnai. Her whole family was back in Thailand. And here she was, all alone in Brooklyn. Probably brought here against her will. A sex slave. He pictured Harold Danko on top of her, fucking her like a store-bought piece of veal.

No ... there was a line. This definitely crossed it.

No way could he be a part of this. *No way!*

He needed to figure out what to do.

A way out.

News Flash: "Accident At Sea"

This just in ...

> *A fire reportedly broke out last night aboard a 55-ton Class D cargo ship in the Indian Ocean, approximately 300 kilometers southeast of Madagascar. One observer on an airborne disaster surveillance plane responding to the cries for assistance broadcast from the ship, claims to have witnessed explosions. The damaged vessel is listing heavily and may be in danger of sinking. It has not been determined how many are aboard but similar cargo boats typically have a 20 to 24-man crew. It is unknown at this time where this ship is registered, its destination, or the nature of its cargo.*

Carnivores

"It's very obvious. I know you get it, Lenny. There's no middle ground here. We consider you family. And family takes care of family. What's there to equivocate about?"

It was Monday. The day after his birthday bash. Though Lenny had slept in at the Plaza until well after the noon check-out time, his head still felt like a big empty oil drum. Walking out of the hotel was like walking into an arc lamp. The taxi ride home seemed like it would never end. Another towelhead to boot, who wouldn't shut the fuck up.

Lenny had only been home a couple hours when he got the call. Danko and Valley were in the city taking care of some business. They wanted to meet for dinner. How very strange. They practically never came to town. Maybe every couple years. Tops.

So here they were, the three of them, at Brooklyn's own New York Steakhouse, the perfect spot for a power meeting, and an orgy of meat eating. Lenny worked on a rack of lamb the size of a birdcage, while his hosts carved away at their seat cushion-size porterhouses.

Danko chomped vigorously on his medium-rare slab of steer hindquarters, spraying into the air droplets of pink juice which tumbled among the syllables of his philosophical diatribe — a ballet of diluted blood and high crime wisdom.

"You either are a good member of the family. And you see how that works out, eh? You had a good birthday. Right? Or you are a bad member, and you do something to hurt the family. Then you end up like Frankie and Martin. There is no middle ground. No grey area. And there's no guesswork here. It's a simple choice. Very straightforward. What I'm sayin' is, if you run into anyone who needs to know that, you tell them. You be our messenger. We're both counting on you."

"I hear you. I hear what you're saying. But I ... I guess I don't quite understand who I'm supposed to tell. Who needs to get this message."

Ed's turn.

"Look, Lenny. This isn't rocket science. You'll know. And I can see what bothers you. First of all, these two, this Frankie and Martin. They were worthless punks. Street shit. You didn't think so and we didn't think so at first. But that's the way it played out. Worthless motherfucking punks who didn't know how good they had it. They go sniffing the behind of that homo Mulcahey. They shoulda known better. And if the Bishop tries anything like that again, he's next. I don't care if he is Peter the Apostle."

Now Harold. "We could've taken him out a long time ago. Back in Minneapolis. Maybe we should have. But we were very merciful about it. And now he's at it again. He's gonna learn a very hard lesson."

Now Lenny was really confused. "Minneapolis? I don't get what you're saying."

"We had some girls working Minneapolis. This was back in the '80s. We were just getting started. And Mulcahey came after us with fire and brimstone, thinking if he got the community behind him, he could run us out of town. But we showed him who he was dealing with."

Ed starts laughing from the bottom of his barrel chest. "That's for sure. And we learned how easy it is to take these self-righteous bastards down off their pedestals."

It was obvious that Ed took special pride in this.

"It was right after this huge child molestation scandal at a school in California. McMartin Pre-School. Big news for months on end. So the public was already in a rage about it. Mulcahey's church was in a poor part of town, so it wasn't hard finding someone who would do it for some decent cash. We only needed one kid to point the finger. And then a bunch came out of the woodwork. It's crazy the way it works. But kids are very suggestible and their parents start badgering them. Pretty soon they're saying all sorts of things happened."

Harold picks up the thread.

"And it never has to come to trial or hearing or anything. People are so nuts about protecting their kids, all you need is suspicion. It sticks like napalm. And a person goes up in flames. Mulcahey was out of there quicker than you could make a sign of the cross."

The tag. Valley's back in the ring.

"So if Mulcahey or anyone tries anything from here on out, they're toast. I'm telling you, no one is going to fuck up anything we're doing. It's totally under control. Getting back to Martin and Frankie, you have to realize that you only used those two fucks occasionally. But we used them a lot. And they knew way too much. When they went over to help out Mulcahey, we had no choice. Bingo."

Another quick tag. Danko comes through the ropes.

"Frankly, I'm glad it happened. It'll end up being a really good thing. Word will get around. And you probably won't have to do or say much of anything. You'll just need to be there. We've drawn a line in the sand. Nobody's gonna cross it if they know what's good for 'em."

Valley jumps over the ropes! Now they're both in the ring. A classic double team effort!

"It's about respect."

"And being on top."

"And keeping on the offensive."

"Greasing the right palms."

"No fear."

Between his hangover and the barrage of non sequitur aphorisms, Lenny felt like he was in a hurricane-driven hailstorm without a helmet. He nodded and tried to look impressed. Struggled to mask his confusion and discomfort with an air of engaged nonchalance.

"Just be there."

"Keep your eyes and ears open."

"You'll know what to do."

"Keep us in the loop."

"We'll take it from there."

Lenny had to jump in here somewhere.

"I got it covered. You know you can count on me."

"Right. Good boy, Lenny."

Harold with a gleam in his eye. "So the Djin Djin girls have shook things up a bit over in your part of town, eh? That's what we hear."

"I guess you could say that."

Harold nodding and theatrically pointing at Ed. "Right there. There's the genius. The man who invented them."

"Come on, Harold. You're only saying that 'cause you know it's true." Horse laugh.

"Humble as Donald Trump. That's my man Ed."

"This was way before even Minneapolis when I got the idea. See I have these friends, they got businesses in Vietnam. I was visiting. Checking things out. And we were in this bar in Ho Chi Minh City. And I'm trying to order gin and tonics. But they keep bringing me vodka. So I keep sayin', 'No no. Gin. Gin!' And they bring me vodka and tonic. It gets to be this big joke. 'Cause every time I yell 'Gin gin!', one of these pretty little sluts would come over and sit on my lap and say, 'Gin gin?' They took turns. And after three more vodka and tonics, I had a boner you could run the stars and stripes up. Goddamn those gook girls are hot! So I'm thinkin' for years, mind you, there's a fuckin' goldmine sitting right there. The 'gin gin' girls. Which I then later polished up and changed the spelling, D-J-I-N. So there you have it."

They ordered a last round of drinks. Lenny joined them in their ritualistic imbibing of what he assumed was some very pricey cognac. He clenched his teeth and smiled to keep from gagging.

Ed got even larger.

"A toast. To the Djin Djin girls!"

Down the hatch. Ugh. Drano. Big testosterone grins.

Lenny wondered if they could see through him. He molded his face into his best Kevin Spacey cool but was feeling increasingly anxious. One consolation. So far they hadn't asked him about the evening at the Plaza. Almost home free.

"We have an early flight. So we better call it a night. But be on standby. We may have a situation developing. Consider yourself on call. Passport current?"

"Yeah. Right after I visited you in Chicago, I took care of it."

"Good. We'll be in touch."

One thing about Valley and Danko. Once their business was finished, they weren't big on parting rituals or dragged-out farewells. Before Lenny could even get up out of his chair, they were halfway across the room and headed towards the door.

He took a gulp of water and swirled away the nauseating remnants of the cognac in his mouth, then spit it back into the glass. He walked out of the restaurant, head spinning.

This is really fucked up. What was he going to do? He needed out. The sooner the better.

Live on CNN: "Shipwrecked! Hundreds Drown

All the major newspapers front-paged it. Online it was the lead story, some sites with live video feeds. The public never could get enough of this stuff. It was garden variety blood sport to lean back in the bleachers of modern media and voyeur the misery and misfortune of others. Pleasant diversion from the pedestrian tedium of most people's lives.

This one would definitely sell a lot of shampoo and gas-guzzling cars, hay fever relief and sports videos. The ad agencies were smacking their lips.

As our own 21st Century version of Herodotus, Wolfe Blitzer of CNN — with his pop tart sense of Shakespearean high drama and Huxleyan somatized lack of wit — expressed it with perfect television-neutered style and grace ...

We are standing here aboard a salvage vessel rescue ship and what we are seeing is gruesome beyond description. The M/V High Petra, a cargo ship registered in Singapore, sank about three hours ago and the bodies of what appears to be young Asians, so far all girls, continue to float to the surface. Before the High Petra went down, three other rescue boats made a heroic effort to get the passengers and crew aboard the sinking ship to safety. It is estimated that as many as

300 may have been on the damaged craft. You will recall that just yesterday, the cargo boat burst into flames. There were reports of violent explosions, which fatally compromised its seaworthiness. It immediately began taking water and then listed and rolled onto its side. Members of the crew and the young passengers could be seen on the starboard side of the sinking ship, screaming for help before she went down. Rescue efforts are continuing here at a frantic pace. But it doesn't look good. Drowned bodies continue to be pulled aboard the rescue crafts. There seems to be no end in sight. Wolf Blitzer here, at the site of a horrible catastrophe here off the coast of Africa. We'll keep you up to date as this tragedy unfolds. Back to you.

Two's Lucky Three's a Charm

"This is perfect."

Why was he whispering? He was alone and certainly no one was anywhere within earshot. Then again, you can't be too careful.

John Harrison was on top of a two-story building behind the parapet, binoculars around his neck and his walkie-talkie in hand.

He held down the talk button. "Second Lieutenant Harrison here. Recon complete. Returning to home base camp to prepare for Zippo. Might need air cover back-up at around 0100. Do you copy?"

Nothing.

The reception out here sucked. Probably jammed with ECM. Fuckers.

"Second Lieutenant Harrison here again. If anybody out there copies, I will report progress at 2300, that's 2-3-0-0. God bless America. Out."

He snaked back to stay out of sight and scrambled down a fire escape.

It took him over an hour but when he got back to headquarters, he got right to work. First he took down one panel of the camouflage netting and attached some rappelling rope and pulleys he had adapted for the job. Then he attached a telescoping aluminum pipe which had a small bracket fastened to the back, fashioned to hook under the lip of any available balustrade. The ropes would cross under the bracket and secure the apparatus well enough to lift a small motor vehicle, if you could provide the pulling power. The jerry-rigged device was amazingly light and compact. Netting and all it fit into his large infantry backpack.

It was approaching 11 pm. Time to move out. He grabbed the walkie-talkie.

"Second Lieutenant Harrison here. Moving out for Zippo strike. Do you copy?"

Nothing.

"Harrison here. Do you copy?"

Fuck it. He'd do this entirely by himself if he had to. That's how it's been. That's how it'll be.

It took an hour to reach delineated zone of operation. He quickly identified the building he had found earlier. Up the fire escape to the spot he had chosen. Weather was getting nippy. But he was feeling good. He knew this would work.

John peered over the parapet to the street. Just as he expected, enemy combatants on foot were turning the corner and coming his way on a regular basis. Maybe too regular. Realistically he could only handle one at a time.

To further complicate matters, there were a lot of enemy vehicles. Every kind. Everywhere. Some of them were painted blue and white. These must be the special ops guys.

"Second Lieutenant Harrison again. I could use some air backup. This place is crawling with humvees and other CVs. They are sitting ducks if you could bring in a couple of Hueys. Do you copy?"

Nothing.

He banged the side of the walkie-talkie against his shoulder, stared at it, and tried again.

"Harrison here. Do you copy? Need air support."

Where the fuck are they when you need them? This could be the shooting gallery at an Indiana carnival if he could get through. No evidence of anti-aircraft placements. Sitting ducks.

Whatever. He'd just have to wait and do his thing. Timing is everything. The enemy was gradually dispersing now. A lull in the battlefield ballet. Soon patrol vehicles seemed to be nowhere in sight. Only a handful of straggling combatants. Unfortunately, they were heading away from him. That's the ebb and flow of it. Opportunities gained. Opportunities lost.

Hold on! Single combatant just came into view rounding the corner windows of a 24-hour laundromat. She was angling across the street, looking in both directions. Pulling out a phone. Probably reporting her position to her battalion CO. She would pass underneath him in less than 45 seconds.

He readied the net.

Checked in both directions.

No one else in sight. No traffic.

Perfect.

Just as she reached the base of the building directly below him, he dropped the net and quickly extended the telescoping boom. His aim was perfect. Caught completely by surprise, she was knocked off-balance and fell to the sidewalk.

"What ... what this?"

The net was light. She immediately stood up and struggled to untangle herself, cursing and grunting with the effort. John swung the boom sideways and yanked hard on one of the rappelling ropes attached to a corner of the net. This upended her and she was now trapped like a helpless fish. She fought to recover her footing but was completely tangled in the net. He wrapped his big hands around all three lines and his forearm muscles bulged as he aggressively started pulling her up. The pulleys whined and groaned, then there she was. Second Lieutenant Harrison had bagged another Vietcong.

She was a tiny thing. Not to say she was any less lethal than any of the others. All of them were trained killers. But getting her over the parapet was easy. And all of her diminutive curses and cries were lost in the background din of Brooklyn, the current theater of operations. Thank the Lord in High Heaven for small favors.

John now took his time. She wasn't going anywhere. He lit a cigarette and took two long, satisfying drags, then removed a small pocket flask from his utility belt.

"Shall we have a toast? One soldier to another, my little POW?"

He removed his handkerchief and soaked it with the contents of the flask.

"To all of my brethren … who died at the hands of you filthy commie vermin."

The chloroform worked quickly and she was unconscious in less than thirty seconds. John quickly cut away the netting and dragged her to a corner of the roof away from the street. To take care of business.

Just after dawn, it was the crows that gave it away. The shrill piercing cries. The building custodian went onto the roof to see what the fuss was all about. That's when he saw them. The crows. At least twenty of them feasting on the fresh meat. Much better than dumpster debris or road kill. A young body, partially filleted and laid out like the main course of a rooftop buffet.

Even the police had trouble handling this one. They had seen it all …

Until now.

It was probably a Djin Djin girl. That had to be just an educated guess. Same body type. But what was left was barely recognizable as a human being. Whole areas of her body had been skinned. Her hands and feet were left intact but wide strips of flesh were laid bare on her legs and arms. And a square was cut into the front of her torso, starting just below her breasts and going down to her hipbones. Her organs were exposed and drying in a pool of coagulating blood.

Her face and scalp had been removed. And her entire head was wrapped in Saran Wrap. On top of her head was a plastic Statue of Liberty crown. Her right arm was positioned upwards in a ghastly welcoming gesture. In her hand she held high a plastic liberty torch.

"Whoever did this is one sick fuck!" The detective who said that, subsequently vomited and was so unsteady he had to be helped back to his car.

Fiori only spent a few minutes at the scene of the crime. This was out of control! And sure to fuck everything up real good. This was number three. In the same number of weeks. Right within the same three city blocks. What were his men doing out there? Not keeping an eye on things, that's for sure. Some psycho, some deranged freak was pulling this shit right under their noses.

This had to stop. Immediately!

When he got back to the station, he stormed into his office, opened the top drawer of his desk and pulled out a file. He knocked over a chair on the way back out to the front desk. Abruptly stopping, he glared at two officers sipping on coffee and leaning back in their chairs with their feet up on their desks.

"What are you guys doing? Are you doing anything right now besides wasting taxpayer money?"

"We're not even on duty yet, sir. I just got here."

"Well, you're on duty now." Handing one of them the folder. "Bring this guy in ASAP. He doesn't exactly live large. You'll find him one of three places. It's all in there. Go!"

For whatever reason, Lenny wasn't that easy to find. After returning to his apartment several times, they finally caught him at home. It had been two days since the murder.

"Captain Fiori at Precinct wants to talk to you. Do you have some time?"

"Is there some trouble? Am I under arrest?"

"No, Mr. Petrocelli. It's a social visit. He just wants to ask you a few questions. Please come with us."

They escorted him to the patrol car. He was at the station within fifteen minutes. Fiori had someone in his office but on hearing that Lenny has arrived, he cut the conversation short and headed out to confront him. He didn't offer to shake hands. No empty courtesies.

"Petrocelli. I need your help." Turning to the dispatcher. "Is Bell on right now?"

"Yes, sir. He's in the bullpen."

"Tell him I need him to drive us. Call Sampson and tell him we're on our way."

"Yes, sir. Right away."

"What's this all about?"

"Don't worry, Petrocelli. You'll see."

Not a word was exchanged in the short ride.

They pulled to the rear of a building, into a parking lot marked Official Vehicles Only. They got out and Fiori led Lenny down some stairs.

The door they entered said, Enforcement and Authorized Personnel Only. Despite a noble attempt at air purification with ionizing ventilators, and a robust A/C system, a sickly disinfectant and chemical smell lingered.

So this is what a morgue looks like. Just like in the movies.

Fiori directed the attendant. "The Asian girl."

The attendant walked them over to a body drawer and pulled it out to expose the full length of a corpse, covered head to toe. He looked at Captain Fiori and raised his eyebrows to ask the obvious question.

"Remove it."

When the sheet was removed, Lenny's face went the color of intestinal lining.

He couldn't bear to look.

He couldn't stop looking.

"Who the fuck did this, Petrocelli?"

"Jesus Christ! You think I'm God? How would I know?"

"You know who your enemies are."

"My enemies. What are you talking about?"

"You're the pit bull running this thing locally. You must have some idea who is pissed off."

"Running what? You've got the wrong man."

"Chicago, Lenny. We have it on good authority. For example, we heard you had a little run in with Mulcahey. We know about your promotion. Now stop fucking with me!"

"Do I have to keep looking at this? You've made your point."

The attendant covered the young girl, or what was left of her, and started to push the drawer back into the wall. Just before it closed, Lenny spotted it.

The foot. A toe was missing on one of her feet. Left foot. The second toe.

Oh my God! Was it her?

His neck felt like he had been karate chopped. Lenny fought for control but the tears pushed from the back of his skull. He started to choke.

Fiori looked at him with contempt. "Come on, Lenny. Pull it in. I hear you're a tough guy. A little carve-em-up shouldn't be a problem for a big man like you. Now are you going to help us or not?"

Lenny forced a halting reply. "Violence is not my thing ... I run an office."

"Tell your friends Franklin and Martin about it."

What a kick in the head! Did they know everything? They had an inside track, alright. Or maybe they *were* the inside track.

Lenny had to keep it together. Show no emotion. He looked at Fiori.

"Do you ... do you know who that is in there? Her name?"

"Funny thing, Petrocelli. She forgot to call to let me know she was on her way to the Brooklyn chainsaw massacre. No, I don't know who it was! And I don't give a flying fuck. I just want this bloodbath to stop."

"Someone must know."

"Yeah, you! Look. These little girls are dropping out of the sky. No identification. Probably no documentation of any kind. So there are no fingerprints. No dental records. Nothing on file. But here they are and I got enough to handle without fingering a bunch of refugees. Let the INS worry about that. We look the other way. Even on your little internet whorehouse. We know what you're doing over there. As long as nobody gets hurt, we look the other way. But when corpses start piling up, that's a different ballgame."

"Let's say I do work for Chicago. Just hypothetically. Now stop and think about it. Chicago would not put me in charge of anything like this. I'm just a sandwich board in this community. A presence. You know more about any of this than I do."

Long pause — Fiori lost in thought but continuing to eyeball Lenny.

"Okay ... for now. What you're saying is a little hard to swallow. But maybe for the first time in your life, you're telling the truth. Maybe this is out of your league."

Way out of my league, thought Lenny.

"But listen, Petrocelli. Like it or not, you are in the thick of it. So just keep your eyes and ears open. And keep me in the loop. Anything. Anything at all which might be useful. We'll take it from there."

Those words sure had a familiar ring.

"If you get something for me, here's my card. I'm here 24/7 for this. My private cell is written on the back. Only my wife and my girlfriend have that. See? You're special."

"And if ... if you find out who the girl ..."

"Petrocelli. She's dead. Extremely dead. I am only interested in making sure there are no more who end up like her. If you are so concerned, find out who does roll call on them. Somebody in your organization must be keeping track."

He was right. But Lenny had been kept so completely in the dark. And so here he was taking heat from an asshole who couldn't protect the girls who were giving him free blowjobs. What a world.

As they left the room, Lenny glanced back over his shoulder. Suddenly, a brutal, numbing pain shot through him. His legs nearly went limp. He couldn't breathe. The back of his eyes burned and his head felt like it was in a huge vise. He nearly doubled over as his stomach twisted and cramped.

Kimnai? Oh my God! Was that Kimnai back there?

Saturday Night Fever

Lenny was batting a thousand.

Another towelhead.

"Drop me up at the next intersection. Right over by that 7-11."

Brooklyn ran the gamut. Right across both the Williamsburg and Brooklyn Bridges from Manhattan, developers had housing prices swinging from the chandeliers. Even some of the dock areas had been gentrified, become the latest characterless victims of new chic, and now were places where swiping credit cards had replaced swapping license plates on stolen vehicles.

The rich and famous, and the rich and not so famous, flocked to these new freshly disinfected haunts for lavish evenings of what they inaccurately characterized as slumming.

Others areas of Brooklyn only minutes away gave the worst of Newark, NJ a run for its money. Abandoned cars rusted and gangs ruled. The neglected and graffitied projects were a playground for only the foolish, fearless and the suicidal. Slumlords armed like Green Berets collected rent and dislodged the past-due. The streetwise drug dealers openly ran their no-prescription curbside pharmacies, eliminating the competition with a bullet in the back of the head. Law enforcement was never considered an option because the cops had long ago ceded this no-mans-land to the thugs and criminals. You'd be more likely to see a blue whale than a blue uniform in this part of town.

The particular area where Lenny just stepped out of a taxi was neither the best and worst of Brooklyn. Granted, it was the area where every evening the street girls turned the sidewalks into a runway show of the latest in cheap and gaudy, the see-through and the see-all, where showing flesh, pushing up breasts and pumping up the heat trumped any considerations of good taste and style. Even so, it had two decent schools in the area, a middle school and a high school. It had flats, condos, and apartments which housed mostly middle-class and lower middle-class working people, young singles, the retired, couples in the start-up years of building a life. It had family-friendly stores and shops, a Community Center, three churches, and a small hospital/outpatient clinic.

It also had two pawn shops, three second-hand stores, a bail bondsman's office, a pool hall, an off-track betting parlor, and several taverns. It had been officially designated an Enterprise Zone by the Mayor in 2004. But most of the enterprise took place in the evening when the girls arrived.

It was Saturday night. He paid the cab driver and got out.

Where to start.

The center of the action was definitely the four corners back two blocks. He didn't want to appear too conspicuous but he'd have to hang around there if he was going scope out the Djin Djin girls. He started to walk casually in that direction.

As he approached the first intersection, he saw five or six Asians on his side of the street. A car pulled up. One got in. Another car pulled up. Two of the Djin Djins talked to the driver through the passenger window. The car pulled away. They stayed. And giggled.

He made it to the next intersection, walked up to a newsstand on the corner, then took to looking over the magazines, maps and newspapers as nonchalantly as he could, all the while glancing sideways at the young Asian girls.

After about twenty minutes, the attendant said, "Hey buddy, this ain't no fuckin' library."

Lenny pulled out a buck and bought a newspaper.

"Big spender! Have a wonderful evening. Say hi to the missus for me."

New York. You gotta love it. Or you'll hate it.

Lenny knew Kimnai's face. Long hair or short hair, he would recognize her. So far none of them had come close.

He couldn't talk to them. That might get back. Chicago had ears everywhere. Was he supposed to be here? He didn't know and couldn't take any chances.

What to do. He needed time to figure something out.

He looked across the street and spotted a bus stop. Directly overhead there was a streetlamp. Enough light that he could plausibly be reading the newspaper.

Lenny crossed the street and sat down. He folded the paper open to the Sports Section.

He read and casually glanced around. Read and glanced. Pretty much the same thing going on. Cars coming and going. No Kimnai. He read some more.

Lenny didn't see or hear them come up behind him.

"If you're waiting for a bus, you got a long wait. Last one went by at about 8:15."

Lenny turned around and saw two black hookers. The one directly behind him totally hot. Too bad he didn't go for the dark meat. The one standing a little further back was a big girl. A really big girl. Renaissance if not rotund.

"I'm ... uh ... um ... just taking a walk."

Shawna in her helium soul-sistah voice and Betty Boop eyes. "Really? Me too. I just love long strolls on the street, dinner by candlelight, poetry readings, Swan Lake and cuddling in front of a fire. We were made for each other!"

Lilly felt she needed to keep a tab on things around here. "If you're ... UH ... UM ... just taking a walk, then why are you sitting on your fat ass? Are you an undercover?"

"Is that a badge in your pocket or are you just glad to see me, Colombo?"

"Believe me, I am the furthest thing from a cop." Lenny pointed across the street. "Happen to know any of those girls? The Djin Djin girls."

That instantly put Shawna in a bad mood. "Now *that* is a very sore subject. This used to be a decent neighborhood, where a respectable, God-fearing 'ho, like myself, could actually make a living. Then those fortune cookies arrived with little pink slips inside for the rest of us. They have turned this once-fine community into a sinkhole."

"Aaahhh! I see what you mean. I remember now. This used to be like Beverly Hills and Miami Beach all rolled into one. I used to come down here to the Rolls dealership every year to buy a new car."

"Oh, a comedian. A not-very-funny comedian."

"Look. I know one of them. I'm just looking for this Asian girl."

"I'll bet you are. You look like the type. What's with you guys? You can't find a little boy to fuck. So you come down here to score one of these no-meat-on-a-stick, titless, tofu types. You make me sick!"

"Well, miss … what's your name?"

"Shawna."

"Well, Miss Shawna, with your attitude and a mouth bigger than your ass. You know what the Bible says, don't you? I think it's Genesis. If you can't take the heat, then get off the street."

Shawna started to lunge at Lenny with bad intentions. "Fuck you, white-ass muthafucker. What the hell you sayin'? You talkin' shit, boy!"

Fortunately, Lilly was right there to step between them and keep her friend from committing another assault-and-battery.

Lenny held up his hands in mock defense. "Whoa whoa. Slow down, mama. Bad joke. Okay? Just a bad joke. Sorry."

"You better be. And you better tell us exactly what you're doin' here, before I make you *real* good and sorry. I'll kick your nutsack all the way back to whatever soup kitchen threw out your pathetic white ass."

Lenny had to hold back to keep from bursting out laughing. This one was definitely a character. Talk about being full of piss and vinegar. And a lot of fried chicken. But who knows, maybe they could help.

"I know one of them. I am sure this sounds kind of strange. But she's … she's just a friend. And she's missing. I came looking for her."

"Well, you better look fast. They been disappearing faster than a nigger at a Ku Klux Klan convention."

That definitely was a kick in the balls. He didn't need to hear that.

"Look, Clark Kent. We'd just love to hook you up. But you are definitely on the wrong side of the street. You want that Asian pussy, go get it. Don't say I didn't warn ya, though. And when you want a real woman, you just come right here to Shawna, baby. I'll do you right."

Lenny stood up. He looked at Shawna. Then at Lilly.

"I'd better be going."

He started walking. How far was he from home? Two maybe three miles. He figured he'd see a cab along the way. Or maybe he'd just walk.

Well, that went well. Why is everything so difficult? This is really fucked up. He had no idea how to go about this. And he had no idea if Kimnai was dead or alive. Maybe he should just face the facts. The painful facts. How many young Asian girls could there possibly around this town with the second toe on their left foot missing?

What a horrible thought! He pictured Kimnai reading one of her children's stories to him. The way her face became so animated and the way she would laugh and cry before even reading a passage, tipping him off to what was coming. What a beautiful little thing she was. Is? Was?

He saw a taxi coming toward him on the opposite side of the street with its 'For Hire' sign lit. He hailed it and the driver did a screeching Hollywood movie style U-turn to pull up next to him.

What? Pinch me to see if I'm awake. An American cabdriver!

"Vair vould jew lok do ko?"

Alright. Not an American in the Forrest Gump sense. At least he could see the guy's hair. Lenny gave him his address.

When they arrived, Lenny tipped him generously. "Arrivederci!"

"Auf Wiedersehen."

A FedEx package was waiting between his doors. From Chicago. He read the cover note.

> Lenny – We have a situation. You need to be at Kennedy (int'l flights) at 6:30 tomorrow a.m. Everything you need is enclosed here. Specifics in envelope marked <u>Take care of this</u>. Read on the plane. Have a safe trip. Call me when you get to Bangkok. – Harold

Oh fuck.

Chapter 8

DANCES WITH WOLVES: The Law of the Jungle

Around the World in Eighty Hours

His driver was waiting for him right outside of the customs and immigration area, holding a sign that said *Mr Lenis Pardoceli.* Close enough. After that flight, who wants to referee a spelling bee.

"Welcome to Bangkok. I will take you hotel. Tomorrow we go early. Hey! You want lady spend night? Nice lady! Boom boom. 2000 baht."

"Uh … I'm a little tired. Some other time."

Clearly not an official member of the Chicago team. Contract labor. Lenny had been warned that most of the taxi drivers over here had "side businesses" that suckled off the sex services industry. This guy was probably on commission. A taxi pimp?

According to the itinerary Danko had provided, he had a meeting first thing in the morning with a Laotian high-roller named Dok Phnom. He was supposed to be a real golden boy, educated in America, a spit-shined Type A achiever, top notch entrepreneur. Word had it that behind the diplomatic gleam of his reassuring smile was ravenous affluenza and sledgehammer ruthlessness. In other words, if money was at stake, Dok got the job done. If things went as smoothly as expected with him, Lenny should be able to go back early.

When he awoke bright and early, his brain fog had partially cleared and he was able to look with not a little wonder at his surroundings. Chicago clearly didn't believe in pinching pennies. The hotel truly was five-star elegant, in the same class with the Plaza in New York. But much more modern. A soaring tower of glass gleaming like a giant urban jewel.

His driver was in the lobby waiting when he stepped out of the elevator.

"I'm sorry. What's your name again?"

"Just call me Danny, sir. Much easier than my Thai name."

"Well, Danny. It says here we are going to a Buddhist Temple. Is that right?"

"Yes, sir. Temple of Dawn. Wat Arun Ratchawararam. Wat means temple. This on other side of river. You take ferry. It go right to temple. I take you now. Wait for you come back."

Quite a little adventure. It only took a few minutes to cross the Chao Phraya River, which seemed to have more debris and floating vines than vessels, though the river traffic was considerable. The temple's ceramic figurines, thousands of them covering the huge spires which reached majestically into to the morning sky, gleamed quietly and mysteriously in the early sun.

Dok was unmistakable. In a country given to casual dress, either Western or traditional, there he stood at the entrance in a perfectly tailored three-piece suit and silk tie, his shoes shined to patent leather perfection. He smiled like he was watching his new bride come down the aisle. When he spotted Lenny, he briskly strode to meet him, hand outstretched and ready to pump.

"Mr. Petrocelli, I presume. I am Dok Phnom, originally from Laos."

"Yes. Yes. Pleased to meet you, Dok. You can just call me Lenny."

"This is my favorite temple of all. You know there are 40,000 temples in Thailand. I always make a point of coming here when I am in Bangkok. Shall I explain?"

Actually, thought Lenny, let's skip the formalities. No time for the dance of the diplomats. Let's get on with this.

"If it's all the same to you Dok, I would like to get right down to business. I'm told we have a situation to deal with."

Dok couldn't conceal the onset of a smirk. "You have a situation, alright. 82 bodies floating in the Indian Ocean, I'd say is a serious problem."

"Excuse me. What are you talking about?"

"What am I talking about? Mr. Lenny, don't you watch the news? A ship bringing your girls went down a few days ago. Off the coast of Madagascar."

Like a shot of smelling salts to his brain, it came to Lenny at once. He had heard something about some shipwreck but at the time really didn't tune in to it. The slipstream of disaster was a crowded highway and the media pumped out the stories faster than any sane person could possibly keep up with. So that's what Chicago in their backhanded way was referring to. 'We may have a situation developing.' Danko's words. What a prevaricating slimeball.

Cover, Lenny. Very bad to look like some third-string gopher to this guy.

"Oh that. Yes. Yes, very bad. So we have to come up with some pitch hitters. I hear you're the right person for the job here. You're our major and most reliable supplier, I understand."

"Thank you, sir. I am humbled by your flattery. Yes, we can replace them. But this will be very expensive, you know. Mr. Danko has very high standards. He usually handpicks them."

"He come here to Thailand?"

"Or Vietnam. Sometimes Malaysia. But by the time he sees them, we have done a lot of the screening. All the difficult work. To give you the very cream of the crop. There are thousands of beautiful young girls here but we make sure they are ready for the new world they enter. Your world."

"What do you mean by ready?"

"Let me ask you Mr. Lenny. Have you ever had any of the girls try to escape? Or go to the authorities?"

"You tell me, Dok."

"Well, you haven't. You see, it's not just fear. We give them the right attitude, train them so that you never have to worry about that. I have three schools where both boys and girls are enlightened and prepared. They are given a very powerful spiritual discipline. They come to you perfected in a way that assures loyalty and obedience."

"I really don't know or care about any of that. I was just told to arrange to bring back 80 plus heavenly bodies. Street ready. For a fair price."

"Mr. Lenny. My prices are always fair. But there is no warehouse here, even if this is Thailand. We may sell sex but it's not like ordering shirts or gift sets of Thai cooking spices. It takes an extraordinary effort to put together a shipment of that many exceptionally beautiful young girls to go halfway around the world. Girls with a good work ethic and the proper attitude."

"So can you do it or not?"

"I will personally guarantee your 80 precious bodies. I will personally select from the best sex workers here, girls that meet Mr. Danko's expectations, both in terms of looks and performance. But on such short notice, I can't guarantee they will not cause trouble. I think he should be patient and wait until we can properly prepare girls for your special line of work. And their new freedom in America. Otherwise, there is no predicting what can happen once they are there."

"He says he can't wait. What's your price?"

"Recognizing what a formidable task this is … $12,000 each."

"Eighty or more girls at 12 Gs a pop, is that right?"

"That has to be my minimum. I should charge more but I respect Mr. Danko and appreciate his business."

"I'll have your answer by tomorrow. Thank you, Dok, for your time."

"I see there is a ferry coming right now if you want to go back. Sure you won't join me for my walk through the temple? It is a most unique creation with a fascinating history."

"I appreciate your offer. But I'll take a rain check."

"It doesn't rain here very often this time of year but I understand. It has been a pleasure."

A pleasant bow from the waist with hands in prayer mode. Dok was the consummate charmer. At his prices I guess he could afford to be, thought Lenny.

Holy fuck. $12,000 each! That's almost a million bucks. How is Danko going to take that? I guess we'll soon find out.

Let's see. Thirteen hours earlier in Chicago. Early evening.

Lenny got hold of Danko on his mobile phone. He was with Valley in the company limo and they were apparently just wondering if Lenny had a face-to-face yet with Dok.

The phone call did not go well. In fact, in all his years working for them, he had never seen either of them lose it so completely. 'Extortion!' 'Fucking opportunist.' 'Thinks he has us by the balls.' 'Tell him to go fuck himself.' These were the key operating phrases.

They passed the phone back and forth between them and Lenny had to listen to their harangue for almost ten minutes before they calmed down enough to make a superficial effort at coming up with something constructive.

Danko said there were other "brokers" in Thailand and they would try to track down some contacts for Lenny. On his end, he should be doing the same.

Right. He should do the same.

But where to start? Lenny had no idea. He was in a strange city with very unfamiliar ways of doing just about everything, from eating to praying to pissing to paying. What was he supposed to do? Ask the concierge at his hotel where he could buy 80 adolescent girls to take back to America with him?

Valley did mention he could start by going to a place called the Nana Entertainment Plaza, apparently the closest thing to a sex worker shopping mall anywhere in the world.

This was really getting out of hand. Buying girls at a public sex mall? Lenny didn't need this. This was not what he had bargained for when he signed on with them originally. But they certainly had a way of manipulating people. One way or another getting everyone to do just what they wanted.

Christ! He really needed to get out of this job. But he was trapped. Now they had him running halfway across the planet to traffic young prostitutes. Incredibly young prostitutes! My god. What were the legalities if he somehow got caught? Don't think about it, Lenny. They probably put you away for life. Fuck. Fuck. Fuck.

"Tragedy at Sea: Vessel Trafficking Children"

Starpower. That's what running a successful primetime network news program was about. Starpower and sexiness. Not the sexiness of southern California porn or Japanese schoolgirl anime. But the sexiness of Princess Di and Michael Jackson, OJ and 9-11, Clinton-Lewinsky and Watergate. And if the crème de la crème sex object wasn't available, occasionally a good celebrity drug bust could be fleshed out to make the grade.

The kidnapping of a beautiful little girl, rescuing a young boy from a deep open well, and hardworking family men trapped in a collapsed copper mine were always sexy television.

Of course, there was a lot of flexibility in the business of dumbing down the public and appealing to lowest common denominator tastes. Lorena's Bobbit's cutting off her husband's penis and brain-dead Terri Shiavo being taken off of life support seemed to have one foot in a latrine and the other in the stately mansions of human drama. These two gruesome affairs, larger-than-life real world soap operas, each monopolized TV screens for weeks, sold to the public as matters of profound urgency and relevance.

They were about as sexy as 24/7 television news ever got!

Network-endorsed G-rated sadomasochistic porn for the dulled and witless.

Of course, the goal was not information but patronage. Thus, there was a method to the apparent madness. When a story had been stroked and massaged with enough foreplay to get the most neutered boob tube drooler excited, then the networks brought in their big guns, folks with perfect accent-neutral delivery, sonorous voices, GQ and Cosmo good looks, flawless Botoxed skin, snowblinding white teeth, and more credibility and public confidence than the President himself could ever hope for. No one could avoid being intoxicated and seduced by the electronic pheromones that these celebrity reporters hotly pumped out over the airwaves. Every major TV station had one or two. Some even had more. Starpower.

Here is how Brian Williams of MSNBC reported on the sea disaster ...

In the wake of the tragedy at sea which we've reported on over the last couple days, this coming Sunday evening NBC will be presenting a special news documentary on the trafficking of children, typically from countries in Southeast Asia. These youth end up exploited as cheap factory labor in sweat shops or as sex slaves in the lucrative and growing sex service industries both overseas and right here in America. Much of this documentary is graphic in nature and only for mature audiences. Viewer discretion is advised. Please consult your local listings for "Bodies For Sale: The Frightening Truth About Child Trafficking".

The final word appears to be in on the M/V High Petra, the 55-ton Class D cargo ship registered in Singapore, which sank in the Indian Ocean, approximately 180 miles southeast of Madagascar. The total number of fatalities is listed at 104, twenty-two crew members and even more shocking, eighty-two adolescent girls who were being smuggled for illicit trade of an undetermined nature. Since this practice of smuggling young bodies is on the rise and becoming the number one concern of many human rights organizations, as I just mentioned, NBC will be running an in-depth program this Sunday exploring this horrifying but very profitable enterprise. Yours truly will be hosting.

The sinking of the Petra was caused by a fire and a series of explosions which opened a gaping hole in its hull. Apparently the cargo included numerous items which contributed to the conflagration and explosions. There were huge containers of flammable clothing, there were tanks of propane, and boxes of incendiaries, fireworks and various detonating devices. It is not known what sparked the initial fire. But after the explosions, the effects of the damage could not be contained and the fate of the ship was sealed. Down she went, a huge coffin for the adolescent girls who were aboard. It is believed that all of the bodies which floated to the surface have been recovered. Salvage teams are still at the site but the vessel is in very deep water making it unlikely that the divers will be able to access the sunken ship to recover the rest of the bodies, if indeed there are more.

We will keep you posted if there are further developments in this alarming and very tragic story.

Headhunter

"Good bye, my little kitten. I will miss you."

Gregor had roughly pulled Dawa out of the lunch line and leered at her like an animal. Tomorrow she was on her way back to Vietnam.

"Maybe we will have a special farewell party tonight, eh?"

A jolt of fear and revulsion ripped through her frail body like an errant bolt of electricity. Her head became light. She felt like she would faint, something which had been happening more and more frequently the last few weeks. She looked down at her feet to steady herself. A desperate clawing roiled her insides. She fumbled for something to say to distract him. Anything.

"I am hungry."

"So am I, little kitten. So am I."

He ran his calloused finger across her lips.

"Go and eat."

Dawa returned to the line to receive her midday allotment of rice and watery soup broth. Earlier that day she had been told that after her work shift she should gather her belongings, meager as they were, and be ready to leave first thing tomorrow morning. She was going back to the toy factory in Da Nang. This launched her emotions on a roller coaster ride. Which place did she hate more? She had reacted violently to the toxic chemicals of the factory. Her frail body had been raised and nurtured in the purity of family farms and remote villages and was totally unaccustomed to the poisons of progress and plenitude. The mere thought of having to again endure the headaches, the nausea, the pus-filled eruptions on her shoulders and back, horrified her. But maybe that was the price she had to pay to get away from Gregor and his obsessive cruelty. He had continued to see her much more frequently than any of the other girls. Her whole loin area throbbed and ached from the bruising of her legs and hips, and the tearing of her vaginal walls caused by his outsized member and convulsive climaxes. Now he wanted to see her again tonight. She had often wondered if this is how she would die, ripped apart by this heaving buffalo. Oh by the grace of Buddha! Why couldn't she just leave right now?

Dawa was one of thirty-seven workers who would be sent back to Vietnam from the fabric works, joining others coming in from all over southeast Asia, to return the toy factory to full force. Hinge was indeed getting back online and they needed bodies. Quickly. There was no time to lose. Orders had been stacking up for weeks. Too much money at stake here to temporize or dally. Just as the board had predicted, the fickle attention of the restless public eye had been diverted. By a disaster at sea. And how ironic! Some of the ones that went down on that cargo ship had actually worked at Hinge in the recent past. Now the public horror at seeing their sea-bloated and lifeless little bodies floating in the Indian Ocean had created the diversion they needed and was putting Hinge back to business as usual.

Since their sudden shut-down, Hinge had been quite busy and was now ready for their grand re-opening. They had had just enough time to put together some nice spin for the media. Some eye-catching Powerpoint graphs, some staged photographs of people lined up to excitedly hand in their applications for employment, a press conference announcing a workers union which had recently been formed — but which in reality was just five stooges Hinge had hired merely to role-play as union leaders for the press — and lastly a huge banner at the entrance gate which promised a new glorious future for everyone involved …

Welcome to the <u>new</u>

HINGE TOY WORKS - DA NANG
"Friend of the worker, guardian of the environment"

The watchdog groups were too myopic or dumbfounded to effectively challenge Hinge's probity on any of this. Of course, they had known all along that Hinge was the enemy, a fierce and uncompromising enemy, and in all aspects an affront to everything they believed in, everything they were fighting for. But this time they really didn't know where to start.

To be entirely candid, they had never actually known how to mount a truly effective campaign in the first place. For example, Hinge had been suspected all along of using trafficked child labor. Unfortunately, no one could prove it. So the watchdogs, as a fall-back position, had protested how badly Hinge treated their extremely young workers, the unhealthy working conditions, the abusively long hours, the exposure to carcinogens and industrial pathogens. Ugly stuff but not really the insidious core of Hinge's practices — the stuff that could bring them to trial, or deal a devastating blow in the court of public opinion.

Even on Hinge's culpability for these human and worker rights violations, though the onsite evidence was incontrovertible, and a whole host of explicit and heinous worker rights abuses were paraded before the public, Hinge's Board of Directors just feigned total ignorance of what was going on, then finessed the watchdog groups by abruptly shutting the plant down.

Now the facility was again ramping up for business but floating this whole new shiny image. As Hinge's Board of Directors had hoped, the major media limelight had since moved on to other gruesome breaking stories. Meaning that the few people still paying attention could only stand impotently by to see what might unfold at the "new Hinge", and perhaps hope for some cracks in the wall. Hinge was even ready for that.

<u>Director #1</u>: "They're so confused, they don't know which hole they shit out of."

<u>Director #2</u>: "And this time, we're completely locking the place down. Anyone who even *tries* to speak up will pay with a lot of pain. Or disappear. No more mister nice guy. We know where that gets us."

<u>Chairman</u>: "What have we done to bolster security?"

<u>Director #2</u>: "We got animals on the inside who are hungry for their next meal. Nothing will get by them."

<u>Director #3</u>: "And we've got people on the outside. Sarawut Kuhn's elite guard."

<u>Chairman</u>: "The drug lord? The Saber?"

<u>Director #3</u>: "None other. He *owns* the streets in Da Nang."

Director #1: "He fucking owns Vietnam. You sure we want to get that heavy? He is one very scary son-of-a-bitch."

Director #3: "Exactly. And it's a handshake deal. Everyone wins. I am sure he won't cross us."

Chairman: "How's that? What have we got that he wants?"

Director #3: "A little space on a cargo ship. He always has serious transportation issues."

Director #1: "Genius! Pure fucking genius!"

Chairman: "What about the fabric works?"

Director #2: "It'll have to run lean. The real money is in toys. The shirts and socks don't make a third of what the toys make."

Director#1: "Which reminds me. The American has some guy in Malaysia right now. Since that ship went down, he is screaming for bodies. He's suppose to be at Kampung Sepetang right now."

Director #2: "Good luck. Very slim pickins now. They really cleaned us out last trip. We're still waiting for the schools to let out."

Director #1: "Fuck 'em. We'll throw him a few bones. He'll take what we give him."

Director #3: "What's he paying?"

Director #1: "6K per twat. You should've heard Danko on the phone! Fucker sounded like a rabid dog. Or like he was having an epileptic fit. But I held him right at six. We don't owe that fucker any favors."

Chairman: "This has been a good year. A very good year."

All of Dawa's worldly possessions were wrapped up in a scarf, sitting next to her mat. It was still early, and if Gregor was true to form, it would be a few hours before he came for her. Usually it was late, right when most everyone else was going to sleep.

But there was a change of plans. Dawa was to be spared the horror of one last night with her rapist tormentor.

Maybe two hours before lights out, with unceremonious abruptness, in marched the "some guy" from America, a personal scout sent by Harold Danko, to scavenge among the adolescent girls working at the apparel plant, the ones who might be promising as potential sex workers.

Lenny was accompanied by the driver of the 40-passenger bus which had just pulled up moments before.

Gregor led the way.

The Russian seemed a little uncomfortable.

But as instructed, he walked Lenny among the mats, the young girls keeping their eyes averted, or occasionally stealing a quick glance after the men had passed.

"How many are you planning on taking, Mr. Petrol?"

"Just call me Lenny. That depends on what you got. They're pushing me hard to bring some bodies back. But that doesn't change anything. We still need some lookers."

"Lookers?"

"Yeah. You know, good on the eyes. Nice to look at. Lookers."

"Right. Ones you want to fuck. Well, it's a bad time you caught us. Kind of in between. Still, there are some nice kittens here."

Lenny gave him an odd look. Kittens? This guy is as strange as he is ugly, Lenny thought.

Lenny continued walking through the dorm, trying to get some fix on the young faces. It started with the face. If that had allure, he would ask them to stand up.

As they strolled casually, moving methodically back and forth through the scattered bedding and personal items next to each individual's sleeping pad and blanket, Lenny grew increasingly discouraged. Danko had told him they were paying a pretty penny for each girl and he should try to get their money's worth. 'Don't bring back any dogs' is the way he put it. So he couldn't just test for life signs and lead them out the door. He had to be selective. It was very clear what Chicago wanted. Seeing first hand the Djin Djin girls back in America left no doubt in his mind what their tastes were. So far, this didn't look very promising. He felt relieved. He didn't want to be doing this in the first place.

Pointing at a frail 14-year-old with her back to him. "What about her?"

"Bad teeth." The girl glanced over her shoulder and Gregor proved right.

Lenny kept walking. Dawa turned and looked at him with shy curiosity. Her eyes reflected the overhead fluorescent lights, tiny pinpoints of stars, one in each pupil. She looked like she wanted to smile but was afraid.

"She looks good. In fact, she is the best looking one yet."

Gregor flushed but deployed his big chin-thrusting Russian smile to try to disguise his disapproval.

"She's a handful. A real troublemaker."

"What happened to her toe?" Lenny reacted with a start. Left foot. Second toe. That can't be a coincidence.

"She had an accident."

"An accident."

"Yes. Trying to escape."

Lenny couldn't stop looking at this little girl. There was some haunting prayer in her eyes. It reached from deep within her, making a beeline for the empathic regions of his conflicted soul. There was such desperation in her face, and the nervous flinching posture of a dog which had been beaten unmercifully. She seemed to beg for his attention. Or his protection.

Whew.

Was he going crazy?

First it was Kimnai. Now this tiny wisp of adolescent innocence. What was going on? Was he in the throes of some twisted delusion, fancying himself as a den mother to a gaggle of frightened girl scouts?

How confusing. How disorienting. How weird.

These sudden surges of conscience were batting him round like a tennis ball. Right now it was as if he was trying to convince himself that sending this girl to the streets of Brooklyn or San Francisco or wherever to turn tricks, was doing her some sort of favor. That he desperately needed to believe he might be doing something to help these pathetic little girls, though the brutal truth was they would be trapped on yet another treadmill of exploitation.

Wasn't he just rationalizing?

True, this one was probably working for pennies a day, twelve or fourteen hours at a stretch, sewing glitter on the six embroidered pockets of bellbottom jeans, sexy grossly over-priced numbers which hung down so low they showed the ass-crack of some spoiled American teenager, till she got tired of them and threw them away. So now he going to make a cosmic improvement in the quality of this little girl's life by consigning her to giving blowjobs to businessmen on their way home to the wife and kids?

What should he do? What the *fuck* should he do?

The equivocating was driving him nuts.

Lenny. Get it together! Stop thinking.

Just do your job as directed.

Walk the line and stop looking for trouble.

Focus.

But what about the missing toe? And the desperate pleading prayer in her beautifully innocent eyes? She had been the only one who looked at him.

Lenny felt so confused. So exposed. So ridiculous. So unhinged. So stupid. He was supposed to be a steely dispassionate buyer of flesh-for-fucking and here he was having a Mother Theresa moment with one unfortunate child. Could they read him? Did this Russian hulk-man sense his unease and dislocation?

He glanced back at Gregor. Lenny shuddered.

Something in the man's face gave it away. The cold granite of his eyes. There were demons lurking in this tank-sized hulk. The man had no soul.

Time for a management decision. Lenny made it.

"She's coming with us." Turning to the driver. "Take her to the bus."

If looks could kill, Gregor's face would have taken Lenny down in a hail of bullets. But it was done. The matter was settled. Lenny just turned and moved on, continuing to survey the sad collection of emaciated bodies and sallow skin.

He weaved back and forth among the young workers, who stole glances at him even as they arranged themselves for a much-needed night of sleep. It was certainly tough going. Not much to choose from. Then he spotted another one, who appeared to be fifteen or sixteen, and sent her and her meager bag of personal things ahead to wait in the bus.

When he finally finished, he had only found four more girls. They were in terms of sexual allure at best borderline, but hopefully close enough that with some decent meals, flashy outfits, and a bit of buffing and grooming, they could at least be second string players. He prayed Danko and Valley wouldn't feel they had been ripped off, and wouldn't take him to task for doing a crappy job.

The one they called Dawa, the first girl he picked and plucked from the clutches of the Russian bull, was definitely first string material. Beautiful face. Long lean body. Nice hair. A bit young. But lots of men went for the young ones, especially if they had at a few curves to their lithe little bodies. He hated to look at her that way but let's face it, that was what he was here for. And whatever she ended up doing there, maybe America was a better alternative than living here and being worked to death in this armpit of a country.

That's what he told himself.

He almost believed it.

Lenny and the driver joined the girls on the bus. Now that was a good move, hiring a bus for forty and only bringing six along. It seemed cavernous inside but the girls were grateful that they could stretch out, comfortable enough to sleep through most of the night.

He was taking them to Singapore. They would take back roads east to Ipoh and judiciously observing the speed limit on the highway, head south through Kuala Lumpur, to Johor Bahru, at the southern tip of Malaysia. The bus had been painted with markings that read *Grace Methodist Church – Ipoh*. They wanted at all costs to avoid brushes with authorities of any shape and size. The driver even wore a dress shirt and tie, with a crucifix tie tack, though he actually was a Muslim.

The drive to Johor Bahru was about 500 kilometers and would take at most seven hours. From Johor Bahru it was a quick jump across the Johore Strait on the causeway to Singapore. They would enter the country through the Woodlands checkpoint, as Malaysian citizens in transit.

It was important to minimize travel as much as possible in Singapore itself. They headed straight for the airport in a hired van. The police were busybodies and he wouldn't have any way to fight the bureaucracy if they were detained. The plan was simple: Through immigration, back into the van, arrive at the airport two hours before the long flight to Seattle, then finally on to Duluth.

He had to hand it to Chicago. They had really planned this out well and taken proper care of business. They arrived in Johor Bahru early in the morning and the entire day was spent putting together the necessary travel documents and doing some light shopping. The girls of course needed identities, passports, visas, etc. Ed and Harold must have some serious connections because each girl would be given a Malaysian passport which included a pre-approved one-year student visa. Passport photos would be taken and forged passports should be ready within 12 hours. After an overnight stay in Johor Bahru, they could begin the final, important leg of their journey on an early morning flight, only one day after they got off the bus and checked into the hotel.

On the journey from Singapore to the U. S. they were being accompanied by a forty-something lay nun, a Sister Francis Maria, who was allegedly taking them for a year-long Bible-study and cultural exchange program at a fellowship church in Minnesota. Sister Francis spoke excellent English. However, a discerning ear would on some of her words discern a Bronx accent poking through her Malaysian-colored drone. It was very subtle. You'd have to be a native New Yorker to hear it. With her veil and dreary complexion, her wire-rim glasses and milky brown eyes, she would certainly roll through passport control in Seattle. Since the girls were being taken through as a group, the nun would do all of the talking for them. No opportunity for slip-ups.

With the accommodations in Johor Bahru, here again, Chicago showed some serious style. The hotel wasn't five-star, but by any measure was luxurious and centrally located in a prime commercial area, with expensive shopping and a breathtaking view of the beach. Lenny tried to imagine how the girls were taking this in. Probably none of them had ever been to a city, much less one which courted tourists, golfers, and others romping at their leisure across the beaches, in such an opulent area as this. They were wide-eyed, at the same time, deaf-mute quiet, visibly stunned into disbelief, rendered totally at a loss for words. When they all went down to the restaurant for a breakfast buffet, they had to be prodded into taking anything. They had never seen food like this and probably couldn't believe that they were allowed to actually eat any of it.

Everything that very busy day went like clockwork. Their hair was styled, photographs taken, decent clothes selected and purchased with assistance from a local lady Chicago had hired to come by and help. By the end of the afternoon their suitcases were filled with the simple nice things that everyone in the developed world took for granted, but was the stuff of dreams and magic to the unworldly young ladies.

They returned to their rooms and, since they were getting up very early, were in bed by nine. Sister Francis Maria arrived around ten and introduced herself to Lenny before retiring to her room. The travel documents for the girls were delivered to him shortly before midnight.

They left the hotel at 4:45 the next morning and everything ran like the trains in Switzerland. Once the girls were at the international terminal in Singapore, Lenny felt he could relax. Nothing could go wrong now, and he was nearing completion of his end of things on this. The van dropped them at Departures and he accompanied them to the Northwest Airlines check-in area.

As they were waiting in line for Sister Francis to get their boarding passes, a process as mysterious and other-worldly to the girls as everything else for the last twenty-four hours, Dawa turned and put her hand on Lenny's sleeve to get his attention. Her voice was so soft it was barely audible.

"Kòp prá koon."

These were the only words she had spoken to him since he had selected her back at the apparel factory in Kampung Sepetang.

Thank you.

The Cattle Drive

Things were not going well. All con artists, these Asians.

No matter what you say, they look at you and smile, nod and assure you. But they understand about 2% of what you're saying. And if that 2% doesn't jibe with their plans, they even ignore that and do whatever the hell they feel like doing. Whatever works out in *their* best interest. Then they spend whatever time it takes to try to convince you that this is what you told them to do in the first place, slaughtering both the English language and the truth in the process.

Lenny had carefully explained, and was sure he had made absolutely clear, exactly what he was looking for. But around and around he went. If they had been intentionally toying with him, had conspired to make his assignment there the punch line to some cruel insider joke, they couldn't have done a better job of totally pissing him off. What a fucking waste of time!

Lenny had been to Vietnam. That was a total bust. The prostitutes in Vietnam, going back to the days of the U. S. war there, have been internationally reputed to be the most perfectly beautiful women on the planet. Lenny wondered where they possibly could have found the mutant strain that they paraded past him. Had any nuclear reactors melted down in the past fifteen or so years in Vietnam?

Then on to Cambodia, stops at both Phnom Penh, the capital, and Sihanoukville, described frequently as the Miami Beach of southeast Asia. What a horror show that turned out to be! Sihanoukville made the shipyards at Galveston, Texas look like the French Riviera. Eight of the "girls" looked like they probably had grandchildren. Three other "girls" brought to him by a local body broker there, turned out to be ladyboys. Thank god his driver in Bangkok had cautioned him. "Always, Mr. Lenny. Look under skirt before you take home." Moreover, Phnom Penh appeared to be the amputee capital of the world. All land mine victims of the Khmer Rouge, one of the bloodiest and most brutal dictatorships in history. Lenny's tortured senses had driven him into a protective cocoon, and he found himself spending more and more time shoegazing. In spite of his frazzled state, he still felt confident that he was being objective, hence making the right decisions. The girls he was seeing definitely were not Djin Djin material. Not even close. It was becoming increasingly obvious that the right thing to do was to leave Cambodia as soon as he could book a plane out of there.

Lenny was tired. He still hadn't adjusted to the time change. Jet lag was like a slow carbon monoxide leak. Not enough to kill you but just enough to keep you tipping in and out of semi-consciousness. The language barrier was another huge drain on his usually abundant energy. Bouncing from one country to another, everywhere straining to understand what anyone was saying, and trying usually with only limited success to make himself understood, certainly was taking its toll.

Then to pour kerosene on his rancid crème brûlée, he got a call from the Laotian king of sting himself, Dok Phnom. How did he get the number? Lenny had switched cell phones three times. Chicago must have given it to him. They must be very desperate. Or Dok was very convincing.

He said in his smooth Princeton English that he might have as many as forty girls, that Lenny needed to come up to one of the more remote Siddartha schools to see and decide for himself. Lenny had his doubts, having been bludgeoned into a permanently state of skepticism by his disappointments in Vietnam and Cambodia. But he reluctantly agreed to make the trip.

He would fly to Vientiane, Laos, cross the border back into Thailand arriving in Nong Khai, which happened to be the site of Dok's most prized monastic school. Dok would then drive Lenny by automobile, southeast from Nong Khai a little over 200 kilometers to Nakhon Phanom Province, also on the Mekong River and right on the Laotian border. Quite removed from the town of Nakhon Phanom itself was a abandoned monastery which had been reclaimed and turned into a Siddartha school. This was the second "educational" facility Dok had set up to draw pliable young minds from the surrounding countryside and from Laos itself, these initiates to the flesh trade being smuggled across the Mekong on longtail fishing boats in the dead of night.

Lenny took the one daily flight from Phnom Penh to Vientiane on Vietnam Airlines, went through customs without a hitch, took a taxi from the airport and was across the Thai-Laos border shortly before 7 pm. There was the master of ceremonies himself, dressed like he was guest-hosting the Miss America Pageant, waiting for him at the border crossing.

"Mr. Petrocelli, how good to see you!"

"Wish I could say the same."

"Excuse me?"

"I said I feel exactly the same. It's good to see me."

"Okay ... I see. Well, a slight change of plans. You will, of course, need to stay overnight. But for a person of your esteem, the accommodations at the monastery are not up to proper standards. Therefore, I thought we could spend the night here in Nong Khai and then go to the school in the morning."

Lenny stared at him with numb incredulity. Was this guy human? Or was he some poorly constructed robot from a laboratory in North Korea?

"Whatever you think is best, Dok. This is your turf. And its your show."

"As a matter of being completely candid, Mr. Petrocelli ..."

"Lenny."

"Yes, Lenny ... sir. To be completely candid, I have arranged for us to use the time very well here tonight. I am always working on your problem and do everything I can to help."

"My problem."

"Well, you know ... the girl problem. The shortage of girls for Mr. Valley and Mr. Danko."

"Right. Right. That problem. Well, let's get on with it. That's what I'm here for."

"First, we get you into your hotel. Relax a couple hours. Have a special meal. I will take care of the bill, Mr. Lenny. You are my guest here."

"Thanks, Dok. You are a true gentleman."

They say that Hitler liked dogs and children. It was already obvious that Dok liked children.

"Do you like dogs, Dok?"

"Ha ha ha, Mr. Lenny. That's just a myth. We don't eat dogs here!"

Dok drove them in a Mercedes that Lenny guessed was three or four years old. Not a bad ride for a bottom dweller in the sordid business he was in. But then Lenny remembered the prices he had quoted Chicago.

"When are you getting a new car, Dok? This one's kind of shabby, wouldn't you say?"

"This car? I just use it here. To run around when I am either here or in Nakhon Phanom. It's good enough for my purposes."

"So you live where?"

"I live here, actually. But most of my time I am in Bangkok. Bangkok or Phuket. When I'm not traveling to meet with the NGOs."

"NGOs?"

"Non-Government Organizations."

"I'm not familiar with any of this. What are they for? How does that fit in with your work?"

"It's very complicated, Mr. Lenny. But even though your bosses, Mr. Valley and Mr. Danko, are using our schools in a special way to staff their service industry … "

"As whores, Dok. Just spit it out."

"Well, yes. However you wish to say it. It's not for me to judge, you see. Anyway, our schools train and provide deserving young people for many other needs. Many different types of work. And the NGOs very much appreciate what we do. They're quite supportive."

"So, would I know any of these organizations? These NGOs."

"You might. But here is your hotel, Mr. Lenny. I hope you will find it pleasant enough."

The Royal Mekong Nongkhai Hotel was a very nice place indeed, considering the location. They were, after all, in one of the more remote, impoverished northern Thai provinces. But since Thailand had become such a popular tourist spot, better hotels were springing up in the most unlikely places.

Lenny checked in and Dok promised to return in about three hours. That would be 10:30 pm.

When he got to his room, a wave of drowsiness engulfed him. He no sooner lay his head on the pillow then he was out cold.

The soft electronic ring of the in-room phone woke him from a bizarre dream. He was inside a submarine which was taking water. Everyone was panicking but he just stayed in his bunk and kept reading a book and writing notes in the margins. The book was about tropical birds. He kept trying to tell his shipmates about a strange bird called a manakin which lives in both Central and South America. 'Guys, this is fascinating. This bird can't sing worth a damn. So when it courts, it beats out a rhythm on its feathers. It says here that Charles Darwin was very intrigued by the manakin.' But no one would pay any attention to him. Though the situation was hopeless, they kept running around frantically. At the precise moment he woke, the water was up level with his bunk and starting to soak his shirt and pants. He knew he was going to die but kept right on reading as if nothing was happening. Or as if he could care less.

He felt almost disappointed to open his eyes and see the light of the bedside lamp illuminating the brightly painted walls of the hotel room.

Was there some profound Jungian message in this? That we're all alone in a sinking ship?

Like he needed to hear that.

Lenny freshened up and met Dok in the hotel restaurant. As they ate two very attractive girls a few tables away made obvious overtures to them.

"Friends of yours, Dok?"

"They're friends of anyone who will shell out a couple thousand baht."

"We're getting a late start. Where are you taking me?"

"The night is very young, Mr. Lenny ..."

"Lenny. Just Lenny."

"You'll see. It's work-related. You have your passport with you?"

"Always."

"Before we get started, I need to explain that there has been a change of plans. We will not be going to the school at Nakhon Phanom tomorrow."

"I don't understand."

"Tonight is the main event. In fact ... it is the only event."

"Look, Dok. Details bore the shit out of me. Just do what you have to do and make it good. Got it?"

"I wouldn't waste your time, Mr. Lenny."

Lenny was actually quite relieved. The less time spent with this greasy asshole the better. Tonight better be good, however. Or at least one shiny-faced Lao head was going to roll.

They got back in the Mercedes and headed to the border, to cross back into Laos on the Friendship Bridge, which spans the Mekong River and connects the two countries. Without any doubt, the border people were very familiar with Dok. They were ushered through with VIP treatment. Lenny was mildly impressed. Big fish in a small pond. Maybe a koi fish in a toilet.

Instead of going west on the main road back to Vientiane, they headed straight north, winding through rural collections of bamboo huts raised on stilts. Men squatted on their porches in the flickering light of kerosene lanterns. Even at this late hour, he could see a number of half-clothed children running around, and cadaverous women doing late-night chores, in and around the huts. Cattle wandered along the side and sometimes onto the gravel and dirt road, requiring Dok to maneuver around them.

They came to an intersection in the midst of a small village and turned east. This road led to a hilly area with rice fields on both sides. They finally turned into a large dirt parking lot. Around the lot were various businesses, as businesses were in this impoverished country. Ramshackle buildings, usually made of corrugated iron siding or basic building blocks fashioned into primitive cubicles, housing whatever meager wares the store might be selling. One appeared to offer hardware supplies, two others displayed various food staples and soda, and an odd assortment of other household items — batteries, balloons, brushes, pencils, soap, matches, candles, can openers. Three or four appeared to be restaurants, with shabby chairs and tables arranged under their overhanging straw and bamboo roofs.

Dok parked in front of one of these "eateries" and Lenny noticed a couple of young girls had come to the open doorway to peer out and see what was happening. The light went on in Lenny's head as he realized what kind of place Dok had taken him to. An anonymous brothel in the middle of nowhere.

A very large woman pushed aside the two girls and waddled like a huge goose towards the car as Dok got out. As she approached the car, she held her arms wide enough to embrace a giant bodhi tree. She beamed like she was seeing the Buddha himself, her ear-to-ear smile puffing her cheeks into two wide white eggplants. An enthusiastic litany of babble in her Laotian tongue riddled the air with giddy high-pitched toy machine gun fire.

"Lenny, we're here. Please. Come and meet Aulii. She is the mama-san and CEO."

He smiled at Lenny, obviously pleased with his own cleverness.

As Dok turned to greet Aulii, she gathered him into her voluminous arms and they embraced and jitterbugged in place, laughing and carrying on in Lao. They sounded to Lenny like two mynah birds on speed.

Then as abruptly as they had begun, they broke off their wrestler's mating dance and Aulii turned and approached Lenny. She became calm, almost blissful, and gracefully extended her hand in the fine style of a graduate of Harvard Business School. The transformation was made even more disconcerting by her addressing Lenny in perfect English, with only a trace of an accent.

"It's an honor to meet you, Mr. Petrocelli. I'm Aulii. Please come in and meet my girls."

"Hmm ... sure. Nice to meet you. Your English is so good."

"That's what I am told. Dok here has taught me well."

The two girls had retreated to join three others on a long wicker lounge sofa. Aulii led Lenny through the door and gestured for him to sit down in another bamboo love seat, apparently the guest of honor spot in the small reception area. There was a low table directly in front of him with two candles and an ashtray.

"Noelani, please bring our guest a drink." The young girl closest to Lenny looked at Aulii with a look of bewilderment on her young face. Aulii repeated her request in Lao. The girl then got up and went through a curtain which covered a door at the rear of the room.

"My name means 'Delicious Emerald' and when I was their age ..." She nodded at the beautiful young lovelies who sat across from them with their hands in their laps and their eyes averted. "... I was a precious jewel to the eyes and a delicately savored dew on the tongues of many men. Too bad they were not all as handsome as you, my new friend."

What a charmer, thought Lenny. And as subtle as a beached whale.

Noelani returned with a glass and a bottle of local Lao beer and placed them on the table directly in front of Lenny. She smiled sweetly at him, then moved directly behind his chair. Apparently the arrival of the drink was a signal to the other young ladies.

The girls now flirted openly with Lenny, assuming he was a potential customer. Being the one chosen to provide the brief erotic release was important, both to earn money and to curry favor with Aulii, so the girls each gave it their best shot. Without actually shoving one another aside or provoking a wrestling match, they sidled up to Lenny, gracefully jousting for the most advantageous position. One lithe and particularly beautiful girl who appeared to be no older than 14 or 15, managed to seat herself right next to him on the arm of his bamboo chair. She put one arm around his shoulders and stroked his neck and hair with her other hand. Another sat at his feet and put both of her hands up into his pant leg onto his calf, caressing him and stroking the hair on his leg with her fingertips. She put her chin on his knee, looked up at him and smiled. She had a lovely petite face and her teeth were charmingly crooked. Her lips were painted cherry blossom pink. Her deep brown eyes sparkled in the dim light and she looked ready for a big night out on the town or a smaller one in the bed.

Four more girls, as alluring and devastatingly beautiful as the ones in the room, came through the curtained door, sat down on the now vacated wicker lounge chair, and casually but flirtatiously watched.

Lenny lunged for his beer and bypassing the formality of the glass took several long gulps.

"Nice, wouldn't you agree? I take great pride in them." Aulii stood up. "Please come."

She took his hand and led him out the way they had come in. The girls seemed confused by this but as Lenny exited, he could hear a soft chorus of whispered 'byes' in Lao. He even heard one or two tentative attempts at 'Mr. Lenny'. Little could he comprehend how much preparation and coaching must have gone into this reception.

Aulii's waddling gate contrasted with the poetic grace of her voice.

"I am moving on, Mr. Lenny. But I cannot just walk away from my girls. They are family to me and I want to pass them along to someone who will appreciate and utilize their talents as much as me. I understand you are looking for many such talented girls."

"Yes. That's true."

They walked to one of the other "restaurants" and the scene was very much the same as their first stop. Here there were at least ten more girls, equally attentive and disposed to send his libido to new untested heights.

By the time they had visited Aulii's third, then headed towards her fourth little eatery, Lenny was both becoming unnerved and very much put off by the way he now felt he was being manipulated. The mild effect of the beer only exacerbated his sense that they were trying much too hard to orchestrate his visit, maybe railroad him into whatever they had in mind.

Aulii a was smooth and very clever lady, that was beyond doubt. They were working both ends. Aulii worked on his brain and the girls worked on his crotch. A deadly strategy designed to outflank his good judgment.

One thing could go without saying. He definitely did not trust Dok as far as he could throw him, drugged on animal tranquilizer and using only his little finger. The guy gave new heightened meaning to disingenuous. He had clearly had a big hand in setting this whole thing up and implementing it to the last detail. What did he have up his sleeve?

Lenny decided he should look a little deeper.

He turned to Aulii. "Can I look around? You know. See where the girls take the men."

"Konane."

She continued talking in Lao to Konane and the girl came over and tentatively edged up to Lenny, putting both her hands on his bicep. She escorted Lenny into the back and clearly assumed he wanted sex from her. She opened a flimsy bamboo-and-woven-thatch door to a tiny room with two candles burning in clay holders sitting in the corner on the dirt floor. There taking up most of the floor space was a small thin mattress, more of a mattress pad, which was too small for someone his height. What looked like an Indian bedspread was thrown over this in an unsuccessful attempt to make it look comfortable and inviting. The bedspread was cream-colored and tie-dyed with a swirling yellow and orange pattern, but despite the complexity of the swirls, several large stains were evident in the center area of the spread. The low-roofed room smelled like peat moss and spoiled milk. Not strong enough to provoke gagging but hardly an invitation for an amorous episode.

The girl slid one of her hands down the front of Lenny's pants and started a slow circular massage of his member. This jolted him back to the incumbent need to take back control of the moment. He took stock of his situation. There he was, alone in a fuck-room of a squalid brothel, with a girl practically young enough to be his grand-daughter giving him a hand job, a girl who was probably about to pull him down onto a disgustingly filthy bed flung on the dirt floor of a room only slightly larger than a steamer trunk, all of this unfolding in a remote rural area, in the midst of a blighted region of Southeast Asia.

Sometimes life seemed so arbitrary. So improbably random. He certainly didn't choose this or have much control over the outcome.

He managed to smile paternally at the girl as he removed her hands from his crotch and turned to leave. Determined to please him and avoid the wrath she feared her mama-san would heap on her if she failed, she persisted desperately in trying to cling to Lenny, but he kept right on going. The sooner he could get out of here, the better.

As he worked his way back out to the lounge are where Aulii was waiting, he couldn't help but notice four more doors. A total of five rooms stuffed into an area the size of a small kitchen. Walls as strong and soundproof as a cardboard box. A real love hotel.

"I appreciate your time, Aulii. You're a wonderful and gracious hostess."

"Safe journey, Mr. Lenny. And may the light of Buddha fill your mind and spirit with happiness and clarity."

"Right. Buddha. Clarity."

Dok was standing with his back to Lenny not far from the entrance. He had one hand on his hip. With the other he was grandly smoking a cigarette.

A skinny Marlboro man in a business suit. A cultural icon who had apparently traded his horse for a Mercedes.

"Nice place. I'm thinking about spending my honeymoon here. Let's go."

Thank God that was over. He had a mild case of blue balls and a headache.

Neither of them spoke as they walked back to the car.

Lenny was deeply troubled and knew precisely why.

No matter how he mulled and massaged all he had seen tonight, there was one red flag which wouldn't go away. Lenny couldn't help but be aware that the entire time he had been there, not a single vehicle had pulled in to the lot. He had been the only potential customer.

"Why would she want to give up a thriving operation like this, Dok?"

"Your sarcasm is not lost on me, Mr. Lenny. Remember I was educated in your country."

"Regardless."

"Based on her impressive entrepreneurship here, Aulii has been offered other opportunities. You might say she's up for a big promotion."

A stone wall. What did he expect?

None of this made much sense. This Aulii would have you believe this is a class operation, that she had the protective instincts of a bitch dog towards the girls. She personally comes off like the Grand Duchess of Windsor. While there was no disputing she had assembled an amazing assortment of sexy young hotties, look at the working conditions. Disgusting. Absolutely unconscionable. How could she claim she actually gave a shit about these girls?

Impressive entrepreneurship? What a charade. No customers? Very fishy.

What was this all about? Was this dog-and-pony-show just put together as a sting? Once he was gone, there was no way to know until it was too late, whether any of these girls would even show up back in the U.S. What about Chicago? What kind of deal were they talking? Were they paying up front?

Okay, Lenny. Slow down.

Just keep it simple. What's your job? Find 'em and approve 'em. That's it. The whole deal. No point attempting quality control here. Or trying to be a hero. Getting a straight story from these circumspect Asians is like trying to stare through a rock. Do your job. Let it be.

"Dok. There's one important item I need to know. Have you and Chicago worked out your differences? What I mean is, have you agreed on the money?"

"Yes. We have a deal. They just want to hear from you."

"And what do I have to do from this point on? I can't be a babysitter."

"Absolutely nothing. As you say in America, it's thumbs up or thumbs down. You decide. I'll take it from there. Everything. Every last detail will be taken care of."

"And how many girls are there? How many have I personally seen tonight?"

"Mr. Lenny, you have met thirty-eight of the most beautiful girls in my country. They're all yours if you want them."

"Alright, Dok." Lenny swallowed and hoped he could actually sound sincere. "You've done a good job here. I'll take them all."

There. He had done it.

Great. Now what?

What was he in store for at the hands of this slimy bastard?

He could only guess.

And hope for the best.

Realistically, was it his fault if Dok pulled a fast one? Chicago put the ball in motion on this. Apparently they were behind Dok's bringing him here. Dok claimed that they had talked out the money issues and come to some agreement. Why shouldn't he believe him? Accept it as that.

He needed to get hold of Chicago immediately. Good luck getting a cellular signal out here in Boomfuk. He'd have to try a landline back at the hotel.

They got back in the car. Big waves from Aulii and a handful of girls as they pulled away.

They retraced their route on the dark, unpaved roads, and now were just a stone's throw from the Mekong River, finally approaching the Friendship Bridge border crossing.

Lenny broke the long silence.

"No bait and switch, Dok. I want the girls I saw this evening."

"Mr. Lenny. I am a man of integrity. You will be getting the girls you saw."

"You never told me, Dok. Do you like dogs?"

"With all due respect, Mr. Lenny, you are a very strange man."

Breakfast at Tiffany's

Christine got out of the taxi. There was Alicia standing in front of Tiffany's, smiling and looking very stylish as usual. She had a paper bag in the palm of each hand.

"Can you loan me $25,000?" She turned and nodded toward a necklace in the display window behind her. "I just adore that one right there. The one with the emeralds."

"I'm a little short today. I just gave all my money to a bag lady at Grand Central Station. How are you?"

"Fine fine. Should we sit down on the sidewalk?"

Christine looked in her bag. A croissant, an organic banana, and a bottle of orange juice. Alicia was such crazy fun. Breakfast at Tiffany's was her idea.

"Let's sit in Central Park. It's a beautiful day."

"Sounds like a plan."

They headed across 57th and up Avenue of the Americas. The leaves were turning and the Park was a Monet in red, orange and yellow under billowing white clouds. They sat down on a bench just inside the south perimeter.

Christine in the throes of culinary bliss. "This croissant is scrumptalicious."

"From my favorite bakery. So how have you been? Busy? The fundraising thing?"

"Oh yes. They keep my calendar full. And my head spinning. It chips away at my soul. Sometimes I wonder if it's such a good idea. Personally, I mean. You know?"

"No, I don't. Not really."

"All the sanctimonious people. So concerned. Actually, they *are* concerned. In their own way. But they lead these protected lives. The bubble of affluence."

"They shell out, don't they?"

"Yeah, they write checks. But realistically, it's nothing to them. And at the same time, everything to them. It makes them feel like they are doing something good. Giving to those in need. 'Give the money to the poor, and you will have treasure in Heaven.' So says the Bible. Which seems to sum up the real motivation. Not deep-in-the-heart caring. Just a small investment to buy a nice condo in the afterlife."

"But they ante up. And you get to take the money to the causes you care about. Right?"

"Do you realize how rich some of these people are? I mean, these donations are like one gazillionth of their personal wealth. And to see the look on their faces when they hand over the check, you'd think they'd just abandoned all their personal possessions to spend the rest of their lives on a pilgrimage through the wadis of Galilee."

"Wow. You keep a lot bottled up. Do you ever feel like slapping them?"

"No. I slap myself instead. For being such a phony. Not that I'd do anything differently. Guess I'm in a rut."

"You are very conflicted about this … "

"Conflicted? What a great word! So merciful. Just this side of neurotic. 'Conundrum' is another word I really like."

"So … Sybil … how do you do it? I mean, having the two of you battling it out in there."

"I could only wish I were a full-on schizo. At least I'd have some official sanction for being such a hypocrite. I mean, I don't hate these people. In their minds, they are leading good Christian lives. But I'll tell you one thing I've learned. The meek have not inherited the Earth. Not the one I live on. The rich own everything lock, stock and barrel."

"You still haven't said how you do it."

"In public, I keep my sleeves rolled up and let people think what they want. In private, I don't wear anything with sleeves."

"Except for today."

"I'm with *you* today. And my arms are hairy."

"What about with your husband?"

"Tom."

"Sorry. I forgot his name. Yes, Tom."

"You're very perceptive. You're right. There's some role-playing there. But he is what you would consider a fanatic. He's an evangelical soldier. And I love his passion — his total devotion to what he believes. He is the Christian Right, but not in a bad way."

"He'd hate someone like me. He'd consider me a slut. Burn in Hell, whore of Babylon!"

"No no no! Tom's not that way. He doesn't judge. Unlike 99% of the others. I really love him. He's a good father. And a good husband."

Alicia studied Christine's face. Christine was beautiful in both ways. On the surface, she had model good-looks, a freshness, a fair-skinned radiance that created an innocent but still sensuous aura — which immediately drew you into her warm hypnotic presence. Then from deep within, she radiated an amaranthine beauty. Her dark blue eyes were windows to a profound intelligence, a deep compassion and caring, a sense of purpose, a pool of goodness.

A deep male voice came from behind them.

"Have you been baptized in the name of the Lord Jesus Christ?"

They both turned around and saw a man dressed in a hooded brown robe, wearing leather sandals which laced up his calves, and sporting a thick, rather frayed cincture around his waste. He carried a large burlap satchel, from which he withdrew a canvas-covered military-issue canteen. "This is the water which is consecrated as only the blessed sacrament of baptism shall be thus sanctified. They call me St. John the Baptist of Hell's Kitchen, but you should just call me John. I am here before you in the name of the Lord Jesus Christ. Have the stains of original sin been washed from your beautiful souls, cursed at birth but deserving the perfect grace of God's love?"

Both Christine and Alicia simultaneously decided he wasn't dangerous and now fought to suppress a laugh. Christine answered first.

"Yes. The answer is most definitely yes. And thank you for asking."

Alicia stood up and started a slow Tai Chi sort of dance. She feigned an exaggerated Asian accent.

"In my tradition, we aspire to the perfect state of nothingness. I think you have a jump on me in that department."

John stared at her intently for almost a minute as she continued her absurd dance. When she stopped, he made a sign of the cross in the air in front of him. She mirrored him. He smiled. A sinister but knowing smile. Then he winked. "I will be on my way now, Saigon Sally." Pointing toward the duck pond a short way from where they were sitting. "This servant's contribution to building God's Holy Kingdom here on Earth is to baptize the unbaptized right over there. And so it is done. God bless you both. And God bless America."

He went on his way. But the strange encounter had silently worked its effect on Christine and Alicia. They were simultaneously both infected with a case of the giggles, becoming two schoolgirls desperately trying to keep it together, as their austere teacher stared them down.

As soon as St. John the Baptist finally was out of earshot, the floodgates of hilarity broke wide. It felt good to let loose and just laugh. Alicia was the first to regain some semblance of composure.

"There you go. Who says there aren't some eligible hunks still around?"

They doubled over again.

"That was quite some dance you were doing. Is there something you haven't told me?"

"Velly good. Make chop chop. You velly good luck. Moon lady lotus flower. Maybe lady want lice? Flied lice. Ah so?"

"Stop! I need to catch my breath." Still giggling, Christine wiped her eyes.

Gradually they settled back into a calm appreciation of the lovely autumn day, the casual strollers, the nannies walking children by the hand or in baby carriages through the park.

"Hey, Alicia. I've been meaning to ask you. What's going on with the adoption?"

The lightness and the calm instantly vanished from Alicia's face. Her brow was a mixture of anger and pain as she turned her head to the side.

"It's a fucking disaster."

Then she lost it. Thank god for no-run mascara. Christine quickly put her arm around her. She gently pulled Alicia closer. A tissue appeared and she wiped away her tears. But they kept coming.

"I'll be alright. Well … I won't be. But I have to. It's not going to happen. They either lost him or they're hiding him. It's really screwed up!"

"I don't understand. What do you mean, lost him?"

"I got this letter. So I called them. And after forty minutes on the phone with five people, none of whom could speak English worth a damn, finally this one lady told me, the boy is gone. He's no longer there."

"Alicia. I'm so sorry. You met him, didn't you?"

"Twice. Like I could afford flying over there even one time. He's such a beautiful little boy. I could tell he loved me. Or maybe he was just desperate for a mommy. But he would have loved me. I wanted so badly just to give him a home. A chance at a real life."

"There's no one you can talk to? Maybe with the government?"

"The government tries to shut them down. They don't like other countries offering to take their children away. It's apparently bad for their international image. Like anyone in the rest of the world gives a shit about what a great job they're doing for the people of Indonesia."

"There's nothing you can do?"

"Christine. These little Asian countries don't play by our rules. It's so screwed up. Oh God! Things you don't know about. Things which, believe me, you don't want to know about."

"Like what? Is this okay? Talking about it?"

"Yeah. It's okay. I need to talk to someone. I am *so* pissed off."

Alicia hesitated. In deep thought about something.

"Christine. I don't know what I should say and what I shouldn't. You are a very smart lady. And I think we are becoming good friends. Even so, maybe you shouldn't hear this."

"Try me."

"Well. Over there, they buy and sell these kids. That's what I'm afraid happened to my boy. I mean, we've got it right here. Right in Brooklyn, there is this whole Asian prostitution thing going on. Young girls abducted and made into little sex slaves."

Christine felt a chill go through her body. Her eyes widened like saucers.

"Some of them are only fourteen, fifteen years old."

"How do you know about this?"

"It's a long story. But there is a Bishop in town here. Bishop Mulcahey."

"Yes. Everyone knows him. He gets in the news a lot."

"Well, I interviewed him on an assignment. A special article I was doing on adopting kids from overseas. He has a support group for prospective parents. And a referral service as part of his church."

"St. Francis of Assisi."

"That's it. Anyway, these girls start showing up on the streets. Manhattan has a bunch. They're in Brooklyn, right in the Bishop's own parish. The Bishop is very concerned and thinks he knows who is behind it all."

"You mean, organized crime types."

"Not exactly. Not the way we think of it. The Mafia and all that. Anyway, I kind of know the guy they think runs it in Brooklyn. So I set him up. It's a long story, but I used to have a massive love jones for this guy in high school, and he treated me like I had bubonic plague. So maybe I was just paying him back. It was a stupid impulse. But I'd get to see him again. Anyway, with my help they brought him in to pump him for information."

"Alicia. You amaze me. You were like an undercover cop."

"Uh … yes. That's what I was. Sort of. Except not for the cops. A favor for the Bishop. So he could try to get out of him who the big kahunas are behind these girls. I mean, this is international in scope. They are bringing them in from all over southeast Asia. Indonesia, Cambodia, Malaysia, Thailand."

Alarm bells were clanging a deafening cacophony in Christine now.

"Thailand?"

"Most of them probably come from Thailand. Sex is the largest single industry there. Anyway, since all of this happened with my little boy, I have been connecting the dots. Bodies are just property over there. Boys, girls, men, women. They buy and sell them like we buy and sell furniture or running shoes. I really think that's what happened. I think they *sold* my little boy."

"Alicia, I'm *so* sorry … I … I wish I could help."

"I know, Christine. I haven't given up. I just don't know where to start now."

After a few moments lost in thought, Christine broke the silence.

"These girls you mentioned."

"Yes. They're called Djin Djin girls. That's what their little business cards say."

"I know this sounds weird. But can we see them?"

"Believe me, that's easily arranged. They're on the streets every night. You just need to know where to look. I grew up in Brooklyn. So I definitely know where to look."

"Can we go? Tonight?"

"Well. Sure. I don't know what the urgency is. But I'm free. Tonight it is."

"I'll use Tom's car. What time? Eight? Nine?"

"Let's make it nine. You know where I live?"

"I will when you write down the address. Alicia, this is really important to me. Maybe I'll try to explain tonight. But I need to know about this."

"Christine, my conflicted Christian friend. I am here for you."

I Wear My Sunglasses at Night

Nine o'clock sharp. Christine knocked softly. Almost immediately the door to Alicia's brownstone opened.

"Alicia! What's this? You look like you just got off the boat from Bulgaria. A babushka?"

"My fashion sense has taken a completely new direction."

"Can you see anything with those sunglasses on?"

"I didn't mention it. This could be a little dangerous for me. But I don't think like this anyone will recognize me."

"That's for sure. I feel like I should have brought a bag of hand-me-downs. Or a blanket. Where is your shopping cart?"

"Hey, don't knock it. This could start a whole new trend. Gutter chic."

They pulled away in Christine's Ford Escape.

"So where are we going?"

"Take the Williamsburg. We'll head south from Bushwick. Do you know Brooklyn at all? You'll get to see my old neighborhood."

"Not really. Music?"

Alicia picked out a Tori Amos CD. The SUV had a great sound system. Neither said anything as both of them seemed to lose themselves in the melancholy space of the songs. *Silent All These Years* was just finishing as they made the final approach to the area where the Djin Djin girls lined the sidewalks.

Christine slowed the car to a crawl.

It was a complete flashback to Sukhumvit Road in Bangkok. Certainly on a much smaller scale, but effectively the exact same visual. She was transfixed. A save-the-world voyeur, mesmerized by an accident on the freeway of her mind.

"Look out!" Alicia grabbed the dashboard.

But it was too late. Christine had rear-ended another vehicle, a new Chrysler New Yorker. A Djin Djin girl had been talking to the driver through the passenger window but now she backed away and plopped her oversized silver platforms back onto the curb, where she shrugged and began walking over to join the other girls.

Christine started to get out but the driver of the New Yorker peeled away in a burst of smoke and squealing tires.

Alicia laughed. "He probably doesn't want anyone to know he's trying to pick up young girls. Usually it doesn't sit well with the wife and kids."

"I couldn't have hurt anything. I was barely moving. Alicia, this is astounding. This is exactly what I saw when I was in Bangkok."

"Why were you trying to pick up young girls in Bangkok?"

"You're funny. It's a long story. A really ugly story. Alicia, you've got to help me out here. Please. I want to talk to them. These girls, I mean."

"Are you crazy? Why?"

"I want to find out if … if they had anything to do with these programs I raise money for."

"You're serious."

"Serious as a heart attack. See, this guy in Bangkok, this friend of Tom and mine, tried to tell me that some of these child sponsorship organizations, particularly ones in Thailand, are feeding this … this sex trafficking business. I didn't believe him but …"

"And you want to talk to them? Right now?"

"I have to. I have to know."

"You think any of those girls are going to talk to you? I mean, if they were brought over here, they're illegal. And they sure as hell aren't going to talk about anything to anyone who looks like they could work for the government authorities — which you definitely do."

"We've got to try."

"I said I'd help. So we can try. But don't get your hopes up."

Christine pulled the car to the first available space along the curb and parked.

They backtracked on foot toward the corner intersection. There were six Djin Djin girls right in close proximity. Paired off. Chatting away. If anything, when Alicia and Christine first approached, they seemed curious. Not very often did a lady engage them in conversation.

"Hello. I'm Christine. Are you from Nong Khai? Have you heard of the Siddartha School?"

The first two just appeared puzzled. "Not know. Sorry." They turned and walked away.

"How about you? Are either of you from Nong Khai?" These two wouldn't even look at her, said nothing, then quickly scampered away. The last two within earshot apparently had been listening and also beat a quick retreat. They nervously confided in hushed high-pitched tones, timidly looking back over their shoulders. It was obvious they didn't want anything to do with these two nosy white women.

Right then a squad car pulled around the corner. The cops looked at the news stand attendant, who nodded in the direction of Alicia and Christine. The driver pulled up to the curb parallel with them and fired a single burst of his siren to get their attention. Both officers jumped out of the vehicle.

Good cop. "Can I help you? Are you lost?"

Bad cop. "If you ladies are looking for trouble, this is the perfect place to find it."

Alicia stayed back but Christine stepped forward and put on her award-winning smile. "Good evening, gentlemen. No. There is no problem here. We're just … just … well, it's a beautiful day in the neighborhood, wouldn't you say?"

Bad cop. "Not really. Not this neighborhood. I think you better move on. There is a lot of suspicious activity around here. The whole area is under intense surveillance."

Good cop. "Hey, you in the shades. Love your outfit. Are you in *Ellis Island The Musical* or is this a dry run for Halloween?"

He was obviously quite amused with himself.

Bad cop. "Maybe we should run them in."

Christine stood her ground.

"Wait a minute. This is a public street. We're just walking on a public sidewalk. Is there a law against that?"

Bad cop. "Lady, there have been three murders here in the past couple weeks. You are *not* safe walking on this particular public sidewalk." Pointing. "Is that your Escape over there?"

Christine nodded.

"Well then, if I were you, I would get back in your vehicle right now and confine your strolling to the aisles of Bloomingdales. Otherwise, we're taking you to the station — if nothing else, for your own good."

Christine was visibly shaken by this last bit of news. Her previous air of cool confidence was suddenly shattered, her demeanor betraying shock and serious misgivings about their little escapade.

"I understand, officer. We'll be going. Sorry to be of any concern."

Good cop. "You ladies have a nice evening."

The cops got back into their patrol car and waited for them to leave. Christine took Alicia's arm and the two of them, now very subdued and humbled by the confrontation, walked back towards the SUV.

As they made their way, a petite figure stepped out of the shadow of a storefront entryway. A very sweet little Asian face, painted in the high tramp gloss and glitter of a Djin Djin girl, looked with sad frightened eyes directly at Christine as she passed. Christine turned.

The girl whispered almost inaudibly.

"I from Nong Khai. Siddartha School."

Christine could never remember the walk back to the car or the drive home. But Alicia always said that she looked like a woman who was cradling her dead child in her arms.

Chapter 9

NO LAUGHING NO CRYING: The Wishing Well

Baptism of Fire

3:12 am. The squad car pulled out of the alley and onto Church Street, quiet and residential. Officer Maggie Thornton was typing a report into the dash-mount computer when her partner, Officer Tim Mackey, interrupted.

"Check this out. Can't say this job isn't interesting at times."

A man who appeared to be in his late forties or early fifties was dragging a crucifix made of long two-by-fours down the sidewalk. He was dressed as if to wander the sacred lands of ancient Israel and was now offering his own symbolic re-enactment of the Passion of Christ, much as Jesus the Lord Savior so long ago walked the bloody path to Golgotha. Those persons encountered along the way here in Brooklyn who were receptive and in need were offered and given the sacred sacrament of Baptism, then sent along to live their lives, renewed with the possibility of redemption and the final reward of eternal residence in the Kingdom of Heaven.

St. John the Baptist of Hell's Kitchen stopped and looked at the two police officers as the window on the driver's side of the patrol car rolled down. Mackey launched a first salvo.

"Jesus. Good to see you. How are you today?"

"Do not blaspheme. You know I am not Jesus Christ."

"Help me out here. Who exactly are you? Can I see some identification?"

"Those who know me know me as St. John the Baptist of Hell's Kitchen, a perhaps frivolous moniker, but one which does not diminish the profundity or sanctity of my holy mission here on Earth."

Both officers were out of the car now. Mackey continued in his mocking tone.

"I'm sure you're right on the money there, Mr. St. John. But fill my partner and I in on this. Just what exactly is that mission?"

"Plain and simple, it is purification. Expunging the stain of original sin and eradication of any and all foulness which has crept into the clear waters of our collective spiritual lives."

"Hmm, I see. Well it sounds to me like you're preaching without a license. And we have strict regulations. Preaching without a license is a very serious offense, you know."

"I do what my Lord and Savior requires of me. No more no less."

It was obvious Mackey was getting bored with his little game. Officer Thornton took over.

"We can talk more about that in a minute. But for now would you mind putting down the cross and stepping over to the squad car with us, please. Do you have a driver's license or identification of any kind?"

"By the grace of God go I — and He knoweth who I am."

"That may be so. But even if Jesus walked these particular streets at this particular time, we would require him to show us some ID." While Thornton spoke, Mackey opened the door and positioned himself for a chokehold, should force be required to get John to cooperate. "Why don't you have a seat here in the car where we can talk more comfortably?"

"But my crucifix ..."

Mackey feigned concern. His acting wouldn't fool the dead.

"I don't think that your crucifix is any danger right now. It's pretty late and the demand for full-size crucifixes seems to be at an all time low right now. Just leave it there and I'll keep an eye on it for you. This should only take a few minutes."

John got into the back seat of the police car and leaned forward with his face right up to the separator between the front and rear seats. He reached into his robe and produced a dog tag. He handed the dog tag to Thornton as soon as she got in.

"I think we're both on the same team here, ma'am. Just out looking around. Same as you."

His tone was all business and he had dropped the pretense of being a time-traveling wanderer of the desert. This sudden change of John's demeanor had certainly caught both officers by surprise. Usually the crazy pretty much stayed crazy. Thornton looked at him curiously.

"So you're ex-military. Is this from Vietnam?"

"Yes. I was in the thick of it. Berin Sac, Binh Dinh Province. Nam Tu'o'ng. Other places I can't talk about."

Right then, they got a call from the station. *"5-1-4, we need an escort over to the warehouse. Chief wants to make sure his little sisters get home all right. Are you available?"*

"Mackey here. We're on it. Back at you from location."

They pulled away from the curb and Mackey made a left at the first intersection. Another right and they pulled up across from the alley which ran behind the STD Prevention Center. They sat and waited. The alley was dark and it was hard to see what was going on.

Thornton turned back to speak to John. "My older brother was there too. Said it was hell. He came back with a serious drug habit and spent over two years in and out of a vet hospital trying to kick it."

Two vehicles pulled out of the alley, but from the back seat it was impossible to get a good look at them. Mackey waited to pull away, apparently wanting to put a few car lengths between his patrol car and the vehicles they were following. Then he radioed in. "We're with 'em now."

John leaned back. Where were they taking him? He decided it would be best to just play along for now and see what happened. He finally replied to Thornton.

"There was a lot of drugs. Never touched the stuff. A lotta guys cracked under the pressure. The ones that didn't? They did what they had to do."

The patrol car rolled through a red traffic signal, briefing flashing its emergency lights to warn any cross traffic. The streets were pretty deserted at this hour. They continued along at a good clip, keeping visual contact with what appeared to be a couple large SUVs, heading north and then west, into an industrial area. John could see they were passing one corrugated iron building after another, all of them enclosed by chain-link fences with spirals of barbwire at the top.

"This dog tag is all the ID you have, Mr. Harrison?"

"It's all I need. I have been and am now in proud service to my country."

"So what's with the ... you know, the outfit you're wearing? Isn't it kind of cold out there? Those robes were made more for the desert in the Middle East than autumn here in Brooklyn, wouldn't you say?"

John reached into his robe again. Thornton's right hand shot back and unbuckled the strap on her gun. She relaxed when John leaned forward and extended a single dollar bill to her through the partition.

Mackey glanced over at the single bill. "If that's a bribe, you'll have to do better than that."

John stared at Thornton with round childlike eyes. "What does it say?"

"What does what say?"

"On the dollar, right there." John indicated with his thumb. She looked at him suspiciously and said nothing.

"In God we trust. That's what it says. In God we trust."

"Mr. Harrison, I'm not following you."

"It's all the same thing. One master. One true God. We are his chosen people. Americans. It doesn't matter what you're wearing. Or what I'm wearing. You follow now?"

Officer Mackey interrupted. "We're here. How does it look to you, Maggie?"

"Smooth as an buttered oyster."

"You make me so hot, baby."

"You're disgusting, Mack."

John looked up and could not believe what he was seeing. His breathing froze and his head reeled with shock and delight. At the same time, he realized it was absolutely critical that he maintain his composure, and completely mask what he was feeling. So he donned what he hoped was his best stone face. There is no way he could give audience to the firestorm of excitement which was raging through him right now.

Right there in front of him were two Lincoln Navigators, one black and one silver. Out of them were pouring little gook sluts, one after another. The fucking enemy! They each filed past two burly bodyguards on through a narrow gate, then apparently headed down a passageway between two buildings.

Mackey eased the cruiser forward and when he pulled up across from the . two guards, nodded and tipped his cap. With a barely discernable movement of his eyebrows, one of the guards returned his assent.

John could now look down the passageway and see that at the end the girls turned left into a door and disappeared. So this is where they bivouacked.

He had spent the last three nights wandering through the streets of Brooklyn trying to get some feel for how it was organized, how it all came together. To see where the enemy was concentrated. How they dispersed. Where and when they came and went. In his travels, he had come nowhere close to wherever they were now, but this place would be easy to locate. If they took him back to where they had picked him up, he sure as hell would make some careful mental notes along the way.

It was just like he had said to the lady officer. They were on the same team. The God team. This was no coincidence. There was no doubt in John's mind who had sent them to him tonight.

It was Him.

Mackey was back on the radio. "All clear here. Tucked in." Then he gave the accelerator an assertive push and they were on their way again.

"Okay. So where were we? What you think, Mag? Whaddya wanna do with Apostle Paul here?"

"Your call."

"Waste of time. He's harmless. Let's drop him back where we found him."

"Should we write it up?"

"Right. Talked to Jesus. He gave us a dollar for the field day fund."

It took maybe twenty minutes for the return trip. They had to stop briefly on the way to check on a report of suspicious activity at the rear of a dry cleaners. When they finally got back and pulled up to the curb, Mackey got out and opened the door for John.

"See! Your crucifix is right where you left it. This is such an upstanding neighborhood. Behave yourself now. We'll be watchin' for ya."

"God bless you both."

Three days later at 5:30 a.m., the warehouse where the Djin Djin girls from all of the boroughs lived, a total of fifty-seven young beauties, went up in flames. By a miracle — some might even suggest there was Divine intervention involved — only one girl was killed. She was overcome by smoke inhalation and had collapsed behind her bunk. Neither of the two guards who were there to protect the girls saw her as they hustled the others to safety. Here's what the New York Post had to say about it …

"WAREHOUSE BURNS TO THE GROUND IN BROOKLYN"

Early Tuesday morning, an old warehouse in the 9th Street and 2nd Avenue industrial area of Brooklyn, apparently housing documents and other highly flammable material, was turned into a pile of smoking ashes and twisted metal siding. The fire raged out of control and completely destroyed the facility before firemen even started to train their hoses on the conflagration. One fireman was quoted as saying, "This had to be going a while before we even got the call. It was a done deal before we even pulled up." Because of the age of the building, it is believed that faulty wiring may have been responsible. There were no injuries reported.

A Prayer Early One Saturday Morning

Almost every American household with a high school age teenager has a ghost in the house. This ghost looks, for all intents and purposes, like someone who has been a member of the family for 15 or so years. But as the pressures of transitioning from childhood through puberty and on into the vast, mysterious, and undefined world of adulthood mount, as peer pressure and the manipulative forces of modern media assault the 16-year old mind, as huge changes in physical appearance unremittingly challenge this young person to try to figure out who he really is and what might be his place in the world, as this unremitting juggernaut continues its predictable assault on the not-a-child-but-not-yet-an-adult, the fully formed but only partly completed organism known as a teenager, withdraws into an alternate universe.

Only an embodied apparition, a fleeting chimera, an elusive poltergeist, makes sporadic cameos, up and down the stairs to the bedroom, in the bathroom in the morning, occasionally at the dinner table, only rarely in the family room, those sightings catalyzed by major holidays like Thanksgiving and Christmas. This ghost-like being is silent and secretive, inhabiting a world on the far fringes of the family with whom he or she shares a surname.

Most well-known adolescent psychologists, at least the ones who regularly appear on talk shows like Oprah, say that the best approach at this age is invisible monitoring, laissez-faire stewardship, a hands-off approach which manages to keep the kid alive and out of trouble, until he can emerge at the other end of the existential tunnel and rejoin the society of kin. Sort of a "trust but verify" policy, like the U.S. had with the Soviet Union in the 80s on missile reductions.

This was the unspoken but concordant policy that Tom and Christine used in relation to their 16-year old son, Daniel. As Danny gradually entered this phase, they had subtly but systematically calibrated their own interactions with him, to adjust to what was happening. Both Tom and Christine were privy to the dynamics of good parenting, much of their understanding coming from church groups and church-sponsored roundtables, where other parents would share in a Christian setting their own experiences raising kids. Some of their ease in adapting came from their own caring and sensitivity as people, and the fact that they were still young, the business of being 16 not so far in the past that it was inaccessible, or had become distorted by time.

Danny was born 9 1/2 months after their wedding day, probably conceived in the last week of their honeymoon. He had always been a bright kid, easygoing, extroverted but pleasant. He was a solid student in school and more importantly took his Bible studies seriously enough to be a constant source of satisfaction and pride to them. Even now in high school, his grades were always As and Bs, so he maintained a solid B+ average in the college-prep program he was enrolled in.

Despite their having to accept at this point in time, Danny's effectively being more of a boarder than a son, they were overall quite gratified and predictably proud of him, hence saw little need to make any uninvited incursions into his private world.

At least until now.

Tom had inadvertently found it. Danny had put his school notebook on the third step of the staircase and rushed out somewhere, probably to meet his friends to do whatever they did together these days.

Tom grabbed it on his way up to his and Christine's room, intending to lean it against Danny's bedroom door, which he did. But the notebook fell ever-so-slightly open and out popped a small piece of paper. Tom picked it up and stared at it in complete and total shock.

He obviously was a grown man. And while he had accepted Jesus Christ as his personal Savior and had devoted his life to living as a devout Christian, he still thought of himself as "worldly". Even if he had chosen a path of righteousness, he was not naïve to what went on in the world around him. You couldn't live in a city like New York, during such troubled times as those of the new Millennium, in a nation which seemed embattled on every front — socially, politically, militarily, and spiritually — and not be aware of every possible sin, of every conceivable iniquity, of every lurking evil, of every potential for wickedness, of every possible transgression of God's Divine Will.

Yet nothing had prepared him for this.

This was right here in their *home* — sacred territory for a man of faith.

It was his *own son*.

He needed to talk to Christine. Immediately.

Was that possible? What horrible timing.

Tom had never seen her like this. How long had they been married? More than 17 years. She usually had more positive energy than the entire stadium full of people at the Super Bowl. But the last several days, something had changed. Dramatically. She was not at all herself. She wandered through the house with a glazed look in her eyes. Totally absorbed in thought. Lost inside some dark world that had descended on her. Her face was drawn down and she had heavy circles under her eyes. If she weren't so beautiful, he would say she looked like a very sad zombie.

He went into the living room looking for her and there she sat. Staring. Brooding about something. What had happened?

She wouldn't talk about it. They had always been very open and candid, so yesterday he asked her what was going on. She said she didn't know what to say. But she'd figure it out.

There wasn't time for that now.

"Christine. I have to talk to you. It's about Danny."

She looked up at him without saying anything.

"I found this in his notebook."

There it was. A business card. Plain white paper. Text printed in bright red. *I'm Djin Djin I'm from Thailand ...*

She barely managed the two words which breathlessly escaped her lips more as a gasp, than an utterance.

"Oh ... God ..."

They sat in silence for what seemed like an eternity. Tom nervously turned the Djin Djin business card over and over in his hands, looking at it, then looking away. His face was a slide show of disbelief, frustration, angst. Christine tried to hide it, but she was sobbing, in the grip of the slow burn of grief, engulfed in an ineffable sense of helplessness.

"Christine. What do you want to do?"

Whispering. "God, please help me." Sobbing again. "I can't deal with this."

"Come on, you know you can. You have to. I need you. We'll figure it out. Together."

"I'm not fit to be a human being, much less a mother."

"Christine, I really don't understand. What's going on with you?"

"What's going on with me? What's going on with *me*? What's going on with the world?"

"The world is what it is. This is our son. We have to do something."

"We should do nothing. It's not his fault."

"Nothing? I don't get it. Nothing."

"Tom, this is my fault. It's your fault. It's everyone's fault. But especially my fault."

"I can't make any sense of what you're saying. We can't just sit here. Danny needs our help. Out prayers. This is horrible. This is evil."

"Exactly. It's about evil. The spread of evil. The inevitability of evil."

"Christine. *'And ye will not suffer your children that they go hungry, or naked; neither will ye suffer that they transgress the laws of God.'*"

"But we have completely failed. This is where *I* in particular have failed. It's not his fault. Danny didn't choose a playing field of filth. He doesn't have anywhere else to play."

"The Bible says, *'Nevertheless we, according to His promise, look for new Heavens and a new Earth, wherein dwelleth righteousness.'* According to His promise, Christine."

"The Bible says. And it says. And it says. Everyone's quoting the Bible. But it says what they want it to say. I finally figured out what has been quietly but steadily eating away at me for the past few years. Going to these fundraisers. Hearing everyone talk about God and how He'll take care of us. Right. He'll make it all better. Just drop a few coins in the basket, burn a votive candle, say a prayer, wear your Sunday best to services, pledge to the building fund. And the Big Guy with the beard will deliver. God is like a mail order catalog of good works. What a pile of crap! What a bunch of lazy, indifferent people Christians have turned out to be. God's all powerful, He loves us, so let Him fix the mess we've made of the world. Well, God doesn't care! He doesn't care, Tom. Or if he cares, He's moved on to something more promising than the human race."

"We as Christians are His chosen people."

"If *we* are His chosen people, then God is not very bright."

"Christine, that is blasphemy. I can't believe I'm—"

"No Tom, it's not blasphemy! It's the truth! *'Thou shalt not bear false witness.'* God is love. God is mercy. God is compassion. But most of all God is truth. He doesn't lie to us. So we shouldn't lie to ourselves. Particularly about Him. Just to make it easier on ourselves. Maybe you forgot. But I can quote the Bible too. *'For the wrath of God is revealed from Heaven against all ungodliness and unrighteousness of men, who hold the truth in unrighteousness; who changed the truth of God into a lie.'* That's Romans 1, 18 and 25."

"This is our son. It's our responsibility to guide him, to—"

"Leave him alone, Tom." Glancing at the Djin Djin card. "Make believe you never saw this. It doesn't matter. If it wasn't this, it would be something else. Evil is everywhere you look. And that's our real job. I just don't know how or where to start."

"We should start at home."

"This is our mess to clean up. But not by humiliating little Danny. I have been contributing to this. Just like everyone else. If you're not the solution, then you're part of the problem. Christians and their self-righteous apathy are absolutely part of the problem. Not anymore. Not for me, Tom. I've got to help fix this. I've got to undo what I've done. The mess I've helped to create. I just feel so helpless. So completely paralyzed."

"This is crazy. I ... I ... feel like I'm talking to a stranger. This is not the Christine I know and love. The one I married because she had committed her life to Christ."

"Tom. Look at me."

But he couldn't.

Instead, for the next 30 seconds he stared at his folded hands.

Tom got up slowly and went up the stairs to their bedroom. It was Saturday and the young sun of morning threw its warm rays through the white translucent drapes onto the soft wool carpet. He knelt down beside the bed and bowed his head in prayer.

"My Savior in Heaven, my merciful Lord Jesus Christ ..."

His mind was a blank. After ten minutes he gave up. He wiped a solitary tear from his right eye, stood up, and looked out the window. A tiny sparrow sat in the tree next to the house. Then it flew away.

The Bully Pulpit – Part I

The flight from Bangkok had taken over 26 hours. Exhausted, Lenny paid the cabbie and pulled his two bags out of the trunk. It was close to midnight and all he could think about was a good night's sleep in his own bed.

Another FedEx waiting as his door. A note from Chicago.

> *Lenny, that shitbag Mulcahey is going public.*
> *He never learns. Be there. I want to know*
> *first hand what BS this guy is floating.*
> *It's this Sunday. — Harold Danko*

How did he get in this deep? They couldn't be serious. After what he'd been through with that sadistic bastard. Now they wanted him back in the lion's den. Alright. He'd be there. Maybe he should bring a shotgun and finish him off for good. Payback time!

Right. Get a grip.

As much rage as he felt, Lenny didn't have a vindictive bone in his body. Not the kind that pulls triggers. Sure it had been hell. But his attitude had always been, it's job part of the job. High risk employment. What the fuck. Think about Martin and Frankie! This wasn't little league baseball. If the worst could happen it would.

Sure Lenny could inflict pain when he had to. He could make someone suffer. But die? Taking Mulcahey out wouldn't accomplish anything, except make the Bishop a celebrity martyr and bring even more attention to his self-righteous harangue.

And more heat on Lenny and anyone else who worked for Chicago.

Everyone! Himself. Keary. Markham.

Who else?

Well … he really didn't know. He was so in the dark. That was a big part of the problem. Here was this huge, complex enterprise and he had no idea how many or who was involved. But however it shook out, a lot of innocent heads would roll if he did anything stupid. Fact is, everyone plays for keeps around here. This whole scene was like a Texas-style death match. Only one man leaves the cage. Sometimes no one was left standing. How Shakespearian.

He definitely would keep his cool for now. He'd get Mulcahey somehow. Eventually. There had to be a court of karmic justice in this world. Otherwise, the world made no sense at all. Then again, did it make any sense? It sure seems like there are a lot of really bad guys running around living large, living the good life, cannibalizing a lot of decent people.

Like himself.

Truth was, this world did not make one ounce of sense. So he'd do what he had to do. But only until he could blow this pop stand once and for all. After all, when all was said and done, what were his options? He had none. Except to grope his way like a blind man through a house of mirrors until he found his way out. He really wasn't cut out for this kind of thing. Maybe he should be glad he wasn't. That might be his supreme redeeming quality.

But that motherfucker Mulcahey! A cruel pig of a man. Sieg heil!

What day is it? Thursday. Meaning he'd be doing the holy holy in three days. In the resplendent Cathedral of St. Francis Assisi.

Sunday turned out to be one of those chilly but crystal clear autumn days that put poetry on a page and watercolors on a wall. Lenny arrived intentionally late, wishing to avoid as much of the service as possible. With the timing of an Olympic gold medal gymnast, he walked in as the Bishop was just starting his keynote address to the entire congregational cast — the clocklike core of regulars and devout do-gooders, the casual and curious, the gazers and gawkers, and finally both the conscientious journalists and the scandal-hungry hacks representing the whole cornucopia of print and broadcast media. It was a motley hierarchy which spoke volumes about the awesome power of the pulpit, wielded as the weapon of choice by a man like the Bishop, even in these Godless times, even in the agnostic megalopolis of New York.

"Recently there have been three horrible murders right here in our local neighborhood. I am loathe to conjoin the term 'typical' with 'murders', since no loss of one of God's children should be seen as commonplace or routine. Having said that, these recent killings were not typical murders. Not gang shootings, not domestic violence, not robbery, none of the characteristic homicides commonly reported in the news, the carnage which — God help us — seems to be part of the fabric of American urban life in these violent times. No, the victims of these killings were not your everyday citizens, probably not citizens of this country at all. They were not people you see in our churches. It is safe to assume they were not even Christians. They were not among those you have grown up with, those who have lived on your street, or gone to your schools over the years. Their families are not here even now. In fact, they all arrived here very recently from far away lands, countries like Thailand, Cambodia, Vietnam.

"The true story of how they got here is very ugly and heartbreaking. These victims were brought here unwillingly, trapped by a brutal system of forced slavery. They were brought here as sex slaves to walk your streets, to sell themselves as prostitutes, and to make a lot of money for those responsible for this grotesque enterprise. More money than you can imagine. You've seen them out there, young Asian girls, flagging down cars over by Turner and 6th Street.

"I don't know if you will find this shocking or not. I certainly do. Some of these girls are as young as 13 years old. The three murder victims, of course, had no documentation, no passports or birth certificates. And two were — God have mercy — gruesomely mutilated.

"But police experts believe two were 16 and the other only 14 years old. Can you grasp this? Look around at the beautiful young faces who are here with us at Mass today. Many of them 13 to 16 years old. The grace of God shines forth and blossoms in the innocence of these youth. This from Psalms 36:7 ...

*'How precious is your steadfast love, O God! The children
of mankind take refuge in the shadow of your wings.'*

"Jesus Himself had a very special place for children in His divine plan. As He is quoted as saying in Mathew 10:14 ...

*'Let the little children come to me, and do not hinder them,
for the kingdom of God belongs to such as these.'*

"Still, some of you may ask — as abominable as this enslavement of children may be, as horrible and unforgivable as these murders are — why should we as a congregation, as Catholics here in the diocese of St. Francis of Assisi, concern ourselves with this? We have so many problems right here in our own backyards, problems which directly impact our own children. Hunger, homelessness, gangs, drugs, teenage pregnancy, broken homes, violence, all right here in Brooklyn and the other boroughs. Why should we divert our attention, our precious time and energy to some cartel which traffics human bodies out of southeast Asia?

"Surely, there are a lot of reasons we must put an end to this blight. The obvious answer is that each of these girls is one of God's children, just like your own. God doesn't see borders or shades of skin or the shape of the eyes. Thus, if it is in our power to help put an end to this horrible and sinful business, to do so is doing God's holy work here on Earth. It is an anointment of the ministry and good works of the Lord Jesus Christ, who showed us by His own example how we must treat others, if we are to be deserving of the grace of God and the Kingdom of Heaven.

"Let me again remind you how old these girls are. Some of them are only thirteen or fourteen years old. It is hard truly to grasp. They are here against their will, sold and bought like cattle into a life of forced prostitution. It is a horrible nightmare which has become real for each and every one of them.

"But even beyond that, this blight is in our own backyard. It directly affects the quality of life here in Brooklyn, for you, and especially for your children. This exhortation from Ephesians 5:3 ...

> 'Among you there must not be even a hint of sexual immorality,
> or of any kind of impurity, or of greed, because these
> are improper for God's holy people.'

"Having what are effectively child sex slaves walking the same streets your children use to go to school, or to play stickball, to skateboard, meet with their friends, and so on, sets the stage for even more appalling behavior. Even more frightening possibilities. If we allow this to continue, the worst is yet to come. The physical safety of your loved ones is at stake. And the spiritual integrity of your community is under assault. This from Ephesians 5:1 and 2 ...

> 'Be imitators of God, therefore, as dearly loved children and live
> a life of love, just as Christ loved us and gave himself up
> for us as a fragrant offering and sacrifice to God.'

"So I turn to you now, and ask each and every one of you to join me in this noble battle to take our community back from these criminal elements, the inhumane and opportunistic devils which have turned our streets into child brothels.

"Let us pray ..."

It was all Lenny could do to keep from yelling out at the top of his lungs, 'Fucking hypocrite!' Listening to that holier-than-thou asshole calling others 'inhumane devils' really took the cake.

He shook his head and got up to leave. Lenny didn't approve of the whole Djin Djin thing either. It made him sick to think of what Kimnai and the other girls must be going through. But if he stayed a minute longer, he might really lose it and attack this evil motherfucker.

What grandstanding! Mulcahey was no better than a gangland thug and he had the audacity to get up there wearing the Good Shepherd's robes. A sickening performance indeed, from someone who should be working for the mob or as a drug-lord mercenary in South America.

Lenny shuddered at the memory of the weeks spent caged and in chains, while Mulcahey tortured him for information he didn't have. No matter how noble the bishop's intentions might have been, they didn't justify what Lenny had suffered — guilty or innocent.

The mass continued now that the sermon was over. Lenny stepped outside, leaned against a marble pillar, the broad steps of the cathedral spread before him.

A young mother leaving early came out. She had toddlers on both hands, two boys maybe three and four struggling to break free from her grip, whining and being little boys. Lenny watched her hail a cab and wrestle her two ninja turtles into the rear seat.

A short while later, two teenage girls roller-bladed by singing some pop tune.

As he stood there thinking, the initial wave of his personal rage against Mulcahey gradually dissipated. He started to consider the other side of the coin.

Without any question, he really needed a way out. If the Djin Djin thing kept on spreading, he would be locked in tighter than a maximum security prison. Truth was, he feared he might already be in too deep to make a clean break. Maybe his only hope was for a total crackdown. Someone who would back this up all the way to southeast Asia. Meaning Chicago wouldn't need him anymore. Maybe then he could just ease out. Disappear.

Lenny started to view Mulcahey in a slightly different light.

Think about it. Right now what were his options? The cops were definitely in bed with Danko and Valley. Who knows how far that went? City hall? No way could he count on any law enforcement organization doing anything. Not the local cops anyway. What about INS? Or the FBI? This operation was breaking every interconnected law in the book. Especially the Federal laws. Immigration. Kidnapping. Transporting minors across state lines. On and on it went.

Unfortunately, if the feds got involved, he himself might face some serious time. He had to be very careful.

On the other hand, while it pained Lenny to consider having to rely on him, if Mulcahey threw his considerable weight around, he might be able to deliver. He carried a big club in this town — a really big club. Mulcahey didn't need to use official channels. The guy created his own channels.

It made Lenny nauseous to think his fate might be in the hands of the Bishop. He hated him more than anyone in his life. Ever! And he had definitely carried some serious grudges along the way.

But there it was. Staring him right in the face. This might be his path to freedom. A way to cut the chains and start fresh.

Lenny knew what he needed to do, at least for now: Keep a clear head, just sit back and wait and see what the reaction to this publicity stunt was. There was certainly a lot of press there. At least three network stations had cameras rolling. And from what he could tell, all of the other usual suspects were there as well. The whole range. From the New York Times keeping its above-the-cut readers informed, down to the scruffiest tabloids, trolling for body parts in the sewer.

For Lenny, at least for now, it was self-evident. Stay sharp, wait and see. Play the game. Let Chicago know they might be in for some bad press — and for very some serious shit if Mulcahey's appeal caught hold.

As he took the marble steps descending from the cathedral's main entrance two-at-a-time, hoping he could just jump in a taxi and be out of there, he heard her voice.

"What's your hurry, Lenny?"

Like the Good Old Days

"Fuck you, Alicia."

"You did. It was nice."

"Nice? It was *nice?*"

"Alright. It wasn't nice. Not nice at all. In fact it happened so fast, if I had coughed I would have missed the whole thing."

Lenny turned his back and continued down the steps at a brisk clip. Writ big and bold on his emergency message board in block letters was that if he didn't get the hell out of here right this minute, he'd be sent up for homicide. This broad had to be crazy even to come within a mile of him, much less try to make small talk.

Small talk? No. She was there to *mock* him. What could she be thinking?

"Lenny ... "

"Alicia. Are you outta your fucking skull? WHAT DO YOU WANT?"

"I ... I ..."

"Eye eye eye. An eye for an eye and a tooth for a tooth. Get away from me, you cunt."

"I'm sorry."

He turned and looked at her. Goddamn she was beautiful! But beautiful like a ballistic missile armed with a nuclear warhead. Elegantly functional. Agile. Sleek. The grace of parabolic flight. Rapture then chaos. The arc of destruction. You couldn't help but to push the button. Then run like hell for cover.

"Do you have any idea ... ?"

"Yes, Lenny. I've gotten bits and pieces. It sounded horrible."

"Alright, pumpkin. You said you're sorry. So everything is great now. It's a lovely day and the birds are singing. Now that you and I are back on lavender terms of endearment, tell you what. I really gotta go. See ya!"

"Lenny. I ... I want to talk to you. I mean, you were always messed up. Always into things you shouldn't have been into. But—"

"Where is this going? Here we had everything patched up, nice and sweet. I started to get the warm and fuzzies inside. And now what? You're bringing up that? Our illustrious educational experience back when. In that fucking prison they called a school. You may be real good on the eyes, Alicia, now that you're all grown up and filled out in the right places. But *you* are the one who is messed up. You were always messed up. And you still are."

"What are you talking about?"

"Just look at you. You dress like some cross between Paris Hilton, Rupaul and Dorothy Parker."

"You know who Dorothy Parker is?"

"And how do you spend your days? Exactly how do you spend your days, Alicia? I don't know for sure. But I can fucking imagine. Writing poetry and plotting the overthrow of the government. Chanting om with a vibrator up your ass. You've probably got a shrine to the Black Madonna and a freezer full of male genitalia. But thank the lord in high heaven that you came here today to tell *me* how sorry you are. Because that puts everything right back in place. Everything all better, mommy. Why it's just like the good old days. And I really can't thank you enough. I wish I could. But I can't. So can I fucking go now?"

"I didn't come here to see you. I came here because of Bishop Mulcahey."

"Oh yes. The Bishop. Glad you brought that up. Now there's a man I really admire. What an inspiring talk that was today. What the hell would we do without Bishop Mulcahey pontificating about returning the streets of Brooklyn to the delightful Garden of Paradise, family-fun playground they used to be back when? Get those filthy little Asian sluts off the sidewalk to make way for Mickey, Daffy and Donald, Big Bird and Dr. Seuss."

"You are so cynical. Do you know that? Do you? You don't … you don't … you don't have one caring bone in your whole body."

"Okay, stop! You've made it almost two minutes without me strangling you. Do you really want to keep pushing your luck?"

Despite her best effort, despite her wanting with every fiber, every single cell, to keep it together and put this asshole in his place, Alicia lost it. Lost it completely. All of her pent up anguish and frustration over losing the little boy she tried to adopt, the whole thing with Christine and the Djin Djin girls, plus a healthy dose of guilt about what had happened to Lenny as a result of her subterfuge, all of it came crashing down on her.

Alicia started to cry. She cried and cried and cried some more.

Lenny, not particularly given to sentimentalism, certainly not disposed to give a shit about someone who almost had him killed, stood there in anguished silence. He had never seen such pain written in the contorted face of such a beautiful woman. Maybe he'd never looked. There was no way he could avoid it now.

"Alicia … I don't know why I am doing this. But come with me."

Lenny could remember her back in high school. Yes, he had noticed her. On more than one occasion, she had put herself in his way, an obvious attempt to get his attention. He was such a ladies boy back then, convinced that every girl on the planet wanted a piece of the Lenny action. So Alicia's subtle and not very competent flirtation amused him, even feeding into whichever artery the ego juice syringe plunged itself. Another shot of the narcissism steroid for the young stud, the BMOC of P.S. 131. But beyond that, he was hardly tempted to do anything other than wink at her and give her a patronizing smirk. She was definitely not his type. There were so many others ripe for the picking, why should he bother with this rag doll?

Alicia was cute back then, but lacking any definition. She had no style. Everybody at school belonged to some clique, the mop head wannabe Brits, the hippies, retro rockers, the frats, yippies, the brains. But Alicia seemed to fall into the none-of-the-above, the miscellaneous group. The 'no match found' category. She was a scruffy doll left in the back of the closet, easily forgotten.

Lenny fancied that he himself was his own clique, a young man of such uniqueness and exclusivity, he made his own rules, set his own agenda, ran his own show. In one respect this was true. If nothing else, he was the founder, president and sole member of his own fan club.

Yet objectively speaking, the reality was that he fell squarely into a very specific, universally recognized and feared social group. This was a loose confederation of adolescents who were too headstrong, too independent, too guarded, and too anti-social to intentionally coalesce into a clique per se. These were the hoodlums, the troublemakers, the juvenile delinquents — the JDs, as the police and school administrators called them. And though they would aggressively tout their rejection of compromise and conformity, they had as many characteristic, high-visibility markings as any of the other cliques had. Black leather jackets, greasy hair combed back off the forehead, pointed leather boots, wife-beater t-shirts — as they would eventually become to be known — sometimes a tattoo high on the bicep. Their meticulously crafted personas were designed to provoke fear in everyone around them. When they walked down the halls of the high school, the others parted like the Red Sea before Moses. If they knew what was good for them, that is.

Even if Lenny had had one iota of interest in Alicia back then, which he didn't, there is absolutely no way he could have shown it. It would have been cosmically bad for his image. A death sentence: *'Lenny's with bottle-lenses? What a homo! What a total fucking loser!'*

But look at her now. She was breathtaking. Stylish. Truly a piece of fine art. Yes indeed! What a difference a few years makes. Growing up. Figuring it out. Becoming a person.

Face it. It was intimidating — looking at Alicia, then realizing where he was at. Running a cyber sex mall. Trafficking little girls. Living every moment in fear of upsetting the big boys in Chicago. Trapped. Pathetically a victim of his own shortsightedness. Ultimately a complete — and possibly soon dead — victim of his own undoing, if he got pulled any deeper into this messy business.

Lenny thought about the evening when he ran into her outside of Tony's. His heart had stopped. His brain had stopped. His dick took over. Wasn't that the way it always was?

Yes, what a class act you turned out to be, Lenny Petrocelli.

Admit it. You haven't changed a bit. You're still the egotistical little shit you were in high school, just a street punk. Only now you wear a tie to dinner.

As they walked, Alicia wiped her eyes, and blew her nose. Only to have to wipe her eyes and blow her nose again. She couldn't look at Lenny. She just kept mopping away all of the liquids pouring out.

As she continued the janitorial work on her face, she kept pace with Lenny. Then without thinking, she put her arm through his.

What's this?

In his mind's eye Lenny was shaking his head, rolling his eyes, and ferociously kicking himself in the head. What's next? Maybe they would go over and meet her parents. Then they could head for a chapel and tie the knot.

As was happening more and more frequently of late, he felt like he had no control over the situation he was in. Particularly no control over himself. This made no sense. He had always prided himself in being in charge. Was he just fooling himself? Massively delusional?

What a bizarre day this was turning out to be! First, sitting in a church. Second, sitting in a church listening to a man who he hated to the very core of his being. Third, going for a Sunday morning stroll, arm-in-arm with a woman who worked with the man who he hated to the very core of his being — a woman who, incidentally, had actually helped to arrange having him nearly tortured to death.

Lenny turned to look at Alicia. Just as she, with her handkerchief pressed to her nose, turned to look at him.

Now she had the hiccups. She still tried to talk.

Hiccup. "Lenny. I'm in no position to judge you." Hiccup.

"What did you have for lunch yesterday?"

Hiccup. "What are you talking about?" Hiccup.

"Just think about it. And tell me. What did you have for lunch yesterday?"

Hiccup. "Well. Let's see. I ate at Mollie's Deli. And … and I had an egg salad sandwich, with herb tea. And then for dessert I had a snickerdoodle."

"Okay. Your hiccups are gone."

She looked at him quizzically.

"You're right. How did you do that?"

"It's an old trick. If you put your mind to some task, it interrupts the synaptic misfirings that cause hiccups. So they go away."

"Lenny. You surprise me at every turn."

"I still hate you."

"Is that a problem?"

"Maybe not, Alicia. Maybe not."

Here we go again, thought Lenny. Here we go again.

Make a Wish

"Lenny, you need to talk to him. Just tell him what you told me."

He had taken her to a restaurant three blocks from the cathedral, one he knew would be open. Popular for post-worship munching across the spectrum of Christians in this part of town. Certainly not his own usual Sunday morning hang out.

The restaurant had both tables in the open and booths. They found some privacy in the back near the entrance to the kitchen in their own booth. Lenny was certain they could not be seen from the street, and it was highly unlikely anyone who knew him would come in to this place, especially on a Sunday morning. People he knew were just crawling *into* bed.

"I shouldn't even be talking to you, Alicia. What am I doing? I must be nuts. Nobody can help me. This is a stupid waste of time."

Lenny suddenly looked angry. His eyes burrowed deeply into Alicia's, with a look that signaled both confrontation and desperation.

"Why did you set me up, Alicia? Why did you get involved?"

"I thought I was doing the right thing. And I wanted to see you. "

"You wanted to see me? What's that supposed to mean?"

"Lenny. Let's not go there. Not right now. The Bishop is a good man."

"He is an insane, pompous, brutal, ruthless asshole!"

"I had no idea … I … I … he said he wanted to bring you in to talk. He needed to find out who was behind it. You know, the girls."

"Well, he could have just brought me in. He had his thugs. I'm not very hard to find. What was with the James Bond thing? The pretty girl seduction scene."

"Sometimes I'm so stupid. It wasn't the way I pictured it. I can't talk about it. It wasn't my best moment, Lenny."

"Alicia, listen to me now. No more games. No double-crosses. These people play for keeps."

"I know. I heard about what happened to those two guys. Bishop Mulcahey told me."

"You really want me to talk to that fucker. What makes you think he wants to talk to me?"

"You say you want out. He'll talk to you. He's a good man. He just wants to put a stop to what's going on. For everybody. For the community. For the girls."

"I'll think about it. But for now, I need to tow the line until I can figure what to do."

"Lenny, I want to make it up to you. I'm so sorry about what happened."

"Right right. You told me."

"Let me talk to him and maybe come up with an arrangement for you to meet."

"Alicia, just stay out of it for now. You'll live longer."

Lenny pulled out a pen, picked up a paper napkin and handed them to her. She wrote down her cell number and email address.

He slipped it into his shirt pocket.

"Keep your nose dry. I'll be in touch."

He was up and out the door before she could even say good-bye. Passing by, the waitress dropped the tab on the table and Alicia reached in her purse and fished out a $20 bill.

There was a single pale yellow daffodil in a small vase at the edge of the table. As she pulled out the last petal, she closed her eyes — and made a wish.

Chapter 10

MANAGEMENT DECISIONS: Building An Empire

In the Lapdance of Luxury

"You know that guy that made the Statue of Liberty disappear."

"You mean the magic guy? David Copperfield?"

"Yeah. David Copperfield. Well, looks like he been at it again. No other way to explain it. That boy been comin' around."

The world according to Shawna.

They were gone again. The Djin Djin girls. But so were the johns. That was the downside.

"I can't be wastin' my time no more. I'd be better doin' bottles and cans than standing here freezin' my butt off on this deserted street."

"Shawna honey, I hear ya like you was shoutin' it."

The warehouse fire was a blessing in disguise. Of course, there was the initial scrambling around to find them housing, making sure whoever had done it could not track them down and make another attempt on their lives. And it obviously meant that they would be off the streets for at least a short while. But what was initially thought would be just a few days, a week at tops, a mere pause in their routine, turned out to be a permanent rearrangement of their living and working habits.

The morning and afternoon of the fire, Ed Valley and Harold Danko were on the phone with everyone they knew in the four boroughs. In a full tilt rage, they initially tried to find out from the underworld grapevine — ever abuzz with rumors of varying reliability on who was up to no good — who was responsible for the blaze. They threatened, bribed, cajoled, and French licked anyone and everyone, but either no one had a clue as to who had torched the warehouse, or somehow a complete blackout had body-bagged all conversations on the matter. By late morning, they realized they were wasting their time, at least for now, trying to find their man. Revenge would have to wait.

Certainly, the more pressing matter was finding housing for the girls, preferably rooms located close to their regular street beats. These would have to have some semblance of built-in security or at least allow the boys Chicago had working it, to set up their own security detail. The two bodyguards from the warehouse, joined by three other of Chicago's trusted hired guns from Manhattan, were already keeping the girls out of sight and looking to put them under a roof of some sort for the day. Every decent but inexpensive hotel was being scouted and given the once-over.

By late afternoon, the girls were still disoriented and shaken by the traumatic ordeal, but safely tucked away, two to a room, in three rather rustic but clean hotels. Two were in Brooklyn itself, the other in Manhattan.

It was during the hiatus of the next few days that the lights went on for Harold and Ed.

The Djin Djin girls had been street-tested and were proving to be a goldmine. Wherever they dropped them, and they had set up similar operations in three other major cities as well — Seattle, San Francisco and Miami — they landed like a nuclear bomb, local competition sent scrambling, wondering what had hit them, the johns flocking to the new girls like hyenas to fresh carrion. Cash was piling up so fast, they had trouble keeping track of it all.

Of course, New York presented special challenges. The weather was turning cold. Within a few short weeks, that would put a serious crimp in their style. And threatening to undermine the whole undertaking, there was some maniac or competing organization out there popping the Djin Djins one by one. This warehouse fire was the latest attempt at Djin Djin cleansing. Here they were, forced now to tuck the girls away secretively in hotels. Money was being lost. The girls were sitting there, two-to-a-room on their beds, with absolutely nothing to do.

That's when the light bulb went on. When the floodlights smacked them. The blinding white light of an epiphany!

Why put them on the streets at all?

Why put them directly in the crosshairs of a killer?

Bring the customers to them! Set them up proper and nice, in relative luxury, make sure the doorman screens who comes and goes, and jack the prices up as high as the market will bear. From the reaction so far to these hot little numbers, it looked like they had a lot of room on the upside before they hit that ceiling.

Ed Valley's mind pumped as fast as his heart.

"Two to an apartment. Each has a bedroom, so you both girls can be working in privacy. But a lot of guys like the two-girl action thing. Bingo. There they are, ready to go."

"A lot of guys, eh?" Harold giving him a poke in the ribs. "I've heard about your two-girl parties, with a third working the handycam. But think about it, Ed. We've got everything we need at the computer shop. I mean, we been running the cyber sex thing for all these indie girls, taking what, 30% for running the switchboard."

"Twenty five."

"Twenty five per cent? That sucks. So now we run it all on cards and keep the whole ball of wax. Just pay expenses and give our little hairy ax wounds some spending money. They'll be much better off than they are now. Better yet, we don't have all this cash to dry clean."

"We can still play dispatcher for the white girls. It practically runs itself anyway. But we'll set up the Djin Djins as their own special thing. Nice website. Discrete paper ads. But only class stuff. None of that girly action shit you see on Broadway up by Times Square."

"This is gonna work big time, Ed. We are fucking geniuses!"

They put their boys to work — everyone but Lenny, who had no clue any of this was going on. Chicago had recruited and mobilized quite a little local militia. Taking care of both military and civilian matters. When the time was right, they'd let Lenny know. When they needed something.

For now the girls could just sit tight.

Until things got done properly.

With class and style.

Two-by-two, over the next week or so, they were moved into condos and flats. To see the smooth young faces of the Djin Djins light up when they saw their new digs would warm the heart of a card-carrying curmudgeon. Completely and elegantly furnished, all of the apartments had beautiful fine art prints on the walls, living rooms with big cozy loveseats and overstuffed pillows on the floor, luxurious bedroom suites, some with mirror-lined canopies over four-post beds, all with plush satin duvets and an assortment of cushy pillows. Each of the bedrooms had its own high-quality stereo to provide amorous background music. Some suites even had jacuzzis in the bathroom for water play and aqueous sex.

Slowly over the next few weeks, the Djin Djins would have their wardrobes of hot flashy street clothes complemented with some Playboy Mansion lingerie, lacey negligées, feathery body veils, sheer baby dolls, and delicious panties. They even threw in some latex and leather, for the borderline kinky.

Ed and Harold were beside themselves with excitement. They were on a roll. This was a whole new phase.

No more boom-boom fucky fucky sex for these girls. This was going to be the best high-end Asian pussy money could buy. They would provide a no-rush hour of eroticism that would keep the hungry boys coming back for more. At a 1000 to 2000 dollars a pop.

If you could say nothing else "nice" about Harold and Ed, it had to be conceded that they were geniuses at spotting opportunity and capitalizing on it. Masters at snatching millions from the jaws of potential catastrophe.

Yes indeed, the fire turned out to be a wake-up call alright. Loud and clear. Like the clanging of the opening bell on Wall Street. Fortunes to be made here. Come and get it.

Spread the risk.

Spread the wealth.

Spread 'em wide, baby.

The Cookie Crumbles

Lenny was nervous.

No … nervous didn't quite get there.

He was very frightened. Not a feeling he often had to deal with.

The Nipponese Agent of Charm, Yoshikaze, showed up unannounced at Lenny's flat, two airline tickets in hand. No explanation.

"Let's go. No need to pack. We'll be coming right back."

In the first place, how did the Jap know he'd be home? Was he staking out the place?

"Right back?"

Lenny scrutinized his face. Just a smirk. Behind that, a slate wall. No clues as to his fate.

As they checked in at LaGuardia, Lenny saw where they were headed.

St. Louis. Stopping in Charlotte, North Carolina. They'd be there in a little over five hours.

Uneventful flight. Lenny just stared at the in-flight television monitor most of the way. Without the sound.

They landed with a thud, in a rancorous cross wind.

Yoshikaze led the way out of the terminal. In a few minutes a black Lexus LS 460 pulled up. The driver, a big guy with a long scar down his left cheek, got in the back, and Yoshikaze took over the wheel.

Forty minutes later the car squealed to a stop in front of a large institutional building, bricks and mortar.

They jumped out. Yoshikaze opened the door at the entrance and led the way down a long hall. They were in a school that had apparently closed down. Somewhere out in the bland suburbs of St. Louis.

There was Harold Danko and Ed Valley.

If looks could kill.

Behind them, sitting on the floor surrounded by duffel bags, overcoats, scarves and various other apparel, were over thirty Asian girls. Not exactly girls. Women.

Spit flew out of Harold's mouth as he spoke.

"What the fuck are you doin' to us, Lenny?"

In a grand sweep of his arm, Harold took in all the Asians. They sat looking frightened. Some hugged their knees desperately trying to avoid being noticed. Several were sobbing.

"What am I looking at?"

"You should recognize at least some of them. Dok says you tried to fuck half of them before your dick finally died."

"Dok? What … ?"

"Come on, Lenny. We're out over 250 Gs. I don't have time to play games. If this isn't the scaggiest, most pathetic bunch of twats I have ever seen, I don't know what."

Walking over to a thirty something woman with a lazy eye, thinning hair, and acne-pocked complexion.

"Is this one you tried to fuck? Did you even look at this puss? For cryin' out loud, Lenny!"

Harold continued stepping over bodies to single out a particularly emaciated creature whose mouth dropped open when she winced, to show a very discolored set of teeth. He yanked her to her feet and she started to whimper.

"Tits, Lenny. Have you heard of tits? This one looks like she was she was put through the planing saw at a lumber mill."

Valley came up on the other side of Lenny, shaking his head. "Why, I wouldn't screw any of these girls with someone else's dick. We counted on you Lenny. What were you thinkin'?"

"I never saw any of these girls. The girls I saw were incredibly beautiful. Some of the most beautiful little Asian babes I'd ever seen."

"Right, Stevie Wonder. Has your terminal case of myopia maybe cleared enough for you to explain this collection of losers? What exactly are we supposed to do with this herd? It's not like throwing out a pair of house slippers."

"I ... uh ..."

"Well, I'll tell you what. The ball's in your court. You're responsible for them now."

"What do you mean? I don't understand."

"You'll understand soon enough. But for now ..."

Harold glanced at Yoshikaze and jerked his thumb. Yoshikaze roughly took Lenny by the arm and hurried him out of the room. They headed back to the Lexus LS 460 they had arrived in.

"Nice work, Lucky Lenny."

"Listen, Japboy. Keep your smart comments to yourself."

Yoshikaze looked at Lenny. An acrimonious heat burned in his slitty eyes.

Pure spite. The caustic lye of disdain.

Yellow Trash

Yoshikaze never broke the silence on either the plane or during the car rides, for the entire eight hours it took to get back to Brooklyn.

Lenny got out of the black Infiniti and didn't look back as he approached the entrance to his flat. Yoshikaze squealed away.

Something didn't sit right. The screen door was open slightly and hanging a little crooked, like it had been partially wrenched from its aluminum hinges.

When Lenny stepped inside, he could see immediately what had happened. The place looked like a tornado had hit full force. Everything that had been shelved or in drawers was strewn all over the floor. Even his refrigerator, which was tipped onto its side, had been emptied, bottles of ketchup and relish, salad dressing and beer lay shattered on the linoleum. His bed was upside down. Dresser drawers dumped and apparently thrown violently at the walls, which showed fresh gouge marks and crumbling plaster at the impact points. His closet had been evacuated, shirts, pants, suits and jackets piled on the floor. It looked like the pockets had been methodically searched, many of them still inside out.

Who would bother trying to rob him? It's not like he had anything worth stealing. Or were they looking for something specific?

Jesus Christ, what a mess!

Should he report this?

Right.

Like Fiori and company would give a shit. Who knows? Maybe it was them.

No. He'd have to figure this out himself.

For the next two days, Lenny put his place back together and tried to see what was missing. That was the strange thing. Nothing seemed to be gone. It definitely wasn't a burglary. Whoever was in here had passed on the few things that could be quickly fenced for an emergency fix in a local shooting gallery.

No. They were looking for something.

But what?

Then something struck him. He was gone for less than 24 hours and in that short time his place had been ransacked. Coincidence? Only Chicago knew he'd be away.

What was going on? Would they do this? Why? Was he on the outs now?

One thing for sure, judging from what happened in St. Louis: They were sure pissed at him.

But then again, they didn't mince words or 'equivocate', to use their term. If he was on their hit list, there wouldn't have been an all-expense-paid trip to St. Louis. They would've just popped him.

His head was swimming with possibilities. Nothing made any sense.

One thing was certain. He was in deep shit. He needed to think. Maybe he needed to hide.

But who from?

Lenny threw on his heavy leather jacket and went for a walk. It was getting on into the evening. He couldn't help but notice that the weather was beginning to take a serious turn. North. Brrr! Here it was only November and already it was starting to feel like winter. Thought they said the Earth was warming up. Maybe that was the rest of the planet. New York? Definitely in its own world.

He wasn't quite sure where he was going. But maybe some fresh air and exercise would help clear his mind.

As he passed a newsstand, he noticed the late afternoon edition of the Post had a headline about some sort of protest rally this weekend ...

BIG MARCH in Brooklyn Saturday!!

What now? Were the peace creeps at it again?

What a fucked up world. We'll never get it right.

Suddenly it occurred to Lenny. He hadn't been to his old haunt lately. Tony's! Ten minutes walk to a cerebral holiday. He could use some lubrication for his thinking machine.

When he entered, there were only five customers in the bar. A young couple at one table. Three guys who looked like they had just gotten off work and were stopping for a quick one. Probably construction workers.

Tony spotted him immediately and gave him a larger-than-life welcome.

"Well! Look who dropped out of the sky! Lucky Lenny, the invisible man. How ya doin', my eye-talian stallion? You're lookin' sharp!"

"Tony. Master of mixology and spiritual advisor to the none-the-wiser. Thought you would have moved this place over to Park Avenue by now. But glad to see ya here. Mighty glad."

"So whad'll you have. The usual?"

"Tony." Lenny venturing his best Al Pacino. "You know what Winston Churchill said? Mr. Winston said, 'Change is the master key.' So tonight I say,

167

we're going where no man has dared go before. Pioneers in the quest for the ultimate imbibing experience."

"You're the boss."

"So tell me, what's foamy? Both sweet and sour. With a blue tint. Chunks of tropical fruit. Bites like a dog and purrs like a kitten."

"A Tahitian Rob Roy, made with Windex and green tea, a cherry lifesaver, and just for you, some anabolic steroids and Prozac thrown in for a nutritional spike."

"You read my mind. You truly are a genius. Stephen Hawking with a fruit blender."

Tony plopped a shot of Cutty Sark and a bottle of Mickey's on the bar.

"So where ya been? Last time I saw you with some Japanese guy. Looked like trouble."

"Oh him? Nah. Just showin' me something related to business. Haven't been around much. They have me traveling all over. Got a bit of a promotion. It's keeping me busy."

"So, you makin' some good bucks?"

"That's what they tell me. We'll see. What's breeding around here?"

"Are you going to the march? Big news around town, you know. You should go. You'll see everyone you don't know. The Tony's regulars are gonna be there. For them, it's just another excuse to start drinking early."

"You know, I'm kinda out of the loop. But I did see a headline. What's this all about?"

"Mulcahey. You know, the Bishop?"

"Yeah, I know him. Not personally."

"There's been this invasion of sweet street stuff, hot little Asian girls, and it's got everybody up in arms. Plus, three of them got snuffed. Three murders, bam bam bam. Very violent. Anyway, Mulcahey wants to clean up the neighborhood. So he's got this big march planned. I think it's like 12 noon on Saturday. Really. You should go, Lenny. You could probably pick up some nice ass there."

"That's my Tony. Always thinkin'."

"Saturday afternoons are slow. I'm pretty sure I'll go. Maybe I'll see you. We'll be a team."

A new patron, an old man with a tattered wool coat which was much too big for his slight, buckled frame, came in. His bulky work shoes had no laces and were the worse for wear. His long greasy hair stuck out in every direction from under a filthy wool aviator hat. He had at least a week's worth of salt and pepper stubble and extremely dark bags under his rheumy, jaundiced eyes.

Lenny leaned to Tony confidentially. "Didn't know you took American Express here."

"We'll take anything. We'll even trade furs and hides."

Either the guy's motor control was severely compromised by age, or he was already three sheets to the wind. Tony eyeballed the creaky old man closely, as he shuffled toward the other end of the bar. When he finally maneuvered himself onto a stool, Tony went over to serve him. After a long struggle to understand what the old guy was saying, Tony poured him what appeared to be a stiff double shot of whiskey. Straight up.

He glanced over at Lenny, with the archetypal expression of Tony stoicism.

Lenny stood up.

"Tony my man. I better be going." Extremely bad Arnold Schwartzenegger. "I'll be back."

With a quick shift in the cinematic metaphor, Tony stepped out from behind the bar like a cowpoke, hooked his thumbs in his pants, and copped a slippery southern drawl.

"You ain't leavin', mister. We gots business to settle."

"Sez who? You and what cavalry, dead man."

They square off.

Lenny has both of his hands dangled out at his sides, fingers wiggling in anticipation of the draw.

"Yew sheer yew wants to dew this? Yew ain't be knowin' wutcha dealin' with here, son."

"Shore as the sun do come up. Ay-nee times you be raidy, stranger."

They draw.

Tony acts like his gun has been shot out of his hand. Lenny blows the end of his barrel and re-holsters his Colt.

"Why … why I ain't never seen anyone as fast as you! You be like lightnin' wit' that gun!"

"That's right. You tell 'em. You tell 'em real good." Lenny theatrically grabs his crotch. "I'm the biggest, the baddest, the fastest. Nobody can touch this barrel … 'n less I lets 'em."

The old man had been staring in rapt attention at the exchange, mouth drooped open, purple tongue lapping at the air like a thirsty dog. He was craning so hard and concentrating so completely on what was going on, he suddenly lost his balance and fell off of the stool.

Tony rushed over to help him up.

"Tell 'em Lucky Lenny is in town."

Lenny tipped his invisible cowboy hat and took wide bowlegged strides into the street, pushing the imaginary panels of the saloon door out of his way as he left.

As soon as he got out, his mood went 180°, his face now tense and anxious.

So much for the calming effects of alcohol.

He recalled that among other things, he'd never reported back to Chicago about the sermon. Everything was happening so fast. Then running into Alicia. He had become so preoccupied with trying figure out how he was going to make an unobtrusive and graceful exit from the messy situation he was trapped in, he hadn't gotten around to deciding exactly what he should say about Mulcahey, then calling in his report to them.

To complicate things, there was going to be this new event on Saturday. Big press. Big media glare.

This was certain to bring some heat. He needed to warn Ed and Harold. Soon. But when?

Another realization smacked him hard. He couldn't think about contacting the Bishop. Not now. Maybe never. It would be suicidal. He would forever be haunted by the image of Frankie and Martin, in the warehouse decapitated.

He saw a taxi approaching and ducked his head to see if it was empty. It was. The driver pulled to the curb and Lenny got in.

"What time is it?"

"My sundial says 9:30, sir. Where can I take you?"

"Not that far. Turner and 6th Street. Hey! You're American."

"Born and raised. Right here. Why?"

"Oh … just … lately …"

"Nope. I'm not al Qaeda. Not an Arab, like 90% of the others. They're okay, though. They're just trying to make a living. Some of my best friends are towelheads."

They both laughed.

Eight minutes and here they were. He handed the driver a ten.

It was a little early. But when Lenny got out, the action was already pretty thick.

Actually, there wasn't any "action" to speak of. But there were a lot of girls. On both sides of the streets. In the entranceways to businesses closed for the evening. Under street lamps. Cruising the curbs.

Something was off. The Djin Djins usually dressed a lot flashier.

He approached three who were leaning against the window of a leather goods store.

Whoa! Not exactly beauty contest material. In fact, they were rather unappealing. Maybe in their 30s. Not fat but certainly not lithe or sensuous. Borderline ugly by hooker standards.

"Mr. Pet … Petro … "

"You know me?"

"Yes. You boss. We know. See?"

She reached into her tiny purse, a shiny vinyl thing, which was the only decent item in her otherwise pedestrian apparel, and pulled out a piece of paper. On the front was a photo.

It was him.

On the back was written 'Lenny Petrocelli' and his cell phone number.

"Are you … are you Djin Djin girls?"

"Din din? No understand. We just saw. You at school with two big boss."

Lenny handed the photo back and walked further on up the sidewalk. And spotted them. Two he *did* recognize from St. Louis. The "no tits" girl, and the one with the history of acne.

They were here. He was their boss.

He recalled the words of Ed Valley.

You're responsible for them now … you'll understand soon enough.

He understood alright. Everything made sense now. This was the storefront. He was the manager in charge.

They were covering their asses. He was the fall guy. If anything went down, and it always eventually did with these things, he'd be the one to take the heat. They would be invisible. And they'd just sail over it like nothing had happened. Move on to something better. Unbelievable. What now?

And where were the Djin Djin girls? Maybe they had *already* moved on to something better.

"Whitey! Didja ever find that little boy you was lookin' for? Your skinny little boy fuck?"

It was the big one. With the big mouth.

"Good evening, miss ... uh ..."

"Lady Shawna to you, wiggah."

"You're lookin' good. Have you been going to the gym?"

"Sweet talk all you want." Licks her middle finger and runs it seductively across her crotch. "You're out of luck. This here honeypot is closed for business. For you, anyway."

"So, what's goin' on here? Looks like some new kids on the block, eh?"

"You're so full of shit! You know what's goin' down. Knew all along. I gotta say, though, one thing's for sure. Pimpin' ain't what it used to be. Cuz you are one sorry-ass, pathetic excuse for a pimp if I ever saw one. Why, a 'ho would be better off with Pee Wee Herman. At least he got a pud to pull."

"What exactly are you talking about? Or are you just blowin' gas? Which you seem to have in abundance."

"Soons as I see that picture, I says to Lilly 'Well lick my ass! That's that empty sack boy scout that was hanging out here by the bus stop a few weeks ago.' You sure had me fooled. Here I thought you was gonna hand me the latest Watchtower magazine. And look at you! Yo! Mr. Big-Fuckin-Deal, in charge of all this yummy Asian pussy. Surprise surprise."

With what was becoming a more and more frequent occurrence lately, Lenny was speechless. Every turn seemed to be fraught with some completely unexpected and paralyzing surprise.

"But I must say this is a new twist, Bruce."

She was on a role.

"Yes?"

"These new chinky-chinks. Not exactly championship material. I done heard of white trash before. But I never in all my days ever hear of yellow trash! What exactly is the plan, Stan?"

Lenny paused, then spoke with the sincerity of a beauty queen contestant.

"I came down here tonight for one reason and one reason alone. And that's to take my cream dream paradise angel girl on the Love Boat to Fantasy Island to live happily ever after in the hairy hammock of my heart. Lady Shawna, that girl is you! Yes, sweet pie ... you! Come here to daddy and tell me you love me. That's the plan."

He held out his arms wide, closed his eyes, and puckered his mouth.

Shawna broke into a laugh that could be heard in the far side of the Bronx. She laughed and laughed. Finally before turning to go, she managed to calm her quaking, jellybag of a body enough to say something.

She batted her big false eyelashes at him.

"Can I wear yellow?"

Chicago on the phone.

"Got it covered. I'll be there."

Like he had a choice.

Lenny absolutely did not want to go to the rally. What was the point? Speeches. Yelling. He hated big crowds, unless it was a ballgame.

This was a prescription for disaster.

But he'd be there.

At Chicago's bidding.

Good boy. Sit up. Roll over.

Now play dead.

At the rate he was going he might not have to fake that last one.

Saturday came way too soon. He decided to arrive early to scope out the scene, and most importantly, find a spot where hopefully he could see and hear everything without being noticed himself.

He got to the front steps of the cathedral, where the initial speeches would take place, and from which the march would proceed to the heart of the Djin Djin enterprise zone. He was about forty minutes early and was surprised how many people were there already. Some were clustered in small groups and chatted away in the clear air of a crisp autumn day, while others put finishing touches on their signs. Some watched expectantly for the arrival of their friends.

The placards ranged from the predictable to the pious to the bizarre. Many featured quotes from the Bible or the kind of slogans one would expect:

God Loves All

Take Back Our Streets

It Takes A Village To Raise A Child

The Sixth Commandment Forbids Promiscuity

A Woman's Body Is God's Temple

Let Us Pray

There Is No Bar Code On Flesh

'Thou shalt not bring the hire of a whore…into the house
of the Lord thy God' – Deuteronomy 23:18

Others struggled for relevance or coherence or both:

Fornicators Are Sheep

Not One Man Ten Whores

What About Mary Magdalene?

Virgin Mary Virgin Jesus

Sodom and Tomorrow

Blame MTV

Save It - Join VWV (Virgins With Vibrators)

One-Way Ticket 2 Hell Half-Price

Can U Spell c-o-n-D-U-M-B?

After surveying the area for maybe twenty minutes, he found what he judged to be the perfect spot. It was kitty-corner from the cathedral with a clear view of the speakers podium. Looked like a tailor's shop from the piles of clothing he could see through the front window. There was a recessed doorway and a thick support pole in the middle of the entranceway, which he could slip behind and be largely out of sight. The march should go right past him, so he would be perfectly positioned to see everyone participating.

As these things usually go, it started over a half-hour late. Then the speeches droned on and on, each speaker scaling the towering battlements of outrage and indignation, slathering huge gobs of self-righteousness on themselves and the attendees of the march, who had to do a lot of heavy lifting on their own just to remain attentive and not appear rude or restless.

Lenny was at first surprised that the Bishop was not among the initial speakers, but then he overheard someone say that Mulcahey was going to close out the march at the other end with his address. There certainly was no shortage of politicos, community leaders, and various celebrities who wanted to ante up their own loose pocket change of indignation and contempt, perhaps chalking up a few photo ops and other PR dividends in the process. The podium was a revolving door of head-shaking, finger-wagging proselytes, calling and raising the bets of the preceding orators, without a merciful end in sight.

Finally, one tall bearded man in the center of the crowd fairly close to the podium, turned around and spontaneously started to lead a yell ...

Djin Djin, send 'em back, send 'em back to Thailand
Djin Djin, send 'em back, send 'em back to Thailand ...

He had a loud voice and the force of his confident leadership was the catalyst which unleashed the crowd's latent but building impatience. People quickly picked up the rhythm of the chant, and waving their protest signs high in the air, turned around and started moving en masse. The march was underway.

For some reason, they headed in the opposite direction Lenny had expected. There were police in both regular uniforms and riot gear positioned all around.

They seemed to subliminally guide the flow. Perhaps the parade permit was very specific about the path the march should take. This was a hot issue. And an extremely high-visibility public protest. They weren't taking any chances.

Whatever the case, if he actually intended to monitor this thing for Chicago, Lenny now found himself in the worst spot he could be in. The crowd was walking away from him and he couldn't see anything but the backs of a multitude of heads some fifty yards away.

He had no choice but to come out of his safe little spot and catch up with the river of bodies, walking and chanting their way down the center of the street. He made a beeline for the rear of the mob, taking the opportunity as he approached them, to turn up the collar of his coat. He figured that maybe if he tucked his head into the turtle shell of his duffel coat, no one would pay any attention to him.

The opposite turned out to be the case.

He drew looks from several of those in his immediate proximity, who were concerned that he was either some over-zealous undercover cop, or maybe some creep with a psychotic agenda. One guy actually grabbed Lenny's arm and forced him to turn so that he could look at Lenny's face. He looked like he could be a college student. But considerably older. Late 20s. Long hair and wispy beard. Cap with a Michael Moore *Fahrenheit 911* logo.

"What are you doing here?"

"Bad thing, these prostitutes on our streets."

"Right."

"Everybody's got to stand up and be heard. So here I am."

"Right."

Lenny glanced over ever so briefly and noticed the guy was walking with a friend, who was a tall Arian dude with dreadlocks and big spacers in his earlobes, the combined effect making him look like some sort of albino tribesman. He pulled a pipe out of his shirt pocket, apparently preloaded and ready to go. Soon the scent of marijuana mixed with the usual smells of the city, auto and bus exhaust, and ambient grime.

The stairway to heaven provided by the ganja considerably mellowed the guy who had just been so suspicious. Now he sidled up to Lenny.

"I'm not so sure about all of this. I mean, granted I got two kids. One's a girl and I sure don't want her to end up being a hooker. But I don't think it's like the worse thing in the world. They always say, the world's oldest profession. If they would just play it a little cool. You know, stay out of sight."

Lenny gave him a thorough once-over to see if he was serious. Definitely seriously stoned.

Lenny politely declined a hit from the pipe, then replied. "It's a fucked-up life. These Asian chicks didn't choose this."

"Whaddya mean?"

"They're slaves. They are owned by the people who make all the money. And forced to do it whether they like it or not."

"You seem to know a lot about this."

"You could say that."

As the crowd moved along, Lenny started to relax. Who was going to see him? It's not like he was a known quantity in these parts. He still pretty much kept to himself. The invisible man.

"You fucking asshole!"

A woman's voice. From the sidewalk. It sounded familiar.

Then pushing through the crowd, there she was. Decked out like she was going to the Fashion Institute of Technology's annual new designer show.

Alicia.

"You said you wanted out! Lying bastard. I know what you're up to."

The guy next to Lenny gave him a whoa-dude look, then smirked. "Friend of yours?"

She was all over him. And waving something in her hand.

Oh my God! It was one of the pictures that the new ugly Asian girls were carrying around. The one with his name and cell phone number on the back. Where the hell did she get that?

"The irony of it all. The fucking audacity. What the hell are you doing here, Lenny?"

"The same as you, Alicia."

"You're writing an article for the Poughkeepsie Journal?"

"Well not—"

"Fucking hypocrite!" She tried to wail on him but her thin arms flailed in the swarms of material she had layered under her ankle-length purple cape.

Lenny backed away but Alicia determined to cause him damage one way or another turned and addressed those in her immediate proximity.

"Do you know who this man is? This slimy bastard right here?"

"Alicia, don't!"

"This is the guy who runs these girls. The very same ones we're marching about."

Runs these girls. No one seemed to get it. They were transfixed by her anger and intensity, but confused about what she was saying.

Lenny suddenly realized that this could turn ugly. He needed to get out of here immediately. He backed away, turned, then started running back toward the cathedral, hoping he could find some place in the vicinity to duck into and hide, if necessary. He looked over his shoulder and could see the crowd had closed circle with Alicia as she pointed to the photo and apparently explained its significance. She made a dramatic gesture in his direction.

Three or four guys took off after him. Fortunately, he had a good head start. But now he'd most certainly have to disappear somehow.

There were a couple of fast food restaurants on the next block. Maybe he could cut through. He pumped his legs as hard as he could and could feel his lungs start to burn. It was times like these that he realized what pathetic shape he was in.

When he reached the first place, a tiny self-serve deli, he realized that his pursuers would see him if he went in, so he kept on running. He reached the next intersection and turned right. As luck would have it, only three doors down was a small pizza shop, the kind that had no stools and looked like the inside of an Airstream camping trailer.

Damn. No back door.

Behind the counter was a short, stocky, Italian man, dressed in an oversized white apron, abundantly stained with red pizza sauce. His eyebrows arched under a billowing paper chef's hat, filthy from weeks of wear, as Lenny jumped behind the counter and crouched down out of sight. Before the man could even react or decide if this was a holdup or just another typical encounter with an anonymous psycho, Lenny reached back and pulled out his wallet, then waved a $100 bill.

The sound of feet pounding pavement.

One of the pursuers stopped abruptly and stuck his face in the shop.

"Did a guy just … ?"

Then he noticed how small the place was. There definitely was no way out.

"Never mind."

The pursuer was gone. Lenny looked up just as the man snatched the hundred bucks out of Lenny's hand.

"You can stay down there if you want, until you're sure they won't come back. Do you want a slice of pizza?"

"Thanks. But I'm not feeling too hungry right now."

"Have it your way. But it's the best pizza in Brooklyn."

"I'm sure it is."

Five or six minutes passed. His pursuers must have kept going.

Lenny slowly got to his feet. His hands, dark coat and black pants had big patches of flour on them, which Lenny tried with little success to brush away.

Thumbs up to the pizza man. "Thanks. I'll recommend your pizza to the Pope next time we get together for some poker."

The man gave a puzzled look, then went back to making pizza dough.

Lenny cautiously stuck his head out and looked both ways. All clear.

Now what?

Should he make a big circle and stake out the area where the rally would terminate? At this point, he didn't have much to report to Chicago.

Wait.

What was he thinking?

This was all a big sham. Chicago had the whole of Brooklyn, certainly the area where the girls worked, crawling with their own people. Well, maybe not crawling. But they had it covered. They had their moles and militia.

Which raised the question: Why were they sending *him* there?

Fall guy. Fall guy. Wasn't it obvious?

He had to keep a clear head and constantly remind himself. He had to bear in mind, regardless of what they said to him on the phone or wherever, what was really going on. He was the beard. When the bill came for dinner, he'd be paying.

Think about it. They had his picture all over the streets. Any one of the new girls could identify him. It was only surprising they had not taken out some full-size billboard ads.

Want some HOT ASIAN action?
Call 'Lucky Len' Petrocelli.
He'll fix you up right!

Chicago never let him in on anything. Just gave him vague directions and hints about what he should be doing there in Brooklyn. It was like being in one of those murder mystery plays. Except everyone else knew who the killer was. He was the only dumb fuck in the room.

Now what?

Play it straight. Talk to Chicago. Be a good boy scout. Wide-eyed and ready to please. While he was doing that, he'd try to figure out exactly how to extricate himself from this horrible mess he was in, one that only promised a lot of prison time or would severely shorten his life span.

It suddenly occurred to him what his next move should be. Chicago wants a report. He'd give it to them. He'd give it to them *in person*. That was the ticket.

But he needed to take care of something first.

Alicia.

How long did it take to survey his vast collection of friends and come up with a list of everyone he could trust? Let's see. About one second.

Alicia was the only one.

If the truth be known, he had no real friends. Only business associates. And they were all connected one way or another to Chicago.

At least Alicia was someone who apparently would listen and understand and empathize. Lenny could not fathom why it was so, but under all her hostility and contempt for him, she seemed after all these years to still like him. That was what he sensed and surmised, after that little breakfast they shared following the Bishop's dreadful sermon. She even offered to talk to the Bishop. To try to help Lenny find a way out.

That, of course, was before this last incident. This time they hadn't exactly parted on great terms.

He needed to straighten this out. Immediately! He needed to convince the one person who he felt might be able to offer some elusive hope, some opening, some potential solution, that the whole 'pimping' business was a horrible misunderstanding, that he was being set up. Then see where that might lead.

Lenny took a taxi back to his place. He'd call her this evening.

Where was her number? She had written it down on a paper napkin.

He started to look for it. And kept thinking about the two days he had spent cleaning up his apartment from the burglary, trying to recall where he had put it. Had he seen it at all? He had made a stack of notes, mail, letters, and put them in the top center drawer of his desk. Over and over he went through them. Then he looked everywhere else. Behind the desk, under the dresser. He even moved the bed. Then went through the living room. Even the kitchen.

Through all of this, he still puzzled what they had been looking for when they turned his place upside down. What, after all of that searching, was missing?

He couldn't think of a single item. Except one.

The paper napkin.

The Bully Pulpit – Part II

The march was more successful than anyone had imagined possible. While only an estimated 500 people actually participated, it happened to take place on a weekend when there was a dearth of sensational news stories at both the national and local level.

There was only one minor altercation, that occurring between some teenagers and, as the press described him, a "holy man" who was dressed like one of the apostles and wandered along the parade route offering baptisms to any takers. The incident was unrelated to the subject matter of the march and dismissed as unruly adolescent behavior. Three boys were reprimanded by police at the scene but not taken into custody.

Otherwise, the march proceeded quite smoothly. The marchers themselves appeared to cover all age groups from toddlers to retirees, and to be, as they say, from all walks of life. They kept the mood upbeat with chants and cheers, occasionally breaking into familiar hymns from their Sunday service hymnals. There were no hecklers to speak of, just the occasional drunk or loony, and the sidewalks were sprinkled with casual well-wishers, enthusiastic supporters, and the idly curious.

After a little over thirty minutes of actual walking, they converged at the intersection which had become so notorious as the heart of nocturnal Djin Djin excess and success.

A sizeable speaker's platform had been erected on one corner, kitty corner from a newsstand, which benefited from the unusual event and did a brisk business. Large public address horns stood atop heavy-duty support tripods, and a sound engineer sat behind the board of an oversized mixing console at the side of the stage.

A folk duo was performing as the marchers arrived. The crowd filled and milled in the intersection, which had been cordoned off and was being monitored by a substantial contingent of area police, including even two equestrian patrol officers. The singer, a tall girl with a floral wreath sitting on top of her waist-length blond hair, wearing a full-length tie-dye dress and a copious collection of shells and beads hanging from her neck and arms, screeched several songs of marginal relevance in a high punishing soprano voice. She was accompanied by an acoustic guitarist, who had a shaved head graffitied with seashell-shaped tattoos, and was incongruously dressed in a hooded 50 Cent pullover and baggie gangbanger pants. They fought their way through *Go Tell It On A Mountain*, *This Land Is Your Land*, and Joni Mitchell's *Sex Kills*, before trying to lead a completely uncooperative audience in an a cappella version of *We Shall Overcome*.

The official emcee thanked them with uncritical and unctuous enthusiasm and managed to wrench a smattering of applause from the audience. He spoke haltingly, stopping often times mid-sentence to clear his throat. His voice didn't project very well and when he attempted to manipulate the microphone to be better heard, he was rebuffed with painful screams of feedback. But good soldier that he was, he forged ahead.

"We all know (ahem) why we're here. And you don't (ahem) need to hear (ahem) any more preachin' to the choir, (ahem) as they say. I do want to (ahem) thank certain individuals who have (ahem) taken the time to be here, and (ahem) to (ahem) generously contribute their energy (ahem) to this cause."

He then went on to point out numerous important attendees. Some waved from the sidelines or came stage center for their nine seconds of fame. Others stood up from their seats at the rear of the platform. There were two rows of 12 or so folding chairs directly behind the podium, where a number of VIPs sat with anchorman smiles affixed to their faces, as they awaited the moment of recognition for their much-appreciated participation in the event. Captain Fiori was there, uniform cleaned and pressed, several commendation badges affixed above his breast pocket. The three plain Janes from the STD Prevention Center sat mop-like at one end. The chairperson of the newly established Ad Hoc Committee To Save Our Neighborhood, an obese woman in her late fifties, sat with her two younger assistants, between a caseworker from County Children Services and a deputy from the Sheriff's Department. Overall, it was a confusing assortment of official representatives on display, their relationship to one another and relevance to the march made more impenetrable by the emcee's consistent misidentification of their titles and departments, and his mispronouncing their names. No one quite knew when to stand up and take a bow because they often had no idea who he was introducing. After a final round of fumbling and apologizing, he got to the person everyone had been waiting for through the entire dragged out VIP ordeal.

"There is no reason (ahem) for me to say (ahem) much about our (ahem) next speaker. (Ahem) You all know (ahem) and admire him (ahem) for his vast, selfless (ahem) contributions to our (ahem) church and community. So without further ado (ahem), may I present the (ahem) esteemed Bishop (ahem) William F. Mulcahey."

The crowd's appreciation was evident as the Bishop stepped onto the stage and approached the podium. There seemed to be no end in sight for the waves of cheering and applause.

"Thank you. Thank you."

Someone in the rear of the audience started a chant: *Mulcahey, Mulcahey, Mulcahey* ...

"Thank you. Thank you for your warm reception. But most of all, let me personally thank each and every one of you for being here."

Thunderous self-congratulatory applause. The sound of backslapping.

"Indeed. For taking time out of you busy schedules, perhaps your much anticipated Saturday off from the hectic pace of the week, to be here in support of this worthy and important cause. God has a very special place in Heaven for those souls who selflessly continue the divine work of his Son here on Earth, for those whose compassion and caring drive them to make great personal sacrifices on behalf of their fellow man, those who know and live these words from the New Testament, Matthew 5:16 ...

'Let your light so shine before men, that they may see your good works, and glorify your Father which is in Heaven.' "

More applause from the audience. There was a subtle glint in his eyes, which revealed that the Bishop was quite pleased with the turnout and commitment of the people before him. But he maintained a solemn and stern demeanor.

"We all know why we are here. You don't need me to — if you'll excuse the term — pontificate here on what we all know to be true. This scourge which has descended on our community has to stop. And stop immediately."

Battle cries soared over the clapping of hands and cheers of approval.

"Let me be very candid with you. This is much worse than has been publicized." He paused for dramatic effect. "It wasn't three girls brutally murdered. It was four. I have it on good authority that the warehouse fire earlier this month, over in the 2nd Avenue industrial area, took the life of a fourth young girl. Now I ask you, why is it that I know about this but we see no mention of it in the papers? Why do we see nothing in the police records of the incident? Why is it that a priest just doing his job in one corner of Brooklyn seems to know more about what's going on here than the New York Times, NBC's Chuck Scarborough, and city hall?"

Hoots and the jeers of disbelief.

"I knew the girl. In fact I knew all four of them. How? Here is something else you won't read about in the papers. Or see on the nightly news. Two months ago, with the help of some brave men from right here in Brooklyn, I attempted to rescue the Asian girls, to get them off the streets and to safety. We hid them in the old convent right next to the cathedral. But before we could get any help from the government agencies to repatriate them, or at least find a safer haven for them, they were kidnapped and returned to their sordid lives of forced prostitution."

Murmurs of awe and shock.

"While they were there, yes, I got to talk with each of them. To hear their stories. To listen to them tell about their families, the villages they came from, how miserable and homesick they are. To pray with them and share with them both the words of Jesus, and the hope that they would not have to live out their days here in America doing what they had been doing.

"But as we know, they are back on the streets, and in a bargain that only benefits those responsible for this ugly and dehumanizing business, both we and these innocents are held hostage to the sinful and criminal behavior that degrades the community and robs spiritual life from all of us.

"I think I know who is running this operation. I don't mean just locally. I am certain that this insult to our community has been masterminded and is being administered from another major city here in the U. S. — that city being Chicago.

"No, I can't prove it, but yes, I do think I know who is responsible. Which adds yet another dimension to my determination to eradicate this plague — a highly personal one.

"Some of you may know this story, and while it pains me to talk about it, it is important here. When I was at St. Joan of Arc in Minneapolis, I was accused of molesting young boys. I was the victim of a smear campaign created to drive me out of the parish and out of Minneapolis. Of course, as has been demonstrated beyond any dispute, there was no truth to the rumors. But it did accomplish its goal of getting rid of me. Why? Why did someone want to get rid of me at that time? Well, there was a small but determined group of gangsters there who were flooding the streets with young girls, adolescent streetwalkers, and the neighborhoods where they worked, right there in my parish, were in a tailspin. Crime was up, and all of the horrible things that go with this kind of open sex trade, had the entire community up in arms. And a naïve, optimistic, perhaps foolish Father Mulcahey took them head on, went toe-to-toe with them in a battle to reclaim the streets for the good people of our parish.

"Does this sound familiar?"

The multitudinous voices of affirmation. Then the single voice of one man broke through with *Let's roll!*, the battle cry made famous by the 9-11 attacks. Immediately there was an outburst of copycat rejoinders and a general roar from the fired-up mob. The Bishop finally smiled. He calmly waited for the burst of enthusiasm to cool a bit before continuing.

"Anyway, I left Minneapolis. I was railroaded out by the thugs who wanted to use our streets, our community, as their own private domain to promote their shameful enterprise. But I was later completely exonerated and all of that is behind me now, a distant if unpleasant memory.

"The thing is, I believe, and again I have no proof ... not yet ... but I believe these are the same shady, ruthless people who now visit this same plague on us here in Brooklyn.

"But let me say this. Regardless of who is responsible, whether it's the evil men I was victimized by in Minneapolis, or someone else, let me make this clear. This is going to stop. This is going to stop and we will have our streets and our community back."

Whoops and hollers.

"Let it be said that the people of Brooklyn saw evil, that the people of Brooklyn stared down that evil, that the people of Brooklyn came together and marshaled all of the forces at their disposal and defeated this evil. This enemy of Christ Our Savior!"

More whoops and hollers.

"As your Bishop, as a member of this community, let me this day, this hour, this moment, make on behalf of everyone here today, a declaration of war.

"We declare war on this evil and we will prevail."

The crowd was now in a frenzy. The Bishop's oratory had captured the imagination of the most skeptical. Even curious bystanders were swept up in the tidal wave of his message.

181

"This is a holy war. A holy war on the unholy elements that have inflicted this community with a scourge which we will no longer tolerate, no longer bear.

"Make no mistake about it. It will be a fierce and vicious war. These men have no scruples, no morals. They recognize none of the boundaries of decency or honor you and I do. These men are protected by layers of thuggery, have their own little army of mercenaries running around doing their bidding, bullying and muscling, even killing those who stand in their way.

"I regret to say this, but these men are even shielded by layers of corruption within the offices of our trusted officials, within our own local government."

Captain Fiori shifted slightly in his chair and crossed the opposite leg.

"Again, I have no proof. But something smells very bad around here. Very bad indeed. There is a stench emanating from certain official buildings here right in Brooklyn. And I intend to find out where this stench is coming from."

The Bishop pointed at a cameraman who was standing slightly off to the side and gestured for him to come over directly in front of him.

"That's right. Point it right at me."

Glaring right into the camera, Mulcahey punctuated each point with a stab of his finger.

"We will find you. We will take you down. This is a war and it's a war we are going to win. A holy war in the name of decency, a holy war in the name of God, in the name of Jesus Christ. God is infinitely wise and infinitely just. He sees all and sees to all. You will not escape Divine Justice. That is for Him to decide.

"Now hear this. Whoever you are, you will not escape earthly justice either. That is for *us* to decide. And we have decided."

The crowd loved it. This was their Bishop and he was right out front leading the crusade. The battle lines had been drawn. This was a historic moment.

The Bishop now looked up and took in the entire audience. He raised his hands in a grand gesture, then slowly lowered them in a calming motion.

The consecrating warrior.

"Let us pray…"

Djin Djin Goes Viral

It was better than their wildest dreams.

They'd have to buy their own bank to have somewhere to put all the money.

It was no fluke. Harold and Ed had thought of everything.

They even hired a top notch public relations firm in New York to get the media thing handled. One that had some experience in flesh. High end porn. Deluxe escort services.

The best photographers and videographers were lined up. Locations weren't a problem. The girls had been set up in luxurious digs. Why not just film them there? It added to the excitement and allure to not only get a preview of the girls, but to see the lush environment which would host the erotic adventure. All part of building the fantasy. A customer might be paying a mighty dollar, but he would be Hugh Hefner for an hour he would never forget, and hopefully want to revisit again and again.

The shoots were easy enough. The girls were so incredibly beautiful and sexy-hot to begin with, it was just a matter of faithfully capturing them on film and video. The director of photography predictably was gay, but that proved to be the crowning asset. He was a man of impeccable taste with a stylish sense of restraint, which kept the visuals exquisitely sensual. He never gave it all away. There was abundant nudity but the kind that delivered just enough to make you want more. A complete complement of hair and make-up artists, lighting technicians, and top-of-the-line equipment produced a final product that would be the envy of many Hollywood professionals.

Once the photo and video shoots were done, the artistic director at the PR firm put his three best designers to work, to come up with an overall 'look', a visual statement that in print and especially on the web would set the Djin Djin girls apart from everything else out there, entirely in a class by themselves.

There are so many sex sites on the internet, from the crude and simple to the flashy and chic, this was no easy task. But these graphic artists were specialists in flesh-for-fantasy, true geniuses in their own right. Frankly, they really outdid themselves this time. The layouts were saturated with beauty and skin, charged with erotic energy and lustful invitation, yet glistening with panache and style. They even secured the rights for several music tracks from an internationally-renowned hip-hop producer, outtakes from a session he had recently done with Mariah Carey, as the bed music for the videos and website pages.

Harold and Ed were beyond themselves with awe and excitement, and looked with hungry fascination at the approval proof package. They could hear the ching ching of a choir of cash registers serenading them.

Ed looked like he had just taken a hit off a crack pipe. "Holy shit! This totally kicks ass! We really got our money's worth for a change."

Big thumbs up from Chicago. It was all systems go.

Now it was just a matter of implementing it, getting the sites up and running, throwing teaser print ads in some of the local entertainment rags. All of the final layouts, mpegs, stills, music tracks, and so on, were delivered to Markham, Chicago's sys-ad guru right there in Brooklyn. He would set up the necessary servers and seat the data files securely behind the partitions and firewalls already in place, integrate the credit card payment functions with their existing secured payments mechanism, then sit back and watch the river of money flowing ultimately into numbered bank accounts in the Cayman Islands.

When Markham received the site files, he immediately set to work. He assembled three new, streamlined, ultra-fast network servers from scratch, anticipating a high volume of curiosity surfing, legitimate queries, and of course, booking and payment. This was a robust addition to their already efficient cyber infrastructure, recognizing that Chicago would most likely want to rapidly grow the Djin Djin operation. Markham then spent several sleepless nights applying the necessary final technical touches, both to the hardware and software. This new business initiative was clearly very important to Harold and Ed, so it had to be failsafe and bulletproof. No tampering from the outside, no stealing of the graphics, videos, text, music, links — none of it. It also had to be invulnerable to the kind of glitches which crop up when computer illiterate or just plain stupid people did incomprehensibly dumb things. He looked at the rates being charged for the girls and knew there was way too much money at stake for the system to lock up or crash, even for a short while.

"Hey Keary, you gotta see this."

"This better be important. I'm playing Chaos Crusade against some guys in Hong Kong."

Kerry strolled over, crossing behind Miss Tourette's chair and sticking his index fingers into her armpits, sending her halfway under her workstation in a burst of giggle laughter.

He bent down to look over Markham's shoulder. "Zip-a-dee-doo-dah! How did you run across that? Good god, those girls are beautiful!"

The Djin Djin Girls ... better than you ever thought possible. Gifts from the erotic gardens of Thailand. This is us. Chicago's latest venture. I'm just getting the sites ready to go public. Should be online tomorrow."

"Hasn't there been a lot of press about them? A couple were murdered maybe or something. But I didn't know we were behind it. Did you?"

"Can't say I did. Not until I got these components last week. Pro stuff, eh? They could be selling fine art or rare antiques."

"Or an Angelina Jolie cloning kit!"

"Not quite."

"Sheets of Paris Hilton's toilet paper?"

"You are so brain dead."

"A channeling session with Anna Nicole Smith?"

"Keary, are you doing drugs again?"

"Is spirulina considered a drug?"

"Spirulina?"

"Yeah, everyone in my Live To Be A Hundred support group uses it. Man! There are some very hot women in their forties. Of course, I see a lot of the same ones at the Saturday night Nip-and-Tuck 4 The New You meeting."

"You of all people, handsome-hungry-young-sex-machine-runway-model that you are, why do you think you need cosmetic surgery? Or is this for some part of you not showing?"

"There have been no complaints down there. Freckles, man. I hate these fucking freckles!"

"Whatever. Tourette's doesn't seem to mind. Are you checking her oil?"

"She's got a nice edge. Very well-read. I'm getting tired of cry-me-a-river silly moo types. And she can suck the chrome off a trailer hitch."

"You are a truly sensitive guy. You're gonna make some girl very happy. The bad news is she will probably have serious immigration issues coming from the steppes of Kazakhstan. Anyway. Down to business. Chicago wants a whole set of separate books. On a discrete off-line computer. I have a new laptop coming. After I delete the games, it'll be all yours."

"Delete the games? Sadistic bitch!"

"You know deep down you love me."

The first three days djindjingirls.com went online saw only what could be characterized as random visits. Markham had installed site activity monitoring software which tracked every page and every component of the site. With a simple keystroke, it would generate elaborate charts which summarized right to that very moment, everything that had been going on — which girls drew the most attention, which photos got the most hits, how long a visitor spent on the site, whether he had bookmarked it, how many times he went back to look at something again. None of the advertising of djindjingirls.com was out yet, and no links from other sexually-oriented adult sites had been created. If anything it was surprising that there was any activity at all.

Then right before noon on the fourth day, things began to happen. The miracle of exponents. Five guys tell five guys who tell five others who tell … and so on. Pretty soon a casual tip offered at the water cooler in an office, or over the wall of a work cubicle, or an e-mail note that includes the hyperlink gets copied and forwarded, copied and forwarded, copied and forwarded. Soon like a nuclear reaction it heats up explosively and spreads. At the speed of light!

Markham first noticed that a couple of the other non-Djin Djin sites seemed to be responding sluggishly and thought that there was something wrong with their individual workstations. He ran a couple quick tests and determined that it was their T-1 connection to the internet for the entire facility that was bottlenecking for some reason. Part hunch and part logic nudged him over to the three Djin Djin workstations. He pulled up the traffic monitoring screen, punched in the command and almost fell over.

"Holy Mother Mary! There have been almost million hits in just the last three hours!"

Djin Djin fever was sweeping the global cyber community.

The first thing that was apparent to Markham was that they needed to beef up their thru-put immediately. No way could their present system configuration handle this. After getting the okay from Chicago, he called in an order for two more high-speed high-capacity T-1 lines. Then he ordered the components to assemble three more desktop computers.

He sat and watched as the numbers kept going up and up. Apparently, the Djin Djin girls were the new cyber celebrities of the hour, the Britney Spears of sex industry idol worship.

It was clear from the extremely high ratio of site visits to actual confirmed calendar entries for sexual services, that they were more the darlings of gawkers and cyber stalkers than paying customers.

Keary had his own analysis of it and was probably dead on. The Djin Djin site appealed to the tastes of the "soft core crowd", the ones who could spend hour upon hour looking at beautiful babes but couldn't handle or weren't particularly attracted to the hard core porno readily available these days at the click of a mouse. There were thousands of other soft core sites out there, but apparently djindjingirls.com had raised the bar into the stratosphere and the word was spreading fast.

This is not to say that there weren't a substantial number of very serious customers, sex shoppers apparently not in the least daunted by the upscale rates — $1000 basic donation (quickly upped to $1500) for one hour, $2000 for two hours, $8000 for the night and breakfast in bed. There were. Calendars were filling up fast, out two months and beyond. It was a gourmet feeding frenzy.

The significance of this Djin Djin mania was not lost on Ed and Harold. They had hit the center of the center of the center of the bull's-eye. It was not some fluke. Yet given the intrinsic fickleness and short attention span of this particular customer and fan base, there was no time like the present to capitalize on the firestorm of lustful devotion they had unleashed.

This prompted some bold decisions and some immediate action.

As quickly as Markham could get the software code in place, public access to the Djin Djin girls site was restricted to "members only". An annual fee of $19.95 gave you full privileges. Within a month, they had over 100,000 card-carrying members. Without removing a single panty, the Djin Djin girls had generated 2 million dollars.

Ed then came up with the ingenious idea of blocking out three hours Saturday evening of each week for the four most popular girls and offering special "Heaven Is A Place On Earth (Called Thailand)" sessions. These were exclusive encounters which included a light but Viagra-laced meal (the men were always amazed and puffed-up proud with their sexual performance), a full body massage with another girl assisting (always a great surprise when a "free" Asian beauty was thrown into the mix), and completely unrushed sex in and out of every orifice, sure to push the limits of endurance and the envelope of pleasure for the most seasoned of escort service users.

They had Markham create an eBay-like interface just for the Heaven-Is-A-Place sessions and they were auctioned to the highest bidder. Right to the close of bidding, the offers went up and up. There seemed to be no rational limits on what men would pay. In what had to be a wallet-flexing battle of titanic egos between two bidders with astronomical limits on their Visa cards, one of the sessions went for $36,650!

All of this took place purely from word-of-mouth. No advertising. No hype. No nothing. Purely on merits, this thing was a ballistic missile firing through hyperspace right before their eyes. What words could you use to describe this? Cash cow? A cow the size of Montana. Gold mine? Better than a gold mine. They really didn't have to do anything. Just keep the girls healthy and reasonably happy, and make sure their djindjingirls.com super-site was always online and functioning smoothly.

The real beauty of this was the growth potential. New York demonstrated in just a few short weeks the power of the Djin Djin concept to create a deluge of cash neither Harold or Ed, who were hardly short on imagination and over-the-top optimism, could not have thought possible. When Ed was sitting there in Vietnam back when and had exclaimed, "Goddamn! These gook girls are hot! There's a fuckin' goldmine sitting right here. Yessiree. The 'gin gin' girls!", little did he know what a clairvoyant and visionary megacapitalist he was being. Bill Gates with a vodka Collins and a boner.

The next obvious step was to replicate the same model in the other cities where they already had a Djin Djin contingent in the streets — Miami, Seattle, San Francisco. From there, who knows? This could be the Starbucks of the sex service industry.

If you build it, they will come. And come and come and come.

Chapter 11

SINK OR SWIM: The Psychology of Quicksand

The Element of Surprise

"Alicia Peters, for chrissake!" Lenny was yelling into the phone. "Sorry. I'm just a little frustrated. She told me she was writing an article for you."

"Sir, I'm going to need some information."

"What information? I just want to leave a message."

"I just work here. We have certain strict policies on incoming calls, sir."

"This is the Poughkeepsie Journal, isn't it?"

"Yes, it is."

"I am an old friend. I need to talk to her. You can't just write it down and pass it along?"

"I just have a couple ..."

"Let me speak to your supervisor! Jesus Christ, I'm not some freak."

"Thank you for calling. Have a nice day."

"Hello. Hello?"

He looked at the phone with disbelief. The stupid assholes had hung up on him.

Now what? He was sure Alicia had said she was writing about the march for the Poughkeepsie Journal. That was a dead end. They sure as hell weren't about to help him track her down. He'd have to figure out something else.

It was time to go. He had booked a flight to Chicago, which was leaving in a couple hours.

He fell asleep on the plane, hit broadside with an unexpected wave of total exhaustion. But as soon as he arrived at O'Hare, his energy rebounded, and in a blink he was out of the plane and into a taxi. He had booked a hotel midtown, not too far from the Willis Tower, where Harold and Ed had their splendid if somewhat pretentious office.

What did they call themselves? He had never given it any thought before. They must have some high-sounding name with an 'Inc' or 'Ltd' or whatever — the tux and tails on their ass crack of an enterprise. He knew the floor and suite number. That was all he needed.

It was mid-afternoon. They should still be there. He knew they kept pretty regular office hours, doing whatever they needed to do to keep everything running smoothly and pumping their coffers full of money.

When he walked into the reception area and stood there smiling, Jessica looked up and for the briefest of moments her face was a video editor's quick cut of emotions. Shock briefly seemed to trump the others — confusion, delight, anxiety.

"Lenny! What a great surprise. Did I know you were coming?"

"That's me. Full of surprises. No, Jessica. I didn't know I was coming. Good to see you."

"So ... what's the occasion? Did you win tickets to a Bulls game?"

"Just reporting in. Doing my job. Are Harold and Ed around? Maybe available for a quick one?"

"Sure. Let me check."

Rather than risk the indiscreetness of the intercom, she disappeared through a door and walked into their private suite area. She was back in three or four minutes. The phone did not ring that entire time. Thriving operation. Well, at least no fires to put out.

"They'll be with you in about twenty minutes. Can I make you comfortable? Coffee?"

"I'm fine, Jessica. Thanks."

In only ten minutes, Jessica's phone buzzed and she got up to escort Lenny into the private and sacrosanct quarters of VAI, Viz Adcom, Inc. That was the official name they went by. What the hell did that mean? Or was it just something they drew out of a hat?

"Lenny. We were just talking about you. So good to see you."

Harold. What was he campaigning for? Grand Hooded Executioner.

Except he wouldn't spoil the fun by wearing a hood.

"Lenny, my boy. Was this on the schedule?"

Ed was tanned. Booth or beach?

"I thought I would bring you up to snuff. You know, the Bishop. The march."

"Exactly what we were talking about. You took it all in?"

"Yes, I was there." Technically not a lie.

"And?"

"Can I sit down?"

The view always caught Lenny unprepared. To walk from the center of the building where there were no windows, into this corner office and see the city spread out and in such dramatic perspective, watch it blend and disappear into the distant infinity of the horizon, was exhilarating, but at the same time created an unsteadiness. Skyscraper legs? The subtle swaying of the building could be felt by the gyroscopics of the inner ear, a pleasant but unbalancing effect.

One unpleasant footnote. The smog. Lenny had no idea that it was so bad here in Chicago. He guessed that even the "windy city" couldn't mount an effective defense against the blight of automobile-fueled pollution. Not enough wind to blow the hydrocarbon soup away. But the visual impact of the skyline was only mildly attenuated by the thin layer of haze.

"I was there. And let me say this. The Bishop carries a big stick. But it's only a stick. And not a very effective one at that. That pulpit thing has seen its day. Too much else going on."

"So what's your take? Have we got anything to worry about?"

"Well, I don't have a crystal ball. And frankly, I am having trouble getting a grip on just what you guys have on the ground there. But I know how you operate. And I am sure you got it covered. The boys in blue still on board?"

Ed gave Lenny a curious look. Hard to read.

"Fiori is a political animal. For now he's doing his part by not doing anything. He even gives us a little logistical support. But he's very concerned about the killings. That makes him look real bad. So he's playing papa bear, hoping there won't be any more blood sport on his watch or in his backyard."

Lenny wanted to say the right thing. He needed to alert them without causing them undue alarm. Without a doubt, these guys were loose cannons. Frankie and Martin again came to mind. It made him exceedingly uneasy to think about the possibilities here. He needed to tread lightly. With Harold and Ed, as they said themselves, there was no gray, only black and white.

"I'm just saying, what's the Bishop gonna do? Make some speeches. Get a few old ladies to hold a bake sale. Then what?"

"You tell us, Lenny. You're our eyes and ears."

You mean, I'm your fall guy. Your local boy with the 'Arrest Me I Did It' sign hanging from his rear end.

"From what I saw, Mulcahey is a bleating sheep. He's got a bullhorn but no real authority. Nobody with a say is going to let him build his career any further, especially on the backs of a few whores. He'll blow a lot of smoke, then go back to handing out communion wafers and this will be over."

Harold and Ed sat silently for a moment. Lenny felt he was being sized up. Finally Harold spoke up.

"Lenny, how long are you in town? Why didn't you call? We take care of this sort of thing, you know. Where are you staying?"

"Staying? Oh yes, with a friend. No problem."

Harold walked over to Ed who was leaning back in an overstuffed leather chair, gazing east out over Lake Michigan, seemingly in a reverie. But a reverie with a sharply furrowed brow. They spoke too softly for Lenny to hear what was being said.

"We want you to come by tonight."

"Come by?"

"Yes. We'll have a good time. Some sin food, a few drinks, a little entertainment." Wink. "You haven't seen our pleasure pad. Lenny, my boy, you're gonna love this. We have this new place, right up on Lake Shore Drive."

Ed's turn. "Whaddya want, Lenny? Blonde, brunette? You want one with a shaved head and a shaved pussy?" That brought on some hearty guffaws from even the usually more reserved Harold.

It had been a while. He was out of town. This was their party. Why not?

"Give me your best shot. Surprise me."

"White or yellow?"

"Got anything in green?" More guffaws. Maybe a little bit forced, but testosterone levels were riding high.

"We'll come up with something good for you. It's not very often we get to entertain our boy from New York. We'll take care of you. Tonight Lucky gets his sucky fucky." Such class. Ed should be auctioning cattle in Nebraska.

"Have Jessica arrange a pick-up. Say around 8:30. And in the meantime, have dinner on us. We'll set you up at Spiaggi. You like Italian, right?"

Harold gives him the razz look. "Ed. Italian? Lenny? Can a penguin walk on ice?"

"Got it. Okay, my boy. We've got to finish up here. See you tonight."

Lenny walked out back into the reception area on his own. How should he feel? It seemed to go fine. But there was always something. He couldn't remember a single meeting or conversation that he had had with Harold and Ed, when he didn't feel like there was some subtext, some subliminal conversation going on. Right below the surface, things always seemed to lurk, hover, taunt. Unsaid, inaudible little hints and translucent shapes of ideas. Usually scary shit.

Maybe that's just them. It wasn't like he was working for the Humane Society or the Hope Foundation. These guys had their feet firmly immersed in the slimy muck of criminal stuff. He had every reason to think that whatever he saw and heard from them on the outside, what was going on inside was worse. What's that behind the curtain? A firing squad? Dante's inferno?

He wouldn't change anything about today. He'd done what he set out to do. He'd appeared. He'd given them reassurances about what was happening in Brooklyn. As long as he just kept playing it cool, everything should be alright. Acceptable, at least for now. It would buy him some time.

Before leaving, Lenny looked at a city street map that Jessica had in her desk, and wrote down the name of an intersection about four blocks from his hotel. That's where they should pick him up for tonight's soirée and orgy buffet.

At this particular moment, he was definitely hungry. He had slept through the plane meal. A healthy if inadvertent choice. So he'd catch a taxi to the Italian place right now and have an early dinner. Then rest up for an evening of delightful debauchery.

Things were turning out better than he had expected. This was a good move on his part. Always take the initiative whenever possible. Keep your adversaries off balance.

And Ed and Harold were adversaries. They were as long as they controlled his life. As long as he was the organ grinder's monkey for Viz Adcom, Inc.

Yes, so far so good. Lenny felt he was gaining some maneuvering room. Maybe even achieving a little tactical leverage, if that was possible.

The dinner was excellent. He asked for the check and they informed him that it had been taken care of.

Back to his hotel. He tried to watch a *Sex In The City* rerun but fell asleep. When he woke up he was slightly disoriented. It was 7:30. Plenty of time to get ready. He got dressed, even put on a tie, a very rare thing for him. Hey, why not? It's Alice In Wonderland tonight. Only without drugs.

A Night at the Movies

Lenny headed to the lobby, allowing himself enough time to walk the four blocks to the point of rendezvous with Harold and Ed's driver. When he exited through the glass revolving door, someone spoke to him.

"Mr. Petrocelli?"

"Yes. And you are?"

"Right this way, sir. I'm your driver."

They found him. How? These guys were uncanny.

"Sure. Thanks."

So they knew he wasn't staying with a friend. Should he try to cover? Come up with some excuse for lying? And what would that be?

This was unnerving.

Lenny decided to just leave it. Not bring it up unless they did. He figured he would just stonewall them. Use their own tactics on them. He just hoped it never came up. Here he had just dropped in on them. Then was staying in an undisclosed location. That would look suspicious even to someone who wasn't usually suspicious. Had he screwed up again? Christ, it seemed impossible to get a leg up on these guys.

They pulled up to what Lenny could only think was one of the most majestic modern skyscrapers he had ever seen. Lake Point Tower. Condos for the ultra rich. It was a giant curvy crystal made of smoky dark glass, reaching up some seventy stories. Right beside the Navy Pier. Unbelievable views of both Lake Michigan and the Chicago skyline.

Up and up he went. These guys sure had a thing for heights. The elevator stopped on the 64th floor and when the door opened, there waiting was an Asian girl in a royal blue kimono.

"Welcome, Mr. Petrocelli. This way please."

She led the way down the regally decorated hallway. She was petite and elegant the way Asians girls typically were but there was something else in her walk. An edge. A feistiness.

She turned to Lenny and smiled. "I am Ying Mae, the closest thing Harold will ever have to a girlfriend. Here we are."

He could have guessed.

Two massive bodyguards stood on either side of the entrance to the suite. They were dressed in light gray three-piece suits. Their neck muscles bulged over the collars of their shirts. Lenny was glad he wore a tie.

The one on the left pulled out a hand-held metal detector and indicated to Lenny his should put his arms up.

"I'm clean."

"I'm sure, Mr. Petrocelli. It's just a formality."

They were very thorough. The detector, then an exhaustive pat-down. As he stood there, he noticed the sign on the door. In beautifully wrought gold bar relief was the name for this party pad. *Shangri-La-La-La*. That had to be Ed's ingenuity.

When he walked in, his senses were completely overwhelmed. Counter to his expectations, it was enormous. He would have thought that such pricey real estate would be parceled out in smaller units. But vast it was. A spacious indoor playground geared to the tastes and whims of a king or a kingpin.

There was a bar and serving counter with five stools, adjacent to the kitchen. In the lounging area, a large circular glass-enclosed fireplace, around which were distributed two creamy leather loveseats, several body-size satin cushions and sculptured glass end tables. At the other end of the room were two plush white cotton and microfiber upholstered sofas, and a glass and chrome coffee table, set facing a flat-screen plasma TV, which looked to Lenny to be the size of a cineplex screen. There were human size vases with wispy frond arrangements reaching up toward the high ceilings. Without cluttering the place in the least, there were also some very modish glass sculptures on stands, several original neo-modern abstract paintings mounted at eye-level, and a glass media component enclosure against the base of the wall.

Two other features captured both the eye and the imagination.

One was an entire wall of floor-to-ceiling glass, offering a breathtaking vista of the sparkling skyline of the Windy City.

The other was a bed. It so perfectly integrated into the atmosphere of the entertaining area that it didn't interrupt the aesthetic balance of the room. But once noticed, it tended to draw a person into a world of imagined possibilities, fantasies which embraced the cosmic view of the skyline and the intimate intensities of personal hedonism. Perfectly circular in shape and perhaps 10 feet in diameter, it was tastefully dressed in a broad-patterned, deep blue and silver silk slipcover. Centered in the room it was positioned next to the wall of glass, facing the panoramic view of the city center. Certainly not the kind of bed you would merely sleep in.

The place looked like it could have been on Hugh Hefner's wish list.

And so could have been the three girls there, sitting and sipping drinks with Ed and Harold.

"Lenny, my boy. You made it. Fantastic!"

The little Asian — and she *was* little — with her graceful arm on Ed's shoulder looked very familiar. Lenny was distracted by the effort to place her.

"You should recognize this hot little fuck. You picked her out. The factory in Malaysia."

"I Dawa." Her face betrayed grateful resignation and an intrinsic shyness.

Lenny remembered now. It was disconcerting to see her here.

Wonderful. He was responsible for this. Apparently she was Ed's little concubine. At least for the night. Bad luck, little girl.

He looked around. The girl that had escorted him from the elevator — what was her name? Ying Mae? — had joined Harold on the divan in front of the fireplace and was playing with his ear with her fingers.

"Look at this. Lucky here's dressed up for his address to the nation. Have a seat, Lenny. What'll you have to drink? Still a cognac man? I have some nice Chateau de Breaulon."

Harold stood up and headed over to the wet bar.

"Just some bourbon would be great. I'm in a bourbon mood tonight."

"You're on. Got a bottle of Kentucky Straight right here."

Lenny then looked at the other two girls. Perfection. Not Asian. Probably American. Wow! Money talks. Real loud.

The blond, who bore a striking resemblance to Uma Therman, was staring right at him.

"You must be the world-famous Lenny Petrocelli. I'm Cassandra."

"Cassandra. Pleased to meet you. Do you go to high school around here?"

Harold shot him a look. Ed remained distracted. Cassandra broke into a laugh, that filled her face with even more kittenish allure.

"You're a funny man! But I'm a little insulted. I'm still in junior high. Guess I'm aging fast. Maybe you could recommend a good cosmetic surgeon?"

Smiles all around now. Harold handed Lenny his drink. He felt pretty good. Maybe she was on the payroll but she seemed to like him. It had been a while. Too long.

"And I am Friderika." Thick German accent. She looked at Ed. "You didn't tell me that he was so good looking."

She gave Lenny the subtlest hint of a wink. Long black hair falling on her heavenly cleavage. Her full-length evening gown was slit up the side almost to her hips. Uncrossing and recrossing her legs, he saw she must not be wearing any panties. He felt the pressure in his pants. It had been way too long.

"A toast!" Ed was the toastmaster. Lenny got ready to cringe. "Let the games begin."

Okay. He could live with that. For once Ed didn't come off like a porn movie director.

They raised their glasses in assent.

Harold sat back down and Ying Mae took his glass and got up to refill it.

"Lenny."

"Yes, Harold."

"Do you like butter?"

"Butter?"

"Yes, butter. It's a simple yes or no question."

"Well, then. Yes, I like butter. Thanks for asking."

"You're very welcome." Harold smiled with a sly glint in his eye. Then he gave an almost imperceptible flick of his eyebrows to Cassandra, who stood up and walked over directly in front of Lenny. She reached over and pulled him by the tie. She whispered.

"You're coming with me."

She led him through a door at the far end of the room Lenny hadn't noticed. They turned left and went through another door. When she flicked on the light, a large bathing room opened before him. It was covered entirely in elegant Italian white tile, except for the floor which was a patterned powder blue design. There was a floor-to-ceiling 12-nozzle glass shower enclosure which could comfortably hold four people, and a small two-person sunken hot tub in the center of the opposite wall, surrounded by a spacious deck. Thick white towels were already spread out on the deck, and next to them an assortment of toiletries, grooming and cosmetic items. There was a large globe-shaped glass bowl sitting on a pewter frame, and underneath Lenny could see the delicate flickering of a votive candle. The bowl held a creamy golden translucent liquid.

Cassandra saw Lenny looking at it. As she started to loosen his tie and unbutton the buttons on his shirt, she brought her lips against his ear and breathily whispered a single word.

"Butter."

By the time she finished undressing him and completely disrobing herself, Lenny's body was raging with the raw heat of anticipation. He was already breathing the deep longing breath of urgent, relentless need. Aching hungry need.

"Just lay down, you beautiful man. On your back."

He was in no position to argue. He was also incapable of taking his eyes off of perhaps the — no, take back the perhaps — the absolutely most perfect body he had ever seen, in person, pictorially, or onscreen.

She straddled him and as she bent down to adjust the towel under his head to make him more comfortable, the tips of her breasts brushed across his chest, then came within an inch of his face. He had never in his life felt so aroused. And they hadn't really started doing anything. It had been *way* too long.

Cassandra reached behind her and brought a lathering brush and a bowl of shaving soap next to them, reached again and grabbed a razor.

"Just relax. I think you'll like this."

She started up near his neck and worked her way down. Inch by inch, she shaved him, chest, stomach, and beyond. She took her time, carefully applying the lubricating soap with the soft bristles of the brush, spending extra time around his nipples, the lower part of his stomach. Lenny, despite his Mediterranean heritage, did not have a lot of body hair. What was there was rather light and wispy. The body shaving served more hedonistic ends than depilatory. He gasped and writhed involuntarily through the whole process, and though she had not yet touched his penis, he thought at several points he was going to orgasm.

She soaped up the brush and started to slowly apply the lather in gentle strokes to his balls, being careful to not touch his member. Then she gently took it between her finger and thumb at the base and shaved the entire region around his genitals. His penis pulsed, begging for release. Lenny just gasped.

"Oh god ... oh god ..."

When she finished shaving him, she dipped her hands in the warm water of the tub, then with the lightest possible touch ran them across the areas which were now baby smooth and free of body hair. Around and around. Even his balls. But not his penis. Not yet.

She straddled him again and lowered her body onto his, gently sliding her delicious skin back and forth ever so slightly, so he could feel the entire hot sensation of her breasts and stomach against him. His penis throbbed, bouncing beckoningly on her ass, and again he was sure he was seconds away from a full and earthshaking climax. She put her tongue in his ear and he felt its wet warmth fill him with a hot surge of pleasure and even more desire.

"Okay. We need to rinse off. The best is yet to come."

She reached for a remote, pressed several buttons, and the shower came to life. They stepped in and were sprayed from every possible angle. The temperature was perfect and the 360 degree aqueous siege licked and lubricated every skin cell on their bodies, except the soles of their feet. They couldn't help but laugh, more like two kids playing in a lawn sprinkler than two adults midcourse in a session of hot sex. They stepped out wet and exhilarated.

Lenny didn't have to do anything but stand there. Cassandra dried him off, removed the towels from the deck which were wet with shaving cream and body hair, and replaced them with fresh ones.

She ran her hands over his chest again, and pressed her mouth to his, in a slow and deeply sensual kiss, her tongue just teasing his and licking the edges of his lips. Her hands worked their way down his torso. Down to his hips, then gently brushing the surface of his thighs, around back to briefly linger on and caress his buttocks. She gave them a gentle squeeze.

"Mmm. Nice and firm. Okay, on your back again."

He lay back and watched her. Her breasts were perfect. Perky. Small pointy pink nipples. The frolic in the shower had taken some of the edge off of the urgency to climax. But he was still very aroused. There was no going back.

It had definitely been way too long.

Cassandra lifted the large bowl with both hands and brought it next to her. She then quickly rinsed the lathering brush in the hot tub and dipped it in the butter.

Dip and drip. Dip and drip. First to the inside of Lenny's wrists. She slowly swirled the butter around, feathering the creamy liquid on the surface of the skin, gentle circular motions designed to send warm surges of lust through the entire body. Then she lowered her face and licked the butter off with her tongue, and generous use of her lips. When she came back up, her mouth glistened with sensuous perfection.

"Mmm. You and butter. The perfect combination."

On to the hands and fingers. The inside of the elbows. Lenny's nipples.

Oh yes. The nipples! Each becoming slick and hard in the magic spell of her mouth.

Lenny's passion built and built. All of the heat emanated from the point of contact with her lips and found its way into the steely craving of his member.

She could feel his pleasure and anticipation and clearly was enjoying it.

After kissing and licking both of his nipples with delicious dedication, more dipping and dripping around bellybutton and downwards.

She blew ever so gently on his penis to let him now she had arrived. The tip was moist with a single drop of semen.

Cassandra appeared fascinated. "Someone is very ready."

Lenny moaned. "Ooohh! Believe me, I've been ready."

She worked slowly … gently … methodically … delicately brushing the warm butter on his testicles, the base of his penis, inch by pleasurable inch up its length. Again he felt the hot sensation of a climax building as she brushed the head with the slippery liquid. Like she had a sixth sense, however, she would ease off just in time to further delay its onset.

She put the brush aside and now concentrated on savoring her man.

He felt her wet tongue explore the inside of his thighs. Then his balls.

"Lenny, you taste good … so good."

Then, ever so slowly and gently, she ran her tongue up the length of his shaft. When she got to the top, she cupped her mouth over it like she was savoring a delicious confectionary treat.

At that very moment, with no further ado, he lost it. Finally and completely, his body experienced the totally consuming paroxysm of orgasm.

It seemed to go on forever, as the pleasure pushed in urgent pulsing waves from the inside of his pelvis and forced the creamy liquid to freedom. He just let it flow and flow.

With the fingers of a pianist or an angel, Cassandra massaged the length of his penis as he climaxed, synchronizing her strokes with the rhythmic convulsions of his abandoned release.

Eventually ... ecstatically ... finally ... it was over.

Lenny closed his eyes and let his body sink relaxed into the soft towel underneath him.

"Ohmigod! *That* was unbelievable. I have never ..."

He stayed that way for a few minutes. Then he opened his eyes to see that Cassandra had her hand between her own legs and was at that very moment experiencing her own release. Her eyes were closed and her head slightly tilted as she softly punctuated a moan with a faint but pleasure-saturated gasp.

Her eyelids slowly and dreamily opened and she saw Lenny looking at her, curious, fascinated, reverential. Lenny's version of a Mona Lisa smile.

"That was *so good!*" She leaned over and placed one last delicate kiss on Lenny's stomach.

"Let's take a shower."

Cassandra took Lenny's hand and led him back into the bathing enclosure, pausing to reach down and tap the resume button on the remote. Using just her hands, she lathered both of them, paying special attention much to his pleasure and delight, to those areas which were oily from the butter.

They got out, dried off, and got dressed.

Lenny put the finishing touches on the knot in his tie as she wrapped her hair in a towel.

"You go ahead. I have to put on my lady face."

Lenny, making every attempt to look casual and cool, rejoined the others in the entertaining area. They had moved from the fireplace and were positioned around the sofas at the other end of the room, which faced the giant flat panel plasma TV. The screen looked active but nothing was playing.

"Lenny. You look like a new man. How do you feel?"

Frankly, he couldn't wipe the smile off his face. He felt renewed, drained, exalted, refreshed, sleepy, exhilarated, ecstatic, spent, edgy — all at once. But he definitely felt good. Real good! It had definitely been way too long.

"Not bad, Harold. Thanks for asking."

"Ying Mae, sweetie, get Lenny a drink. The Kentucky."

"Yes, your highness."

"Here. Sit down, Lenny. Just relax. Enjoy. Let's watch some video."

Ying Mae handed Lenny a drink. A very stiff drink. Bourbon straight up. Several shots.

"Thanks, Ying Mae."

She bowed graciously to Lenny. Then gave Harold an obviously contrived smile, and sat down on the floor in front of and next to him. Ed and Dawa joined them on the divan. Cassandra finally came out and sat behind Lenny on a large floor pillow. She leaned on the back of the divan, and Lenny could sense her presence, almost feel her breath on the back of his head. He felt a warm connection.

"Go for it, Ed." Ed had the remote in his hand. He started the video and the huge flat panel screen came to life.

It's very strange watching yourself on film. Seeing for the first time a video of yourself having an orgasm is an out-of-body experience. You are right there — because you were there — feeling and savoring every sensation, the deep plunge of pleasure, the hot aching surges which fill the body and explode outwards.

At the same time, you are on the sidelines, given the very best seats in the house.

You are divided, existing simultaneously in two space-time continuums.

Nevertheless, in the end reality finally trumps all and you are *here*, a detached spectator, watching the other you, the you perpetually trapped by the magic of technology in a moment which has explosively passed. A binding temporal seal has been placed on everything which happened then, preventing you from actually experiencing it in the present. Or ever again.

All Lenny could think right now was how messy it was. Not something he normally would tune into, that's for sure. But he had ejaculated gobs and gobs. Amazing. Disgusting.

They had probably filmed the whole thing. But they now watched only from the butter in the bellybutton through the climactic ending.

The quality was stunning. Where was the camera? From the angle, it must have been up near the ceiling. And they were able to remotely control where it pointed, and the zoom. The sound was brilliant. You could hear every breath, lick, and moan.

They watched maybe three or four minutes. The best part. Unless they filmed them taking a shower, they should be near the end.

Lenny saw Cassandra lick the back of her hand and reach down to touch herself. Ed stopped the video. The screen went to a metallic pool of blackness.

Ed sat there with a shit-eating grin plastered on his face. Harold just stared straight ahead. His expression was an impenetrable slate. Lenny thought he heard from behind him a few words whispered by a female voice. Then a faint giggle.

Lenny stretched his arms and faked a yawn.

"Did Spielberg do that?"

Blindsided by Lenny's crack, Ed snorted. "Yeah, it's a side of him most people don't know."

Harold lifted his glass. Paternalistic diplomacy.

"Kudos, Lenny. I'm don't usually comment on other men's peckers. But that was alright. You've got a decent joystick working for you there."

Ed unconsciously eased his pants. Then offered his characteristic strip club worldview.

"My man. You shoot your wad like a fucking sperm whale!"

Deep lungs exhaling chunks of guffaw.

The light melody of conversation could again be heard floating in the air. Then slowly it began to dissipate and segue into the soft tinkle of ice jostling in overpriced booze and pretentious crystal. Harold reached over and put his hand on Lenny's shoulder to garner his full attention.

"Quite frankly, Lenny, that's not really what we brought you here to see."

He pressed two more buttons on the remote.

Filling the screen was a mob. Above their heads, the waving arms, and hand-painted banners and signs, could be seen none other than Bishop Mulcahey. He was midway in the speech which had closed the rally. The camera was able to faithfully record the thundering sound of the Bishop's oratory, as well as the energetic response of the marchers. Ed and Harold had the volume up high, so it was almost more overwhelming than actually being there.

The crowd cheered and went wild as the Bishop fired off some of his more spectacular lines.

"This scourge which has descended on our community
has to stop. And stop immediately."

"Let it be said that the people of Brooklyn saw evil, that the people of
Brooklyn stared down that evil, that the people of Brooklyn came
together and marshaled all of the forces at their disposal
and defeated this evil. This enemy of Christ!"

"We declare war on this evil and we will prevail."

In the middle of the harangue were other statements that were particularly ominous. Ed and Harold both visibly tensed.

"I think I know who is running this operation. I don't mean just locally.
I am certain that this insult to our community has been masterminded
and is being administered from another major city here
in the U. S. — that city being Chicago."

The Bishop's oration continued building to its final crescendo.

Somebody had then cut into the video a segment of footage from the nightly news covering the march. It was the end of the Bishop's speech, the point-of-view camera shot from the audience, with the Bishop at a high-oratory zenith, putting the criminal elements on notice. His finger stabbed at the camera like a huge battering ram, and the crowd shouted at the very peak of their enthusiasm as he drew the lines of battle:

"We will find you. We will take you down. This is a war and it's a war we
are going to win. A holy war in the name of decency, a holy war in
the name of God, in the name of Jesus Christ Our Savior."

The video then cut back to the live footage, showing the Bishop leading the crowd in prayer, and the huge rock-star ovation for him that seemed to go on forever, as he waved and shook hands from the stage, then finally made his way down to a white limousine that was waiting to take him back to the parish offices.

The screen went blank and the DVD player clicked itself back into play ready mode.

"It didn't look that way from where I was."

Ed looked him squarely in the face and spoke in a cool, steady voice.

"And where was that, Lenny?"

Stonewall. Just keep quiet, Lenny told himself. They probably know anyway. There's no need to play that card.

A long minute went by. Finally, Lenny broke the tense silence.

"Surely you're not intimidated by that display of bluster."

Ed looked at him curiously. "Well, someone has taken a vocabulary building course, I see."

"I'm not as stupid as you look." Lenny immediately laughed to show he was joking.

Ed obviously did not think Lenny was clever or funny or long for this world.

"I only have to say one word ... and poof!"

"You mean bingo?"

Stiff silence.

What had gotten into him? Here he was in the den of lions and he was smearing himself with meat tenderizer. Lenny hadn't noticed this suicidal streak in himself before. This was new. Were there more surprises lurking? Maybe next he'd be loading a gun and handing it to them. Truth or dare, motherfuckers.

No. Stop. It's none of the above. It was just a moment of stupidity. His understandable but impulsive reaction to the video of him in the most private of all possible moments. Another example of his too-frequent relapse into self-sabotaging defiance, a pattern which had set the tone for his adolescence and way too many years beyond. The same self-sabotaging defiance which inextricably entangled him in Harold's and Ed's labyrinthine employ in the first place, and now had him entirely caged as a victim of their manipulations and whim.

It was time to get a grip. These guys play for keeps. He had gone toe-to-toe with them. After the briefest exchange of blows, he could see he was badly outgunned, if not completely out of his league. It was time to back off. Time to hit the rewind button. But how?

He sat and waited. Saying nothing suddenly seemed brilliant beyond words.

Harold broke the icy chill that had filled the room.

"We gotta tell ya, Lenny. We expected more of you. You've let us down. Having said that, we still need you. We do like you, Lenny. We see potential. Maybe you're just a slow starter. Ed and I both like to think that we know what you're capable of."

"You think I'm capable of peddling a bunch of second rate hookers after you've spoiled the customers with the Djin Djin girls?"

"Listen, Lenny. It's all just pieces of the puzzle. We got it handled, see. Those girls. Maybe they got beat with the ugly stick. But not everybody can handle the high-class pussy. Some guys are Walmart shoppers. The Djin Djin girls, that's somethin' else. When we get done, they're gonna be in a class by themselves. Don't you worry about it."

Harold picked up the thread.

"Your girls will pay for themselves. It might take a while. But you got guys sniffin' around 'em and when they get that sex smell in their nostrils, they think they're seeing Pamela Anderson. So don't fret the details. You just keep them healthy and alive. A stiff cock has no conscience and is usually as blind as a lawn mole."

Ed stood up and started pacing. Lenny could tell he was becoming agitated.

"You want to do your job? There's two things you gotta do. That's two, Lenny! One-two. First, find the sick fuck who is poppin' our girls. That's your first job. It's bad enough we had a whole boat load of them go to Davy Jones's locker. But to have somebody sniping them right under our noses. That's a complete fucking outrage! Have you heard the gruesome details?"

Lenny thought about the girl in the morgue. Then about Kimnai.

"Yes. I know."

"This motherfucker is out of his mind. He's a psychotic butcher!"

"Right right. I'll do what I can."

Ed didn't seem to hear. His anger was still ramping up.

"I gotta tell ya. I ain't never seen anything like this. We got eyes and ears everywhere and there isn't even a whisper out there. This guy is invisible. You find him, Petrocelli! I know you can do it. You find that motherfucker and strangle him with your own two hands, goddammit! Take him out!"

Lenny glanced at Ed. He looked crazed. Was this a trap? Or was Ed actually completely out of his mind? Barring a miracle, he would never find the killer. Not if they couldn't, with everything they had at their disposal. The street team, grapevine, even the goddamn police. On his own, he was guaranteed to fail. They must know that.

"And what's the second thing? You said there were two things."

Harold's turn. He always took on the more global issues.

"The Bishop, Lenny. Mulcahey. How should I put this?"

Rationally, I hope, thought Lenny.

"We don't share your optimistic assessment. You know, what you said earlier. We think he's dangerous. Very dangerous. Whatever he says makes headlines. Headlines make opportunities for local politicians. If the Bishop gets his way, they're going to come down on us hard. Very hard."

A slightly calmer Ed.

"That's right. Just when the gettin' is good. They'll make sausage out of us. Then probably turn around and open their own operation. That's how these politicos work. They work with us now. It's easy pocket change for them. But who knows."

So there *were* people on the take. Just as Lenny had suspected. But who?

"After we've gone and done the legwork, these ruthless fuckers have no qualms about shutting us down, so they can look like heroes. Then, guess what? The store opens again. New owners. It's a sick goddamn world, Lenny. A sick world."

The irony was not lost on Lenny. He almost laughed in Ed's face. Survival instincts saved the hour. A sick world indeed. And here he was with two of the sickest.

"Listen, Lenny. You don't have to be humble. We're family. You're doing a great job."

"But what am I doing?"

"Whatever you're doing. We've seen some of the numbers. It's holding it's own."

Ed could spew this stuff effortlessly. His mouth always seemed two paces ahead of his brain. Or was it calculated?

"Numbers? What numbers? How come I don't see the numbers?"

"Lenny, there's no need for you to get your hands dirty. We got grunts out there doing the messy stuff. Carting the girls around. Counting the money. Crap detail. You're the general. You don't need to go running around the front lines with a pop gun in your hands to get the job done."

"But you've got my picture and phone number on every one of those girls."

"And they know that they only bother you when the shit seriously hits the fan. Not every time their eyeliner smears or they get a run in their stockings. It's like we told you before. Nobody is gonna fuck with us with you there. You're like our early warning system."

The capper from Harold himself. The patron saint of patronizing. "You're creative, Lenny. A take-charge kind of guy. Exactly what we need in this organization."

Right. They invited him here to rub his face in video footage which spelled out in clear and unambiguous terms that everything he had told them about the situation with the Bishop was completely wrong. That he apparently had his head inserted entirely and unequivocally up his poop hole. Now he was 'creative' and a 'take-charge kind of guy'?

If bullshit could roar, everyone in Chicago would be running for cover right now.

And if he had ever had any doubt about what his real purpose was in Harold and Ed's master plan, that doubt was completely gone now. If he wasn't being set up to take the fall, then camels could quote Shakespeare, and Larry Flynt could run a four-minute mile.

He was take-charge alright. When they arrested him, they would charge him with a litany of felonies and he would take it in the ass, all by himself. When they strapped him in an electric chair, he would take the charge, all 880 volts from the headgear down to the soles of his feet.

Yeah. They had him. They had him good. For now.

But the time for fun and games was over.

Shangri-La-La-La.

Sin food, a few drinks, beautiful women, a room with a view. Was this Heaven on Earth? Or a living Hell?

They say the caged bird sings. But what if it could fly?

Ying Mae walked Lenny to the elevator. The door opened but Ying touched his arm and stopped him before he entered.

"Yes?"

"You deserve better, Mr. Petrocelli. We all do."

Every Mother's Son

Christine was home a lot these days. Well, maybe not a lot. But a lot more.

She had scheduled no new fundraising appearances for several weeks now. Her heart just wasn't in it. She wasn't really sure where her heart was these days. She couldn't feel much. Certainly her passion for the child sponsorship programs was completely gone, and she had little sense of exactly what she should be doing.

Of course, there were a few fundraisers that were already on her calendar when the truth came crashing down on her, and these she didn't feel comfortable canceling. But if the truth be known, going to them, standing up at the podium usually as the featured speaker, and extolling the virtues of sending money into those black holes overseas where God knows where the money would end up or what would happen to the poor kids after they were used to bilk the public, going to these feel-good events and putting on her happy face was one of the hardest things she had ever done.

She was so lost. She needed to figure things out. She needed to talk to someone.

Alicia.

"Mom."

"Danny. Come in."

Christine was sitting at her desk and half-heartedly going through some mail. Her laptop computer was open in front of her, and she had been reading a report she had done a couple years ago for one of her church's Christ Awareness groups.

"Mom. I have to talk to you."

"You know you can always talk to us. Your father and I love you."

"Dad won't talk to me. He hasn't since … I know what he found. In my notebook. It was stupid of me to keep that."

"So. Where did you get that um … that advertisement?"

"It's the guys. You know. Just curious."

"Curious about what?"

"Come on, mom. Do you have to ask?"

"I understand. There are better ways to go about it. You can always talk to us about sex."

"Mom. I know what I need to know. I'm not going to sleep with any girls. Not until we're married, anyway. That's not what I wanted to talk about."

"Then what?"

"The murders, mom … the girls that were murdered."

"Yes? It's horrible, Danny—"

"Mom! We think we know who did it."

"Who? I don't—"

"We saw him. I mean, I think we saw him. We have been following this … well, he's an older guy. He's probably crazy and …"

The fear and horror written across Christine's face stopped Danny mid-sentence.

"God bless you, Danny, for whatever reason. I trust you and believe you mean well. I don't know what or why you and your friends are up to. But, please, please. Promise me you won't do this anymore. If this man *is* crazy, anything could happen. Anything!"

"Listen. We've been careful. It was just a coincidence. But we saw some things."

Christine was fighting for control. She couldn't lose it now.

Be strong. Be strong.

"Danny. I can't explain. But I know about these Djin Djin girls. I can't really tell you why. This is a very painful subject for me. And now, you're somehow connected … I don't know what to say. But nothing good can come of it."

"So we should just let this go on. What if he kills some more? He probably will. Isn't that the way it works? He's a psycho!"

"Let me think about it. But for now, promise me you won't do anything else. Please, Danny. For me. Just stop. You have to stop."

"Okay. But don't talk to dad about this. He's so out of touch. He probably thinks I've been doing it with them. I mean, Phil keeps saying how he'd like to, you know, do something. But that's not me. I know it would be wrong."

"Stay away from Phil. He's always been trouble. As long as you've hung out with him, nothing but trouble."

"I'll try, mom. But we go to the same school."

Phil was not a bad kid. But full of mischief. A lot of teen angst and bravado. A need to rebel and confront the older generation with what spineless, safe and uninteresting lives they led. Always coming up with one crazy adolescent adventure after another. He and Danny had over the last couple years become best friends, though in many ways they were like black and white. Or gray and white, anyway. Phil's family was Christian but they had no where near as devout a home life as Christine and Tom had created for Danny and Megan. Phil talked in expletives. Danny never swore. Phil boasted about real and imaginary sexual conquests. Danny was shy and sex with a girl right now was about as inconceivable as time travel. Phil always seemed to need to prove something, impress his friends, shock his parents and teachers, affirm in his own mind what an ultra-cool dude he was. Danny had a healthy curiosity, an adolescent innocence, the sense of invulnerability that was typical for his age, but no agenda.

Now this.

"Danny, do you want to tell me how ... how you ran across this crazy man?"

"It doesn't matter, mom. I'll stay away from him. But he's definitely stalking those girls. Sometimes he dresses like a soldier. You know, like he thinks he's in a war. Then one time we saw him leave his place — he like lives in a warehouse or something like that, it's not a real home — anyway, he comes out dressed like someone from the Bible. Like Jesus or one of His disciples."

"Did you talk to him?"

"No way! This guy's a total creep. One time he saw us. And came after us. Man, we were so scared. Even Phil. I've never seen him run so fast in my life!"

"So what happened?"

"Nothing, mom. He just scared us, that's all. It was no big deal."

"Danny. You have to promise me."

"I did. I have homework to do. Later."

He went back to his room.

Christine felt uneasy. Danny might mean it now, in the moment. But she could tell he felt he was being forced into something. She wasn't as convincing as she wanted to be. She doubted that Danny really understood that this was not something to fool around about. This wasn't the movies or some video game. This was real life and very dangerous.

She picked up the phone and dialed.

"Alicia. Is this a good time?"

"Ohmigod! I've been thinking about you. Constantly."

"I'm sorry I've been a stranger. It's ... it's ... well, you know. Can we get together? Soon? I really need to talk to someone. I mean ..."

"Of course. That would be fantastic. I've been trying to give you some space. I'm just finishing an article. But I'm free tomorrow. How about it?"

"Tomorrow? That would be great! Again, I'm sorry ..."

"Christine. Who are you talking to? No sorries allowed. How about noon?"

"Perfect. See you then. Bye."

Strawberries Are Out of Season

"Damn. I've been having these cravings. Maybe I'm pregnant. Though considering the state of my sex life, it would be more on the order of a virgin birth."

Christine looked across the table at her friend. The waiter, with almost a condescending what-planet-are-you-from attitude, had just delivered the cosmically horrifying verdict.

Alicia's strawberry shortcake fix would have to wait, at least till the next growing season.

"I've missed you."

"It's only been a couple weeks."

"Longer than that."

"I'm sure you're right. I've been in a fog. And things are really weird right now with Tom and I. And my son. Well, that's a whole other story."

"Always is. But you look good."

"Because I sleep twelve hours a day. Okay. A slight exaggeration. But I've been escaping."

"They say that our best thinking occurs in our sleep. The mind is undistracted by the routine humdrum of life. Unpaid bills, bad TV reception, chipped fingernail polish. So it gets down to business. All at the subconscious level."

"If anyone is living at the subconscious level, it's me right now. But I realized, I don't have time for a vacation in a coma. What are we going to do, Alicia? We have to do something."

"'Something' is kind of big. A bit vague. What's bothering you?"

"Everything. The prostitutes. The money I've been raising. My son. Is there ever an end to all of this? Do the good guys ever win? Or is that just another fairy tale?"

"Christine. What we saw that night is business as usual. At least for the rest of the world. You live a very sheltered life. Sorry to be so blunt."

"That's what friends are for."

"I mean, ever since high school — even in high school — I thought, 'Alicia Krysynski, you are going to make a difference. You are going to make the world a better place.' And—"

"Alicia Krysynski?"

"Yes. I'm Polish. Don't knock it. All Polacks aren't losers. Just the majority of them. Anyway, you have these big dreams and every breath is another shot of hope, every day you cartwheel towards those idealistic visions that seem so perfect and so doable. Then, one day this big garbage truck backs up to your house and dumps the biggest heap of reality right there in your front yard. You sit and stare at this stinking heap, wondering 'where the fuck did that come from?'. You keep thinking you have to do something about it. But what? Where do you begin?"

"That's kind of where I'm at right now."

"I'm just trying to survive, and solve this one little problem — so miniscule in the grander scheme of things — my little boy in Indonesia. And I can't seem to do either one very well."

"What if we were to go over there?"

"Over there? You mean Indonesia?"

"Thailand. Indonesia. There are good people there. I'm sure we could look around and make some connections. We could look for your little boy. We could talk to the government and whoever else we could find. When I was there, I met some very high officials. They all said that if I needed something I should let them know. They were very excited about the work we were doing in Thailand. They held this big banquet to celebrate our efforts."

"First of all, those are two very different countries. So whatever you do in Thailand isn't going to help me find the boy. But if there's something we could do, we should do it. I'm all for it. But ..."

"But?"

"But we have to have a plan. We just can't go off half-cocked. We'll get swallowed up. Believe me, I know. I went to Jakarta and four other God-forsaken cities and they had me spinning around like a circus elephant. They have their own rules, which probably don't make sense even to them, much less people like us. The Third World is nutso, Christine."

"The plan is to get to the bottom of who is trafficking all these kids, then put them out of business for good."

"That's the goal. We don't have a plan. But I think we should talk to Bishop Mulcahey."

"Why? What can he do?"

"He'll know people, organizations, volunteer groups. The Catholic Church, as evil as it is, does a lot of good things. He helped me get to some of the people in Indonesia during my last ill-fated trip."

"But it didn't do any good. I mean, at least so far."

"That's what I'm saying. You talk and talk till you're blue in the face. You go round and round with them and never get anywhere. It's just the way it is."

"You sound so pessimistic. Why would you want to go with me then?"

"Because ultimately I'm a hopeless optimist who believes in fairy tale endings. If you don't try, you only have yourself to blame for failing. So I'm in. Let me check my calendar. There. Checked it. I'm wide open. When do we leave?"

"You're right. We need to think about this. Let's meet with the Bishop and anyone else you can think of. We'll figure something out."

The waiter returned with a smug look of satisfaction on his face. He set a bowl down in front of Alicia with a clunk.

"Frozen. And it's not shortcake. It's a crumbled donut. But it's on the house."

"Can I kiss you?"

"Thanks anyway, but my boyfriend took care of that this morning. He kissed my G-spot."

"Way too much information."

The Silent Hell of War

John Harrison had the feeling that high command was really miffed at him. Or at the very least disappointed. He had seriously botched his assault on the barracks of the enemy. Granted that the fire itself was a masterpiece of a deliberate conflagration. But they had escaped — from what he could tell, every last one of them — and probably were out there spreading the filth of their corrupt ideology throughout the region.

Sometimes he would stare for hours at his walkie-talkie, almost believing that the sheer force of his determination and will would elicit a response from headquarters. But no such luck.

Silence.

Thick, unnerving, enervating silence.

John was hungry to show them that he was still on top of it all. That the warehouse incident was just a fluke. That he was as solid a soldier as any out there. He just needed an opportunity to show what he was made of.

But nothing.

Deadly, maddening, incapacitating silence.

What was even worse was that he could make no sense of the lines of engagement anymore. Chaos now seemed to reign supreme, grinding his normally perceptive and analytic military mind to an ineffective halt.

He had been back many times to Brooklyn. For a while he watched the girly agents of the Vietcong come and go. There was a new batch. Not as succulent and tempting as their predecessors but probably as crafty and vicious. Maybe more so.

He was thinking it was time to mount another Zippo. He was putting the finishing touches on the mission plan and hoped to be in a position to deploy in a couple weeks.

He regularly did extensive recon to fine tune his tactical sensibilities.

One time he had stumbled on some sort of crazy rally.

This particular day was also one of his designated baptism days. Lately he had been subjected to a lot of harassment in Central Park by some godless hooligans. So he decided to take the glory of the sacrament elsewhere.

Since he had grown very familiar with the terrain of Brooklyn, he thought he would give that a try. A Saturday in Brooklyn seemed like an excellent way to put the unpleasantness of Central Park behind him. Besides, there seemed to be no shortage of souls craving the mercy of atonement, wherever you went.

He was really looking forward to it.

As he was leaving his quarters that Saturday, John sensed the translucent presence of angels — a very positive spiritual sign. He loved the way their wings waved so gracefully, a Divine gesture, the soft nod of God's approval.

God was sure an enigmatic dude. But John couldn't complain. At least He kept in touch.

When he had arrived in Brooklyn shortly after noon, there was a march going down the center of the street, hundreds of people carrying signs and shouting their support for a holy man, a Bishop. Which in and of itself was good. Here was a man of the cloth, like John himself, leading the flock in prayer and promoting an effort to cleanse the community of the blight of sin.

Despite a lukewarm reception at the rally itself — in fact John got into a minor scuffle with some young punks — he decided Brooklyn was indeed an excellent place for him to dispense the sacred sacrament of baptism, a deliverance from eternal damnation and a bold commitment to walk the path of righteousness.

Coupling that with his ongoing effective military actions to dispatch the onerous messengers of political and moral poison, he had the perfect one-two punch in the palms of his hands — all in the service of God and country.

All very promising.

But then things started to get confusing. Shortly after the rally, John saw there was some sort of photo reconnaissance effort going on. Then, before he could get his bearings, the entire new crop of Vietcong completely disappeared. The very ones targeted for his upcoming Zippo mission! Not a one in sight.

It was puzzling and frustrating.

He knew they were still around. But where?

These commies were a cagey and formidable adversary. A vicious and unscrupulous enemy. For them to pull a Harry Houdini right when he most needed to demonstrate to high command that he was still in charge here, that he had not lost his magic touch, really sucked!

Damn damn damn.

Was this really happening?

John went back several nights in a row, but only to confirm his worst suspicions. Still no sign of them. They had vanished into thin air.

At this point, his options were very limited. He bided his time and continued to hone the specifics of his tactical plan. That's all he could do.

Of course, he was still hoping to hear from high command, perhaps get their always valuable insights, maybe even obtain some logistical support for whenever and wherever he would mount the attack. But nothing …

Silence.

The kind of silence that invited demons and malicious sprites to fill the void with whispered innuendos and conspiratorial asides.

He heard them sometimes. Their wicked hissing murmurs.

He hated them.

These were times when it was all he could do to keep focused. Hold on to the iron discipline which was the spinal cord to every great soldier.

High command certainly wasn't helping matters by leaving him in a vacuum.

John was a by-the-book soldier. The thought of insubordination was an impossibility to him. There were damn good reasons for chain of command. The hierarchy served a greater good. It was not for him to question, much less challenge, with his own ill-informed decisions.

On the other hand, he was really stuck. And he had to consider all possible scenarios.

What if high command had been cut off? As loath as he was to consider it, perhaps headquarters had come under some unforeseen and diabolical assault and at least temporarily was inoperable. Nuclear? Motherfucking Red China! They had *The Bomb*. Bastards!

John heard something.

He stopped and listened. It wasn't the demons this time. They apparently had been driven away by something else.

It was the gentle beating wings and soft playful whispering of the angels!

They say God works in mysterious ways. Not really. Not if you know Him. Quirky yes. But not mysterious. He just had this … well … He just liked surprises. The offbeat prank. A burning bush. A big flood. The Cain and Abel bit — which God now on His own will admit went a little too far. The Seven Plagues. Ha! That was sure a wake up call. Egyptians are such knuckleheads.

Here He goes again. Angels. Unmistakable. The fluttering feather duster effect of the wings. The faint sound of warbling, contented pigeons. Coo coo coo. The piquant smell of myrrh.

God obviously liked John or He wouldn't take the time. Go to all this trouble.

And John took no time figuring out exactly what the Big Guy was saying.

It was: Stop banging your head against the wall. Lighten up!

As if the floodgates of the Hoover Dam had just suddenly opened, a holy water of cool refreshing comprehension flooded John's mind. He was instantly baptized in a new understanding of his circumstances.

What did chain of command have to do with it? God wasn't just another cog in the military machine, even though He expressed in no uncertain terms an endearment for armies which marched in His Divine Name and for His Divine Purposes.

No, the reality was that God was His *own* chain of command. A singular divine assertion of Infinite Wisdom and Judgment.

God was a layer of Ultimate Power which lay like a celestial blanket, over all of the inventions of men, including the rules and regulations of the U.S. military. His strategic and tactical discretion functioned on an entirely different plane than that of mere mortals, regardless of their rank, or what obedience was due them as a consequence of manmade structures and systems.

John decided, then, that it could hardly be construed a violation of military protocol to speak personally — or even professionally for that matter — to God Himself about his present quandary and concerns.

John now knew what he had to do.

He had questions. He needed answers.

It was time to appeal to a Higher Authority.

Chapter 12

BLOOD ON THE TRACKS: Red Flags and Visions

Housekeeping

What to do? Lenny couldn't seem to get a leg up on Chicago. That was becoming obvious. But what were his options? He needed to come up with a plan. Until then, it was all about buying time.

For now, he would walk the straight and true, a semblance of exactly what they expected, giving them no reason to question his loyalty. That was a given.

But Lenny also concluded he needed to go way beyond that, that the very best defense was a good offense. Just as he had set out to do with his last visit to Chicago, he'd walk the extra mile and give them a stunning and gratifying show. He would awe them with his complete subservience and overwhelm them with a display of his energy and commitment. He would actually be the take-charge kind of guy, they had patronizingly accused him of being. He would be their ecstatic dancing bear until he could figure out how to get out of the cage.

That would have to be the plan. At least for now.

He didn't have to wait long for an opportunity. In a short few days, he had a fire to put out.

A big fire.

Inspired by the rally, and organized by the Ad Hoc Committee To Save Our Neighborhood, the community went to work. Every evening they took turns in the working girl enterprise zone. Waiting in the shadows, as soon as a car pulled up to the curb and the negotiations began, they would leap out, small digital cameras or photo-capable cell phones in hand, then quickly take two or three incriminating shots. *Flash!! Flash!!* Typically, the guy was in gear and peeling off in a cloud of burning rubber before they could say 'smile'.

As if being photographed wasn't bad enough, the next day the pictures were put on fliers with big bold text, that proffered a range of intimidating, mocking, humiliating captions:

Is this your daddy?

Do you know where your husband is tonight?

Buy him something special for Father's Day! ... an <u>HIV test</u>.

The mister bought a little something extra on the way home last night.

He said he was working late at the office. Does <u>this</u> look like he was working late? Is this his office?

Your daddy's such a friendly guy. Here he is making some <u>new friends</u>.

Do you think he'll bring <u>her</u> home to meet the family?

The fliers were then posted on a huge bulletin board that had been put up in the front window of the STD Prevention Center, both officially on board with the initiative, and serving as the unofficial headquarters for the street team patrolling the area to photograph the cruisers in the act of soliciting sex.

The campaign was phenomenally successful. Within three days, the johns were nowhere to be seen. There was such a reduction in traffic, it looked like martial law had been declared.

The Bishop applauded and thanked the activists from the pulpit the following Sunday, declaring that this was the kind of exemplary work which could and would make a big difference. But he also reminded them that this was just the beginning.

"Yes, the first battle has been won, but the war is far from over."

He then told them about the Djin Djin website. While certainly their efforts would make the neighborhood a more decent and fitting place to raise a family and live a Christian life …

"Until we find the wicked men behind this scourge, much of the same thing will still be going on, merely driven into the less visible but no less sinful seclusion of a computer screen and a stealthy 30 minutes in a slimy hotel. Off the streets, yes. But not off the map of innocent souls. These 14, 15, 16-year-old girls walked the same sidewalks that you and I and our children walk, thus they have become part of our community. They are and always have been members of that vast congregation and ministry of Jesus Christ. As a result, they are our responsibility. We must continue to safeguard our streets, as many courageous activists have done over this past week, while at the same time we redouble our efforts to track down and bring to justice the men who chain these young girls to a life of forced prostitution. Let us pray."

For Lenny's part, he had a number of problems to solve immediately. First, though there hadn't been any incident yet, things were getting crazy out there, meaning there was an ominous potential for physical violence inherent in the situation. From the angry johns, if they thought the girls were setting them up for the photo entrapment. From maybe even the working girls themselves, being deprived of their meager share of the livelihood they earned. This was serious. Someone could definitely get hurt. Or killed. Though he hadn't been heard from for a few weeks, there was still a brutal killer loose in Brooklyn somewhere.

Moreover, if Chicago said the initial numbers looked good, that sure as hell wouldn't be the case now, as all of the numbers inevitably would plunge to a big fat zero. The borough's little sex enterprise zone was in free fall.

He decided he needed to move them out of Brooklyn immediately. Somewhere safer for sure. Somewhere which at least would appear to have the potential to create some revenue. Chicago had dumped this squarely onto Lenny, making it crystal clear that the new uglies were entirely his responsibility. One thing was even more clear. The Bishop had won this round. He had won it big. Chicago, with their huff-and-puff egos, were going to be very pissed.

Time for damage control.

He got Jessica on the phone and actually managed to get the names and cell phone numbers of the two grunts Chicago had on the ground working there in Brooklyn with the new Asians. He got hold of them immediately and explained that he was going to move the girls, that they should have them ready to do just that within the next 48 hours.

But where?

Lenny took the subway into town. He got out at Times Square and just started to walk.

Times Square had, of course, changed dramatically over the years. Once a haven for drug dealers, hustlers, hookers, and every shape and size of con man and petty thief, the streets had been lined with porn theaters, strip clubs, cheap eateries and pawn shops. Unsavory squeegee men and women in various states of sobriety would leap into the stream of passing traffic and try to eke out a living by washing windshields.

Then the 80s heralded a new long term effort by mayors Ed Koch and David Dinkins to reinvent the area as a tourist-friendly, Disneyfied zone of family fun. Eventually, the procession of smiling yuppies filing in and out of the upscale restaurants and renovated historic theaters, drove the scum away. But only into the adjacent city blocks, particularly those west of 42nd Street and 8th Avenue, on the back side of the Port Authority Bus Terminal. Everything that was available in the old Times Square could still be found back in these dingy, characterless streets.

This is where Lenny headed now.

Sure enough, he saw hookers and hermaphrodites, drug dealers and garish queens, punks and slick con men, the sick, the psychotic, the sinister, the homeless. The whole underbelly of the city, its street scum and lunatic fringe, was represented in every rank and wretched mutation.

Perfect.

He found in the back of a 24-hour diner next to the restroom what has become an anomaly in this era of cell phones, a telephone booth, with a Yellow Pages directory to boot, and spent the next hour looking up dive hotels which had addresses close by. These were the flophouses which typically attracted the transients, the indigents, the recipients of a sole social security check, living hand-to-mouth each day of their miserable lives. Not that he wanted to put the girls up in such squalid conditions, but because he knew that despite the proximity of these establishments to the heart of Broadway, in view of their rundown condition and suspect clientele, they would have high vacancy rates. After all, he was looking to plop down 37 girls out of nowhere with no advance notice whatsoever. In a city which for nicer apartments there were two and three year waiting lists, this was no insignificant challenge.

Once he found them shelter, he figured he could cobble together some sort of small budget from Chicago to buy some new bed clothes and throw rugs, maybe fix their rooms up enough to get them above the gag threshold.

The most important thing at this point was to get them out of Brooklyn as soon as possible. And as marginal as it was, there was some potential for the girls to make some money here around Port Authority, with its established, high traffic customer base.

He spent the next several hours visiting nine of the sleaze hotels which were within walking distance. Though it was getting late, a night clerk could be found at each, ready if somewhat reluctant, to show Lenny a room. The pattern was usually the same. Some unkempt guy in his 30s, either reading a porn magazine or slumped over next to an ashtray overflowing with cigarette butts. Real life can be such a cliché.

He found three hotels that would do the job. Combined they had enough vacancies to handle forty new occupants, barring a sudden influx of tourists from Somalia or the shanty ghettos of Mumbai.

Chicago's two street boys, a Puerto Rican named Oswaldo and a Costa Rican who went by Pablo, with their shift supervisor, a huge block of muscle from Belarus who called himself Wedge, started moving the girls in the next afternoon.

Having to keep a low profile when carting 37 Asian hookers around, presents some unusual challenges. But as Lenny observed and monitored the performance of their duties — albeit somewhat from a distance — he had to admire the stealthy professionalism of his crew. He really didn't have to do much. As the girls filed past him with their scuffed luggage, shabby satchels and shopping bags full of personals, Wedge pulled an enormous wad of money out of his pants pocket and peeled off enough to cover their rooms a month in advance. He then handed it to the clerk on duty, whose eyes bulged and darted around anxiously, in light of the size of the transaction taking place.

After all the girls were tucked away and presumably getting settled into their new digs, Lenny turned to Wedge and extended his hand.

"Good work, my man. Bi-a-shoy-ah spa-see-ba."

Wedge broke out in a huge grin, showcasing a gleaming silver incisor, and gripped Lenny's outstretched hand in a bone-crunching handshake.

As Lenny left the last hotel and turned to head to the subway station which would get him back to Brooklyn, he looked across the street and beheld a sight which had more of the aspect of a hallucination, than the stark stuff of reality.

A man standing perfectly still.

Staring.

There was something eerie about him. And familiar, though Lenny couldn't recall ever having seen him before. Surely he'd remember someone dressed like this.

He thought it was worth a closer look, though he couldn't say why.

Crossing the street as casually as he could, attempting to make it appear as unintentional as possible, he passed about ten feet in front of the strange character, stealing a glance or two along the way.

Lenny decided he was harmless. Just another kook. This city sure had its share of them.

Lenny was past him now but not out of earshot. A low, even voice followed him down the sidewalk.

"Have you been baptized in the name of Jesus Christ?"

"I can't believe we're doing this!"

"Believe it. Here they are."

Christine placed the two envelopes containing the airline tickets between them on the table. They were back at the restaurant-deli on Amsterdam and 73rd Street, a place Christine really had come to like, mainly because it was so off her beaten path.

"I'll pay you back as soon as I—"

"Don't worry about it Alicia, this is important."

"But what are we doing? What do you think we can accomplish?"

"I'm still figuring it out. We have to do *something*, don't we?"

"You shouldn't beat yourself up, Chris. It's not like you had any idea. Besides, a lot of good comes out of your work, I'm sure. There are many very respectable organizations, operating all over the world. It can't be all bad."

"No, just the ones I raise money for. So what does your friend the Bishop have to say?"

"Well, we'll find out when we meet with him. The specifics, I mean. But he thinks that every little bit helps. On the other hand, he recommends that we not be too optimistic. He says that there are many, many organizations over there working right now to try to put a halt to the trafficking. It's a huge enterprise, turning enormous profits. He thinks that the governments themselves, or at least the government officials, if they're not making money from it, then they have reasons to look the other way. They play by very different rules over there."

"I'm not so sure it's so different. Look at our own politicians. Say one thing, do another. Anyway, when can we talk to the Bishop in person? Gosh, we're leaving in three weeks. That will go fast."

"A week from Thursday at 2:30. He says he can spend a whole hour. In the meantime, he has his staff looking into who is doing what, and who appears to be most effective. He says it won't be a very long list."

"When I was there last, I collected the names of some officials that were very high up in the government in Thailand. Several I met personally, and they all said that if I needed anything I could look them up. I'll put together a list. It's worth a try."

"From what I've seen, that kind of promise is a lot of smiley air. They all said the same thing to me, but when you leave their office they forget who you are and what they told you."

"No no, I know what you mean. I'm trying to be realistic. I mean, it was at one of these gala receptions when everyone is on their best behavior, putting forward their best foot. And a lot of that is for image, for their reputations in the international press. I understand that. But maybe we can get to the right people by going through the wrong people. Know what I mean?"

"I'm game to try anything. So after Bangkok we go to Jakarta. Three weeks total, right? How long are we in Bangkok?"

"We'll be there for twelve days. Then off to Indonesia."

"Christine, you are great! I have all these shit grin friends who talk about doing something. Everybody says the right things. But you actually get off your ass and do it."

"And you, my fashion exemplar with the mouth of a truck driver, are my best friend ever."

The Nice Thing About God

The nice thing about God was that he didn't fuck around. No himming and hawing. None of that equivocating or doubletalk. The Man said what He meant and meant what He said. You definitely knew who was in charge. And where He stood. No futzin' around.

Another nice thing about God was that He hated middlemen. God being the *ultimate autocrat* that He in fact was, hated bureaucracy. Despised it with a passion. All those Catholic Popes were in store for a huge shock and a painful tongue-lashing when push came to shove. They would have to just sit there and grimly endure God's fury as He dressed them down for acting as gatekeepers through all those centuries, telling the humble congregants along the way, that God didn't have time for any of them personally, that if they had any matters to take up with the Big Guy in Heaven, they had to go through them. Fuck that!

And here's something that would probably surprise most people.

It wasn't easy being God. So much to do. Billions and billions of souls to worry about. Angels and saints and sinners and even the fallen. He cared about every single one of them. So many to look after, so little time. Sure He had eternity, but that still wouldn't cover it. He'd blink His eyes and whoa! Another billion years down the drain. The 'In' basket still full.

And another thing that would surprise most people was this. Being God was a lonely job. Despite the extreme high visibility of the position, the constant behests, prayers, appeals, supplications, sacrifices, the Sunday services, singing and worshipping, masses and prayer circles, sacraments and invocations — all in *His* name — overall, it tended to be very impersonal.

Frankly, sometimes God just wanted someone he could just hang out with, pop a few brewskies, shoot the shit, have a little God-to-man face-to-face. It could be anyone, perhaps someone in an "official" position, but despite that, someone who could give God that warm fuzzy feeling that you only get from a *real* friend, that special person who you can just talk to and let it all hang out.

Thank God — God just *loved* using that expression! — He had found John Harrison. Out of all of the billions of people out there — just here on Earth! — a lot for even God to get a handle on, he stumbled on John and they had really hit it off. God was more than aware of the crazies popping up from time to time who midleadingly claimed to know Him personally. Some blasphemously or in the chaotic tumble of their dementia even claimed to *be* Him. God of course new better. But have you ever tried to talk sense to a crazy person? Good luck with that!

Of course, it — meaning the friendship with God — went both ways. John was sure one helluva lucky guy. To be able to chitchat with the Creator of the

Universe, get the Big Guy's take on things, bounce ideas back and forth. Whoa! Very cool.

Which brings to mind the whole John The Baptist thing. God and John had a lot of laughs about that one. The whole bit of dressing like a fashion faux pas from 100 BC. God gave credit where it was due, however. To be fair about it, it was John who first tossed the idea out. But God knew a brilliant stroke when he saw one. And this was a brilliant stroke alright. A great PR stunt for sure.

"Go for it, Johnny, my man. That'll sure grab some attention down there!"

God, when He had a break in His demanding routine, would look down with amused omniscience, checking out the expressions on people's faces when John would shuffle up with that hilarious look of mortification plastered on his puss and ask, 'Have you been baptized in the name of Jesus Christ?' That shook the big Divine belly quite a few times with hardy haw haws. Better than Letterman, it was.

God knew how ridiculous the whole thing was. But He had a great sense of street theater. Look at the crucifying of His Son. If that wasn't street theater at its best, then what was? Hollywood still couldn't top that one!

God loved the 'St. John the Baptist of Hell's Kitchen' tag too. Kind of ironic. Nice and punchy. John had become a minor celebrity, no mean feat in the Big Apple.

Best of all, a lot of real good came out of it. Quite a few baptisms chalked up along the way.

To top it off, it put someone God really trusted and liked a lot, right in the thick of things. No matter how you slice it, New York was the center of the Universe when it came to planet Earth. They sure had that right. And here He had his hang bud, his dear and close friend — what did they call it now, His 'homeboy'? — John Maximilian Harrison as His Own number one emissary, His Own personally selected and approved hoodie, gettin' the job done.

God realized that John had to break a few eggs along the way. That's the way it always is. Putting things right gets messy sometimes. But all in all, it was good, clean, productive fun. With some great laughs to boot.

Ha ha ha ha ha ha ha ha.

Knock knock.

"Come in! Oh Peter. How is it, my old friend? Hey, I love the coloring of the hair thing. You look two thousand years younger."

Slaughterhouse Five

Here is how one local television talking head in a live-broadcast dialogue with the host of a network news-at-noon program described it ...

Pamela Kelly here in the Bronx at the scene of a gruesome multiple homicide. Employees of Musa Karoop & Sons walked into their meat processing facility early this morning to find the bodies of five Asian women hanging by meat hooks, their blood drained and their bodies disemboweled. Police have the entire city block where the facility is located, cordoned off and there is a team of forensic experts on the scene. It is expected that they will be here for at least the next 24 hours looking for some clues which will lead to the perpetrator. There is speculation that the five Asians were prostitutes and that this latest killing spree is related to a series of equally grotesque homicides recently in Brooklyn, also of Asian streetwalkers.

Pam, we understand that there were two other bodies found in the area.

That's correct, Chuck. The bodies of two adolescent boys, 16 years old, were discovered three blocks away lying in an alley. Police have not determined nor will they speculate at this time whether they are connected to the mutilated Asian women here at the slaughterhouse. The identity of the two boys has not yet been established, as no identification was found at the scene.

Well, this has been quite a disturbing and frightening day there in the Bronx. Will you be keeping us up to date as this horrible tragedy unfolds?

Yes, Chuck, I will. Later this afternoon, I am covering the reception at the Trump Tower for several visiting dignitaries from the Middle-Eastern country of Bahrain, men who are currently business partners with Michael Jackson. But I will be back here to report to our viewers any new leads and information which might result in the apprehension of the sadistic murderer, who turned this respectable butchery into a sickening scene of human carnage. This is Pamela Kelly signing off from the Bronx for Channel 3. Back to you, Chuck.

Fade to Black

Christine had to admit it. The Bishop was an awe-inspiring figure up-close and personal. She had, like every other New Yorker with eyes and a television set, seen Bishop Mulcahey on the news making a public statement or being interviewed. He was always impressive and commanding. But sitting here in his office took it to an entirely different level. She had always been puzzled by the popular expression 'larger than life'. What could be larger than life?

Now she knew.

"Ladies. I want to be able to speak with absolute frankness, because this whole child trafficking business is horrifying, despicable, immoral, sinister, on and on. That makes *anything* anyone tries to do to stop it vastly important and worthy of God's highest blessing. It is especially important to me personally, the very uppermost of my priorities as a human and as a priest. If I accomplish nothing else on this blighted planet of ours over the course of my life, to vanquish this horrific enterprise would be enough. However, though I am a man of the cloth, as they say, I am not naïve or out of touch with the ways of the world. Sex sells. It does now and always has. The Bible itself is full of sex, prostitutes, adultery. Maybe that's one of the reasons it's so popular, eh?"

The girls quietly giggled at that one.

"What I'm saying is this. We can't make all the bad go away. Sins of every variety exist as part of God's greater design. He has given man the choice of good and evil. Even the best and holiest among us sometimes makes the wrong choice. So until the final redemption, when the entire checkerboard history of humankind is behind us, there will be wrongdoing and human error. To err is human. Truer words do not come to mind. But what we can and must do is take on the very worst, the most abominable manifestations of human failing and try to eliminate those, try to make those go away. Trafficking is the vile core of human failure at its worst. The capture and enslavement of innocents like the Djin Djin girls and the thousands of other youths who are held in forced labor camps and sweatshop factories around the world — this we must try to stop. It is sin of the blackest kind by the men with the blackest hearts, men who respect no limits, who recognize no spiritual value in anyone, not even the most innocent child, men who will stop at nothing to enrich themselves.

"But I also want you to understand that you are facing formidable, possibly insurmountable obstacles. Just look at the situation locally. How difficult should it have been to get these girls off the streets? It's not like they were hard to find. Little Asian teens dressed the way they dress. About as hard to spot as the Statue of Liberty. Why, I myself took a couple vans and three men one night, and actually got them into relative safety for a few weeks. Until they were taken back. What I'm saying is, the authorities and agencies who are supposed to take care of these matters are doing absolutely nothing. Why?

"The truth is that the people who could with a stroke of a pen, a simple action-item order — people in power who could remedy this situation immediately — don't want it to go away. Now I don't know how high up this goes, but I have my suspicions. Certainly, the local police precincts are in on it. But it could go all the way up to City Hall. Who knows?

"My point is this. You're going to run up against the same thing overseas. Only worse. And you will not have the benefit of being a citizen, or even knowing the local language. Thailand makes a lot of money off of sex. They estimate that 3% of the entire economy of Thailand is generated by the sex industry there. We're talking several billions of dollars annually. For many of the sex workers, it's a great way to make a living, one that provides them with more income than they ever dreamed possible, a life full of the material things they grew up wanting. But for the ones you and I are talking about, as you already know, it's a whole different story.

"I have a fairly close friend who works at FACE, which stands for the *Fight Against Child Exploitation*. They are the United Nations' key ally in the fight. A great organization. Another one is the *International Justice Mission*, a Christian organization, which the Church ties into there in Bangkok. I'm still trying to get a good contact for you on that one."

Christine was taken aback. Her eyes betrayed the anxiety building inside her.

"Christine. What's bothering you?"

"Frankly, I just feel … I feel so small. From what you're saying, there are all these people out there working full-time on these issues. And it still just keeps going on. I apologize if this offends you. But the more you talk about it, the more hopeless it appears. I can't speak for Alicia. But for my part, I feel overwhelmed. I have, ever since I realized what was going on and how my own work was feeding this horrible system."

"This is a huge problem. While there are substantial resources being committed to solving it, it's never enough. Every little bit helps. Estimates vary but conservatively there are over 25,000,000 children held captive as slaves in the world today. Let's face it. It's not like this is some big secret. The issue of trafficking has had its five minutes in the limelight. Oprah did a whole show on it. It even occasionally pops up as a feature segment on the major network news shows. But it gets lost in the deluge. You watch TV. You know better than I. So many problems, so much horror, so much violence and pain.

"I'm not here to judge people. I understand why this is item number seventy-seven. People are getting compassion fatigue. They're getting numb from seeing and hearing so much tragedy. From wars to famine to AIDS, on and on. Moreover, it's out-of-sight-out-of-mind. Most of us have our hands full just trying to keep our own communities safe and orderly. Until it ends up in our back yards, it's hard to get motivated. That's what makes our own struggle unique. As you've seen with your own eyes, it *is* right here in our backyards. The good people of our own community saw and experienced firsthand the consequences of letting this go unchallenged. When the two of you come back from your trip, you'll be able to feed into the concern and anger that already exists right here in this parish about the abuse of these children. You can help people connect the dots. *That* is an enormous contribution."

Alicia leaned over and took Christine's hand.

"We can only do what we can do. Some good will come of this."

"I know, Alicia. We're definitely going. That's been decided. I really want to go. I mean, more than I've wanted anything in a long time. It's what I need to do. I just …"

"You just want to make a difference. Believe me, I understand. As a priest, I am there at the crossroads of people's lives. Their baptisms, weddings, funerals. Often times, key critical moments in between as well. But as someone merely to officiate. To administer the unction of the Church's sacrament or blessing. Most of the time I feel like a helpless spectator. Especially when it comes to funerals. All I can say is I believe Alicia's right. We can only do what we can do. Ultimately it comes down to each of us making a very personal decision. You two have made a courageous decision. I personally believe it's the right decision."

Christine looked squarely at the Bishop. "I hope so. You know, I wasn't able to attend your rally. But I hear it was a great success."

"It was a positive step. A lot of enthusiasm. And the community has banded together and are out patrolling the streets. It's a good start."

Alicia's face simultaneously livened and darkened as she remembered something.

"Lenny Petrocelli. That guy I went to high school with was there."

"Believe me, I know who you're talking about. Remember? We detained him for a while, thanks to your help. He was at the rally?"

"Yes, and we almost got him. I had some guys chase him but he got away."

"Chase him?"

"He's running girls again. I *hate* him so much. He told me he wanted out. Next thing I know he's like the head pimp. He's such a devious prick."

She covered her mouth embarrassed.

"Don't worry about it, Alicia. The profanity police are in the field. And I won't turn you in. This time. So what was he doing there?"

"Probably something evil. Spying. Maybe he had a bomb strapped to his chest. I wouldn't put it past him. He makes me sick. You should have killed him when you had the chance."

Christine was a little startled by the turn the conversation had taken.

"Christine. Lenny works for the people behind this. I held him here for a few weeks and tried to pry some information out of him. Things got a little nasty. Perhaps I went a bit overboard. I am human. My anger was running pretty high at that point. That's when I had the girls right here with me and was hearing the sordid details of their lives. Sometimes, as they say, the ends justify the means. But I don't go around killing people, whatever the reason."

"You missed a great opportunity." Alicia looked wounded and angry.

Christine almost in a whisper.

"There's more to it. He obviously hurt you."

"I must be out of my mind. He is the scum of the earth. But yes, I've had these … these feelings for him. All these years. It makes no sense. He's not my type. I'm not a Satanist."

"All of my life I have studied the Scriptures and theological writings of the Church. They are filled with the so-called mysteries of the relationship between man and God. But from what I have seen, the greatest mystery is the relationship between a man and a woman. Honestly, I'm not sure it's supposed to make sense. It certainly wouldn't be the exciting roller coaster ride without all of the intrigue. The intensity comes from the irrationality, unpredictability, the craziness. The heart is a visceral organ. Often — perhaps most of the time — it ignores the brain."

"Men have a brain?"

Alicia's mind. Being with her was like throwing a match into a box of fireworks.

The Bishop played along. "There was one isolated instance reported around 1620 in Bavaria. A violinmaker."

Christine's cell phone rang and she reached in her purse to mute it until she saw who it was.

"I'm sorry. I better take this."

She flipped it open and turned her head for a modicum of privacy.

"Tom. I'm in a meeting right now …"

"This is important, Christine. I … I … something's happened to Danny. The police are here right now."

"What? What are you saying?"

"They found him. Danny's been killed. I—"

"No! No! It can't be! Oh God no!! NO NO NO …"

She was screaming and crying. Her hands were flailing wildly. She doubled over, burying her face in her knees, and continued to cry out.

"No no no … it can't be …"

She had dropped the cell phone on the floor. Alicia reached over and picked it up.

"Hello?"

"I'm going with the police. They want me to identify the body."

"I'll tell her." She closed it and put her arm around her friend.

The Bishop, hardly a stranger to witnessing personal grief, sat immobilized. Then he stood up slowly and came around from behind the desk.

Alicia pressed her head against Christine's.

The Bishop knelt and took her hand.

"Christine?"

"My baby my baby … my son has been killed."

Chapter 13

IF WOMEN RAN THE WORLD: Sugar and Spice

Televandalism

Christine learned everything she wanted to know and everything she didn't from television.

Hour after hour, days upon days, of television. Thousands of pixelated images flashing in a Möbius strip of storytelling. A story with no beginning and no end, just scene after scene of moments, vignettes, thin slices of the space-time continuum, presented for the numbing edification of TV viewers — citizens of a nebulous electromagnetic community, spectators, potato chip munching voyeurs — whose own lives were now just a pancaking collage of other people's lives, an evaporating flat-screen diary of images and illusion.

Alone with her television. She even had her bag of chips. And a half-empty bottle of wine. Next to many empty bottles.

The morning after Danny's funeral, Tom packed up Megan and headed to Pennsylvania to stay with his parents. Needed to take some time he said.

To think. Sort things out.

This was the same man who had vowed to be by her side, through sickness and health, for richer or poorer, through joy and sorrow, the good times and the bad.

At least she had her TV.

And she was learning so much.

For example, she learned that she wasn't just a mother who had lost her beloved boy and was now fighting for her survival against a swallowing vortex of grief, the pain of loss worse than anything she could have imagined possible. No, not at all. She was actually the courageous mother of a young hero who had sacrificed his life to try to save some helpless victims of a merciless psychopath. She herself was a strong woman who led her own battles against the pernicious spread of poverty in the Third World, a savior of young orphans, a real Manhattan-based Mother Theresa.

She also learned from interviews of Danny's classmates that a lot of the other kids knew what Danny and Phil were up to, their following the Djin Djin girls around. For sure their friends did. Some thought it was real weird, while others just knew in their hearts that they were trying to do something heroic. That's the kind of guys they were.

Heroes.

She learned about the inevitability of falseness. She saw politicians and community leaders with ambitious dreams of promotions and higher office, deplore from the bottom of their hearts the senseless loss of such fine young men, tearfully claiming they felt that one of their own children had been murdered. She saw neighbors who she had never met or even seen, garrulously share the details of their intimate friendship with Danny and his entire family.

She learned about how ratings trumped truth on television. That no story was so good that it couldn't be improved on by the creative team at newsroom headquarters. That the name of the game was feeding the public's insatiable appetite for real-life drama, so that it could go head-to-head in the battle for ratings with the pulp fiction pumped out of Hollywood — the fairy tales and visions of hell that filled their screens between reality shows and the news.

She learned that just like the body of a human being, the soul of a human being could also be autopsied with cool dispassionate calculation. She watched as her own soul was dissected and probed and analyzed like an earthworm or any other laboratory specimen. Her suffering was the science project of the week, with the scalpel of the camera cutting into the deep cavities of her pain, holding up for a fascinating look the dripping tendrils of her misery, sucking the slimy marrow of her despair from her still-alive body, in a pre-death autopsy of her agony and desolation.

She learned so much.

She learned that the strings of the heart could be plucked and bowed and drawn into long, melancholy passages, or whipped and excited into frenetic high-drama flourishes. She saw this happen right there on her TV screen, this magical illuminated window on the grand stage of life. She learned that all of us sitting in front of our televisions are members of a huge orchestra, each adding our own dissonant wail and nervous rhythms to the grand symphony of human emotion. She learned when to laugh on cue, when to cry, when to feel important and superior, when to sneer and when to just sit back and ooh-and-aah, and when to burn with rage and contempt, when to accept with fatalistic and cool indifference, when to hoot and cheer and when to rear back her head and scream, when to feel camaraderie and fraternity, and even when harmonize her own back-of-the-throat purr and giggle with the laugh-track of life. She learned how to surrender to the gentle, hypnotic sine wave of the conductor's baton.

She watched and learned. Watched and learned. But also …

She learned that regardless of how it was packaged and gussied up, it was all entertainment.

The death of her precious boy was the Top News Story of the night, Today's Most eMailed, this week's CSI Buzz Bomb. To her disgust and distress, she saw reporters clawing at each other to get an exclusive interview, photographers jostling, elbowing, shoving, to get that one great shot, bloggers reaching for more and more outrageous and surreal hyperbole to grab the attention of other bloggers, who would then try to top them, talk show hosts scrambling to realign their program guest schedules to get in on the story while it was hot. Poor little Danny was being cannibalized by the feeding frenzy of a media industry gone mad.

What she wanted to know.

And what she didn't want to know.

Sometimes she couldn't tell them apart.

They explained everything. She understood nothing.

Sometimes she didn't think she wanted to understand after all.

The irony of it. The sick, invasive, humiliating, debasing, excruciating irony of it was this: Here was a time in life which begged more desperately than any other for privacy, for the dignity of solitude, and it was during this same brief torturous pause in her life that she was overrun by news-hungry media mercenaries, crude, invasive, bullying, pitiless types who would sell their own children or grandmother for a pint of the sticky juice of someone else's suffering, as long as it sold newspapers or made viewers press their slack-jaw faces closer to their television sets.

They were at the funeral. They were in front of her house. They tailed her SUV.

At night she would sit numb and exhausted, and watch with detached curiosity, footage of herself looking comatose, eyes sunk into the deep shadows of despair. Slow-motion close ups of herself, crying getting into her car, crying getting out of her car, crying walking from the gravesite, crying, crying, crying.

After a while she didn't even recognize this person who bore an uncanny resemblance to herself. This television image of a person torn and tormented by grief. This image who would not even acknowledge the existence of the hounding reporters, hungry for some quotable murmur, some drama-drenched whisper or groan, which they could play and replay until it was completely stripped of any tangible connection with real human suffering. This image who walked like a disembodied spirit through the laughing circus, the giddy costume ball, the freewheeling, frivolous, fatuous, carnival barking of an unhinged world she could no longer comprehend, much less be a part of.

A world where her little boy Danny once breathed and laughed and lived.

She thought of Terry Shiavo.

The irony of it.

Here was a woman who had the foresight and took the time to create a living will. The main request of that living will was that if she ever became mentally incapacitated, if she were ever effectively declared brain dead, then they were to pull the plug and let her die. She was not to suffer the indignity of being observed by anyone, even friends and family, in a vegetative state.

And here was a woman who for weeks on end was seen on television screens all across the globe by millions and millions of people, as a blind, brain dead, completely dysfunctional vegetable. All so that politicians could make political grist, strike their monument-friendly poses, flex their oratorical muscles in sound bite chunks of grandstanding for their respective constituents to see, and nod with approval and pride. So that pundits could pound their competitors to the mat in the boxing ring of viewer ratings.

She was this week's Terry Shiavo.

The irony of it.

The bitter, faith-shattering, gut-wrenching, mocking irony of it. It made her want to raise her eyes to God in Heaven and tell Him to go fuck Himself and his misguided, sadistic plan for His gentle little fawning creatures here on earth.

Her little boy was raised in the purest tradition of the love of Christ, absolute deference to the will of God, respect for the Holy Commandments, love of humankind, praise for the Lord.

Just to be cut down in some sick, senseless homicide of young sex slaves forced into prostitution.

God had the heart and humor of Adolph Hitler.

The irony of it. The sadistic irony.

The unspeakable pain.

The Bunker

The girls were afraid to leave their hotels. And Lenny couldn't blame them. Nor was he about to force them to.

There was a mad killer out there. One who was targeting Asian prostitutes. The numbers be damned. He couldn't put them in harm's way. He'd be signing their death warrants.

What to do? He couldn't go to the police. The girls effectively were undocumented, though they carried passports and other docs, ID which only a complete moron would think was real. At very most, these forgeries allowed some irresponsible official to claim that he had seen something and saw no reason to press the matter.

The point was, alerting any of the enforcement authorities was tantamount to turning them in, and probably getting busted himself for his complicity.

He called Chicago and asked that enough guys be put on security detail for a 24-hour watch on the three hotels housing the girls. Ed's response was, "Hey Len, if you can pay for it, you can hire the fucking U.S. Marines to guard them."

Pay for it? The girls wouldn't be generating any income. Not for the foreseeable future. Obviously these guys, Harold and Ed, didn't give a flying fuck about anyone or anything. Except lining their own pockets. The real question was, why were they bothering with this anyway? It made no sense. These weren't Djin Djin girls. If he had to look at it with a crude and calculating eye, they were nothing more than two-bit hookers. Ugly ones at that. But Chicago still had him running them, as if the paltry income they could possibly generate would make any difference.

He had to keep reminding himself. It wasn't that at all. This was a setup. When the shit hit the fan, the news would report ...

Asian Prostitute Ring Busted, Local Brooklyn Man Arrested

And that would be that. The real culprits would go untouched.

Fall guy. That's all he was in this whole arrangement. Someone to take the heat. That guy Fiori or whoever spoke for city hall could point to and say, there he is, we've done our job.

How many times had he come to this same inescapable conclusion? But he always got sidetracked, sucked in further by Harold's and Ed's unpredictable and convoluted tricks. Masters of manipulation. But now he had no choice. The writing was on the wall. He had thirty-two homely Asian women frightened out of their skulls, cowering in their rooms. Practically begging to get busted.

Time to make a phone call.
Time to get out.
Whatever it took.

Intervention

Alicia and the Bishop sat in silence. He was thinking.

After she called, he had his new secretary reschedule his next appointment so he could see her immediately.

"We can help Christine. Eventually. I'm here to do everything I can. But she needs to work this through on her own for a while. All of us have experienced loss, but what another person personally goes through remains incomprehensible from the outside. At this point, Christine's grief is only shared by her and God."

"That's a nice theory. But we can't just leave her there. She won't talk to anyone."

"From what I saw, she is a strong woman. She'll get through it. And she will come out of it. There's a long road beyond this initial stage of shock. That is where you can be there for her as a friend. Please invite her in then. I'll be more than happy to talk to her. For now we can only wait. And pray for her. That her sorrow becomes bearable and that she will not become bitter."

Alicia knew the Bishop was right. But it didn't temper the pain she felt for her friend or alleviate the desperate clawing need to do something for her.

"Lenny Petrocelli has been calling. He left five messages. I was either out or in a meeting. What does he want?"

"Ugh! Probably to put poison in the communion wafers."

"You, young lady, have a very active imagination."

"Genetic defect."

"One of them said, please give my number to Alicia."

"He has my number. Thank God, he hasn't called."

"Thank God for favors, large and small, eh? I know you dislike him."

"Forgive me, Bishop, but *hate* is the word."

"I will make believe I didn't hear that and leave it to you make peace with both God and yourself."

"You can't be serious."

"Just between you and me, no. I understand your feelings. But something bothers me about this. I can't figure out why he would want to talk to me. On the other hand, if the information I have is correct, he is the linchpin to the Djin Djin operation here, all of the Asian prostitutes. "

"Maybe he wants to invite you to go bowling. Or give you free tickets to Asian Orgy Night."

The Bishop laughed out loud.

"It is so refreshing to be around someone who is so irreverent, who's not intimidated by my being a Bishop."

"You're a Bishop? I thought you just had eccentric taste in clothes."

"Stop, please! I'm having too much fun. The Church frowns on that, you know."

Becoming serious.

"Alicia, my friend. There is a special favor I need to ask of you. Obviously, you can say no. I want you to call him and find out what he wants. I know this is asking a lot. But I just have this feeling … I sense this might be important."

"Only if you let me stand on the altar with you completely naked, the next time you say mass. Christmas Eve would be perfect."

"Wow. You drive a hard bargain. On the other hand, it might boost attendance."

"You're a funny man, Bishop. Who would have known? But your secret is good with me. What should I say to him? I mean, what do you want to know?"

"I guess that's the problem. I have no idea. It depends on what he says. Just feel him out. See what he's up to. Why he might be trying to get ahold of me. Without saying so in so many words."

"We both have to be naked. Christmas Eve and Easter services both."

"Alicia. Please."

"Okay."

"Here's his number. Let me know as soon as you find out anything. I'll tell uh … whatever her name is out there … I'll tell my assistant-of-the-week to put you through, whenever."

"You owe me."

"Yes, I do. I appreciate this. And if you get through to Christine, let me know that as well. God bless you, Alicia."

"Thanks for seeing me on such short notice, Bishop."

As she walked from the rectory office, she reeled in a tumble of emotions.

Lenny. She hated him so!

She was trying to imagine the conversation. She was having trouble even imagining herself dialing the number. Could any good possibly come of this? But the Bishop had been so generous to her, through everything. He was a good man. She would keep her promise. But not without a little anxiety.

Actually a lot.

She reached the street. Not a cab in sight. Her phone rang. She looked at the caller ID. Could this really be happening?

"Christine!!"

"I need someone to talk to. Could you come over?"

Her prayers had been answered. And she hadn't even said any.

Girl Talk

Unlikely as it would seem, considering how close they had become, Alicia had never been to Christine's house. It was both exactly as she had pictured it and completely opposite what she could have imagined.

Sure, the décor and physical appointment was as expected. Middle-class but very tasteful.

But it felt like a mortuary. Or a catacomb. Some physical space which had abandoned hope and embraced the opposite of life.

Christine looked terrible. But somehow still beautiful. The way that priceless and perfect works of art somehow survive the ravages of time and stand before us as pure manifestations of what is possible when genius and vision marry and produce a perfect child.

Alicia loved Christine as friends should love one another.

"I'm ready to live again." Christine said this sincerely but tentatively, as if she were floating the idea out in the real world to see if it was truly viable.

"It's so good to see you. You have no idea."

"I think I do. One favor. Let's not talk about … you know."

"I know."

Christine and Alicia sat down on the sofa facing each other.

"So, Alicia … what have you been doing? Sorry about the trip. I wish we could have gone."

"I have been doing what I always do. I talked with the Bishop again. He is a hoot. Really. I mean that!"

"You bring out the best. Even in a man who walks around in a bedspread from the court of Louis the XIV."

"That's funny you said that. I told him he had eccentric taste in clothes."

The faintest hint of a smile from Christine.

"Alicia, you're very funny."

Christine's unfocused gaze drifted toward the window. Several moments passed.

"Tom is gone."

"Gone? For good?"

"I think so. In a way, I hope so. He's … he's not there for me anymore. Maybe for Megan. He has Megan with him in Pennsylvania."

Alicia tried not to react. She just let Christine talk.

"My life is shit."

That was a first. Alicia blinked but tried not to look too surprised.

Christine now reached and put her hand on Alicia's face. She caressed her cheek with the back of her fingers. Slowly she leaned forward and kissed Alicia on the lips. A lingering, soft and longing kiss, that perhaps lasted thirty seconds.

Christine slowly pulled back, eyes still closed and lips glistening slightly from the moistness of Alicia's mouth. Had Christine been a man, the kiss would have been a romantic prelude to foreplay. But as she pulled back, Alicia only saw a face suffused with an innocent plea, a radiant melancholy beckoning her to fill the vast emptiness which had now taken purchase of Christine's heart.

Christine opened her eyes.

There was a moment of awkwardness.

"Christine, I am craving banana crème pie."

"I don't think I have any."

Reaching down and picking up a wine bottle.

"Want some?"

"Tempting. But it's gotta be the pie. At least for now. Let's go. Our favorite deli."

It took Christine a while to get herself together. Almost an hour. She hadn't been out for over a week. She had bathed regularly, but hadn't bothered with make-up or given even cursory attention to her hair. She looked slightly feral.

As she got ready, Alicia straightened up the living room, taking the dishes back into the kitchen, throwing away the empty snack bags, gathering the empty wine and soda bottles for recycling, then dusting and vacuuming.

"What are you doing down there?"

"Don't worry about it. Just get ready. I'm having severe symptoms of banana crème pie withdrawal. Very serious. If you don't hurry, we'll have to call 9-1-1."

Alicia moved on to the kitchen, did the dishes, gave a sponge bath to the stove and other appliances. As she was folding and hanging up the dish towel, Christine appeared in the doorway.

"You look great!"

"Let's not go overboard."

They headed out. Tom had taken the SUV. No choice but to taxi it.

Christine had hardly spoken to anyone since the funeral. Now that her incidental vow of silence was broken, she was like a dam bursting. Alicia mostly listened and smiled.

"You think you have choices. And they are choices. But just two tiny narrow options from thousands of possibilities, none of which you are aware of at the time, because you are living in a box. So what kind of choice is that? I've been kidding myself about everything. Certainly, I don't regret anything. Especially not the kids. But where does it go? Where do you end up? You think you're dealing with eternity. But it's the flash of a camera. There better be a Heaven. There better be a real shot at happiness. Otherwise, why bother being a good person? Why try to make a difference? Most differences don't make any difference. Did you really say banana crème pie? I love banana crème pie!"

"And here we are."

As they entered, beloved frequenters that they were, the expressions of the bartender and two waiters on duty lit up like the royal family had just dropped by for tea. Of course, no one had escaped seeing Christine on television, so none of them could entirely hide their empathies. Thus the pure glitter of their delight was flecked with a bit of dolefulness, which they all did their best to hide.

"I knew this was a special day. Miss Alicia, you have finally resigned yourself to the fact that I would look better in your clothes than you do. So what have you brought me? I am hoping the Elbaz bolero jacket. Maybe the Peter Jensen chiffon dress?"

"Did someone put LSD in your jasmine tea, Carl?"

"So what will it be, ladies? We have an exquisite squid salad on the menu today."

"Two slices of banana crème pie would be multi-orgasmic."

"We close in about seven hours. Will that be enough time?"

"For us it's like machine gun fire."

"I should be so lucky."

Carl left to get their desserts.

"Have you ever?"

"Eaten banana crème pie? That's kind of personal, Christine. But I guess, if I'm going to share that with anyone, it should be you … yes, I have."

"We never talked about it. Tom and I. Isn't strange to make love with someone hundreds of times but never once ever actually talk about it?"

"I think that's more common than not. But it's changing. With the younger generation. Wow. I'm talking like an old lady."

"You *are* an old lady, Miss Alicia. Just deal with it." Carl was back.

All conversation stopped as they savored their desserts. Unless moaning could be considered elements of a conversation.

They both decided to have coffee. Christine took a sip and put down her cup.

"Alicia. I can't go back. Everything's changed. I've changed. Whether I wanted to or not. But it's for the better. I think it is, anyway."

"The Bishop asks about you. You are welcome anytime. Just to visit or if you want to talk."

"I may take him up on that. Now that I've rolled the stone away from my cave."

"Christine, I have a favor to ask."

"Of course. What?"

"Just to go with me to meet with someone. That Lenny guy. He's been calling the Bishop. It's very suspicious. I don't trust him."

"Is this set up? When?"

"No, I haven't called him yet. But I will. Soon."

"Just let me know."

"More coffee?"

"Sure. Did he ever bring us the pie? I don't think so. I see no evidence of there ever being any pie on this table."

"Carl! Quick! We need some pie."

Girl Talk 2

Ying Mae and Dawa shared a deluxe suite on the 45th floor of Four Seasons Hotel Chicago. It was opulently furnished and had two huge bedrooms, each with its own marble bathroom. One bedroom they shared. The other was the "play room", used when either Ed or Harold wanted to swing by for a quick one, though even for this Harold usually sent a car around and had Ying Mae taken over to the Lake Point Tower. It was just before noon and she had just come back from there. She was sitting on her bed, brushing and bobby-pinning her hair.

"I'm gonna put broken glass in my cunt next time."

"Ying Mae, how come you speak so good English?"

"Very funny."

"Mean. Really!"

"Whatever. How can you stand it? That Ed is a disgusting pig. A pig might be better."

"I have very bad. Much bad."

"Much worse, Dawa. You mean 'much worse'. I had an American boyfriend when I was in Taiwan. For three years. A soldier boy. He was crazy about me and wanted to get married. I got pregnant. I wasn't ready. So I got rid of it. He never forgave me. Boy was I stupid! Look at me now."

"You beautiful."

"Thanks. But that will only get you into trouble. So you've had worse than Ed? Is that even possible? A water buffalo? An AIDS-infected gorilla?"

"Lenny come get me. Save. I like him. Not like them."

"Yes … I know. There's something special there. So what's he doing with them? Ed and Harold, they're gangsters. Lenny has class."

"Oooooh. You want …"

"Dawa you sweet and simple little girl. It's not always about sex."

"Yes it is!"

Laughing uncontrollably as only a 14-year old girl can laugh, Dawa ran over to Ying Mae's bed, jumped on, grabbed and started tickling her.

"You want! You want! Me see! You want!"

"Well … I wouldn't say no. He's a good-looking man."

Ten years separated them in age. But they giggled and rolled around on the bed like a couple of schoolgirls.

Prison is a great leveler.

Chapter 14

THE LIGHTS GO ON: The Shades Come Down

Technophobia

Something about technology rubbed Lenny the wrong way.

Sure he used his cell phone. But just barely. And only occasionally. To him it was just a landline which didn't have a cord to get tangled up or pull your cup of coffee off the table.

Computers. Email. The internet. Even though the control center which he used to manage and which now housed the Djin Djin girls websites, was packed with state-of-the-art computing and networking equipment, his vision blurred when he looked at all that "stuff". And as far as he was concerned, people who practically spent their lives surfing, chatting, gambling online, playing games, and so on, well, were incomprehensible. What was with these online games, anyway? To him a game was in the real world with tangible items — a pool cue, a hockey stick, a deck of cards — or they didn't exist, except in maybe the deranged minds of the geeks who sat hypnotized in front of their monitors for days on end. Frankly, he didn't even like watching TV. Too removed from real life, the real action.

But suddenly, it all became clear. He stared at his cell phone. He had used it so little, it still had the protective film on the clear plastic readout panels.

Now he knew. This was the key. This was how he could get done what he needed to get done, without anyone being any the wiser. It was portable. Anonymous. Discrete.

First, he had to learn how to operate it. People were always tapping on their phones, making what he thought were wild claims about all the things they could do with them. There must be something to it. He looked in his "everything else drawer" and sure enough, still sealed in cellophane was the instruction manual. Over the course of the evening, Lenny emerged from the primitive cave of pre-history and joined the ranks of sophisticated mobile phone users worldwide. And he discovered that indeed these little multifunctional pieces of electronic ingenuity packed a lot of punch.

A few simple text messages had snapped him out of his Luddite stupor. They were from Ying Mae. He wasn't sure how she got his number. Maybe she lifted it off of Harold's phone or Rolodex when he wasn't looking. Did people still uses Rolodexes? However she had gotten it, she subsequently sent him several messages in what looked like pidgin to him.

Want to take thm down. Dont care
wat happens 2 me. YM

Taking big risk. U mite tell thm.
Thnk i can trust u. I hate them! YM

> I cn take care of sefl. Others so
> young. I really hurt 4 thm. YM

Who was YM? He couldn't make any connection there.

Finally, one arrived signed 'Ying'. YM. Ying Mae. That's it!

At first he was very suspicious. Was this yet another from the trick bag of Harold Danko and Ed Valley? Was he being sucker-punched? They were so wily and unpredictable.

Moreover, even if he were able to make sense out of Ying Mae's cryptograms, he wouldn't have known how to reply or what to say.

Her most recent message sounded desperate.

> Cant take this anymore. Will
> u help? Cn I call? Plz. Ying

It had been four days.

Should he risk it? What did he have to lose? Only his life.

He sent he a text message back. Better late than never.

> Yes. Len

Then the jitters set in. Second thoughts. Fear and trembling.

Beneath that anxiety, however, he was constantly being hammered with the humiliating and painful urgency of his situation, his dire and desperate need to get out. To finally escape the frightening clutches of these two men who had trapped him, were now using him, and who would ultimately send him to slaughter in order to protect their own asses.

He had to take the chance. She had an inside track. Christ, she was sleeping with the enemy! And she said she wanted to take them down. Take them down? What was going on? Why?

He sent her another text message.

> Need proof. Lenny

An hour later, he got a reply.

> Kimnai is in SF. Still has short
> hair. Vry sweet girl. YM

Kimnai was alive!! They had shipped her off to San Francisco. How often he had thought of her, a longing shot through with the pain of loss, the dread that she was the victim of the horrible murder, the flayed corpse in the morgue. How often he had tried to not think of her.

But she was okay. Okay? At least alive.

The shock and euphoria subsided enough for Lenny to again focus on the solicitation from Ying Mae. Apparently to join forces.

He recalled her comment that night in Chicago — the night of butter, his debut as a porn star, the confrontation over the Bishop — just as he was getting on the elevator to leave.

You deserve better, Mr. Petrocelli. We all do.

Yes. We certainly do.

He texted his reply.

Call me. Lenny

His cell phone didn't ring for the next two days. But his doorbell did. The next morning.

"FedEx for Mr. Lenny Petrocelli. Sign here, sir."

From Chicago. What was with this these guys and their goddamn FedEx notes? Handwritten.

The fat lady sings, Lenny. The Bishop claims to speak for God Almighty. It's time he met Him in person. Make necessary arrangements. You know what to do. — Harold

A snuff order for Bishop William Flynt Mulcahey. He had signed for it. Wonders never cease.

The Call

"He won't tell me who he is. He insists on talking to you and says you will definitely want to talk to him."

"Okay, Miss Shilling. Please close the door. Which line?"

"The only one that's blinking."

Miss Shilling closed the door behind her. Was that an attitude? Or are these young ones all like that?

He punched the speakerphone button. Then the only other one that was blinking.

"This is Bishop Mulcahey. Who may I ask is calling?"

"We both had it completely wrong. You were wrong about me. I was wrong about you."

"You have ten seconds to stop being enigmatic and just say who you are."

"When you had me as your guest ..."

"Lenny Petrocelli?"

"... I didn't know anything. I had no idea we were mixed up with the Thailand girls. They're all ..."

"I know all about it. They have told me their stories."

"And I thought you were a child-molesting pervert, preying on little boys. I stand corrected. My bosses admitted to setting you up. They hate you with their every fiber."

235

"What about the girls? You say you know about this now?"

"They have put me in the middle of it. I see it from the outside, the inside, every side. They've put me in charge of the new girls you just ran off the streets."

"Congratulations on your promotion."

"It's not my choice. But ... but I need to talk to you. Immediately."

"This very flattering. You want to be friends. I'm supposed to believe you've come around. That you want to help. After what happened to Frankie and Martin. Do you take me for a complete idiot?"

"No. Do you take me for a total slimeball?"

"Lenny, I've never thought of you any other way."

"Bishop. Listen. We need to meet as soon as possible."

"I need to think about this. What do you really want, Petrocelli? You got your little girls back. The police won't lift a finger. In fact, I'm sure they're part of it, taking their own piece of the pie. So what's the game?"

"You're making my point. I have nothing at all in terms of the girls to gain by talking to you. I only have one reason for risking my neck, my very life calling you. This whole thing is sick. These guys are bottom-dwellers. I want out. But I need your help. And you need mine. Listen to me. You are in grave danger."

"Are you threatening me?"

"No, I'm trying to save your self-righteous ass. They've put a hit out on you."

"How do you know that?"

"Bishop ... they ordered me to do it."

"If we meet, I'll have protection. No way am I walking into my own execution chamber."

"On your terms. On your turf. But you gotta protect me too. If this gets back, I'm history."

"I'll be in touch. Is this caller ID a good number?"

"The only good number. If I can't talk, I'll say you have a wrong number. But I will get back to you. As soon as I shake loose. Agreed?"

"This better not be a trick, Lenny. Next time I'll let you die."

"God bless you too, Bishop."

Click.

Love is a Four-Letter Word

The call to Lenny did not go well. Not from Alicia's perspective. Lenny refuse to talk about anything on the phone and insisted they meet face-to-face. He kept saying the same things over and over about a gazillion times. He sounded frantic.

"You have to believe me!"

"It's not what you think."

"Please meet with me."

"I need your help!"

"Please trust me."

She agreed to meet with him but only if she could bring someone.

Was she afraid of him?

Yes.

He frightened her. He had betrayed her. He filled her with anger. Shame. Vindictiveness. She reviled him. She loathed him. She despised him. She hated him ...

She loved him.

There. She said it.

Hearing his voice on the phone. Desperate. Pleading. Certainly not the cocksure, fearless, brazen Lenny she had always known. A completely different side of the man.

But still him. And as always happened, his voice went crashing through all of her feigned indifference, the real antipathy, the anger, the hurt, the protective walls, the Kevlar around her heart, and reached deep deep deep inside of her and unleashed the hot fury of ... love.

It was an inexplicable, irrational, nonsensical, counterintuitive, destructive passion.

She hated him for it.

She loved him for it.

He was her poison pill.

He was her gateway to Paradise.

He was her arsenic-spiked Kool-Aid.

He was the sweet liqueur which nourished her heart.

People who take a cynical, fatalistic view of the human condition — or was it a realistic one? — suggest that there is hard-wired into the human organism, into each and every one of us without exception, a self-destructive flaw. Something lurking as a recessive gene or a subconscious latency. Some crack in the tile. Sometimes microscopic and nearly invisible. But there.

It was this defining glitch which ran as a silent partner to the fine-tuned rationalizations, beautifully-architected systems of thought, brilliantly-wrought and highly-sophisticated political and moral philosophies, heaven-embracing theologies, breathtaking mythologies and analogies and paradigms and models and hierarchies — all of which allegedly set man apart from the beasts of the jungle — then went on to propel him toward the most hideous and shameful testimony of his presence in the world: war, genocide, torture, ethnic cleansing, serial killing, rape. Allegedly for some perceived greater or smaller good.

It was the congenital flaw that allowed high-minded God-fearing men to exterminate whole native populations to put in place settlements to glorify the very same God who commanded their morality and high-mindedness.

It was the glint and gleam of suicidal curiosity in the eye of the five-star general with his finger on the launch button.

It was the all-or-nothing bet, the dirty needle, the no-condom ass-fuck.

It was the kid in school with the AR-15, the cop with the junk habit, the model wife with her Thursday lover, the perfect family man addicted to porn.

It was the grenade with the pin pulled at the center of all of our souls.

Under the Dior, Versace, Gabbana, Donna Karan, de la Renta and Dolce, we all had a bomb strapped to our chests.

Lenny was Alicia's bomb.

How else could it be?

This was the tortured confidence that Alicia was sharing with Christine right now, in a rambling, barely coherent monologue at the Mangiami Café in the Lower East Side of Manhattan.

It was late Saturday afternoon, a few minutes before 6:00, the time she had agreed to meet Lenny. And Christine — sweet dear Christine, God bless her — had agreed to come along. They had arrived a little early. Christine was quiet so Alicia was doing all the talking.

Christine still didn't look very good. But at least she was out.

"I don't understand it. Lenny is so completely the wrong person for me. But that's the way it is. I'm going to tell you something I have never ever told anyone. I can barely admit this to myself. But you know I was married. For almost three years. Do you know that on my wedding night, in the honeymoon suite of our hotel — I can see this like it was just yesterday — there we were, making love, the end of an exhausting but truly beautiful day. Sean was on top of me and my eyes were closed. And with my new husband inside me I was imagining that it was Lenny I was making love to. That's right, Lenny. I'm so fucked up."

"Alicia. I don't think we ever love someone for who they are. We love them for what we think they could be. And then we try to bring that out of them. That is the real joy of love."

"God, Christine. That is so you. So brilliant. So incomprehensible ..."

Alicia's train of thought was halted by the sight of Lenny coming through the door.

Christine saw the look in her eyes and turned to see for herself.

Lenny was much better looking than she had imagined. Though he had a worried look on his face, he still seemed confident, in command. His face even more striking the closer he got. There was character and intelligence in his eyes. Not the thug or rough character she had expected.

Lenny got halfway into the long narrow café and spotted them. His eyes locked on Alicia. She met his gaze and tried to give nothing away. She was feeling such a wild mix of emotions, she wasn't sure where one ended and the next began.

Lenny sat down. No one spoke for a full two minutes. The silence was as thick as cement. Alicia just continued to stare at him. He looked at her. Looked away. Looked at her.

Christine broke the deadlock. Stating the obvious.

"I'm Christine. Alicia's friend."

Correction from Alicia.

"Best friend."

"Pleased to meet you. I wish the circumstances were better."

Alicia. "So do I."

"It's not what you think."

"You already said that."

"Alicia. We both know that I've been a fuck-up. Most of my life. So maybe I get what I deserve. But what has happened … this is not what I bargained for."

"You're a well-paid sleazeball. What could be better?"

"Okay. Touché. I can't go toe-to-toe with you in a battle of words. You're way too clever for me. So just let me lay out a simple proposition. You can take it or leave it."

"Twenty words or less."

"Okay. Better than that. Here it goes."

"That's seven."

Lenny looked squarely into Alicia's eyes. It was so intense it was all she could do to hold on and return his gaze.

"I want to do better."

"That's twelve."

"That's it."

"Why are you calling the Bishop, Lenny?" So much for tip-toeing around the issue.

"He knows everybody. The people I need to get to. My only way out is to blow this thing apart. Take it down. I can't do this anymore. I've got to get out. Before they kill me."

"So you want to save your own precious hide. What if your hide is not worth saving?"

"Then the least I can do is set free a lot of very sweet innocent young girls who deserve better than the hand they've been dealt. If I get blown away, call it collateral damage."

Two more minutes of dead silence. This time Alicia was looking down. She didn't want Lenny to see that she was crying.

"Alicia. I talked to the Bishop. Very briefly."

Whispering. "I hope it went well for you."

"It went. We'll see."

Christine stared straight ahead. Not knowing what to think. A newsreel played in her mind. A disconnected collage. Nong Khai. Bishop Mulcahey. Bangkok. The Djin Djin girls. Danny's funeral.

Alicia still could not bring herself to look at Lenny.

His phone rang.

"Fuck. I hate these things." Popped it open.

"Yes?"

"Ed here. You're going to San Francisco. We'll meet you there."

"When?"

"You leave in three hours. Maybe it's a little short notice. But that's the way it is, Petrocelli. You're on US Airways 5966 leaving Kennedy at 9:10. That's Kennedy. You got that?"

"Right. Right. US Airways 5966. Kennedy. I'll call you as I'm boarding."

He closed the phone and slipped it into his coat pocket.

"I'm sorry. I gotta go."

He was out the door. It was 6:15 and the long-anticipated, much-dreaded meeting was over. Alicia was still looking at her hands, palms up in her lap. Christine watched Lenny all the way out the door, then turned to Alicia and put her finger softly to her cheek.

"He's a very handsome man. Whatever he's done in the past, I think he's a good man."

"Christine, with my whole heart and soul, I hope you're right."

Confessions of an Assassin

It was unusual for a priest of the stature and reputation of Bishop Mulcahey to still hear confessions. But the Bishop was an unusual man.

Typically as a priest rose through the hierarchy of the church to the upper command posts of responsibility, the administrative tasks put increasing demands on time and energy, shrinking the store of those precious resources for the nuts-and-bolts aspects of priesthood — saying mass, hearing confession, doing baptisms and marriages, conducting pre-marital and even marriage counseling. Some bishops, inflated with their own sense of grandeur and eminence, meted out these basic priestly tasks, as monarchs might have done so in times past, either tossing them on rare and special occasions as undeserved love trinkets to an unworthy peasantry, or doling them out as highly precious jewels to high-ranking patrons of the throne.

Thus, saying mass for a bishop or archbishop might be confined to a High Mass service at Christmas or Easter, with production value and media attention which might rival a new Broadway staging of *West Side Story*, starring Brad Pitt and Angelina Jolie, music played live by the Rolling Stones. Or the most holy-of-holies bishop would perform the baptism for the newborn of a local district congressman or U. S. senator in the glare of live television coverage, with the tacit understanding that there would be favorable nods in Washington for bills directly affecting the parish community.

The Catholic Church has historically been a titan on the world political stage, a bullying giant which usually gets its way one way or another, and while in contemporary times it is not the monstrous mover-and-shaker it once had been, it still jockeys for position and is a formidable and respected player in the international political community. Many believe that even today, more than saving souls, political power is the top priority of the Catholic Church in Rome.

At the same time, people are power and strength is in numbers. Meaning that, saving souls by offering a ready-made, God-approved path to Heaven is a way of accumulating and maintaining power. The Church gathers into the protective folds of its sacred garments, the sinful-seeking-salvation souls of the Earth, offering them the eternal light of God's Kingdom. A saved soul is a grateful and loyal soul.

With a seemingly infinite supply of sinners out there, the already gargantuan ranks of the Church's army is constantly being stocked with new recruits. It is reported that there are currently 1,100,000,000 Catholics in the world.

Power.

Bishop Mulcahey's conscience and personally-held values, however, required him to balance out the pressures which flowed down from the Papacy itself to exercise the social control and political authority of the Church, with a need to be a spiritual force in the personal lives of those in his congregation. He believed that Christ Himself set the standard for a truly sacred ministry here on Earth. That attending to individual needs was the highest expression of service to God and fulfillment of His mandate to men of the cloth like himself.

Unfortunately, it was this face-to-face approach, the highly individual attention he gave to each of his congregants, which made him vulnerable to the trumped-up charges of child molestation leveled against him in Minneapolis. He did indeed give personal one-on-one attention to those who sought his counsel. He did indeed spend time alone with many in need of his spiritual advice, some of them pre-adolescent boys and girls.

But even after the nightmare he endured in Minneapolis under the slanderous assault of the men running prostitutes and drugs in the community there, even after being promoted to the highly prestigious position he now had at St. Francis of Assisi, he felt as committed as ever to being in the trenches with the people who attended his church, and dispensing those sacred sacraments which had drawn him to his divine calling as a priest in the first place.

He still said mass at least once a week, he did the occasional baptism, he presided over Confirmations of the young ones who had just come of age, often even performed marriages.

And he heard confessions on the second and third Saturdays of each month.

All of this served in his mind two invaluable purposes. Not only did it create a special connection for many congregants with the man who preached God's word to them from the pulpit every Sunday. But it kept him in touch with *them*. In touch with those particulars, the trials and foibles of Everyman and Everywoman as they lived out their lives and struggled against both the earthly and the spiritual challenges each and every day. It kept him in touch with their hopes, their dreams, their sins.

December 8, 2007.

It was a very cold afternoon. The confessional lacked a heating vent and here at the end of his three hours of listening to litanies of generally quite innocent breaches of both Biblical and Church commandments, Bishop Mulcahey's legs and feet were numb. As it approached 6 pm, there were fewer and fewer waiting to see him, so two or three minutes after the hour, he peaked out and was relieved that from what he could see, he was at last done. Then he heard someone enter the confessional booth on his left. He slid open the small privacy door and bent toward the gauze-shrouded opening.

"I have sinned often in the past, father. Very serious sins."

"We all are sinners. God in His mercy offers us His forgiveness and an opportunity to begin again without the stain of previous transgressions. Do you wish to confess these sins?"

"Well, actually, I have a question."

"Go ahead, my son."

"What about future sins? I mean, if I know I am going to commit a serious sin, how does this work then?"

"Are you asking to be forgiven for something you haven't done yet? I would pray for you, and offer to pray with you, for God to give you the strength to turn away from this, to stand up to the temptation and in God's name say no."

"It's not a temptation. More of an order."

"An order? Who is ordering you to sin? The Devil? That's to be expected."

"Look at you, father. I mean, you take orders from up above. The Pope, for example. Maybe the Archbishop over there in Manhattan. What's his name?"

"I only answer to my Creator and my Savior, just as you also are only to answer to God Himself. There is no earthly authority that can override God's commands. His holy Ten Commandments are his direct instructions to you. And if you are asking me to arrange God's forgiveness in advance, sort of a credit on the ledger for your salvation, I'm sorry. That is completely out of the question. That would be asking God to put His divine imprimatur on your anticipated sin."

"Well, I'm under orders. And I have to do what I have to do. That's that."

"I see. So now I guess I'm puzzled as to why you're here. Confession is a sacrament for those who wish, despite prior weakness and failure, to again walk a righteous path, free of sin. You apparently are determined to sin again. "

Yoshikaze had quietly slipped the handgun from its holster and now retrieved the long silencer from his jacket pocket. Slowly and silently he screwed it onto the end of the barrel.

"Well, thanks for the tip, father. I guess I had it all twisted around in my head and thought you could help. Sorry. My bad."

There was something very strange in this man's tone that the Bishop now started to sense. Granted he was tired from hearing confessions for three hours. But this went beyond that. His chest tensed and squeezed his next words.

"May the enlightening spirit of the Lord Savior be with you during these troublesome times." He blessed the air between them with a sign of the cross. "Is there anything further?"

Yoshikaze could faintly see the outline of the Bishop's face through the confessional gauze. Mulcahey was looking straight at him, probably trying to get a look at who he was talking to. Since Yoshikaze's tiny portion of the confessional was unlit, this was entirely a fruitless effort. With a firm and steady grip, Yoshikaze held the gun pointed directly at the center of the Bishop's forehead. His index finger was moist against the trigger.

"Well yes … there is something. Bye bye, Bishop."

And it was done.

Bondage

Lenny was on the phone with Ed Valley. Fifteen minutes into the boarding for his flight to San Francisco.

"I have to tell you, Lenny, the numbers haven't been good. I don't know what your strategy is but we're hemorrhaging money from your end of town. So now there are five less ugly ducklings in the pond. You should be celebrating. Maybe you'll owe us less money at the end of the year."

This is his reaction to five women hanging from meat hooks like baby veal?

These conversations were so painful. He had always fancied himself streetwise and battle seasoned. The streets were tough. But had he even heard of anyone as cruel and insensitive as these guys? Not that he could remember.

"They didn't stand a chance in Brooklyn. The vigilantes shut everything down there. I put them where they at least they could do some business."

"And hung a sign up that said 'Home of the Ugly Asian Sluts, Homicidal Maniac Wanted.' Don't worry about it. We've got bigger fish to fry."

That sounded ominous.

"What's up?"

"Just be there. Harold and I will arrive somewhere around noon. You're at the Warwick."

"Should I bring my bellhop uniform?"

"Cool it, wise ass. We take care of you. Probably better than you deserve."

Right.

Lenny handed his boarding pass to the attendant and off he was to San Francisco.

As he sat down in the first class cabin, his phone beeped. Text message.

**Careful n SF. They r fuckng wth u.
B sure 2 delete all messges. YM**

Fucking with me? What a shocker.

The flight was almost seven hours. But he'd get there before midnight.

There was an incredibly stupid movie on the plane. *Herbie Fully Loaded.* Did people really find this stuff entertaining? Funny? No wonder kids were growing up retarded.

He arranged his own taxi to the hotel.

Again he had to admit, in terms of accommodations they certainly did take care of him. Warwick San Francisco Hotel. Absolutely five stars. Spacious, beautifully decorated room. Very Louis XVI. Like their brochure said 'a touch of Europe'. Located right downtown in the heart of the theater district and within walking distance of most everything you'd want to see on your first visit to the city as a tourist. This was his first time.

Even if he was on New York time, he didn't feel like going to bed. Mind churning away. His body full of nervous energy.

He threw his bag onto the bed and headed back out. He walked east to Union Square, then north to Chinatown, finally back through Nob Hill, stopping for half an hour or so, at an Irish pub for two bottles of stout. It was a pleasant change from his usual Mickey's Malt Liquor.

When he got back to the room, the accumulated fatigue body-slammed him and he was out cold, face down on top of the duvet with his clothes on.

He awoke groggy and disoriented. The digital clock said 11:08.

Perfect. A good night's sleep and still time to maybe order some breakfast and get himself showered and ready to meet with Chicago. They said they were getting in at noon.

Noon passed. Then one. Three. Five. Evening.

No word from them.

They were so enigmatic. Unpredictable. But by now Lenny recognized it was always by plan. Every move by cool calculation.

Text message.

R u ok? YM

He replied.

Fine. Where are Ed Harold? Len

Almost instantaneously.

Comng 2morrow gotta go. YM

So apparently they hadn't even left yet.

Both relieved and puzzled, he started to pace. Then he began to feel the anxiety build.

He wondered what in the world he was doing here. Apparently a day early. Why did they have him fly out in the first place? Why was he sitting in a hotel room on the other end of the country when he was under the impression he was supposed to be taking care of business back in New York, before things got worse and really imploded?

Lenny was bored and tense but not restless enough to go for a walk.

As a mild distraction he turned on the television and flipped the channel to CNN, always perfect for a non-intrusive bed of chatter, a companionable aural wallpaper. Lenny thumbed distractedly through a USA Today as he sat on the deluxe leather chesterfield. He sipped on a wine cooler he found in the mini-fridge.

A segment called "News Across the Nation" came on. Something in the sonorous voice of the newscaster pulled his attention …

In what has been described as a gangland-style murder, a renowned and highly-regarded Bishop and community activist was killed in cold blood, late yesterday afternoon as he heard confession at St. Francis of Assisi Cathedral in Brooklyn, New York. Bishop William Mulcahey was found slumped over in his confessional by a member of the custodial staff. The cause of death was a bullet fired at close range to his head.

Except for the killer, the cathedral was apparently empty at the time of the murder, so no one was observed leaving the scene of the crime.

A picture of Lenny appeared as an inset the upper corner of the screen.

However, New York City Police have identified a suspect in the case, a Lenny Petrocelli, also based in Brooklyn. He is considered extremely dangerous. Authorities are requesting any and all information which might lead to the apprehension and arrest of this man, pictured here.

Expressions of condolence and tribute are pouring in from all corners of the country, especially from Minneapolis-St. Paul, Minnesota, where the Bishop spent the greater part of his career. Funeral services will be held on Thursday.

Bishop Mulcahey was 63 years old at the time of his death.

They say when you are drowning, your whole life passes before you. As he watched the news about the Bishop, Lenny experienced a variation of that.

Lenny had his whole future pass before him. It was a very short future.

And it had a very unhappy ending.

All he could think now was that he needed to disappear. Escape.

Who was he escaping from? Certainly the police. At least until he cleared himself.

Who else was he escaping from? Ed and Harold?

Definitely. They ordered him to cap the Bishop. Now somebody else had already done it. But the police had fingered him anyway. How did that happen? He couldn't be sure nor could he begin to make any sense out of any of this.

But Harold and Ed must figure in somehow.

He had no alternative.

Escape.

Escape to where? Should he go back to the city? Should he get the fuck out of the country? That would look bad. Leaving the country now — if he could even get out, since they would probably red-flag his passport — would be like signing a confession.

Could he go back to New York now? He was a wanted man. 'Very dangerous' they said. What did that mean? Do not operate heavy machinery? If swallowed, immediately induce vomiting and call a physician? Keep away from children? Shoot on sight?

He saw only one option. Go. Just go! The impulse was becoming more and more compelling. Get away from these creeps before they take you completely apart. It was now a matter of life or death.

Lenny threw his things into his bag. He was making a last quick check around the room to make sure he got everything, when there was a knock at the door.

Room service? They must have the wrong room.

He opened the door. There beaming like the house of the rising sun was the face of Yoshikaze, life insurance salesman smile straining both Yoshikaze's lips and Lenny's credulity.

"Good evening, Mr. Petrocelli. Just wanted to make sure everything was okay."

"Everything is beautiful."

"If you need anything, I'll be right here. Mr. Danko and Mr. Valley will see you tomorrow afternoon at 2:30. There will be a car to pick us up. Have a pleasant sleep."

So he was locked down. These guys were relentless. They thought of everything. It was like they could read his mind. Even anticipate what he would soon be thinking.

As unsettled as he was, he settled in for what was going to be a long night.

He tried to sleep.

He couldn't.

This must be what it was like trying to get some shut-eye lying in a foxhole on the front lines of a raging battle. Just as he would drift off, a bomb would drop next to him. For Lenny, the bombs were images. Harold Danko's smug self-congratulatory grin. Ed Valley's vulgar mocking laugh. Kimnai's missing toe. Djin Djin girls curbside. His "uglies" crying. The flayed corpse. His buttered penis on the big screen. Yoshikaze's slitty predatory eyes. Dok Phnom. The Bishop.

The Bishop.

He had hated him more than he thought possible.

The Bishop. Dead.

Lenny now felt a strange remorse. For a crime he hadn't committed. A remorse for ever even thinking he wanted the Bishop gone.

Death. So absolute. So final. No do overs.

Lenny awoke from what had been a very bad facsimile of sleep. He went down to the hotel restaurant. It was 10:30 and they had stopped serving breakfast. He headed in anyway. Yoshikaze was close behind.

"May I join you?"

"Thanks anyway."

"Suit yourself."

Yoshikaze continued on, then sat watching Lenny from a corner table. Smiling. Always smiling that inscrutable faux smile.

Lenny didn't feel hungry anymore. He got up and went back to his room.

Four hours seemed like forever. His room phone finally rang. Down to the lobby.

There they were. Big welcoming. The family. Back together.

"Lenny! Lookin' good lookin' good." Harold. They must have left him in a vat of tanning dye overnight.

"How's our favorite assassin?" Ed. Charm with a bullet.

Assassin? Did they really think it was him that popped the Bishop?

"Right this way, Lenny. We have a very big day ahead of us." Harold led the way.

They got into a white stretch limo suitable for a high-ranking politician or a high-rolling thug — often times one and the same — and headed off. Lenny could not help but be awed with the view as they navigated the busy streets.

Magnificent architecture, striking, purposeful people. So much character and class. He could see why people were charmed by this city, why so many songs had been written about San Francisco.

Harold was sitting across Lenny. He popped the cap off of a bottle of tonic water.

"We've got a great setup here. You'll see. We thought we'd show you around."

Ed leaned forward and patted his stomach. "Gentlemen, I could eat a steer. Two if they cooked them. Let's get some lunch. We got plenty of time."

"You're on." Harold picked up the in-car phone and told the driver to head to the Bix.

Ed shook his head and slapped Lenny's knee.

"Saw your mug on TV last night, Lenny. Holy shit. All the way over here on the west coast. You're fucking famous."

"Listen, Lenny. Ed and I have no idea now how that happened. How it got so completely out of hand. Fiori's getting checks. He was supposed to have this handled."

"Just don't worry. We'll take care of it. It might a little while to smooth things out. Probably best if you hang here a few days. When's the funeral? Did they say?"

"Thursday."

"You better stay here till, I'd say, the end of the week. You like the room? Nice, eh?"

"Just enjoy yourself. And when we get the burners turned down, then you can go back. We'll let you now." Harold patted Lenny on the shoulder.

Ed with his shit-eating grin. "Be careful what you smack your balls up against around here. Lot of cross-dressers. Best advice I ever heard? Look under the tail before you put it in the male." M-A-L-E. Get it?"

"Got it." Lenny did his best to effect a genuine laugh. Not very convincing. Ed did his best to mask his disdain for Lenny. Also not very convincing.

They arrived at Bix, a financial district favorite among the martini and cigar crowd.

As they walked into the foyer, Lenny's phone beeped. Text message. Very bad timing.

Lenny tried to look as casual as possible as he glanced at it.

Talk 2 Kimnai. She's knows everythng.
Careful what u say. Wires. YM

Options. Delete message? Yes.

Wires? What did *that* mean? And how would he get hold of Kimnai?

Ed pulled up next to him glancing at the phone.

"Local action? Way to go."

"The old lady. Remind me later to bring home a loaf of bread and a half-gallon of milk."

"Petrocelli, you're a homo."

Lunch was uneventful. Ed was completely consumed in devouring a bloody New York strip steak that at best might have been passed under a reading lamp. Harold hovered over a Reuben sandwich, seemed distracted, and was atypically quiet. Lenny ate his Cobb Salad and tried not to show how uncomfortable he was, an effort which made him look even more uncomfortable.

When they got back into the limousine, refueled and refocused, Ed and Harold slowly started to reconfigure into their more familiar selves — bullish, opinionated, self-proclaimed experts on everything worldly and criminal. Ed offered a silent belch and got started.

"Look at this city, Lenny. Beautiful, eh? But what makes it tick, I ask you. Is it really any different than New York or London or Tokyo? I don't think so. And I'll tell you why. Every single one of those people out there are driven by the same thing. And you know what that is, Lenny? You want to take a guess?"

"Let's see, Ed. It's you talkin' and it's me listenin'. So let me take a wild stab at it. Sex? Could it be sex that makes the whole world go round?"

"For once in your life you got something right, Lenny. Though I'm hearin' some serious sarcasm in your voice. Which has been happening a lot lately. And so I'm wondering, and maybe Harold here is wondering too, just where this fucked up attitude is coming from, eh? This head bloat problem that seems to be creeping into recent interactions. Because for a guy to walk around with a big fucking halo taking up a lot of real estate, he'd sure better have his act together *or* he better have some very important friends in high places. Otherwise this motherfucker with the big sarcastic rain cloud raining on everyone else's parade, is just begging to be cut down to size. Way down to size, in the present cited example, if you get my meaning."

"Come on, Ed. Can't you take some friendly ribbing?"

"I could … if we were friends."

"Well, I don't know what to say. I'm in some deep shit here. And the two of you are all I have to turn to. Does this mean you're going to help me out or not?"

Harold, who had been listening with a sober amusement, jumped in to play peacemaker.

"We are family and we take care of family. Fact is, Ed and I always go to the mat for you. But in view of your performance the last several weeks, starting with the fiasco in Thailand with Dok Phnom, and especially now with the girls we put you in charge of, I'd say the ball is in your court."

"What ball?"

"The loyalty ball, Lenny. It would be real helpful for us to know that you are serious about what you're doing. That you're committed. And we can count on you."

A slightly calmer Ed. "That's why we brought you out here."

Harold couldn't temper his excitement. Money was his oxygen.

"This thing is growing so fast we can barely keep up with it. We want you to see what's going on. We need your help. But you have to be ready to step up to the plate."

"I'm ready. I'm ready. I'm here, aren't I?"

As if I had a choice.

Ed's hand shot out. "Alright, clean slate. Let's just go forward. No looking back."

Lenny returned Ed's firm handshake, only to see Harold holding his hand out as well. Another spring steel grip from a man who was clearly no stranger to the gym. And then of course, Harold's predictable-as-the-sunrise whap on the back.

Hopefully they wouldn't opt for a big group hug. Like any of this meant anything. However it was gift-wrapped, as a gentleman's agreement or as a rite of ceremonial male bonding, bullshit was still bullshit.

Ed the poet laureate then started to expound.

"We have two buildings set up in San Mateo. Exclusive playgrounds for the sucky-fucky. They're making a bundle. But this is only the beginning."

"The sky's the limit, Lenny. And the introductions are under the radar. All on the internet."

"Which you know better than anyone. Harold and I leave all that technology to the experts. First and foremost you. You ran a tight ship back in New York. So you obviously know how to put together a team and keep it on track."

"That Markham kid is a genius. Completely solid. They report like clockwork. Even the nigger boy, what's his name … ?"

"Keary."

"Yes, Keary. Rock solid."

Which one was the ventriloquist and which one the dummy?

"So this is what you should be keeping in mind here. We'll show you the visible stuff."

"But you're gonna build the invisible stuff."

Lenny tried not to give away what he was thinking. Were they just confused? They couldn't possibly be serious. What exactly was their game? He thought of Ying Mae's text message. *They r fuckng wth u.* Kind of said it all.

Maybe this is what they do to alleviate boredom.

The limousine had worked its way over to the 101 Freeway South. As they left downtown, the charm factor quickly dissipated as the landscape succumbed to the anonymous functionality of modern urban sprawl and cookie cutter development.

Still quite a contrast to the dense verticality of metropolitan New York.

They took the first San Mateo exit and proceeded on clean orderly streets to a gated community on the west edge of town. It was a large complex, an alphabet city of condos. Finally they pulled up to Buildings Q and R.

Harold was clearly very proud. "There you have it. Those two buildings. That's our World Trade Center."

Lenny suddenly found himself wishing he knew how to fly a Boeing 767.

"So here's what we're gonna do. Harold and I gotta go upstairs and make sure things are okay for a visit. You're gonna wait here. Yoshikaze can keep you company if you like. I know you guys are bosom buddies. Anyway, maybe in about an hour or so we can begin the tour."

"I'll be here. I'm on your clock."

"You got that right."

Perks

So he was going to be in San Francisco for at least a week. His initial panic had subsided. He had thought about it. This was fine. He could do what he needed to do from wherever. He just needed to get organized.

Lenny really wanted to call Ying Mae. It was time they had a serious talk. But he couldn't risk it now, with the driver in the car and Yoshikaze pacing close by.

Lenny sat there thinking, trying to come up with a plan of attack. He watched two workmen go about their business near the buildings. One was doing some gardening in front of Q and the other appeared to be replacing some wiring on the exterior of R.

Eventually, Harold and Ed came out. They were talking fast and gesticulating large.

"Alright, Lenny. Come on in."

They led him into Building R. As they went up the steps, Lenny glanced down at the worker bent over a circuit box. He could just see the handle of a large-caliber handgun, probably a Glock Sig Sauer P220, sticking out of his tool belt. Security. Harold and Ed didn't leave any loose ends.

The entranceway was beautifully decorated with two huge floor vases holding tall feathery plumes, a cream lacquer table with a lavish flower arrangement, two cut crystal sculptures and a jeweled ashtray. Lenny was surprised to see a formally dressed doorman right inside.

"Mr. Danko, Mr. Valley." He dismissed Lenny with a peremptory nod.

They crowded into the elevator and within seconds were on the top floor.

Lenny had to admit, the place reeked of class. It was as opulent and tasteful as any of the hotels they had put him up in and even boasted a homey feel. Customers would feel more like they were going to their girlfriend's pad than a whorehouse.

"We have a bit of a surprise for you, Lenny."

They entered an apartment suite at the end of a hall. There sitting on the living room sofa, smiling her little-girl-big-girl smile, was Kimnai.

Kimnai!

He was glad to see her, of course — extremely glad — but it suddenly hit him that he didn't know how to play this for Ed and Harold. They had no clue that he had been so worried that she was dead and no way of knowing that Ying Mae had already told him Kimnai was alive. But how did Ying Mae know that Kimnai was so important to him? Did she overhear Ed and Harold talking? And what could they possibly think his and Kimnai's relationship was? Exactly why were they arranging this 'surprise'?

Stop and think about who you're dealing with here, Lenny. Ed and Harold are sewer scum.

"My little friend. How have you been?"

"Just okay till now. Now I very happy. I have my big New York guy back."

She licked her lips and did a seductive thing with her shoulders.

Right. Sex. It's what makes the world go around.

"See I told you." Ed looked like he had just won a bet. "Petrocelli's a fucking pedophile."

Look who's talking. Can you spell Dawa?

"She's my special girl, Ed."

"I'll bet she is."

Kimnai came over and sat next to Lenny. She put her arms around him, whispered in his ear. Lenny looked over at Harold.

"Anything important on the schedule for the next hour or so?"

"You've had a rough day. Take some time and enjoy yourself." The paternalistic wink.

Kimnai stood and led Lenny by the hand to one of the bedrooms. She closed the door behind them. Lenny felt awkward.

"Kimnai, I don't ..."

She put her child's hand to his mouth to silence him. Then led him to the bed. He lay down and she lay down beside him, bringing her lips next to his ear. She whispered softly.

"The room is wired. You have to talk very softly. But for now just listen."

Wired! Ying Mae's message.

"Ying was out here too for a while. I told her you were my friend. A good man. I told her what Bishop did to you. Mr. Danko is very cruel to her. And they make me ... they make me do bad things. I am afraid. But it must stop. We must stop them. The other girls very afraid and so it is just me. But ..."

"Kimnai, you have to be so careful. These men are killers."

"I would rather be dead, Mr. Lenny. It so good to see you. Ever think we hold each other like lovers? My good friend. Can I read you a story? A Bible story?"

"No! No Bible stories! Listen, Kimnai. I want out too. I am trying. But I have no plan."

"I have a list. People here you call. But we have to help Ying Mae. All at the same time. Harold is such a bad man. We must do this together. But I have no way to make phone calls. They don't give me a phone. I leave sometimes. No money phones around anywhere."

"I will do what I can, Kimnai. I am so glad you're ... I was afraid something very bad had happened to you."

"Can you do me a favor, Mr. Lenny?"

"If I can."

"Just hold me. I want to feel like someone loves me."

"I love you, my precious child. My special little girl who saved my life."

And that is how they spent the next hour. In an embrace. An expression of love that hovered in the spaces between the usual categories. Not boy-girl. Not man-woman. Perhaps more like father-daughter but not even quite that. Not sexual but too intimate and physical to be purely Platonic. Big man arms and little girl arms.

If Lenny had been up till now wavering in his resolve to bring Harold and Ed and their sex empire down, that absolutely ended now.

It was time for the meek to inherit this portion of the Earth, these grasslands of the soul that these two monsters had been prowling, destroying lives and dreams — trashing the innocence of hope and the hope of innocence.

It was time for these girls to reclaim what was left of the youth and energy that these two men had been stealing and selling.

As he lay there holding Kimnai in his arms, he felt his strength and certainty grow and a purposeful, knowing calm settled over him.

He *could* and *would* do this.

She reached inside her blouse and pulled out a small folded piece of paper. She whispered.

"I have a regular who say he loves me. He works at a government office."

Lenny looked at it quickly. Handwritten names, phone numbers, email addresses. He put it in his pocket.

"Better to hide."

He slipped it inside of the front of his shorts.

"Thank you, Lenny, for being my friend."

He got up to leave and Kimnai remained behind. When he reached the living room, he saw that Yoshikaze had joined them, and that he, Ed and Harold were engaged in some serious, nail-hard discussion.

Busting balls was the topic.

Ed broke ranks to glance over at Lenny with that look of locker-room camaraderie that Lenny found so annoying.

"Hey! How was that, Lenny my boy? Did she slick lick your dick? Some girls just have a natural talent, eh? Born with it, I guess.

"We're getting married next month, Ed. Will you be my best man?"

"Always a comedian. Funny as a bullet in the head."

Harold was becoming impatient with this ongoing jousting match between Lenny and Ed, and again was more interested in getting down to business.

He gestured for Lenny to sit across from him.

"What you see here? This is where we're heading. Most guys who go through that door pay at least $2000 for the pussy you just got for free. We're having no problem keeping the calendars full. It's all packaging. Putting the right spin on it. These little Asians are the Rolls Royce of humping. That's the perception. We just need to make sure that message stays fresh and gets to the right people. You know, the guys that can afford it."

"Looks like you got it handled pretty well."

"It's never handled. Always got to stay ahead of the game. We're already seeing copycats. Easy to put up a storefront these days, with the internet and all. That's where you come in, Lenny."

"I'm not savvy when it comes to the internet. My techies do that stuff."

"You're missing my point. We need to make sure the competition never gets a foothold. Shut them down as fast as they open."

"Shut them down?"

"Damn right. This shit's illegal. Shut them down. You're gonna be doing a little onsite inspection for us, see how these places operate, find the unlocked basement window."

"Then bingo! Bye-bye." Ed. The Ernest Hemingway of pimpdom.

"So Lenny, you need to do some research. Since you're here, you can start with San Fran. Find out whose in charge, who commandeers the storm troopers. Who we can count on to do the busts. One by one. You can be our ambassador of good will to the SFPD."

Wait. This was beyond bizarre. They were telling him he should try to track down the very people he probably had on the list in his undies, in order to bust up any operations which might now or in the future compete with theirs.

This was too good to be true!

Exactly.

It was too good to be true. What was the flaw in all of this? Was this another set-up?

"Can I have a car? I need to get around."

"Yoshikaze can take you where you want to go."

Fuck.

"And after San Francisco?"

Ed laughed his Mr. Ed horse laugh. "You certainly know who to talk to in New York. They're the same ones who are looking for you right now."

Haw haw haw haw.

"We've got Seattle. Then Miami. We'll keep you moving. You need to be away from home for a while. Let the dust settle."

Double fuck. Triple fuck.

"Like I said. I'm on your clock."

Kimnai appeared in the doorway. She looked at Lenny. There was a faint smile on her face. Her eyes were soft and kind, but sad.

And he could see the fear.

Not for herself.

But for him.

Chapter 15

RUSSIAN ROULETTE: One Bullet On The Table

Conspiracy Theories

Lenny sat in the back seat. Yoshikaze drove and hummed along with some very annoying Japanese punk rock CD.

The day had really slammed him hard. Lenny's head was swarming with possibilities. When is the last time he felt certain about something? Anything? Everything seemed to have two contradictory sides.

There was one certainty: He needed to be very careful.

As soon as he got back to Warwick, apparently Yoshikaze had been told to back off the close watch, as he merely dropped him off and went on his way. Lenny immediately went to the reception desk and demanded a different room, claiming he had earlier found a huge cockroach on his pillow when he came out from his shower. They fawningly appeased him by upgrading him at no extra charge, to a suite located on a different floor.

That should take care of the risk of the room being bugged, at least for now. He wouldn't put it past Harold and Ed to try to eavesdrop on his every conversation.

When he got in his new room, he immediately called Ying Mae. This is the first time they had spoken since his night at Lake Point Tower in Chicago.

"No. They're just that stupid."

"They hardly seem stupid."

"Appearances are deceiving. I've spent a lot of time around them. Trust me, they're stupid. They think they're invulnerable. Just because things have been going so well."

"It's like you said. They're fucking with me, right? But why?"

"I've heard them talk. All along they've been testing you. And they're testing you now. Maybe you haven't figured it out. But you're the smartest guy in their entire organization. They've surrounded themselves with a bunch of yes-men who can't think their way out of a candy wrapper. So they need someone like you. But they also think you are way too gullible. You get sucked into every little game they lay on you."

"And if I don't pass the test."

"Gee, let's try to figure this out. Mr. Lenny, listen. You must know by now. With these guys, it's either to the top or to the bottom. They don't split hairs. If they decide they don't need you, you go out with the trash."

"I'm on trial. But they are giving me carte blanche to pull the heat into play. They must trust me somewhat to hand me a loaded gun. One that I could turn on them."

"They don't trust anyone. And if you take even one step out of line, you're history. Just stop and think about it. Who are you going to turn to? Ed brags all the time. One phone call. That's all it takes. You've hardly covered your ass."

"What's that supposed to mean?"

"They ship girls in from Asia. Who's the guy who arranged that? Girls walking the street. Who's the guy running that show? They kill the Bishop. Who are the cops looking for?"

"They framed me? But how?"

"I don't know. But that's been planned for weeks."

"What should I do?"

"Don't you see how perfect this is? You can be a double agent. Just do it, Mr. Lenny. What have you got to lose? You're in front of a firing squad. You might as well take your chances and make a break for it."

"How about Kimnai? She gave me a list."

"Kimnai would die before she would do anything to hurt you. She and I were gonna do this. So she got some squeeze to put together some people to call. But we can't do this alone. There are too many eyes and ears. Both here and there. We're constantly being watched."

"What's your stake in this? You've got it made. You have the life of a harem princess."

"I can't talk about it. Let's just say that I have been making my living on my back for many years but never ... never have I ... I don't want to talk about it, Mr. Lenny. It's disgusting. And Ed. He's almost as sick as Harold."

He waited. But she wasn't going to say any more.

"Okay."

"I can give you their movements. You've got to make the arrangements."

"Can you talk?"

"Text me. Less of a trail. Make sure you delete everything. Everything!"

"I'll be in touch."

"Thanks, Mr. Lenny. You can do this."

It was so hard to put all he had seen and heard for the past two days into some perspective. First he had the whipsaw of Harold's and Ed's games to deal with. He felt like a tiny fly in the hands of two sadistic boys who were trying to figure out the best way to dismember it.

Then just seeing Kimnai as a "working girl" was very painful. But there she was. He saw her with his own eyes right in the environment where, as a fifteen year old girl, she was being pedaled as a piece of young flesh, to men who liked the young ones and were willing to pay big dollars for jailbait sex.

Of course, the flipside was at least she was alive and, at least on the surface, healthy. He had feared in his most pessimistic moments she hadn't made it. But she did say she would rather die than go on like this. She needed his help.

Kimnai had been his guardian angel. Now it was his turn to be hers.

If that emotional whirlpool weren't enough, he found himself thrust into an ongoing conspiracy to take down his criminal sex slave-trading bosses. The train had already left the station. All he could hope for now was that it was on the right track.

Ying Mae. He had sensed something in her that first time in Chicago. Then the urgent text messages arrived. She said all of the right things.

Could he trust her? He had to.

The cherry of irony placed on top the huge indigestible sundae dessert sitting on his plate, was that these same criminal sex slave-trading bosses were actually handing him the very weapons he could use to take them down, at the same time hedging their bets by setting him up for a major fall if he did anything to cross them.

Russian roulette.

What were the odds?

One bullet on the table.

The rest in the chamber, ready for a good spin.

He could mull this over, shake his head, gasp and wonder and swoon at the improbability and horribly bad dumb luck of his situation. But overriding all considerations was this simple conclusion: He had no choice. Not about the position he was in or what he had to do about it.

Time to go to work.

Pomp and Eulogy

There would be three days of services, ceremonies, tributes, eulogies, and other solemn and awe-inspiring observances in New York City. Then the body would be flown back to Thief River Falls, Minnesota, the Bishop's childhood hometown and final resting place.

Pope Benedict XVI, of course, was booked over a year in advance and could not himself attend any of the elaborate events. But the Catholic Church was nevertheless well-represented. New York's own Cardinal Edward Egan, in the honored company of Cardinal Justin Rigali from Philadelphia and Cardinal Sean O'Malley from Boston, led the attendees in solemn prayer and then offered grand visions of hope, predicated on all of us carrying on the good Bishop's unfinished work. Of course, there were dozens of priests and nuns from the boroughs, even from numerous outlying communities, there to mourn and offer their devotions.

Many television and Hollywood celebrities paid their cameo respects to the fallen hero. Lavish bouquets and wreaths, sized to shout loud plaudits as to the generosity of their donors, were carried and presented, paraded and placed during the photo ops generously sprinkled across the three days of lamentations.

Local and even national politicians weighed in on what a tragic loss his death represented to both the Brooklyn community and the national struggle against the moral disintegration of our great nation. Mayor Bloomberg was prominent at the front of local government officialdom. Governor Spitzer dropped by. Senator Charles Schumer gave a solemn speech and even passed along the sincere regrets of his colleague, Senator Clinton, as to her not being able to attend. All the way from Minnesota came Lt. Governor Carol Molnau, who spoke through a tsunami of tears about the loss of one of their native sons.

Most impressive to those who appreciated the refined quality of the Bishop as a man and his closely held values as a spiritual leader, were the throngs of ordinary people who lined the streets for the last day's funeral procession. Officials estimated over 5,000 were in attendance.

Police lined both sides of the ceremonial route, restricting the crowd to the sidewalks. Heads craned and digital cameras were held high as the Bishop's coffin passed by, lying on an open-bed carriage gracefully drawn by four beautifully-groomed white horses, dressed in black and purple funereal vestments.

Most attendees stood and gazed reflectively, faces fixed with solemn curiosity or mournful respect, as the polished bronze casket wheeled slowly past. Some openly cried, while others moved their lips in pantomimed prayer, as the beads of the rosaries they held passed through their fingertips.

There was one incident.

A deranged girl with a shaved head and black Satanic symbols tattooed on her skull, broke through the police line. Before she was apprehended, she exposed her breasts and dumped a milk bottle filled with human blood, or something which looked a lot like it, onto the casket. Then she screamed, *'God fucks the Pope in the ass!'* ... over and over at the top of her lungs.

Police quickly subdued her and attendants ran over and wiped the blood off the casket. Within two minutes, it was as if the bizarre bit of street theater had never happened.

The body of the Bishop continued its journey on a designated route, through the streets of Brooklyn, so that the people who loved him and looked to him for leadership and blessings, could say their final good-bye, and perhaps attach a wish or prayer message to his soul, to be taken to the Creator Himself.

Besides the politicos and celebs, there were two other notables in the audience.

One had developed a close friendship with the Bishop, a friendship characterized by candor and mutual respect.

The other person, also a man of the cloth, had learned of the Bishop only recently, but had grown not only to admire him, but to draw a great deal of inspiration from him.

The first was Alicia.

She was there as a grieving friend and confidant.

The other was none other than St. John the Baptist of Hell's Kitchen.

He was there on orders. Orders from as high in the chain of command as you can get.

Another Nice Thing About God

Another nice thing about ... wait, John thought. Not nice. But cool ... really cool.

Start again.

Another really cool thing about God was He had these big hands.

Really huge hands!

John felt sorry for the millions and millions of people in the world who couldn't see them. They could if they knew how. I mean, there they were. As plain as day. As big as the sky. But as happened with so many things in everyday life, people couldn't see what was right there in front of them, staring right back.

But John could.

John was on top of a three-story building and had watched the entire ceremonial procession peering over the cement parapet down to the mournful crowd below. Those escorting the coffin and even the rear honor guard had passed, and were now far down the street and almost out of sight.

He stepped back and looked up. They were still there. God's hands. Strong and elegant. Steady in the comfort they extended to an often unworthy flock. Majestic and abounding in their embrace of … everything.

Yes, God's cupped hands hovered from one horizon to the other, over the whole surface of the planet, as if the Earth was a big levitation trick conjured by some cosmic magician.

And it got better. Sometimes when He wanted to be more "hands-on" in the affairs of men — and to be blunt about it, God did have these momentary fits of micro-management, kind of a nervous tic or nail-biting thing at a God-level — He did something which was really amazing. He shrunk those gigantic hands down down down, so that now they were so small, they could barely be seen with the naked eye. This way, His hands could move unnoticed as they ambled across the chess board of human affairs, delicately and invisibly nudging the players this way and that, as God enjoyed His favorite Divine diversion: Directly manipulating the human drama, its events now guided by and purely at the mercy of His Wisdom, His Fancy, His Omniscience, His Whim.

People would often say: "I don't now why. I just had this feeling I should call." Or maybe: "This impulse just hit me and so I … (insert some act of kindness here)." There you have it. The subtle push, the sudden urge, the random impetus to do something. Out of nowhere.

Not quite. The Big Guy had His finger in everything. At least sometimes.

For John — him and God being buds and all — there was no wiliness or invisibility or any of that silly game playing God reserved for His more anonymous subjects, your average Joe. Nope. God would just lay it on him big and straight. Exactly the way He was doing right this very minute.

God was pointing at something.

John followed the graceful arc of the Divine hand and Sacred index finger. His eyes judiciously walked the path of the implied trajectory to a spot in front of the building he was standing on. Something down there must be important. He concentrated. There! Yes, right there. That's where God is pointing. Right at that girl with the strange hat and long burgundy coat.

Wait! He knew her. That's Saigon Sally. That bitch that did the oriental break dance routine in the park that one day. Tried to execute a little mind fuck on St. John the Baptist, she did.

She was the worst kind. An American. A fucking turncoat. A treacherous, malevolent, pus-filled Benedict Arnold. In the service of the vilest enemy America has ever known. Doing her cryptic little dance to seduce, bewitch and woo. Trying to hypnotize and trick innocent God-fearing patriots like him into cavorting with the demons of her corrupt political system. So I've found you. At last I've found you.

Thanks, God. I'll take it from here.

Now that the crowd was dispersing, Alicia like everyone else, was starting to leave. John was three floors up, so he'd have to move fast.

Last time he was here at a march, he had been harassed by some punks, so he had decided to wear "civvies" under his robes, in case he needed to become incognito. Off came the robes, the sash, the crucifix. He balled them up quickly and stuffed them against the parapet right by the fire escape ladder. He could come back and get them later.

Down he went. Slip stepping down the ladder in semi-freefall. Gravity was on his side and he was down at surface level in just over a minute. He bolted out into the street and spotted her. She was maybe fifty or sixty yards ahead, just crossing to the opposite sidewalk.

He followed her to a line of taxis, getting in the one right behind hers.

"Follow that one, please. God bless."

Twenty minutes later they arrived.

As John's taxi glided past, Alicia got out and was paying the driver. She then headed up the steps of her flat. John had his driver let him out a block further up the street.

He walked back and found a spot under a tree directly across from her place, from which he could watch inconspicuously. It was approaching dusk and as it darkened, a light finally went on in one of Alicia's windows.

What to do? He knew this wasn't the time. Taking out someone like this involved some planning. It demanded the proper ritual motif. Like the five girls in the slaughterhouse. Perfect example. There was a beautiful aesthetic to that. A grace and symmetry — poetic, balletic, if not ecclesiastical. He wished he had thought to bring votive candles.

John looked heavenward. The vapor trail of a recent jet airliner started writhing like a giant eel. Then it coiled and codified into a huge thunderhead, with boiling vaporous escarpments. From which emerged God!

The Guy loved dramatic entrances. He was a natural showman.

God was evidently very pleased with John's work. He nodded and smiled.

Then He started tapping His temple with His index finger. Still nodding. God had an almost devilish look in His eye ... oops! Devilish. Bad choice there. Mischievous. That was it. God was in one of His *mischievous* moods.

What a character He was!

Ha ha ha ha ha ha ha.

God's big hands.

Really cool.

Crime Stoppers

Lenny could never have imagined how hard it was to report a crime.

Apparently there were thousands of people who, when they got bored with looking at Zircon jewelry on the Home Shopping Channel, amused themselves by phoning in phony crimes. This flooded incoming lines at all levels with crank calls, rumors, and disinformation, guaranteeing that legitimate tips would be fielded with derision, skepticism, even scorn.

This also produced an inversion of the commonly accepted belief that cops took bribes to overlook crimes. Apparently, you actually had to bribe them to get them to *pay attention* to criminal activity.

He went down the list one by one. Call after call after call.

An obstacle course.

If the call was answered on the first ring, he knew he was at the starting layer of a series of menus. Each option would then introduce another layer of menus: *If this is related to an ongoing investigatory matter, press 1. If this is ...*

This went on for hours. Which added up to days. On the rare occasion he was lucky and persistent enough to forge his way through the exhausting bingo game of menu flips, flops, detours and dead ends, he might actually stumble on something promising: *If you wish to speak to someone, please stay on the line.*

Finally, after several minutes of formless, cloying, completely unlistenable elevator music, there would be the payoff for hours of tenacity and endurance: *No one is here right now but your call is very important to us ...*

No one was ever in. Ever!

Even, when as a result of perhaps divine intervention or some technical malfunction, he got some indifferent life form on the line, whose attention was more focused on what he or she would be doing after work hours than providing one whit of actual assistance, inevitably the person he was trying to reach was in-a-meeting, out-of-the-office, not-available-at-this-time, so on and so forth.

Of course, even if he were to eventually talk to someone who might be in a position and at a level to do something, in Lenny's situation there would be serious credibility issues as well on his end.

He couldn't tell them — at least not yet — who he was, the exact location of the high-rolling whorehouses, when the perpetrators would be at a location where they could be apprehended, where that location would be, and most importantly why he had become a whistleblower.

All of which meant that they would dismiss him like he was another delusional crackpot. He really couldn't really blame them. Wild claims of conspiracies, tales of victimization by marauding gangbangers or organized crime lords, any and all first-hand accounts of crime scene gore or subsequent investigations, had become the preferred currency for buying fifteen minutes of fame, as if that fifteen minutes had not become completely trivialized by the deluge of sensational but increasingly repetitive nonsense on television.

Nevertheless, in view of how dangerous Chicago was, he could brook no compromise here. He would have to just keep going and — most importantly — to play it his way.

Timing was everything. If he was going to bring in the storm troopers, they had to come in at the same time, in San Francisco and Chicago for sure. He was positive he couldn't trust them to hold off on his say so alone. So the idea was to have them primed and ready, then when it was time, load them up with all of the necessary vitals, and let them roll.

Lenny kept hammering away on the phone. Persistence actually paid off. On the third day, he got a detective in the Special Investigations unit on the phone who seemed to take him seriously. At least seriously enough to take his introductory call.

"I've got seven messages here from you. What is this all about?"

"Prostitution."

"Not a high priority. Elections are a ways off."

"Fourteen, fifteen year old girls. Trafficked illegally from Thailand."

"You've got my attention. But I hate to break it to ya. This is old news."

"Lives are at stake. These guys are killers."

"No one running a whorehouse typically is a member of the Kiwanis Club. That's why we carry guns. What's your stake in this? Just being a good citizen? Or maybe you're one of their targets. Maybe you're turning in the competition. We're tired of fighting everyone else's battles here. We have parking tickets to issue. And oh, I forgot. Serious gang problems, drug pushers dropping like its hunting season in Chinatown, at least one serial killer, three hate crimes just last week, several death threats on the mayor and city council, and a White House that wants us to haul in a bunch of Muslims."

Lenny was taken back by the one bit. *Turning in the competition.* Exactly what Harold and Ed had told him he would be doing. Apparently a familiar game to the local police, and one they didn't intend to play.

"Are you going to help me or what?"

"Tell you what ... what did you say your name was?"

"Charlie Watts."

"Right. Charlie Watts. There's nothing in this for us. Not until the cannons start firing. Tell you what, though. I got a friend at INS. He's an old college buddy. They might want to look at this. Being it's illegals. His name is Phil Coltern. Let me get his number ... here it is. 650-330-6137. Give me a few minutes to get hold of him and tell him you're gonna call. Otherwise, you won't get through."

"Believe me, I know."

"And Charlie?"

"Yes?"

"Tell Mick to hang it up. He's getting too old."

Lenny's cell rang. Caller ID blocked. He thought of not answering it but he had a lot of calls out. This could be someone he needed to talk to.

"Hello?"

"Mr. Lenny, it's Kimnai. They're crazy."

"Who's phone is this?"

"My customer. He's in the bathroom. I gotta be quick. They burned me. They wanted to know why you and I ... you know ..."

"What?"

"They listened to the tape. There were microphones."

"Oh yeah yeah. But what ... ?"

"Gotta go. Be careful."

Click.

What did they hear?

Maybe it was what they didn't hear.

What significance could they read into his abstinence with Kimnai? These guys were tripped out, to say the least. So? If I didn't fuck like a dog in heat every opportunity I got, there was reason to suspect I was up to something?

There had to be more to it than that.

Shit. There was no way to reach her.

Burned? What did that mean?

Lenny tried to call Ying Mae. Phone not available. Twenty minutes later …

They're gettng crazy. Watching me.
Must be creful. YM

Phil Coltern. It was a little after 5:00. Would they still be in? Lenny dialed.
"Field Office."

"This is Charlie Watts calling for Phil Coltern."

"I'm sorry. He's gone for the day …"

Lenny heard off in the background … *'If that's some guy called Charlie Watts, I want to talk to him.'* His assistant came back on.

"One moment, please. I'll transfer you."

Phil Coltern had been at Immigration and Naturalization Services for over 35 years. He had seen it all and frankly he was tired of looking at it. He was a solid, commendable civil servant, recently promoted to G14, and had been eligible for early retirement for two years. Early retirement would mean a slight reduction in his pension benefits but a substantial reduction in his stress levels.

Immigration enforcement wasn't what it used to be. Budgets had been repeatedly slashed under the last two administrations, and the sheer numbers of immigrants coming in one way or another only promised more failures by an overworked and overwhelmed staff. Official estimates reported over 29,000,000 foreign-borns in the country right now. Who knew what the real number was? They'd have to expand INS by a factor of ten to even begin to get the job done. With things as they were, the only thing they could count on was more public finger-pointing and humiliation as a loud xenophobic sector of the population screamed about the problem, and the politicians exploited this anger and fear, amassing votes by making unrealistic promises and floating unworkable plans.

So, here he was at the very tail end of a long career of public service in about as thankless a job as could be imagined. Waiting. Waiting for what?

For Coltern, a solid and proud man with the thick skin that forms over decades in the tough job of enforcement and the sometimes dangerous job of investigation, there was one last but important item on his action list. Only one more thing to do before realizing his retirement fantasy of a small farm in Montana and salmon fishing in the rivers under the Big Sky.

That one thing was to put a big jewel in the otherwise ordinary crown of his life-long career with the INS. One final achievement which would be the rafter-shaking finale, the huge orchestral flourish, the explosive climactic exclamation point, for the long tedious symphony that had dragged out for over 35 years.

He was looking for some high-visibility bust or raid or roundup, which would capture the eye of the media and the mercurial attention of the public. He had to be picky about this. It had to be right. But he could and would be patient. And he would field any and all queries which appeared to have merit and big bang potential.

For two years now, he had kept a watchful, discerning eye. It was difficult to be optimistic. The days of the headline-grabbing factory raid, the featured news story wetback cattle drive, the television-friendly swamped and sinking boats from Cuba, were pretty much gone. Immigrants got in using professional brokers, highly-trained special task smugglers, holes in fences and gaps in the law. In fact, it was a big and growing business. The interests of immigrants, both legal and illegal, were now represented by law firms, large and small. Bursts of gunfire had been replaced by whacks of a gavel, the battles to enforce the basically unenforceable laws, now fought on polished wood floors, rather than desert sand and industrial concrete.

For two years and counting, Coltern watched and waited and nothing remotely promising had come his way. He was wondering if he was going to just have to resign himself to walking out the door with his Timex watch and a cardboard box of his personal memorabilia, and calling it a day.

Then he started talking to this latest guy. Some snitch who called himself Charlie Watts — boy if that didn't win the prize for worst pseudonym, then what did? It wasn't even funny.

Anyway, the more Coltern listened, the more he came to believe that this operation he was describing had all the right elements. The usual stuff, illegals forced into the sex service industry, everything done online. But these girls were way underage and were apparently getting very high dollars. Commanding that kind of money, being set up Playboy Mansion style, meant they were pulling prominent citizens, at least on occasion. Celebrity fucks. Which also possibly meant some political action figures. They always go together. Always. Like flies to dog shit.

If this was for real, this definitely smelled like the kind of bust that could end up as bold print in both the Examiner and the National Enquirer. Charlie Watts also mentioned similar scenarios in Miami, New York and Seattle. Definitely big bang material.

"Tell you what, Mr. Watts. I'll play along with your guessing game for now. But there is a limit to my patience."

"It's not a game. I just need to get all my ducks in a row. If you guys go in to early, then it stops there. My bosses ..."

Oops. Didn't mean to say that. Maybe it slipped by.

"The guys behind this are shrewd. This keeps going if you don't get them. And a lot of people get hurt."

"Like you, for example."

"Like certain girls on the inside I'm working with. Just give me a few days. Do you have anyone I can call in New York or Chicago?"

"Yeah. I've got everyone you need. But I don't waste other people's time. You really have not convinced me, yet. I'm listening but you're not telling me anything."

"Give me a name and three days."

"I'll give you three days."

"Give me a name."

"Give me something and I'll give you the whole directory."

This guy drove an impossible bargain.

"I'll see what I can do."

No wonder shit kept happening and organized crime was a blue chip investment. You try to deliver something on a silver platter to these enforcement guys and they send it back to the chef for more Béarnaise sauce and steamed okra.

He sent a text to Ying Mae.

> SF getting closer. Need proof.
> Kimnai? Pics? What? LP

Lenny felt bogged down. Three days on the phone and he was only marginally closer to getting someone on his side. He'd have to move faster.

But from here? Staying in San Francisco felt like he was pushing his luck.

Lenny decided that whatever happened, he would leave by Sunday. That was in three days. Chicago said he should stay into next week. But he had a feeling, they would either further detain him or send him off on some wild goose-chase, making it impossible for him to do what he needed to do.

For now, he needed to keep a full-court press. This Coltern guy was his best hope so far. But even he was an uncertainty. Maybe if he kept going, he could find someone better.

What about the FBI? Or the ATF? Worth a shot.

Not really. Another morning and the better part of an afternoon wasted.

Text message.

> Aaron Preston. Ask hm about
> Kimnai. He not cut. YM

Lenny dialed.

"Coltern here."

"Charlie Watts. Here's a name. Aaron Preston. Ask him about a little Thai girl named Kimnai Djin Djin. That's K-I-M-N-A-I, then D-J-I-N and D-J-I-N again. She's fifteen. And, oh yeah … he's not cut."

"Not cut? What's that supposed to mean?"

"How should I know? You're the investigator."

Coltern didn't know any Aaron Preston. He had his assistant run a search. "He's on the Board of Supervisors for the City of San Francisco, Mr. Coltern. In fact, he's the President of the Board."

"Make an appointment for me. Right away. Tell him it will only take a few minutes and it's an urgent matter."

As luck would have it, an anticipated speaking engagement had been canceled and the City Supervisors Board President had a nice window in his late afternoon schedule. He agreed to a meeting if Coltern could be there within the hour. He jumped in a government sedan and headed right over to City Hall.

Aaron Preston was a very distinguished looking man. Almost professorial. But unlike many academicians, he had an easy outgoing personality. Cordial gracious smile. Firm handshake. He poured on the diplomatic charm.

"It's important that we all work together, I say. At all levels. The city government here is always ready to help you boys out there at the Federal level. Is this some terrorist thing?"

"No. A fairly routine matter. People from other countries wanting in. God bless America. Land of opportunity. This person I've come here about, claims you can vouch for her."

"No problem. Shoot."

"I have a few things to go over. But before we start, sir, I have kind of a personal question."

"Go right ahead."

"Mr. Preston, are you cut? You know, circumcised?"

That should throw him off his footing.

It did.

"What the hell kind of question is … ?"

"You're right. The girl. That's what I'm here about. A very close personal friend of yours. Her name, Mr. Preston, is … Kimnai Djin Djin."

As if a thick vault door had been closed and sealed, the room became an anechoic vacuum. The smiley camaraderie of two public servants doing their jobs was shattered, replaced by a chasm of hostility and suspicion. Preston's face was a map of vitriol, fear, bewilderment.

After an eternal minute, he spoke in a guttural whisper.

"You're not here on official business. What exactly do you want? Money? I have a family. A reputation."

"To be honest with you, you've given me what I needed. Thank you for your time."

On his way back to the office, Coltern called Lenny.

"I checked out that name. He seemed to know your Kimnai girl. I'm hesitant at this point to do this, Mr. Watts, but I'm going to give you a couple names."

"What happened to the whole directory?"

"Not conclusive, Mr. Watts. But enough to proceed cautiously. Baby steps, eh?"

"I could give you conclusive, Coltern. I could book you an hour with a luscious 14-year old Asian girl who would fuck you until it hurt. But then you'd bring your troops in and I'd be the one who got fucked, wouldn't I?"

"Whatever you say. Do you want the names or not?"

"Let's get on with it."

The truth of the matter was, Coltern was now about 99% sure that Charlie Watts was telling the truth and that this was going to be a spectacular display of what the INS could do as an agency, and what he could accomplish as an agent. And for that reason and that reason alone, he couldn't lose control of this by getting too many other agents involved. Certainly none that he didn't personally know. In the rare instances when something of major consequence went down, credit had a way of migrating up the food chain and some supervisor or department manager got all the credit. He wasn't going to let that happen if he could help it. He'd play his cards real close and not let this one get away.

This was the big one.

The jewel in the crown.

The Invisible Man

Two names. Both FBI. Henry Sutter in Chicago and George Rabinski in New York.

Coltern had given Lenny direct dial numbers for both of them.

He got hold of Sutter. He was definitely the right man to be talking to. He headed up a sizable investigational unit, including a formidable field force, covering Illinois, Wisconsin and Minnesota. Apparently, he had been the point man for the Chicago end of Operation Site Down, an enormous international anti-piracy effort, and also the main investigatory agent for a huge white-collar crime bust of Chicago Stock Exchange commodities traders in the late 80s — both of which made big headlines locally and nationally.

Unfortunately, Sutter had talked only briefly with Coltern and wanted to hold off on the matter for the time being.

"Regardless. What you're saying is the actual centers of activity are in these other cities. Chicago may be where we can find the big honchos but I can't go busting into someone's home just because he poking an underage girl. There's probably more of that going on than you care to know about. It's a local matter. But I'll tell you what. When I see what turns up in San Francisco and New York, and see a real connection to the people you're pointing at here, I'll do whatever I need to do. But not before. Keep working with Coltern and Rabinski. I know them both well."

Rabinski in New York was more receptive. But tough as nails.

"Charlie Watts ain't gonna cut it, mystery man. Either I know who I'm dealing with or we forget about the whole thing."

Lenny thought about it. He was getting closer. It was worth the risk.

"Lenny Petrocelli. I live in Brooklyn. Just call me Lenny."

"Okay. Now you need to give me something to go on. All I know is the table of contents. What's the story?"

Lenny went through what he knew. Leaving out the things which would directly implicate him in prosecutable crimes of a serious nature, didn't leave very much. It was a short story. He did name the two main characters, Harold Danko and Ed Valley.

"Not much to go on. A couple names and some sketchy details. And I understand your need to protect your own ass. But I also know, Lenny, that you had to be at the center of some of this stuff or you wouldn't know so much about

it. *Frankly, we're not interested in worker bees. We go for the chiefs, not the indians. And we'll make you a deal where you can walk, if you give us what we need. I'll check some of this out, though what you've told me is pretty thin in terms of substance.*

"In the meantime, you've got to be thinking about getting serious with me. I can't commit a bunch of my people to what at this point amounts to idle gossip. For all I know, you've got some personal ax to grind."

"I'm prepared to give you everything. But I am not the martyr type. If this gets back ..."

"We'll talk again. Within 48 hours. Have a nice day."

Lenny sent a message to Ying Mae.

> ### Things starting to move. What
> ### did they do to Kimnai? LP

Next he moved up his flight to New York. Tomorrow morning. Saturday. 9:30 am.

If he stayed here, he would just be prey to the whims of Harold and Ed. Maybe he was a wanted man in New York but at least he knew the lay of the land and the rules of the game. Here he knew neither one. Harold and Ed made up their own rules.

Of course they would eventually catch up with him. What should he tell them? They'd want to know what he was doing, why he was walking right into a citywide manhunt.

He'd just have to call them when he arrived back in New York, and was off their radar screens. In the meantime, he'd try to think of something to say.

His cell phone rang. Ying Mae.

"They're going to Seattle tonight."

"What did they do to Kimnai?"

"Sick motherfuckers! They played one of their torture games. Burned her with a cigarette. They're sick. Very sick!"

"But why? Is she alright?"

"They don't need a reason. To them it's like going to an pinball arcade. She's okay for now. But she's really frightened. They are suspicious."

"Of what?"

"Of everything. Of everyone. You. Me. Just be careful."

"I'm bailing out of here tomorrow. There's a federal guy in New York. I've got to make this happen. I think I'll be better off there."

"What are you going to tell them? Is the Jap guy on your ass?"

"I haven't seen him. But I suspect the worst. We'll see when I try to leave."

"Mr. Lenny, I know you don't know me. Maybe you don't entirely trust me. Please! Please! At the very least do this for Kimnai and yourself. I'll figure a way out if you can just—"

"This is the only way. For all of us. I'll do everything I can."

"As soon as possible. I don't know for sure. But I have a bad feeling about ... about you. I mean what they might do to you. Something feels off. They'll be

back here Monday or Tuesday. I'll find out what I can. You're our only hope, Mr. Lenny."

"Talk to you later."

He'd have to move fast. To keep an eye on him, they would probably want him to come to Seattle with them. He had to avoid them at all costs.

Lenny turned off his phone. Then he packed and took a stairway which allowed him to slip out of the lobby without being observed by the concierge or the receptionists.

He circled around to the guest receiving zone in front of the lobby. Off to one side he found a taxi. Slumped behind the wheel, the driver was reading a newspaper.

"Are you waiting for someone?"

"You! If you want to go somewhere."

"Any hotel near the airport where I can get a room this late."

Lenny checked into Bay Landing Airport Hotel and collapsed back onto the bed to collect his thoughts. Was this the right move at the right time?

There wasn't a right move and there wasn't any time except for the present. The only move was survival, now and the foreseeable future. He had no future at this point. He'd have to build one from scratch.

He also had to think about where he was going to stay in New York. Obviously, he couldn't go back to his own place. The NYC blues had probably moved in and were watching Miami Vice reruns on his TV.

It was too late now, after midnight in New York. But he figured as soon as he got up tomorrow, he'd try to call Alicia. Maybe she could help him out with a place to crash for a couple days. That was probably pushing his luck with her. But at least worth a try.

Lenny spent a restless night, more time pacing and looking out through his window at the hotel's parking lot, than in the bed itself. He was wide awake when the alarm was supposed to go off, and just got up on his own and made a cup of instant coffee.

He powered up his cell phone. Two missed calls from Harold. He dialed Alicia.

"Hello."

"This is Lenny. I'm on my way back. I need your help."

She became hysterical.

"How could you? You are the vilest, most evil person on Earth. How could you do that?"

"Alicia. You don't understand. The police are—"

"The police called me. I told them it was you."

Click.

"Alicia. Hello? Hello?"

Redial.

The number you are trying to reach is not available. Please try your call again later.

Redial.

The number you are trying to reach is not available ...

Jesus Christ! She thought I did it. She told them I did it. Where is that coming from?

Lenny sat down on the bed. He needed to think. Regroup. Alicia's screaming at him was a needed bucket of cold water in his face. Much needed. Objectively speaking, he realized he had been stumbling around in a dream world the last 24 hours.

What was he thinking? Going back was fine, or would have to be. But he hadn't been looking clearly at what a hornet's nest he was walking into. The police probably had an APB out, his picture at the airport, stake-outs everywhere he could possibly show up. He needed to make some serious changes in his approach. To think about every step, every possible ramification, every outcome, think it through and through, then think about it even more.

Forget shaving. He had shaved practically every day since puberty. A beard would go a long way towards preventing immediate identification, at least to the casual passing observer, perhaps even with people who knew him.

And no way could he fly in to any of the three New York airports. That would be tantamount to turning himself in. He grabbed his phone and made some hasty calls to the airline. Within fifteen minutes, his ticket had been changed to Philadelphia. Now he would be leaving at 11:15 am, getting in to Philly around 10 pm. He could stay overnight and take a bus from there the following day.

The gigantic, bustling NYC Port Authority Bus Terminal, grossly understaffed with security personnel, would afford him the best chances of getting into the city undetected. And he would arrive in the heart of the Times Square area, where there was plenty of cheap, anonymous accommodations, as he had discovered when he was looking for a new place to put up the Asian uglies.

Lastly, he either had to cut off all contact with Chicago, or he needed to put them off his trail. Without a doubt, they were going to be pissed when they found out he had left San Francisco without telling them. How long would it take before they became suspicious and came looking for him? The way things had been going, it would only take one misstep to set off their hair trigger. There was certainly no room for error.

Probably best if he made himself invisible. To both Chicago and the blues.

That was it for starters. Then, as things unfolded, he'd have to feel his way.

The prevailing winds were working overtime and his plane arrived in Philadelphia slightly ahead of schedule. A taxi took him to a seedy but secure flophouse within walking distance of the bus depot. He slept in his clothes, hoping that the layer of protection would dissuade whatever insects had already claimed the bed, from taking up residence on him.

As he stepped through the reception area in the morning, there were two old men sitting in the lobby on the wood bench against the wall. Both were unshaven, probably not very recently bathed, and dressed in Salvation Army Store discards. One was slumped over in what could have been an early start on a day of complete inebriation, or just the paralyzed somnambulism of old age. The other was actively engaging in a conversation with an invisible someone, who had apparently shared the trenches with him in World War II. Using the trembling limbs of his Parkinson's Disease-ravaged body, he gesticulated and twisted himself in a St. Vitus Dance of recounted glory. Yellow gobs of saliva flew out between his broken teeth, and a demonic glee possessed his baggy leather face, as he recalled in his mind's eye, the cruelties he had inflicted on the 'Gerries' in the long final push to Berlin.

Lenny glanced at them in passing and embraced the pathetic irony of the moment.

There's always someone worse off than you.

Chapter 16

LAST EXIT TO BROOKLYN: Closed For Repairs

Home Sweet Home

Lenny arrived in New York shortly after noon. He found a room at a hostel housed in what had to be a condemned building. It made the place he stayed at in Philadelphia look like a Marriot. Located off 8th Avenue, west on 37th Street, its main advantage was its entrance from an alley on the south end of the building. It was easy to get in and out of along pathways that had virtually no traffic and limited visibility.

His room was about twice the size of the twin bed shoved in a corner under a wood frame window, which if slid open would permit an escape, if that proved necessary. Right outside the window was the rusted lattice framework of a fire escape. It was doubtful, considering the deteriorated condition of the metal, that this would support the weight of a grown man, but it was only a one-story drop to the surface of a narrow passage next to the building.

The room had not been cleaned in preparation for his new tenancy and reeked of stale beer and partially smoked cigarettes. He tidied up the best he could, scooting the dirt and several fist-sized dust balls under the bed, then the piling newspapers which had been left behind, onto the wrought iron night stand, which tottered on bent legs next to the bed.

Lenny left briefly to buy some new bed sheets. Conveniently, there was a small shop selling household goods just two blocks away on 9th Avenue.

He was in and settled. It was Sunday late afternoon. He couldn't get anything done today. He should eat. Try to get some sleep. Hit it hard first thing in the morning.

Lenny waited till it was totally dark, then slipped out and found a small tavern on 35th Street, opting for a booth in the back corner. By the time he returned to his room, slightly nauseous from greasy bar food and a couple ritual shots of scotch chased with a Mickey's Malt Liquor, it was a little after midnight.

He spent anxious night, interrupted by occasional superficial brushes with actual sleep. Every noise arrived as a harbinger of the storm troopers his paranoia conjured as having surrounded the building, pulling his exposed and defenseless body into their crosshairs. When he finally forced himself out of bed at 9:35 am, he was more exhausted than when he had climbed in.

Nevertheless, it was time to go to work.

Mainly it was time for Lenny to see where he stood in terms of local enforcement, i.e. the NYC Police Department. He decided on a direct approach. Confront the enemy one-on-one to size up the battle which lay ahead. He would determine if he had any wiggle room at all.

He didn't.

The call to Fiori did not go well.

"Look Lenny. Just turn yourself in and this will end better for you. City hall is screaming for your head. My men are very nervous right now. Trigger-happy nervous."

"It wasn't me."

"The game is up. If you're around, we'll find you. Just stick your head out of whatever manhole you're hiding under and you're ours. Every cop in New York has your picture."

"I couldn't ... and I wouldn't. I'm a lot of things. But I'm not a murderer."

"Maybe you should tell that to the Bishop. Oh wait. I just remembered. He's dead."

"They wanted me to. But no way. They FedExed me a note. I can show you. It's at my flat. They're the ones ..."

"Lenny. I'm looking at a copy of the note."

"Then it's obvious who wanted to get rid of the Bishop."

"Crystal clear. This is like a signed confession."

"Then go after them."

"You're very confused, Petrocelli. The writing is on the wall. You had the motive and you went off half-cocked and killed the Bishop. Right now, you're wasting my time and squandering any hope you have for leniency. Just bring yourself in nice and peaceful like. Or we'll drag your ass in, kicking and screaming."

"Fuck you, Captain."

Click.

In his office, Fiori picked up the note Chicago had FAXed him just yesterday.

> Don't go off the deep end, Lenny. We know you
> hate the man but if you pop the Bishop, it's gonna
> bring too much heat. Don't do anything till we talk.
>
> — Harold

Fiori scowled. Petrocelli. You lying prick.

After they hung up, Lenny felt a knife of angst shoot through his body. That was a dead end. Deader than dead.

Somehow, Chicago had sealed his fate. Just as he had always suspected would happen.

At least now he knew that it was just a matter of time before the cops would nail him — which confirmed his presumption that the less time he spent out on the streets, the better off he'd be.

He tried Alicia again.

The number you are trying to reach is not available ...

He called Rabinski.

"I'm still working it. Just let me do my job. Don't call me. I'll call you."

What a pal.

He lay down to let his frustration pass. And try to think. His phone rang. Area 312.

"Lenny. How is Philly?" Ed Valley.

"Historical. Rocky Balboa just ran by."

"We missed you. You should have come to Seattle with Harold and me. We each had a sushi sampler. Yours is still smelling like raw fish. Right between her legs." Haw haw haw.

"I'm staying low, Ed. When can I go back home? Can you get that taken care of?"

"What's your hurry? We were thinking that maybe you should be back in Thailand. We got a lot of beds to fill."

"Right. Thailand. Just let me know."

"Believe me, we will. Make sure you keep your phone on from now on."

"Oh that. Battery was down. I'll stay on top of it. Tell Harold I have his cigarette lighter."

"I see. You're a pickpocket and a homo, eh Lenny?"

Apparently they thought he was in Philadelphia. Good. Maybe there's an advantage there. Or maybe it didn't make one bit of difference. At least Ed didn't sound upset. Or was he just setting Lenny up for another one of their twisted games?

Even if they figured out he was in New York, this is the last place they would look, that was for damn sure. I wouldn't make my worst enemy stay in this shit hole.

What next?

I wonder if there's a band playing in the lounge tonight. I'm sure this place attracts some very classy ladies. Or maybe I should go to the spa and get a massage and take a sauna. You've come a long way, baby.

The Fugitive

When Lenny decided to turn to the law for help, he fully expected they would patronize him. It was in their breeding. Only a self-righteous bastard with a sense of entitlement that bordered on megalomania would feel comfortable with, would actually seek out a job, where he had life-or-death say over another person. And what the master race genetics fell short of accomplishing, actual experience in enforcing the law guaranteed a full realization of their sense of omnipotence and preeminence, which for the likes of Coltern, Rabinski and Sutter, left everyone else — especially the Lennys of the world — in the lowest caste of irrelevance.

The problem wasn't just psychological. These guys were dangerous.

Lenny had this in mind at all times when he was talking to these bull necks. Besides himself, he had to worry about Kimnai and Ying Mae, and any of the other innocent girls that might get caught in the crossfire.

Lenny firmly believed that these government types could care less about any casualties they inflicted along the way, as long as they made the bust. All they cared about was kudos. Kudos meant promotions. Any loss of life and limb along the way, outside of their immediate team, was just the cost of doing business, a price they themselves didn't have to pay.

In a word, they were dangerous.

But there was something he had not at all expected: That was that every single one of them would refuse to acknowledge his innocence, and as a result he would end up on everyone's hit list. By every measure, it was in their own best interest to protect him and go after Harold and Ed. But convincing them of that was a whole other ballgame.

Rabinski — Lenny's best and only hope so far — finally got back to him. It took four days, not 48 hours.

"At first I thought your name sounded familiar. Now I see you got a lot of TV exposure. Anyway, I didn't put two and two together until I did a ICPN search on you and made a few calls. You're the guy who killed the Brooklyn bishop."

"I didn't kill him."

"You've got a lot of people fooled. There are more guys looking for you than Osama bin Laden, my friend."

"It's a setup."

"Right. Every high-security prison in America is full of guys who were set up."

"Why doesn't anyone believe me?"

"Because you're not very believable."

"I've got everything you need to bust up an enormous prostitution ring, operating in four major cities, with probably more than three hundred sex slave teens, illegally smuggled into the country. Do you think you have time in your busy fucking schedule to tackle that?"

"Do you have dates? Times? Locations? Where do they bring them in? What port of call or airport?"

"I don't know."

"Are they smuggling them? Or do they have documents?"

"I don't know."

"Well, what do you know, Mr. Petrocelli, other than that you are up to your eyebrows in your own shit? Give me one single thing to go on. How many were brought in, when and from where to where? I'll settle for one installment."

Lenny realized that the only transfer he could give specifics on was the one which would incriminate him and him alone, the Malaysia to Singapore.

"I don't know what I can say."

"So here I am, talking to a man who I know only one thing about. And that is that he desperately needs to save his ass from a murder rap. This guy wants me to bust wide open some real or imagined child smuggling ring, and wants all sorts of protection and assurances and immunity from prosecution, but he can't give me one shred of evidence, not a hint of a detail of what might have gone down. This guy wants his freedom and all he has in trade are the names of two men who allegedly are the big bad wolf. Two men, I might add, who happen to be leading citizens in the corporate financial community of Chicago, widely regarded as highly civic-minded gentlemen. Does this sound at all familiar, Mr. Petrocelli? And you expect me to believe for one second that you're telling me the truth?"

"I didn't murder the Bishop. I've never killed anyone."

"Not so fast. I've been doing my homework, like a good little cop. I had a very nice talk with the homicide inspector on the case there. They have some rather damning evidence. Are you aware of what they found at the scene of the crime, Mr. Petrocelli? I'd say you've got a rough road ahead of you in court."

"What are you talking about? How could they have anything?"

"At the cathedral where the Bishop was murdered, Mr. Petrocelli, they found a napkin, with a name and phone number written on it. They called the lady and yes indeed, she knows you. She wishes she didn't but she does. You went to high school with her."

The napkin. Alicia's number. Stolen from his apartment.

"She tells quite a tale of a run-in you had with said murder victim, Bishop Mulcahey. So ... do you still expect me to accept your line of bullshit, Mr. Petrocelli? If you want to make a deal, you better call Captain Fiori and the person in charge of the case. They've made it clear that you should turn yourself in. I would take that advice. It will substantially improve your chances of survival. It's hunting season there in Brooklyn. You're the game."

"They won't find me."

"It's not that hard. The tracker I have on this call puts you in Hell's Kitchen right now. Near 37th and 8th Avenue. Frankly, I can tell you within 50 feet of where you are sitting. Now, down there at precinct headquarters in Brooklyn, they don't have these sophisticated toys we big boys have, but you should be aware, these days ... no one is invisible."

"So are you turning me in for the reward money?"

"Not interested. We don't throw this stuff up for grabs unless we're asked. And on the .001% chance that you have something for me, for the present, I am looking the other way. But if you're serious, and you're for real, you better come up with something very soon. I'm an impatient man."

Come up with something very soon. Lenny was stymied. He was hoping he could count on the rich investigational resources of the FBI to do his legwork. But they hoarded them like they were the panties Princess Di was wearing the day of the crash.

Think. Think. Think.

He was sweating like he had malaria. Christ, it's hot in here. The only good thing you can say about this place. They keep the heat cranked. He cracked the window open half an inch. As foul as the air of the city was, it was a Vermont mountain retreat Spring breeze compared to the stifling near-stench of the hostel.

He was getting extremely hungry. How long had it been since he actually had a meal?

Perhaps he could have something delivered to his room. He didn't want to risk being seen. Anything would do, as long as it was edible.

He grabbed the papers from the night stand and dropped them on the floor. He picked them up one by one and started paging through them. Maybe he could find an ad for a takeout with local delivery.

They were dailies from the previous two weeks. A lot of coverage of the Bishop's murder. He saw his picture a couple times. Then something in one of the articles caught his eye.

Police have determined the Bishop was murdered at shortly after 6:00 pm last Saturday, having just completed hearing three hours of confessions at the church.

Last Saturday. 6:00 pm.

Lenny bolted out the door. He remembered the telephone booth in the diner and headed straight up 8th Avenue.

Alicia was trying to restore some order to her apartment — she had neglected the bigger share of basic household chores over the past two weeks of turmoil — when she got the call. A Manhattan number she did not recognize.

"Alicia, don't hang up. Just listen. Either look in the newspapers or call Fiori and ask him exactly when the Bishop was killed."

"Fuck you, murderer."

She threw her cell phone across the room. Intentionally or not, it bounced harmlessly off of the curtain and fell to the floor. No damage done.

She wanted to scream. He was like a yeast infection that kept coming back.

Why would he want to torture me with knowing exactly when the Bishop had his brains blown out? Was he some kind of sick sadist?

Alicia grabbed her purse, threw on a heavy wool Navy peacoat, and headed out the door. She momentarily backtracked to grab her cell phone, then as she went out to the street to hail a taxi, she called Christine.

"Can I come over?"

"Please do. I was just thinking about you."

Christine met her at the door.

"I'm so pissed off. Lenny called me."

"I thought you were avoiding him."

"He dialed from some number I didn't recognize. Then he says I should find out the precise time that he killed the Bishop. What a crazy fucker!"

"Wait, Alicia. There something missing. Nobody's that random. Why would he say that?"

"Because he's demented, that's why. I wish I knew where he was. I'd either turn him in or go there myself and strangle him."

"I was just trying to do some work. I'm online right now."

Christine went over to her desk and typed something into her computer.

"The New York Times quotes the police as saying that the time of the murder was 6:00 pm or very shortly thereafter. Saturday December 8th. Wait. Why does that sound so familiar?"

"The whole city has been grieving about what happened. It should sound familiar."

"No, I meant the time."

Christine picked up her PDA and punched away at the mini-keyboard.

"Oh my God!"

"What? What is it?"

"Do you know what we were doing? Right then? We were sitting in that café with Lenny. That was when you had me come with you to meet with him."

"Christine, are you sure?"

"Yes. Absolutely. We were right there with him when the Bishop was murdered. It couldn't have been him."

"Ohmigod. I … I … I've been so upset, I hadn't even stopped to think. I just assumed …"

"Of course, they've had his picture all over the newspapers, the TV."

"What should I do?"

"Call him. See what he wants. Tell him you—"

"I can't call him. I should talk to the police. Captain Fiori. They need to know."

Fiori had given her his personal 24-hour cell number. He was certain that Lenny would try to contact her and if that happened, she was to alert him immediately.

"Captain, this is Alicia. Alicia Peters. Lenny just called."

"Where is he?"

"The news says that the Bishop was murdered at 6:00 o'clock. I was with Lenny at 6:00 o'clock that day."

"And you decided to wait until now to bring this up. Is he there with you? Has he got a gun pointed at your head?"

"No, of course not. I … I just found out—"

"Or maybe now you have a soft spot in your heart for the fucker. Gone sweet on him all of a sudden, have you?"

"No! No! No! It's just that he couldn't have done it. I was right there with him at the time. We were at a café in Lower Manhattan."

"How do you explain the napkin? With your name and number?"

"I … I can't. All I know is he couldn't be two places at the same time."

"Tell you what, Miss Alicia Peters. If I find out that you are hiding his whereabouts, I'm arresting you for aiding and abetting. You got that?"

This was not going at all as she expected.

"Got it."

"Lenny's our man, lady. Don't interfere in police matters."

"Thanks for the advice, Captain."

Lenny had told her some time ago — it was in the restaurant where she had given him the napkin with her number on it — that the police were working with Chicago and protecting the Djin Djin girls. She also remembered him saying that he was in the middle, that he might be being set up to take the fall, if the operation somehow got busted.

Lenny's our man, lady. It was a foregone conclusion. Fiori certainly didn't want to hear that Lenny might be innocent. What was the only thing could you read from that?

She rebelled against calling Lenny, not entirely sure what she would say, or whether she could keep a clear head. What a roller coaster ride of emotions. From stratospheric heights to the depths of Hell.

How could she bring herself to do it? But she had to.

"Christine. I need you. I'm going to call him."

"Lenny?"

She nodded as genuinely as her bilious dread would allow. Christine came over and sat next to her, putting her hand on Alicia's free forearm. She stared strength into Alicia's eyes.

Tap tap tap. Ringing. His voice.

"Hello."

"Lenny. This is Alicia."

"You put it together? Us? The time? Will you help me now?"

"How do you explain the napkin? You know … the napkin with my name and number?"

"Are you going to believe anything I tell you?"

"I'm listening, Lenny. I called you, didn't I?"

"My place was burglarized. I should say it was broken into. They didn't take anything from what I could tell. Except one piece of incriminating evidence. They must have planted it at the cathedral."

"Who? Why would they do this?"

"My bosses, Harold Danko and Ed Valley in Chicago, have had it in for the Bishop forever. They needed someone to take the blame for killing him. Yours truly. Everything they do is a big game. I'm just another pawn."

"I told Captain Fiori you were innocent. He wouldn't listen."

"He's paid well to not listen. The cops have been on the take through all of this — anything Chicago comes up with here in Brooklyn — for a long time. Alicia, you've got to be careful. If they think you are siding with me …"

"Lenny. I want to believe you. Sometimes you make it … very difficult."

"I told you before. You and your friend at the restaurant. Take it or leave it. It's the truth."

"What should we do?"

"I know you'd better make yourself real scarce. They'll come looking for you."

"Who?"

"Fiori in particular. Chicago if they figure out what I'm doing. I've been talking to the feds. San Francisco, Chicago, here. It's like trying to move a mountain. I'm the bad guy because I'm trying to do the right thing. Am I making any sense?"

"Yes, Lenny. Unfortunately, you are making sense. Everything is backwards. I've been going through the same thing. Same with my friend, Christine. She's a good person. Now her son has been killed and her family has fallen apart."

"I better go. Can I call you?"

"Yes. You can call me. Lenny. I'm sorry I …"

"Forget about it. No more hiccups?"

Alicia smiled as she remembered.

"No more hiccups."

She put the phone down. Christine took her hand.

"Well?"

"Christine, can I stay here for a while?"

"Of course. Is there trouble?"

"Yeah. I think I screwed up. The police are on the wrong team. They will probably come looking for me."

"Listen, Alicia. You can stay here for as long as you want. What about Lenny?"

"He's hiding too. He didn't say very much."

"I wouldn't want to be in his shoes. Or yours."

Lenny had nailed the situation quite accurately. Using back channels, Fiori alerted Harold and Ed that there was a monkey wrench in the blame machine, a person who seemed bent on asserting Lenny's innocence. He passed along enough information to make her easy for Chicago's men on the ground to identify and locate. Then he put out an low-level APB on her with his own men. Without making it look like some military mission, they were to keep an eye out for her and bring her in for "questioning" — possibly for harboring information and abetting a wanted criminal, potentially as an accessory to the felony itself.

Harold contacted Yoshikaze, always glad to have more gruesome assignments added to his list, and told him he should dispatch this Alicia Peters and make it look like a random act of violence, not that uncommon in the part of Brooklyn where she lived.

All Work No Play

Rabinski might be hard as nails but he was no slacker. He was tough, driven, thorough, meticulous. Over thirty years in the highest investigative agency in the U.S. had taught him to leave no stone unturned, no lead unexamined, no questions unanswered, no informer dangling, and no anomaly unresolved.

There was something about Lenny's story which played on both Rabinski's intuitions and his imagination. Enough to take a closer look. Not that he would let Lenny know that. A big part of Rabinski's effectiveness was the product of keeping everyone guessing as to his interest and his intentions. He didn't play his hand close. He made it invisible.

On the first pass, he had gotten the skinny on Lenny himself and some of the local activity. There was a lot that didn't seem right. Petrocelli was most definitely a two-bit player. Whether he had killed the Bishop or not, he was most certainly rank-and-file, not a manager.

It would hardly be surprising to see him as a fall guy. The evidence of his guilt was strong but it always is when someone is set up properly. Frankly, Fiori almost seemed a little too exuberant about the matter. A little too sure of himself.

Rabinski also had assigned two of his best street guys to hang out in Brooklyn's little hooker haven just to see what they could come up with. Maybe put together a little background to get some picture of what had been going on over the past few months there.

Today was Wednesday. It would turn out to be a very big day.

An intern who was assisting him, had just uploaded to his workstation shared folder, the video file of Bishop Mulcahey's last public interview, just two days before he was killed. Though only about five minutes long, it had some revealing moments. The Bishop was being interviewed by a local news celebrity, WABC's Diana Williams, in a special spotlight segment of her regular *Up Close* news show.

Williams: So you're saying, Bishop, that these young Asian girls, undocumented and underage were walking the streets and the police didn't stop it.

Bishop: I'm not here to name names. But I can say, that apparently issuing parking citations and monitoring the dog leash laws seemed to be a much higher priority than enforcing the statutes against prostitution or doing something to help these girls. They are, after all, here against their will, slaves to the people who brought them here and forced them into working as prostitutes. These poor girls are desperate for any kind of intervention or help they can get.

Williams: Why didn't the authorities do anything?

Bishop: You would have to ask the authorities that question. All I know is that none of them were ever detained or arrested or even questioned by the area police. The girls told me, in fact, that they did favors for some of the officers, either at the station or in the patrol vehicles themselves.

Williams: Favors?

Bishop: Sexual favors.

Williams: And you used the phrase 'told me'. You talked to these young girls?

Bishop: On numerous occasions. We tried to rescue them and had them right at my parish for a short while. They were staying in the old convent. So what I am telling you right now is not hearsay. I experienced this first-hand or verified independently the things that the girls said.

Williams: Who's behind all of this?

Bishop: I have no proof but I can say with a great deal of certainty, based on prior confrontations with them, that this is being run by two gangsters out of Chicago. These men have made their fortunes over the years in the sex service industry and continue to poison communities across the nation with prostitution and all of the crime and spiritual degradation that goes with it. They have been at this for years and are masters at the game. In all this time, they have never been brought to justice. Not arrested even once. This will just go on until someone stops it.

Williams: And you are that person?

Bishop: I am part of a community which has taken upon itself to remove this evil from our own community, and hopefully free these poor girls from their chains of bondage. We feel that though they were dropped on us with no choice on their part or ours, we still have some responsibility in the matter. Caring for others in need is fundamental to the teachings of Jesus Christ.

Williams: Well, Bishop Mulcahey, I want to thank you on behalf of WABC and its viewing audience, for coming here and sharing with us your brave and remarkable work. We wish you the best of luck in your noble effort.

Bishop: May God be with us all.

Undocumented and underage Asian slave prostitutes run by two gangsters from Chicago. Local police indifferent to, if not supportive of, open acts of sexual pandering in the streets. Rabinski knew the Bishop's impeccable credentials and sterling reputation. These were not accusations to be taken lightly.

"Get me my friend Coltern on the phone. The INS guy in San Francisco."

Coltern wasn't in but returned Rabinski's call within the hour.

"What's your take on this Petrocelli guy?"

"Who?"

"Charlie Watts. His real name is Lenny Petrocelli."

"My gut tells me there's something to what he's saying. Have you gotten him to open up?"

"Honestly, no. But I've been looking at some things on my own. What little he says seems to add up. There was ... is ... some strange shit going on around here."

"He gave me a name of one of the girls here. She's working in San Mateo. I'll have one of my guys check it out and I'll get back to you."

"Thanks, Phil."

Within five minutes of that call, his intern buzzed him and said a Lenny Petrocelli was calling.

"Petrocelli. Have you got anything to say worth hearing?"

"I can prove I didn't kill the Bishop. I have two witnesses who were with me at the time of the murder."

"That's pretty easy. I can come up with two witnesses who say they saw me at a restaurant with Hans Solo."

"Maybe you could cut me some slack here and at least talk to them. The girl you mentioned that went to high school with me? Her name is Alicia Peters. And her friend is Christine. They were with me."

"Tell you what, Petrocelli—"

"Lenny."

"Tell you what, Lenny. We'll make this an all or nothing proposition. If they're telling the truth and you couldn't have killed the Bishop, you and I will make a deal. But if I find out that somehow you put these witnesses up to this, I will personally have my men find you and haul you in for Fiori and company. And believe me, we will find you, if you are anywhere in North America."

"You're ready to make a deal?"

"I've been ready to talk seriously all along. It's you that hasn't come to the table. I will concede that looking at this closer, I have been able to verify that there appears to be a pretty sophisticated operation doing what you've been saying they're doing. So you've got my attention. But I'm not going to help you beat a murder rap. We can take this Asian girl prostitution thing apart with or without you."

"I can make it easy for you. And less people will get hurt along the way."

"That remains to be seen. "

Rabinski called the number Lenny gave him and talked briefly to Alicia. She sounded on the level and he asked her for her maiden name and Christine's full name as well. They agreed to meet the next morning at Christine's place.

Rabinski's aides did a thorough background search on both of them. There wasn't much in the public record and nothing in Bureau files on Alicia Peters. Christine Lindholm was a whole other story.

Christine appeared in a number of low-circulation Christian publications, as a guest contributor for numerous websites, and was even mentioned in some of the large circulation New York region dailies in articles about child sponsorship and other philanthropic endeavors. No matter how you cut it, she was as upright as a church steeple, hardly the type to get involved in shady cover-ups or mercenary prevarications.

When Christine opened the door of her brownstone the next morning at the appointed time, her clear, intelligent eyes and cordial but no-nonsense smile further confirmed in Rabinski's mind that she was a dependable deponent. In terms of Alicia, though he had little advance material input, just superficial impressions on the phone, likewise meeting her in person gave pause to any suspicions that she harbored some ulterior motive for defending Lenny.

He would still play it on the safe side.

"Would you be willing to make a sworn statement and take a polygraph test to confirm the accuracy of what you've told me?"

Alicia practically didn't let him finish his question.

"You mean a lie detector test? Of course. There's nothing to detect."

Christine nodded reassuringly. "Absolutely. I have nothing to hide."

"Okay. I'll be in touch. And by the way, if you talk to Lenny, encourage him to come in to see me. So far he has been reluctant. I think he's afraid I'll arrest him. Truth is, I am very worried for his safety."

"His safety? I guess! Everyone's looking for him."

"Exactly, Ms. Peters. Probably more than he realizes. But I can put him out of reach."

"I'll pass along your message, if I hear from him. Just so you know, I have no idea where he is right now. His phone is off and on. I think he's rather afraid to say where he is."

"Thanks for your time. Both of you have been very helpful."

When Rabinski left, he realized that his safeguarding skepticism about Lenny was beginning to melt, that the frozen block of incredulity which he always put up to prevent hasty and imprudent decisions, was getting watery around the edges.

Just the fact that the two ladies were willing without any hesitation to undergo a polygraph, was a strong indicator that they were telling the truth. Lenny apparently was with them at the time of the murder. They told him he was at a Lower Eastside café, far from the murder scene, sharing with them his desperation to get free of his gangster bosses, and his desire and intention to try to bust up the operation and free the young girls.

Whether Lenny Petrocelli was a saint or a con man, it was becoming more and more evident that he could be pivotal in taking this slimy business empire apart. Lenny probably knew a lot. He probably knew everything the state would need to know to stick these guys with a number of major indictments. After that it would be like dominoes.

Rabinski was starting to sense both the scale and urgency of the message, and even warming up to the messenger himself — Lenny Petrocelli, aka Charlie Watts.

But while the picture was indeed beginning to fill out, at least in broad strokes, Rabinski still felt he needed more specifics, more unassailable details. Putting together this sort of massive multi-front raid required committing a lot of man-hours over a short slice of time, meaning other ongoing investigations would in the near term suffer. It was a big decision and he had to be sure it would be successful and produce some impressive results.

Lenny remained holed up. He left his phone off a lot of the time, not being fully aware of what technology might be capable of, fearing that an active cellular might make it possible to track him down.

He decided he needed to let Ying Mae know what was going on.

When he switched on his phone, there were five calls from Harold. Three from Ying Mae. He sent her a text.

> Rabinski FBI NY. 12125504317.
> Give him something. ANYTHING.
> He s best hope. LP

Ying Mae had been trying to get hold of Lenny. She had something alright.

She wrote down the number, deleted the message and immediately dialed New York.

"Mr. Rabinski, there is a lady on the phone for you. A Chicago number. It came in on the secure non-public line. She won't tell me who she is."

He picked up the extension.

"Rabinski here. Who is this?"

"I'm Ying Mae. I'm originally from Taiwan. Mr. Lenny told me to call."

"And where do you fit in?"

"I am the personal concubine for Harold Danko. He and Ed Valley run this whole thing. The Djin Djin girls."

"Go on."

"*Harold Danko is a sick man. I want to punish him. For what he has done to me and for everything else.*"

"I am not interested in getting involved in a lovers quarrel, Miss Mae."

"*Don't question my motives. This is not a 'lovers quarrel' as you say it.*"

"So what do you have for me?"

"*They just got back last night. Him and Ed. I overheard them talking about a shipment of more than twenty new girls. They will arrive tonight at shipyards in Duluth. Around 9 pm. Dock B19.*"

"Thank you, Miss Mae. How can I reach you? This number?"

"*No, please. It is very dangerous. I will try to call you if I have anything more. Do not try to call me, please.*"

"Take care of yourself, Miss Mae."

By a stroke of good luck and preternatural timing, Rabinski got right through to Sutter and relayed the details of the Duluth arrival.

"*I've got two men doing some surveillance work at the docks right now. That port is a mess. You got all sorts of illegal transport going on. I'll have them take a look. What's with those Knicks, Rabinski? I didn't know Alzheimer's was contagious. They apparently forgot how to play the game.*"

"To give the rest of you guys a chance, we're only putting four guys on the court. What the Bulls' excuse? Are they getting high in the locker room?"

Rabinski immediately called Lenny. He must have major phone karma working for him today. Lenny picked up on the second ring.

"*Rabinski here. So who is Ying Mae?*"

"She called you? She's Harold's #1 wife in Chicago."

"*Wife?*"

"Figuratively speaking. They each keep a favorite piece of ass in each city. Ying is Chinese. Maybe Taiwan? What did she say?"

"*Lenny, when are you coming in? Your chances of survival are not very good out there.*"

"Are you giving me immunity?"

"*We're close. I'll know within 48 hours. I don't want anything to happen to you.*"

"Wow. I've been upgraded from a murderer to an asset. Are you the great and powerful Wizard of Oz?"

"*You've got a great sense of humor for a man with a death warrant hanging over his head.*"

"48 hours or four days. Last time—"

"*Probably sooner. Leave your phone on tomorrow around 12 noon. We'll talk.*"

Lenny spent the afternoon pacing. What else could he be doing? This had to move and it had to move fast. 48 hours? Did he have that long? So many times when he thought he had a firm grip on a situation, something completely unexpected came blasting out of nowhere. That was the feeling he had right now. Waiting for the other shoe to drop. Time was not on his side. It was a mortal enemy.

What was Rabinski looking into now? What was he waiting for?
He texted Ying Mae.

Rabinski said you talked. What did
you tell him? There is fed guy Chicago.
Sutter 13128857709. Not on board yet.

She entered her reply.

Shipment Duluth. Frsh girls.
Dock B19. Thursday.

She heard Harold coming in. Quick! Delete message without sending? Yes.
She closed the phone and put it down on the nightstand, then went into the
bathroom to get ready.

"Are we leaving soon?"

"Yes. I'll have the car take you back."

He picked up his phone. Or what he thought was his phone. He had given
Ying a white Nokia, a very similar model to his own. He popped it open to
make a call.

Rabinski said you talked. What did
you tell him? There is fed guy Chicago.
Sutter 13128857709. Not on board yet.

He pressed the options button. Details? Select. A New York number. One
he recognized.

Lenny.

Lenny Petrocelli? Feds? Who the fuck does he think he is?

That ungrateful prick. And Ying Mae. The little cunt. The soon-to-be-dead
little cunt. Traitors. Motherfuckers! How long has this shit been going on?

Harold picked up the other — his own — phone. Autodial #1.

"Ed. Whatever you're doing, stop. We have a code red."

Autodial #3.

"Yoshikaze, my loyal Nipponese associate. How would you like to make a
$100,000 bonus?"

When It Rains It Pours

The next morning, Rabinski got hit from all sides. Good hits.

Henry Sutter's boys out of Chicago had done some excellent work.

They had staked out the Duluth Dock B19, recorded on video the unloading
over several hours of a cargo ship flying under an Indonesian flag. One steel
container had been set to one side and without attracting any attention had been
lifted onto a waiting 18-wheel flatbed. A customs officer appeared to have
signed off on it, after giving it a brief visual once-over. Away it went.

Making sure they weren't detected, the agents followed it to a warehouse in
a new industrial park on the outskirts of the city. The hauler backed the steel

container up to the loading dock but they couldn't maintain visual contact. They pulled out their portable high-resolution infrared and long wave high-density penetrating radar imagers. Certainly too far away and too occluded to get detailed images, there was little doubt about what they were picking up. The shapes of around thirty human bodies scurried into and about the inside of the building.

Human cargo.

Definitely not Club Med.

Likewise, Coltern had come through. He didn't share the details of the encounter. But one of his men had set up a session with a Djin Djin girl. He had tried to get Kimnai but was told she was in Seattle to make her debut as a movie star, whatever that meant. He saw what he needed to see. The complex appeared to be teeming with very young Asian girls, none of whom he could imagine were anywhere near eighteen. However they were spinning it, the place was a high-end whorehouse stocked with underage prostitutes. The Djin Djin he met with, freely and explicitly volunteered to perform a wide variety of sexual acts. She told him she was from Thailand, though her parents were originally from Myanmar.

It was a very classy operation indeed, which had to have a lot of capital behind it.

Then two of Rabinski's investigative analysts reported something very strange. Something which was at the very least anomalous.

They noticed that very recently a Brooklyn precinct office of the Guardian Angels, the one that worked Fiori's part of town, had been busted by the local drug enforcement team for allegedly being a huge regional drug dealing warehouse. If it was really on the scale claimed in the arrest report, which also listed sizable cache of unregistered weapons, then both the ATF and FBI should have been notified and officially brought into the case. It was highly doubtful that a locally run 'drug ring' could support the quantities of heroin and cocaine mentioned. Meaning out-of-state and/or out-of-country supply lines. There was a tacit understanding that in these situations federal authorities were always consulted, since they had greater legal authority and more effective institutional resources to pursue the matter across state lines and national borders, and successfully prosecute large-scale perpetrators. No one had filed any request with either federal bureau. Moreover, the Guardian Angels had since their inception an impeccable public file. While controversy surrounded their philosophy of community enforcement, there wasn't a single incident on record of them running afoul of the law. They were lily white and perfume pure.

But with this Brooklyn precinct affair, Rabinski smelled a decomposing rat. In fact, the bust and arrest of the two Angels reeked of the kind of local heroics usually associated with a frame up, prompted by some special agenda, political or otherwise. Another black mark for Fiori and company.

The last thing for Rabinski to process landed on him unsolicited and out of left field.

Peter, his intern ran into his office without even knocking.

"Sir, I think you're gonna want to see this. It's a live television feed."

Rabinski followed him to the media surveillance area where banks of screens monitored a variety of television and internet sites the bureau used for archiving background data and monitoring breaking news.

They were viewing a live broadcast, using handheld cameras, of a situation on a street in Manhattan. There a crowd watched as police intervened in a quarrel between some former residents of a hotel and the manager who had just evicted them, apparently for non-payment. There were boxes and bags of clothing and other personals scattered on the street, with several Asian ladies trying to sort through and gather their belongings. Two or three others were being restrained by the police as they tried to rip the manager to shreds, cursing and yelling at him in their native tongues. The manager was screaming back at them to "go back where you came from" and "come back when you can pay your bill", as well as some racist epithets and slurs about their illicit profession, calling them "a bunch of filthy whores". A female field reporter from one of the local TV stations had beaten her competitors to the scoop …

The manager of this very low-budget hotel who will only identify himself as Billy, claims that these girls are prostitutes and against the stated policy of the hotel regularly brought clients upstairs, despite many warnings that they stop. Then they fell behind on paying for their rooms, so he and a security guard put the ladies and their personal things on the street. That was approximately forty minutes ago.

The girls regrouped and tried to re-enter the building forcefully, but Billy stood his ground. That's when the fight really started and police were summoned to the scene.

In an intriguing aside to this story, several of the ladies have been waving one of these, a flier with a name and phone number on it, saying from what we can understand of their broken English and through their crying, that this man is supposed to be taking care of the rental of their rooms. If the camera can get a close shot of this, you can see that on the front of the flier is this photo and on the back is the name of the pictured man, who is Lenny Petrocelli. This man is currently the target of a city-wide manhunt and is alleged to be responsible for the murder of Bishop Mulcahey, of St. Francis Assisi in Brooklyn.

Police have briefly talked to several of the women and suspect they are here in the U.S. illegally, lacking any proper documentation. If we can pan over to the street there behind me to my left, you can see that the INS has just arrived with three paddy wagons. It appears that the Asian women will be taken into custody until authorities can sort through this.

We will stay on the scene …

"Thanks, Peter. Good eye."

And good timing. It was 11:50 and he had intended to call Lenny at noon.

Lenny's phone rang. He scrutinized the read-out to see who it was. Since he had turned it back on a half hour ago, it had rung at least twenty times. People he didn't want to talk to. Two calls from Chicago, and one right after another from Manhattan numbers he did not recognize.

This is the one he was waiting for.

"Rabinski."

"Petrocelli, where did you get those fliers printed? Kinko's? Nice job. But I think you look better in person than in that photograph."

"What the hell are you talking about … ?"

"Right now I'm watching on live TV a scene in front of a sleazebag hotel in Hell's Kitchen. This is hysterical. I should say, the girls are hysterical. They've been evicted because some guy named Lenny Petrocelli isn't taking care of business and paying the bills. They are being put into paddy wagons right now and hauled off. Tsk tsk, Lenny. You've got to start treating your girls better. They don't look too happy."

"Shit."

Was Rabinski laughing? If he was, that was sure a first.

"So, are you placing in doubt my spotless reputation here by implying that I'm some sort of pimp daddy?"

"No, I'm saying that the people you work for are not very bright."

"Usually they are."

"Correct me if I'm wrong but I'm assuming you didn't have those fliers made up yourself."

"Of course not."

"Then thanks to the brain trust in Chicago, a bunch of Asian prostitutes are running around effectively carrying your arrest warrant. The only thing missing is the date. I assume your bosses would just have to make a phone call and you'd be looking at the outside world through some bars. Ray Charles could see through this. Pretty amateur stuff."

"Then you're on my side?"

"I'm on the side of the law, Mr. Petrocelli. I'm on the side of taking this down down down. If you're going to help, then you're on <u>my</u> side."

"That's been the idea all along. But I don't want to fry just from being in the kitchen."

"I'm going to be open with you. But then you've gotta be open with me. The reports have been coming in. The Bishop himself fingered two heavy hitters in Chicago right before he died. A cargo ship with some fresh bodies docked in Duluth, Minnesota last night. Then as you promised, we found Alice in wonderland party Bangkok-style in San Mateo. Now there's this thing with your little harem in Hell's Kitchen. I'm not sure where that last item fits in, but in my mind this all adds up to one thing. You and I need to meet. And we've got to get you out of circulation before someone gets to you. I'm ready to move on this."

For the briefest moment a comforting hand of cautious optimism caressed Lenny's frazzled psyche, and the tight-wound springs of tension and fear relaxed and released him from the gut-wrench that had clutched him for weeks. Then almost as instantly, the fierce grip of anxiety and dread reclaimed him.

"Tomorrow. Let's meet tomorrow. If the terms are right, I go with you."

They agreed to meet at Tony's, Lenny's old haunt in Brooklyn. Between 9:30 and 10:00 pm.

This was it. No turning back.

Paperwork

With the new laws in place — designed in response to the 911 terrorist attacks — it took less than 48 hours to arrange and get court approval on federal search and arrest warrants. Lightning fast by previous bureaucratic standards, but painfully slow in many situations.

This was one of those situations.

If the Chicago bosses got wind of Lenny's switch of allegiance, they'd probably have the best of the worst out looking for him. As it was, the NYPD was on high-alert. Lenny had been aggressively portrayed as an extremely dangerous suspect. That was a euphemism for shoot to kill. No matter how you looked at it, there was already a hit out on Lenny Petrocelli, which would silence the key witness and make life difficult for Rabinski.

Time was of the essence.

So was a carefully coordinated bust, to minimize the risk that the guys they were really after would get away.

Rabinski got on the phone with Coltern. No problem there. The veteran INS agent reported that it appeared there were only two or three guys on security detail at the San Mateo place. He could have his men ready to go in, as soon as he got the word from Rabinski.

Then he talked to Sutter. Sutter was an interesting guy. Though he had indicated little initial enthusiasm in their first few phone calls, he had been busy doing some 'unofficial' work using his discretionary man-hour dockets. He had put tails on both Valley and Danko. Indeed, despite their sterling reputations in the Chicago business community and their impressive offices in the prestigious Willis Tower, their personal movements raised some question marks. Both were seen accompanied by young Asian girls, the one getting out of a limo with Valley no more than fourteen or fifteen years old. Performing a close scrutiny of their Dunn and Bradstreet documentation, their SEC filings, then correlating other public records and corporate data available in Bureau files, one could only conclude that Viz Adcom, Inc. was a publicly traded company that did nothing except trade publicly. This type of shell was a typical gambit used by the underworld to front for some other cash-intense business or businesses.

Sutter's men had of course done the surveillance in Duluth and had a semi-permanent presence there, as part of a team that had been assembled to try to plug the holes in the porous framework of international shipping at the port. Sutter said he could commit an additional five 'heavy hitters' from his Chicago special ops group any time over the next few days, if Rabinski required it. Plus he could have several Chicago-based special agents ready to apprehend Valley and Danko once the warrants were ready and in his hands.

Now it was just a matter of putting it in writing.

Rabinski had his staff prepare the requests and they went out by the end of the work day.

He set himself to putting together the operational plan and then deconstructing it into discrete and specific action item orders. This would be ready by noon tomorrow.

When was the last time he had turned his computer off?

Paperwork.

Good-Bye Hello

It was Saturday afternoon and Lenny would be meeting with Rabinski tonight.

There was one thing he needed to do before he disappeared into the black hole of federal custody and protection.

He switched on his cell phone. There were no voice or text messages. After the deluge just yesterday, this was a bit of a surprise. Not even Chicago. Bad sign.

He dialed.

"Alicia. Lenny. Can I see you?"

"Lenny. Where are you? Are you okay?"

"I think so. I've been in New York. Listen, Alicia. I'm turning myself in tonight to the FBI. They are supposed to offer me some help if I cooperate in bringing down the Djin Djin operation. I may be gone for a while and I wanted to see you. To ..."

"Of course, Lenny. Are you sure it's safe?"

"Yeah. I think it'll be okay. Where are you? Brooklyn?"

"No. I'm hiding too. I'm with Christine. No one knows about her."

Alicia gave Lenny the address. He would come by around 6 pm. Another fateful Saturday night meeting at six.

It was hard for Lenny to believe it was only two weeks ago that he had been in the café with Alicia and Christine, that the Bishop was now dead, that he was a wanted man, that Chicago had finally pushed him so far that he was now the point man with two federal agencies working to take down their operation and bring them to justice. Two weeks can change everything.

Lenny had no problems making his way to see Alicia. The streets were teeming with people. He pushed his coat collar high around his face, pulled his hat low, and didn't look much different than anyone else fighting the cold December wind.

Alicia must have been watching for him. She opened the door as he climbed the porch steps.

"Merry Christmas, stranger."

"Merry Christmas? What's the date?"

"Christmas is Tuesday."

"I've been living in a cave. At least that explains why everyone is carrying around so many shopping bags."

"I like the rugged look. You say a cave? I believe it."

They sat down across from one another. For the longest time they just looked into one another's eyes. Lenny seemed to be struggling to find the right words.

"Alicia ... thank you."

"For what? I would have killed you a week ago."

"But you believed me. In the end, you believed me."

"Lenny, I ..."

"I've had a lot of time to think. I see what's going on. I don't understand it. I probably don't deserve it. But I understand how you feel."

She came over and sat next to him but was too shy to touch him.

"You're very beautiful, Alicia. But it's takes much more."

"How much more?"

"I'd say you've got plenty."

He stood up to leave. She stood as well. They were standing there — a short uncomfortable distance between them — like two school kids who had never been on a date.

Alicia's timid stare took the slow journey from her own hands, browsing up the length of his body, his chest, his neck, chin, lips. To the soft pools of his waiting eyes. Behind the tension, fear of the unknown, the torment which pulled at the edges of his face — deep inside the space of those eyes — she saw what she had wanted to see. For all these years.

"See ya soon."

"Take care of yourself, Lenny. I'll be waiting."

He kissed her delicately on the forehead, then was out the door.

This last parting moment had gone by so quickly. But Alicia felt good. Frightened and anxious and concerned and unsettled. But still good. For as she watched Lenny disappear into the shadows beyond the last streetlight she could see from the porch, she knew that if he got through this, they would be together.

Everyone Has a Price

Lenny walked into Tony's at a little before 9:30. As expected, the place was almost full, it being a Saturday night, and the empties on the tables showed that the regulars had gotten a good head start along the road to oblivion. Tony glanced up at Lenny but gave no sign of recognition and started pouring a round of shots for three weekend bikers sitting at the bar.

Lenny had on a trench coat and was uncharacteristically wearing a hat, which was pulled down low over his face. He had not shaved now in eight days and had a nice start on a beard. He looked like a cross between Sam Spade and Luciano Pavarotti. It apparently changed his appearance enough to fool Tony at a distance.

He headed to the one empty stool at the end of the bar, keeping his head down and face turned slightly to the side.

"What can I get you?"

"Tony, it's me. Lenny. I didn't kill anyone. I need a favor."

"Ohmigod. I didn't ... are you okay? I mean, the cops have been in here a hundred times."

"Listen. I am meeting someone. Can I use the back room?"

"Sure. Go ahead. No one's in there. If I see a stranger, I'll send him in."

"Thanks, Tony. Really. I'm innocent. You'll see."

"Don't worry about it. I believe you. Do you want your usual?"

"Pass on that. Thanks."

Lenny cut into the hall leading to the toilets and went to the end, where there was a door for entering the "poker den", a modest room which could hold eight to ten people and was used for small parties and the occasional high-stakes card game.

He sat and waited.

As soon as Lenny had turned the corner, Tony stepped to a nook at the far end of the bar, where he kept extra mixes, glasses and other bartending accessories. He picked up the phone and dialed. He turned and began speaking with his hand cupped around the mouthpiece.

"This is Tony. Petrocelli's in New York. He's here right now."

Lenny sat wondering what he should do. How do you know if the feds are going to keep their end of a deal? There were a lot of guys doing ten to twenty who had made a deal.

He was impatient, anxious, a little nervous. Time seemed to have ground to a slow crawl. Every time he checked his watch, only one minute had passed. Rabinski said he would be there between 9:30 and 10:00. What was taking so long?

The door swung open and Lenny looked up.

"Mr. Petrocelli. We meet again."

"Yoshikaze! I—"

"Your car is waiting. But as a courtesy, I'd like you to put your weapon on the table, please. Very slowly. We don't want anything unfortunate to happen."

Lenny knew the routine. With grand, highly visible movements, he pulled back his coat, popped the restraining strap on his holster, and inch-at-a-time lifted his Beretta using only the tip of his index finger, finally laying it on the table at arms-length directly in front of him. Yoshikaze stepped over cautiously and slipped the gun into his coat.

"Let's just leave nice and casually. We are, after all, old friends ... aren't we?"

"Where are you taking me?"

"Mr. Lenny, our bosses wish to have a word with you. They miss your fine company."

Yoshikaze was managing at great effort but with sarcastic delight, his own facsimile of a smile, all that was possible of the frozen rictus of his round face. Lenny could read nothing from it.

"How nice."

"Right. Nice."

Just before he and Yoshikaze walked out, Lenny looked back. Tony caught his glance but turned and quickly headed the length of the bar to take a drink order from a table in the corner.

Less than five minutes after Yoshikaze had escorted Lenny out, Rabinski walked in and headed directly to the bar. Lenny had told him just to ask Tony where he was.

Tony knew immediately this was the man Lenny had been waiting for.

"Lenny left a few minutes ago. He told me to tell you. He didn't say anything else."

"Thanks. If he comes back ... never mind."

Rabinski was confused. He prided himself on being able to read people and situations. Without being boastful, he was usually right about 98% of the time. This made no sense. Why would Lenny disappear? Especially now?

He tried calling him. Lenny's phone was off. What's new?

What now?

Anyone who has been in the investigatory field will tell you, the action is the easy part. It's the waiting that will drive you nuts. It was being able to keep focus, clarity, determination and readiness through the seemingly interminable, undefined stretches of waiting, that separated the men from the boys. The top guns from the also runs.

Things were running. Running silent running deep. The plans of action were being readied. Warrants were being processed. Paperwork going through signature cycles. The slow steady grind of the bureaucratic process. For now he would just have to remain calm and ready.

And wait.

And hope his key witness would be around when he needed him.

Several blocks away, Yoshikaze drove the black Infiniti G35 with steely calm. Wedge sat in the back with Lenny, taking up more than his share of space. Where were they going?

Yoshikaze's phone rang.

"Did you get the slimy motherfucker?"

"Like giving candy to a baby."

"Put him in storage. Don't let him out of your sight. We'll let you know what to do next."

"What about the girl?"

"Don't worry about her. We've got what we need. Merry Christmas, Mr. Yoshikaze. You've earned a nice holiday bonus."

They drove another twenty minutes and pulled into a warehouse complex. Lenny recognized it immediately. It was the same place Yoshikaze had taken him to view Martin and Frankie. Lenny's special birthday surprise.

They took him inside. The concrete floor had been mopped but the two blood-stained chairs still sat in the middle of the bay. Yoshikaze directed Lenny to sit down and Wedge duct-taped his upper body and legs. There was a sickening smell which crept into Lenny's nostrils and found its way into the linings of his mouth and the recoiling surface of his tongue.

It smelled and tasted like death.

Chapter 17

THE SUN NEVER SETS ON DESPAIR

Tea for Two

Sunday morning.

Alicia and Christine were finishing breakfast. Each on their second cup of tea.

"I hope he's alright."

"If he's in custody, at least he's safe. How are you doing? You've been so quiet."

"I feel like I need to wear my own clothes. I'm thinking I should slip into my apartment and pick up a few things later this afternoon."

"You sure?"

"I'll be careful. Yeah, I think if I go after dark no one will see me. It's been how long? They've probably given up on finding me there."

"Five days."

In that very same moment at the warehouse, Yoshikaze was fielding a call from Harold Danko. He gestured broadly to Wedge, who then started removing the duct tape.

"We'll bring him. I'll take Wedge — you know, the Russian guy — to make sure he doesn't try any funny business. We'll be there tonight."

Yoshikaze closed the phone.

"Take him to the toilet. We've got a long drive ahead of us."

Sitting in a coffee shop on Park Avenue, Rabinski was beside himself. He had his men look for Lenny in all of the obvious and the not-so-obvious places. Not a sign of him.

He checked with his office. The warrants were still pending. It was hard enough trying to get this done on a regular weekend. But this was the last weekend before Christmas. Apparently, even judges go shopping.

He told his assistant to fax a request for expediting the orders. Tell them the matter was urgent. Like they hadn't heard that a million times before.

His men had reported that the local police had dropped the stake-out on Lenny's residence.

Interesting.

He tried to call Fiori. Not available at this time.

What did they know that he didn't?

All the President's Men

At first John Harrison was startled.

It had been so long since his walkie-talkie had made the crackling sound of an incoming transmission.

Second Lieutenant John Harrison, do you read? Admiral Michael Mullen, Chairman of the Joint Chiefs of Staff, trying to reach Second Lieutenant John Harrison. Come in, please.

"Second Lieutenant Harrison here, sir."

Please hold on. Admiral Michael Mullen will be right with you.

Could this really be happening? Mullen? Chairman of the Joint Chiefs of Staff, the man who reports directly to the President of the United States!

He came on and even through the static, his voice sounded resonant and commanding.

I'll make this short and sweet. You've been doing fantastic work out there, even without much support from our end, as I understand it. We're stretched real thin in some sectors, to put it mildly. If it weren't for men like you, Harrison, there are areas we couldn't hold. What I have is a very special assignment, one that only a few men could be trusted with.

"I'm here to serve. God bless America, sir."

We can put these commies in full retreat if we play our cards right. First, let me share some highly classified info with you. The World Trade Center. 911. The official line on this is that the destruction of those towers was the work of Islamics. Not true, Second Lieutenant. It has been established by army intelligence that this unfortunate blemish on our nation's history was the direct result of Cong infiltrators. The Cong have been tenacious, to say the least, Second Lieutenant, but we can break them. This is where you come in.

"Yes, sir. I will do everything I can. What are my orders, sir?"

We need to fire a shot, a loud resounding shot, a shot that will thunder across the entire land. We need to let the infiltrators know that their days are numbered. They will be terminated. Do you understand, Harrison?

"Yes sir, I do."

Use your discretion and good judgment. We have complete faith in you. Just take care of it. I will let the President know that the matter is in good hands.

"You can count on me, sir. We will prevail. God bless America, sir."

And that was that.

The World Trade Center Twin Towers had been completed three years after John had arrived in New York, set up his military base in Hell's Kitchen, and began his ministry in Manhattan. They had for decades towered over the skyline of the city and gleamed symbolically as a testament to America's greatness as a power and nucleus of financial and political leadership.

Now he knew the truth about their destruction. The one and only barbaric horde which had over the same decades continued to challenge America's destiny and world leadership, had made a final desperate attempt to shake the moral and political will our nation, to tear the fiber of its determination, to obstruct its sacred historic mission to spread freedom and foster democratic values throughout the world. But this cheap act of sabotage had only reaffirmed America's supremacy and reinforced her resolve. It was time for irrefutable closure.

High command had chosen well.

He — John Maximilian Harrison — would let them know all right!

He would send a bold message. He would fire a shot to be heard around the world.

You are history, commie scum!

It was all coming together. Starting to make complete sense. John knew what he had to do. God Himself had pointed the way. Literally.

Saigon Sally.

At the time he wondered why it didn't feel right to just take her out on the spot. Why he so strongly felt the need to prepare some sort of special ritual. Why this particular target begged for a sacrificial splendor which surpassed all his previous ones.

But now he understood. He could see the plan now. Masterminded at the highest levels.

It was time for reconnaissance, capture and confinement of the designated target.

John carefully staked out her place. There was a lot of coming and going. Police patrol cars. Plainclothes types as well. Some Asian guy, who maybe looked Japanese, sat in a black Infiniti, hunkered down for hours on end watching the apartment. Lot of interest in the lady. But no lady.

No sign of Saigon Sally for almost three days.

Then he saw her.

It was early in the evening but already dark. She seemed to be both in a big hurry, and very concerned about being seen. She looked around anxiously under the brim of a floppy wool hat and had a long cape on, which made her look like the Phantom of the Opera coming to pay a visit. She was only in her apartment about twenty minutes, when the last light went off and she appeared at the building entrance with an overnight and a clothes bag. When she turned to make sure the door was secure, John slipped out from behind the tree and shrubbery which had created a blind from which to observe. He came up behind her with the nearly invisible stealth he had learned doing ambushes as an infantryman.

She never knew what hit her.

More than just painful, a sudden unexpected blow, particularly to the head, renders a person disoriented and extremely obliging. John Harrison hit her hard enough to accomplish just that, but not knock her unconscious. He hooked the weapon — a military issue truncheon — back on his utility belt and grabbed Alicia's arm firmly and started heading to the subway entrance which after only a single transfer would take them back to Hell's Kitchen.

He steadied her as they walked down the street, aggressively moving along at a good pace. He reached in his pocket and pressed the barrel of a service handgun into her ribs.

"One peep out of you, I'll fill you full of holes. Nothing could make this evening sweeter. Am I clear?"

She nodded without looking at him. She was too frightened to look.

When they arrived at the huge, chaotic Times Square station complex, the late hour had not significantly lessened the number of people swarming through the tunnels. John guided them through the bustling swarm toward 8th Avenue and exited onto the bustling street. Within fifteen minutes, they were at his warehouse command bunker.

John instructed her to remove her outer garments, stood outside the door guarding her as she went to the toilet, then roughly pushed her to the floor and wrapped fiberglass shipping tape around her arms and ankles. She would be going nowhere for a while.

He picked up his walkie-talkie.

"Second Lieutenant Harrison reporting. Enemy combatant secured and ready for mission. Over and out."

He sat back in a folding chair, unlit cigarette dangling from his mouth, looking at his quarry.

"Aren't you the lucky lady? Tomorrow you make it into the history books next to your buddies, Trotsky and Che Guevara."

The Midnight Hour

Late Sunday evening.

"Christine Lindholm? This is FBI Agent Rabinski. We met. Sorry to bother you so late."

"It's fine. I'm glad you called. I'm very worried. I—"

"Have you seen or heard from Lenny Petrocelli?"

"He was here yesterday. Around 6 o'clock. He was talking to Alicia. But now she's gone. She was supposed to be back by now.

"Back? Where did she go? I've been trying to reach her."

"She just went to her apartment to pick up a few things. That was over five hours ago. She hasn't come back."

"What did Lenny tell her? Do you know?"

"He was on his way to meet you. To turn himself in."

"Anything else?"

"That was it, as far as I know. He was only here a few minutes."

"Thanks for your help, Ms. Lindholm. Try not to worry. We'll find Ms. Peters for you."

Empty promises. This was a business of promising things you had no idea you could deliver on, just to offer reassurances which had nothing to back them.

Who was going to reassure him?

A key witness gone. His supporting witness missing.

Just to make sure things didn't get worse, Rabinski immediately called in a request for two agents to stake out Christine's home and make sure that nothing bad happened to her.

More phone calls.

Fiori not available.

His field men reported no trace of Lenny Petrocelli.

His office reported that warrant approvals still hadn't come through.

It was going to be a long night.

"See what you've done to America. And you think you can get away with this?"

John Harrison, dressed in formal military dress attire, stood behind Alicia, as they looked at the Ground Zero Memorial. Her arms were tightly bound under her full-length alpaca cape. She felt the hard barrel of John's handgun poking her lower ribs. John kept himself insinuated against her. Making a break for it out of the question.

"What are you saying? I'm not from the Middle East."

"And neither am I. But you and the members of your sinister cabal are responsible for this. So you will pay. You will be the poster girl, Saigon Sally."

"Why do you keep calling me that?"

John gave her a conspiratorial leer.

"We both know, now don't we?"

There was no negotiating with a madman. Alicia was frightened but knew that she needed to wait for the right moment. This wasn't it. Yes, there were a few people around but New Yorkers were legendary for their indifference to violence. People were robbed and beaten while others walked around them, going on about their own business. With her arms tied and a gun pointed at her the whole time, she would make it about ten feet before he cut her down. She had no viable options at this point. She had no idea where he was taking them. She just hoped that something would offer a possible escape or … or what?

"If you try anything, I know where your friend lives."

"What friend?"

"Your lady friend. The one you were with in Central Park."

Where were the cops when you needed them? Supposedly at any given time there were several hundred police out on the beat. She hadn't seen a single one. Not one. On the street. In the subway. Here at the memorial.

"Let's go."

He nudged her with the barrel again. She didn't know much about guns. But it looked to her like some semi-automatic weapon. It could be held in one hand, was small enough for him to conceal it under his jacket, but it had a curved clip, which she supposed held quite a few bullets. If it was like the ones she saw in the movies, he could kill a lot of people in under 30 seconds, she being the first of his victims. How many more ammunition clips did he have in that duffel bag he was carrying?

They boarded a city bus. Within fifteen minutes they were at Battery Park. He took them to the ferry dock and they were on their way to the Statue of Liberty.

It was a holiday weekend, early afternoon, cold and wintry. Last minute Christmas shopping had taken its toll on attendance. The ferry was far below capacity. John made them sit outside, toward the rear of the vessel. There was no opportunity that she could see, to try to attract anyone's attention, much less solicit anyone's help.

But as they approached the entrance to the lift and stairwell to top of the Statue pedestal, her heart quickened as she spotted the thick rectangular frame of a metal detector and the conveyor belt of a bag X-ray machine. There was no way with the gun and whatever back-up armaments he had with him, they would get through. A guard stood to one side. If the metal detector alarm went off, his job was to inspect bags and do a sensitive wand detector pass, close-range over the entire body. A girl sat at the X-ray monitor, sipping coffee, glancing at the screen, and making jokes with another uniformed attendant. Both of them were wearing Santa's helper hats. When John's bag came up, she stopped the belt momentarily, reversed it to take another look, then forwarded it again. No reaction.

Alicia stepped through the metal detector. No buzzer. John stepped through. No buzzer. The guard smiled and nodded in what appeared to be respectful awe of John's pressed and dashing uniform, perhaps as well of the elegant and beautiful lady which accompanied him. After they stepped through, the guard bent down to make sure the power plug to the metal detector was tight in the socket. It had been giving them trouble recently and maintenance wasn't going to be back until after the Christmas holidays.

John grabbed his bag, then pushed her toward the entrance of the stairs. As they stepped into the stairwell, he turned around suddenly and put his hand up to those in line behind them. They looked puzzled but waited, assuming he must have some authority in the matter. He turned back around, took the first few steps two at a time and coming right behind Alicia, prodded her to move along. Up they went.

When they finally arrived at the pedestal, John pushed Alicia roughly to the ground, pulled out the weapon and fired several bursts into the sky. He pulled a bullhorn out of his bag and as he continued to wave the gun menacingly over his head, started yelling his oration.

"I am here to draw a line in the sand of Creation. To pace off the perfection that is the greatest country in history. God bless America. Glory to God in His militant loyalty to America. I am here to consecrate that vision of America which is under attack. Here with me I have a member of the military corps who only exists to poison and plunder that vision. Let all of you vile infiltrators know that this is total war. A war which will vanquish you and render America pure again, free of the foul cancer of communism. You are on notice. This comes from the highest authority of our land and the highest authority in the Universe. It is God who sends me today to fire the shot into the heart of evil. At midnight tonight, on the eve of the birth of our Lord Savior Jesus Christ, the tide is turned and the slaughter begins. Our forces are infinitely powerful and good, backed by the blessing of God Himself and the sacred prayer on the dollar itself. In God we trust. In God we trust. God bless America. Glory to God. God bless America. Glory to God ..."

At the first sound of gunfire, everyone on the pedestal started scrambling for exits. No one needed to stop and analyze the situation to recognize its lethality. It was full-on panic. One portly security guard, one of those heroic minor characters who always seem to be at the scene of disasters and other bursts of random violence, was right in the same area as John and Alicia, and hurriedly assisted people to the exits, attempting to get as many out as possible. John pointed the gun directly at him.

"You! Come here."

To let him know he was serious, John unleashed three shots on the wall right above the man's head. Stucco powdered and tumbled onto his shoulders.

He slowly approached John, fear written across his face in bold terror-filled strokes.

John indicated the walkie-talkie on the man's belt.

"Tell them I want to go to the top. Now! Or I'll kill you."

The guard fumbled with the radio. Then, in a trembling voice, he passed along the demand.

"He's got an automatic weapon. He wants access to the crown. Or … or he'll kill me."

"Just stay calm, George. We'll get you out of this. Tell him we're checking."

"Fuck you! What's there to check on? I said I want to go to the top!"

Within thirty seconds, they came back.

"Okay. We'll unlock it."

There were twelve security people on the island at the time. Only four were armed. Others included an office clerk and the security screening personnel. Back-up was on its way but that would take up to 45 minutes. They had to accept John's terms.

John held the gun to the man's head. Alicia was helpless, arms taped tightly to her body under her cape. It was all she could do just to get herself sitting upright after John had pushed her to the floor. She could offer no comfort to the guard, who lay there trembling and grabbing his breath in short panicky pants. She feared he was going to have a heart attack.

His radio crackled to life.

"The door is open. Are you okay?"

"So far. Yes. I'm okay."

"Tell him he's got a clear path. The area has been vacated."

The guard led the way and very shortly they were at the base of the spiral staircase leading to the crown of Lady Liberty, which had been closed to the public since 911. The padlocks to the gate had been removed and it was open.

"Thanks, old man."

John raised his gun and fired a single shot, splattering the guard's brains across the floor.

"That's a warning to anyone who tries to follow."

He prodded Alicia up the steep twisting 168 stairs to the crown viewing deck. Unable to use her arms, she nearly lost her balance several times. They finally arrived.

He shoved her harshly and she sprawled on the floor. The sound of several speedboats in the distance and at least one helicopter could be heard over the wind which buffeted the Statue's metal skin at the nearly 30 stories above the waters of the bay.

John ran frantically from one side to the other trying to see what was going on. He leaned and craned his neck but the helicopter was not visible, apparently hovering behind the crown. He then inexplicably fired several rounds of bullets and blew out the protective windows. The wind now blew cold air in fierce gusts, sending the temperature in the viewing area plunging. Regardless, John appeared to be sweating and wiped his face with his free hand.

Alicia had reached a state of dissociation. She was past fear, resigned to whatever happened. The feeling was as if she were somewhere else in the room, looking at herself in a movie. She squirmed as inconspicuously as she could to see if the bindings on her arms had loosened but they had not. With a great deal of effort, she managed to upright herself and with no alternative, she slumped against the wall and continued to watch her psychotic captor.

John reached in to his duffel bag and produced his army walkie-talkie.

"This is Second Lieutenant Harrison reporting. Demonstration zone now secured."

Silence.

"That is affirmative. I have Saigon Sally with me. She is restrained and will be dispatched at the appropriate time. Please coordinate media coverage."

Silence.

"No sir. It is not a problem. It is an honor to serve in such a worthy capacity."

Silence.

"God bless America. Out."

Who was he talking to? Or who did he *think* he was talking to?

He put the walkie-talkie back in the bag and took out a small crucifix, about the size of his forearm. He took a few short steps and stood over Alicia.

"Christ died on the cross for America. Taste His blood, viper!" He swung the cross wildly and grazed Alicia's forehead and shoulder. The cape protected her body but blood started running down her face from a shallow cut right above her left eye.

"Now we wait. We wait for the perfect moment to deliver the message and send you to Hell where you belong."

Maybe twenty minutes passed. John stood there, staring out, simultaneously appearing to be in possession of his senses and possessed by some haunting spirit. He periodically glanced over at Alicia and struggled to suppress a smile, whatever prompting it his own kept secret. She never took her eyes off of him.

Alicia had said nothing to him since they left the Ground Zero Monument, certain as she was of his instability and uncertain as to what effect the wrong choice of words might have. But now she felt she had nothing to lose by engaging him, insane as he obviously was.

"Who do you think I am? Why have you dragged me here?"

"I know exactly who and what you are. You are Saigon Sally and represent the vilest of the vile. An American who has turned on her own country."

"I'm Alicia Peters and I'm a freelance writer, a loyal American."

"I am on orders directly from the Commander In Chief to let you and your commie slime conspirators know, exactly where you stand. You think you can just march in and take over, do you? Well, you've got another think coming, Saigon Sally. This is the beginning of the end for all of you. Today you take the fall. Tomorrow all of you vermin will tumble into the dustbin of history. Today we herald the greatest military victory of our time, Saigon Sally. We cannot fail. God is on our side."

The sound of the helicopter engine suddenly became deafening. There was a loud thud directly over them and then some clanging sounds. John became frantic and again craned his head out the viewing apertures in an attempt to see exactly what was going on. Then without any apparent reason, he ran to the top of the stairwell and started firing wildly. The report of the weapon was deafening and bullets could be heard ricocheting off the metal interior.

Then his weapon went silent. Out of bullets.

He rushed over and looked out at the sky.

"See the hand! See the hand! See I told you. You probably thought I was crazy."

He started whooping and laughing hysterically, jumping up and down, easily abandoning the mostly fierce but controlled intensity which had characterized his comportment until now. He thrust the gun in front of himself, holding it like an offering to whatever he was seeing in the sky, looking expectant.

"God in Heaven, Savior of saviors, Your infinite love is the divine bread of your warriors. Reload! Reload!"

John pulled the weapon to his chest and tried to fire it but nothing happened.

"God in Heaven, this is your servant John Maximilian Harrison, St. John the Baptist of Hell's Kitchen, your friend and confidant. Reload! I pray to your Infinite Grace. Reload!"

As he became more frenzied, real fear finally started fill Alicia's body. With a squirming snakelike motion, she slid herself around the containment wall, edging slowly toward the stairwell.

"Reload! Reload! The hour is at hand to vanquish the enemy and baptize the Eden of our earthly triumph, Your Kingdom, this great land of America, with the blood of our victory!"

He pointed his weapon directly at Alicia, halting her slow progress. He repeatedly pulled the trigger. Nothing happened.

Consumed by the pure agony only possible in those who dived into a chasm of despair of their own making, his eyes almost bursting from their sockets and his face twisted in an epileptic spasm of pain and horror, John howled and cried like a wolf choking on its own blood. He fell to his knees, his shaking outstretched hands beseeching some vaporous vision only he could see.

"My God, my God. In our hour of perfect triumph over the great evil, the communist Satan, the beast of filthy lies. Why oh why have You forsaken me? Why have You forsaken me? Why have You ..."

Alicia heard loud noises from opposite sides of the metal crown. A soldier in full battle gear dropped down on rappelling cable to position himself directly in front of the viewing window. And up from the stairwell came three similarly outfitted enforcement officers, each wearing bulging bulletproof helmets and thick Kevlar-reinforced vests, automatic weapons ready to fire. The first saw Alicia, now only a few feet from the stairs, and threw himself in front of her on the floor as the other two rushed John.

With stealth and caution quite unnecessary in light of John's immobilizing despair — but nevertheless prudent — they approached him, keeping their barrels on him, though he now was curled forward, head in hands, weeping. The first to get to him kicked his weapon aside and pounced on him.

John offered no resistance but continued to moan like a helpless child. As a preventive measure, one of the heavily armored and helmeted officers plunged a syringe into John's neck, causing him to instantly fall limp under the sledgehammer of an animal-size dose of a tranquilizing chemical.

"Are you alright, ma'am?"

The officer who had thrown himself protectively on Alicia turned around and helped her to her feet, as the other two continued to restrain John, until they were sure that the incapacitating effect of the tranquilizer was going to hold. Parting her cape, they cut through the fiberglass tape which had manacled and numbed her arms. Slowly and gently they assisted her descent back to the safety and sanity of the ground floor of the monument.

Then down the steep stairs, they dragged the sedated mass of a finely-tuned fighting machine, now a limp hulking rag doll — John Maximilian Harrison himself, the last fateful victim of the madness that had possessed him since the slaughter-filled bloodlust days of the Vietnam War.

Lost and Found

Never had Rabinski ever felt like a case was so completely out of his control.

He did find Alicia Peters for Christine. The same way that Christine had probably found her.

There she was on television being escorted out of the Statue of Liberty, after a dramatic rescue by a paramilitary team from the Department of Homeland Security.

How would Lenny Petrocelli show up? Maybe in a spaceship commanded by an alien force from a remote solar system?

He could wish.

For at this point, there was no sign of him.

His phone rang.

"Halloway here. We got Justice approval on every request."

"Did you forward them?"

"Yes, sir. As per your instructions, Mr. Sutter in Chicago and Mr. Coltern in San Francisco both have verified copies. I spoke to Mr. Sutter right after transmission and he said they will go forward immediately."

Immediately.

But was that soon enough?

Where was Lenny Petrocelli?

Was there a Guinness Book of World Records for the longest held shit-eating grin?

If it was under thirteen hours, then Yoshikaze was now in the record books.

Of course, to describe the twisted configuration of his severely compressed lips and fixed grimace required some artistic license. But it was there. An independent panel of judges would look at the expression on the man's face over the entire drive from New York City to Chicago and declare: *'It fulfills the minimum requirements and is indeed a shit-eating grin.'*

Yoshikaze only glanced at Lenny occasionally to make sure that the bindings on his hands had not loosened, or on his way to making eye-contact with Wedge to confirm that everything was under control. Of course, they both watched him with a prison guard's obsessive attention when making restroom and fast food stops along the way.

Logistics of a prisoner-in-transport functioning properly, there remained a stone dead silence between the three men for over thirteen hours.

Finally, Yoshikaze uttered two fateful words.

"We're here."

They had arrived in the lower parking structure beneath the Lake Point Tower complex, which housed Harold's and Ed's Shangri-La-La-La. It was Sunday evening a bit past 11 pm.

They entered the players pad, then sat and waited for two hours. Wedge stood off to one side and kept what looked like a Glock 9 mm pointed at him. Yoshikaze sat at a table and toyed with Lenny's Beretta.

Finally the bosses came high-stepping in, rather boisterous and cheerful even for them.

"Love the Abe Lincoln look, Lenny!"

"Thanks, Ed. I was hoping you'd approve. So why am I here? Why the special treatment?"

Harold looked at him with a caricature of paternal concern.

"Why? Why? You have to ask?"

"You had me in the perfect cage in New York. The entire NYPD was after me."

"Lenny. You insult me. You know Ed and I. We like to make sure business is taken care of properly. We are very particular. We don't believe in leaving anything to chance."

Ed stepped directly in front of Lenny, taking off his heavy wool coat.

"Harold and I have learned that no one does a job as good as yourself. So when something really important comes along, we prefer to be very hands-on about it."

Harold wandered back from the bar with a drink in his hand.

"So here you are. To answer your question, we brought you here to talk about the future."

Ed went into his high-theater mode. He was clearly enjoying this.

"You're a big expert on pop culture, Lenny. How does that song go? 'The future's so bright I have to wear sunglasses.' Love that. Well, it happens to be true. Harold and I have really been doing well. Right now, we're gonna show you our latest money printing machine."

Harold again. "By the way, Ed and I did this while we were in Seattle. Some very talented people up there. The arts are a big priority with those Pacific Northwest types."

Ed picked up the remote and brought the flat-panel monitor to life. For Lenny, this little diversion, whatever they were up to, had a very uncomfortable familiarity about it.

"We're breaking into the movies, Lenny my boy. Hollywood here we come."

The screen exploded to life and high-energy music roared from the speakers. It began with a quick-edit montage of scenes probably culled from the rest of the movie, settling on one showing an Asian girl with back to the camera who apparently was giving head to some bull stud, who groaned ecstatically over the thump thump of bad disco music. A porn movie.

The title then was emblazoned across the screen in a font drooling a creamy fluid …

Djin Djin Films presents: His Cock Runneth Over

As the title dissolved, suddenly dripping and pooling at the bottom of the screen, then disappearing by running away in little rivulets, the girl slowly turned around and bit the lower of her cum-lubricated lips.

The camera zoomed to a full-face close-up. Her eyes were drugged and sad. It was Kimnai.

Instantly, Lenny thought his heart would explode. It was all he could do to keep himself from attacking one or both of them, probably getting shot full of lead in the process.

If they thought he was watching the rest of the video, they were wrong. His eyes had glazed and he sat there in the self-imposed exile of a man who knew his world was ending. Despite his best efforts, tears ran down his cheeks and dripped onto his shirt.

Gratefully, porn videos are short and this one was soon over.

Harold poured himself another drink and stood with his back to Lenny, looking out at the Chicago skyline.

"I can see you are deeply touched by this little cinematic masterpiece, Lenny. I thought you, above all, would appreciate it. You really are the sensitive guy we always knew you to be."

Ed managed to pull himself out of the erotic reverie the porn video had wrapped him in.

"So where was I? Oh yes … now I remember. The bright future. That is very very true. We are looking at a brighter and brighter future. No doubt about it. But the thing is, that only applies to us. You, on the other hand … nope. Not so bright at all, I'd say. What would you say about that, Harold? Lenny's future." Haw haw haw.

"Without a doubt, we could have left you in New York and it was surely just a matter of time before you got hauled in for multiple counts of criminal behavior. Probably would have served 10, 20, 30. But like I said, we hate to leave anything to chance. Besides, a nice comfortable cell is too good for you. You might just get all sentimental and goose bumpy grateful and next thing you know, you start talking and telling things you shouldn't. Certainly Ed and I don't think you should be telling these things. Right, Ed?"

"The way we're understanding it, you've already made some friends and that loose mouth of yours has already been put on the federal payroll. To make a long story short, this must stop. And it will stop. Our loyal friend Yoshikaze here, is going to put a stop to it tomorrow."

Yoshikaze offered a humble Japanese bow and smiled his wired-jaw smile.

"It's puzzling to Ed and I, Lenny, why you turned on us. We've always treated you right. Took you to the best restaurants. Put you up in the finest style. But I guess it just wasn't good enough for you. And frankly it really hurts, when someone doesn't show the appreciation and respect we think we rightfully deserve."

"Everybody should get what they deserve. Don't you think, Lenny?"

Harold's familiar whap on the back, this time an ominous punctuation mark of finality.

"We'll see you in the morning."

Lenny watched them as they walked out the door. Harold turned to Yoshikaze and indicated he should follow. Wedge stood immobile, eyes frozen in a robotic focus, his steely gaze fixed on his prisoner, handgun pointed straight and true at Lenny's head.

After about three minutes, Yoshikaze came back in and took over the gun from Wedge.

"Wrap him up."

As Wedge wound the fiberglass-backed tape around his arms and legs, Lenny's mind flashed on many things. It was a fast-cut montage of the chaotic events of the past five months. Then it stopped and to his surprise, a portrait of Alicia's face froze in his mind's eye. It was the face from two nights ago. In the silent soundtrack and floating virtual screen of his mind, he could see her lips moving and forming her last words to him.

I'll be waiting for you.

Deadwood

A writer of bad detective novels would say that Yoshikaze had a hard heart.

This description, if not wholly inadequate, would be highly inaccurate. Yoshikaze had no heart. Not the kind of heart that feels remorse, that pulses with pangs of conscience, that picks up pace and beats more rapidly when confronted with responsibility for a morally reprehensible act, or pumps sadness or regret or remorse into the bloodstream over prior sins or misdeeds.

In fact, it was not his heart which came into play when he did housecleaning for his bosses in Chicago. It was his adrenal gland. He loved the rush, the thrill, the amphetamine ecstasy, the 20 G joyride of pure exhilaration, the intoxicating full-body buzz that came with every new bloody assignment.

Right now he was absolutely beside himself, so filled with cluster bombs of energy in anticipation of the next few days, he felt like he himself might explode. If he weren't so constrained by the conservatism of his Japanese upbringing, he'd be skipping, dancing, jumping up and down, maybe even singing the Queen anthem *We Will Rock You.*

He had just been given his new orders from Harold and Ed. His assignment? Four hits at his earliest convenience, starting bright and early tomorrow.

The targets were: Ying Mae, the feisty little concubine, who was Harold Danko's own personal fuck buddy. Alicia Peters, a bohemian cunt that lived in Brooklyn and had the audacity to stick up for Lenny. Christine Lindholm, a do-gooder Christian bitch in New York who had a soft-spot for the Asian girls. And the pinnacle in the glorious trajectory of slaughter, the pathetic man who sat helplessly in front of him right now. Leonis Petrocelli.

Lucky Lenny. That's supposedly what his friends called him. Like he had any friends. Ha. The first time he had met this overrated loser, he had taken a serious disliking to the guy. What a lightweight. Deadwood. Maybe Ed and Harold had had some use for him along the way. But no more. Check out time. Yoshikaze would take special care and great satisfaction in whacking this fucking loser, that was for sure.

The assignment started with Lenny. Tomorrow morning, he would take him to Duluth, to the charm school they had there for the Djin Djin girls-in-training. There were several rooms in the back of the warehouse not currently used for anything. No one would be able to hear the screaming. After Lenny was slowly and painfully dispatched, he would be cut up into nice bite-sized pieces and dumped into plastic bags and loaded onto one of the shipments of toxic waste that regularly left for third world countries from the docks there. How perfect.

Yoshikaze then was supposed to return on Christmas Day to take care of the other traitor, the little bitch Ying Mae, silencing her smart-ass little puckered lips forever. Harold said he had a special party planned for her tomorrow. He could only imagine what that would be like. While it would be a distant second to killing Petrocelli, Yoshikaze knew he would have some fun there as well.

Then it was off to New York. Take out the other two, part of Lenny's sewing circle and admiration society.

Yes, this next week was going to be as good as it gets. The bosses really came through.

Just in time for the holidays.

Harold and Ed sure knew how to throw a Christmas party.

Chapter 18

IT WAS THE NIGHT BEFORE CHRISTMAS

I Left My Heart in San Francisco

It was Christmas Eve.

Kimnai had the inside information. She knew exactly when they were coming. Thanks to a man she only knew as Jim. A man who worked for a federal agency and had committed the professional indiscretion of falling in love with her.

The INS was coming in the day after Christmas. 2 o'clock in the afternoon.

She told the select few around her when to be gone. Hopefully they wouldn't be in the middle of a session and could casually claim they needed to run to the store for something. Or needed to go to the clinic for birth control pills. Or just try to slip out and run like hell. After all, this would be the last time they would ever see this place. They could burn bridges.

She would like to have warned all of the girls but that was impossible for two reasons.

First, it made no sense. Someone had to be there. If the INS authorities came in and no one was there, they would just come back. There had to be lambs for the sacrifice.

Secondly, while the two buildings which their bosses had set up as adult playgrounds housed over fifty girls, Kimnai and five others were kept very separate. They were the Djin Djin Elite, and they got a minimum of $2000 for a single hour. Kimnai often commanded $3000 or more from men who were tantalized enough by the idea of having sex with a 15-year old. As Djin Djin Elite, they had their very plush quarters on the penthouse floor of one of the buildings. Contact with the "regular" Djin Djin girls was minimal. They were watched closely by the three security guards on duty around the two building at any given time. Frankly, they really had little reason to visit the other girls, except for social interaction, which was discouraged.

Unfortunately for Kimnai and her close confidants, her admirer and inside man had it wrong. It wasn't set for the day after Christmas, but the day before.

The raid went smoothly. After the finely dressed doorman and the on-duty guards were subdued, cuffed and put into transport vehicles, a team of female agents and social service workers, including a doctor and a psychologist, swept through the buildings, accompanied by four weapon-toting male agents, rounding up everyone who was there at the time.

The Djin Djin girls themselves were treated with great professional courtesy and tenderness. They were, after all the victims in this.

It did not go so well for the men caught with their pants down in the rooms at the time. Not a single Djin Djin girl was eighteen years old. Countless laws came into play. Statutory rape. Soliciting and procuring sex from minors. These customers were facing a very long hard road and many years behind bars.

The exclusive condominium buildings were in a development complex, serviced by only one main entrance road. This made it easy to restrict access to the two buildings. Of course, once it became evident that there was a major police action underway, someone would play hero to the news-hungry world and alert the media. But the INS with the cooperation of the San Mateo police were able to keep the reporting teams at bay, giving them assurances that they would have full access to the story within eight to ten hours.

Coltern, who was responsible for coordinating all aspects of the raid, was confident that the big boys in Chicago would not get word of what had happened.

One down. Two to go.

The Great White North

It was unseasonably cold. The Arctic winds in a bold sweeping gesture had dumped sub-zero air down the center of the continent. It was going to be a chilly Christmas.

In contrast to his playful self the night before, this morning Ed was a full-tilt ranting hate machine. He alternated like some possessed, wounded beast, between shivering from cold and quivering with rage.

"Put him to sleep, Yoshikaze. Like a rabid dog. First torture him. Then empty your guns into this traitorous fuck. Use both hands. Turn this motherfucker into Swiss cheese. We want no traces of Mr. Petrocelli laying around, stinking up the air. Put him on one of those garbage dump ships that they run out of there. Give someone a hundred and they'll give Benedict Fucking Arnold here, a burial at sea."

Lenny, bound and gagged, was thrown roughly into the trunk. It should take Yoshikaze about eight or nine hours to get to Duluth. There would still be plenty of time to do the job right. He would finish the job in the security and privacy of their warehouse there. Building 7. Yoshikaze had been up all night deciding and savoring what he might do to make Lenny suffer. The best ways to create a slow and excruciating crawl towards death.

They say timing is everything. Coincidence the loins of fate. Serendipity the bastard child of good planning. Whatever.

Timing was either good or bad.

Yoshikaze's timing was bad that day.

Real bad.

In the first place, the cold arctic winds which had plunged Chicago into subzero weather, had dumped about 10 inches of snow north of Minneapolis. It was completely unexpected. Moreover, it was Christmas Eve, making it virtually impossible for the normally efficient Department of Highways to assemble the staff necessary to effectively plow the snowbound roads. What should have been an eight or nine hour drive ended up being over twelve hours. When he got to Duluth, it was almost 9 pm.

When finally he pulled into the gate of the industrial park zone set aside for Buildings 5 – 8, he saw no less than fourteen vehicles which definitely didn't belong there — squad cars, assault vehicles, personnel transports, vans, an ambulance.

They had been there for only ten minutes.

Without hesitating or even slowing, he whipped his vehicle into a U-turn to make a beeline back out of the lot. Too late. They had posted guards on both sides of the gate, armed with rapid-fire urban assault rifles. They quickly stepped into his path and now stood directly in front of him, weapons aimed, ready to fire.

Other agents ran and closed in from behind him and his sides, handguns drawn, safeties off. They had Yoshikaze cold.

After they frisked and handcuffed him, he lay face down at gunpoint on the snow-covered asphalt. They then opened the trunk and lifted a bewildered, breathless, exhausted, but immensely relieved Lenny up and out of the vehicle. They traded fur-lined gloves and a heavy down parka for his tape bindings and helped him to his feet.

Lenny was put into the ambulance along with two agents. Since they had no idea exactly what his role was — victim or perpetrator — it was not clear if they were protecting him or preventing him from escaping. They weren't taking any chances. They remained with him as the medics gave him a brief examination and a mild sedative. He was then moved to one of the squad cars.

Both Yoshikaze and Lenny were taken into custody.

There Is A God

Harold was drunk.

Tonight was special. That's what he had told Ying Mae. In his inebriated state, this could only mean trouble. A prescient shudder of revulsion had stirred her insides when he said it.

As they were leaving the living room, she saw that Ed had Dawa bent forward over a chair. Grunting. Something he did well. He called Dawa his "sweet little backdoor girl".

Ying Mae now was in the beautifully decorated bathing room of the Lake Point Towers suite. Shangri-La-La-La.

Harold stood over her fully clothed. She was naked, on her knees, crouched on the tile floor, hands smeared with a brown goo. She was shaking. Crying.

"Come on now, let's eat some chocolate. That's right. Put it in your mouth. Um, yummy. Now let me hear you say it. Tell me how good it is."

"It's good." She gagged and vomit spilled onto her thighs. "It's so good."

"Now tell me you want some lemonade with that. Come on. Ask me for some lemonade."

"Can I have some lemonade?"

"Please."

"Can I please have some lemonade?"

Harold took another swig from the bottle of Heineken he held in his left hand, as he unzipped his trousers with his right. This was the third beer he'd had in the last half hour after two snifters of brandy, so he had no problem providing the 'lemonade'. He went long and hard, then shook off the last drops onto the back of Ying Mae's head.

"Oh Ying Mae. You are such a treasure. I think I will keep you forever."

At that very moment, even through the thick oak door, he heard some sort of commotion. Before he could even wonder what it was, much less put his pecker back in his pants, he heard the deafening thud of a military-style boot kicking the door open.

"Freeze!"

He stood there dumbfounded, staring into the barrel of a semi-automatic carbine.

"You have the right to remain silent ..."

The Way to a Man's Heart

All Rabinski could think was that he must be doing something wrong. The only other people working on Christmas Eve are standing in front of cash registers in convenience stores.

What does that say about his professional development? His place in the world?

He checked his email. Again. For the gazillionth time.

What a surprise.

Nothing.

Obsessive Compulsive Disorder. OCD. That was it. He was becoming OCD.

He had heard from San Francisco. It was what they had expected. Everything went fine.

And the Sutter's Chicago guys bagged their men. Right in the middle of some sick shit. Details later.

What about Duluth? There was a big blizzard up there. Hopefully that didn't muck things up for them.

And where was Lenny Petrocelli?

His cell phone rang.

"Sutter again. You'll never believe who popped out of an automobile trunk in Duluth."

"Posh Spice?"

"Try again."

"The Dalai Lama?"

"One more."

"Angelina Jolie?"

"Not as good on the eyes but better for your case. Lenny Petrocelli."

"I warned him about hitchhiking."

"I'll have him there on Wednesday."

"Good work."

"Merry Christmas."

Rabinski dialed.

"Hey."

"Do I know you?"

"We have the same last name. I believe we're married. Aren't we?"

"Come home, my brave hard-working FBI man. I baked a lemon meringue pie. Special for you."

New York is for Lovers

Lenny felt like a new man. At least a newer version of an older version.

Six months and he was free and clear. It was an ugly business going through it all, trying to establish his relative innocence. Of course, technically he was culpable for his role as an accessory to and active participant in a variety of Harold Danko's and Ed Valley's felonious activities, irrespective of how he had been unwittingly and unwillingly sucked in by them. But the indispensable part he played in bringing them down was heavily weighted, and the several "states witness deals" he had made along the way kicked in decisively, ultimately exempting him after weeks of pre-litigation from further legal action. He walked out of his final hearing, not exactly holding his head high, but unburdened by the risk of prosecution.

He had a fresh start.

Lenny and Alicia were now 38,000 feet above the Pacific in a Boeing 747 on their way to Jakarta, Indonesia. The entire flight would take over 27 hours.

Alicia was sleeping and Lenny was reading an news article from the New York Times.

She stirred and opened her eyes. They were moist and glistened with the chiffon of dreams. As she leaned over to cuddle against Lenny's arm, she gave him a wan but warm smile.

"It says here that health care expenditures in America for retired baby boomers are growing so astronomically that the country will be bankrupt by the year 2025."

"Lenny, you make me so hot. Goo' nite, sweetie."

Epilogue

AND THE MEEK SHALL INHERIT THE WORLD:
Hope Upon Hope To Do Better Next Time

In a sick world, no one gets to be completely healthy. Some do better than others.

Lenny and Alicia stayed in Jakarta. Despite his checkered past and because of his inside and intimate familiarity with the methods used in trafficking, he was hired as an expert consultant by KAKAK Foundation, an NGO fighting child slavery in partnership with UNICEF and Save The Children. Using every contact he made through this work, Lenny and Alicia continued their search for the little boy she wanted to adopt. After two years, their diligence and persistence paid off. They located him and as Alicia's foster child, he watched them exchange wedding vows on a beach in Semarang on the north Java coast. After six more months of bureaucratic haggling, an adoption was approved and Alicia finally had her not-so-little boy. He would soon turn 13.

Christine filed for divorce three months after the break up of the Djin Djin enterprise. Tom did not contest it. They now share custody of their daughter Megan. Christine moved to Queens and started working as a program coordinator at a local office of Catholic Social Services. A few months later, she and a co-worker, a 29-year old black girl named Maxine, moved into a condo together in Kew Gardens. When questioned about their relationship, Christine always replied that "it's nobody else's business". But it is commonly accepted knowledge that they are an item. Maybe once or twice a day, expletives can be heard issuing from Christine's compact and extremely messy office. Someone claims to have actually even heard the F word once.

Harold Danko and Ed Valley are somewhere in Vietnam, living in a villa on the water of the South China Sea, as guests of Chairman #1 of the Hinge Company, a man named Frank Horton, who shared with both Ed and Harold self-delusions that they were men of sophisticated tastes, as well as their passion for raw hedonistic adventure. The three avail themselves frequently and with total abandon the hottest brothels and street girls in the city, even sometimes boarding a plane for Thailand, to provide some incidental variety to their anonymous orgies with adolescent prostitutes. Harold and Ed had skipped out on their $2,000,000 bail and are on the U. S. Government's Top 20 list for most wanted. Their America-based assets and what bankrolled money could be located in a number of offshore accounts were of course impounded. Rough initial estimates suggested that they had amassed over $46 million in the six months of their meteoric success and excess.

St. John the Baptist of Hell's Kitchen, in a brief but conclusive meeting of the New York Presbyterian Hospital Psychiatric Legal Advisory Committee, was declared unfit for trial. He is still living in a secured cell in the Mid-Hudson

Forensic Psychiatric Center in New Hampton. His restraints only come off for the afternoon meal on Sunday and monthly medical examinations. He considers himself a prisoner of war and is waiting to be liberated by the Special Forces Assault Squad attached to 9th Infantry Division, his old unit back in Vietnam.

The Catholic Church, by declaration of Pope Benedict himself, began the long process of conferring sainthood on Bishop Mulcahey. Initially, there was a public furor in the Minneapolis-St. Paul Catholic community, whose memories were long enough to recall that he had been accused of molesting little boys in his parish there, but too nebulous or selective to remember that after a thorough investigation as required by the local archdiocese, he had been exonerated. After the outcry had been tamped down with the abundant and proactive efforts of Father Justin Peter McCormick, an energetic Jesuit who had committed his career to the reification of the truth as much as to his holy vows, many came forward from that same community to attest to the miraculous things Father Mulcahey had done while he was on Earth. Many predicted and invited even more supernatural displays now that the Bishop sat in the company of God Himself in Heaven. The request lines for his divine intervention in the affairs of common men were ringing continuously. A local radio DJ even took it upon himself to devote an hour of program time three times a week to hearing pleas and prayers from the locals calling in. Requested miracles ranged from the predictable — new cars and boats, chic wardrobes, losing weight, dates with movie stars — to the antic and bizarre — putting a hex on a neighbor suspected of cheating with someone's spouse, an exorcism for a demented grandparent, penis-reduction surgery, a nuclear strike on Mexico, even a sex change operation. All seemed certain that Mulcahey was listening, would instantly see the merit of the requested miracle, and insisted he was their own personal saint-elect in that glorious House of Representatives in the sky.

Dok had told Lenny that Aulii, the enigmatic mama-san that had assembled over thirty absolutely beautiful creatures for Lenny to view in Laos, was up for a big promotion. Well, she got a promotion alright. The girls promised to Lenny, of course, never showed up in America. Rather they went with Aulii to her new sex show night club in Phuket, what became a hugely successful hotspot for tourists from around the world. It was called Bûi Bpàak, which is Thai for 'puckered or protruding lips'. The club was underwritten by Dok and some his underworld friends, and thrived under Aulii's artistic direction. She was the master of ceremonies, introducing the acts, sometimes doing her own lascivious hump and grind on the young men to warm them up for their choreographed fornication. Tired of the usual tricks displayed at these types of establishments — vaginas shooting ping pong balls across the room, picking up coins and cufflinks, smoking cigarettes — she became internationally recognized as the inventor of a whole new generation of sex-oriented stunts. Her hilarious dueling-penises and dove-flying-out-of-an-asshole segments were huge crowd-pleasers. She is reputed to have been working in rehearsal on a spectacular trick where a girl would shoot a long jet of flame from her vagina, lighting a cigarette held in the butt hole of her sex partner (male or female depending who she had just had sex with), when she was cut down by a massive cerebral hemorrhage and died instantly.

Dok himself was the kind of person who always landed on his feet. Unfortunately, that was not especially helpful when he was dropped from the observation deck of a 30-story building in Bangkok. After selling his three "schools" in northern Thailand, he invested the money in franchising Aulii's Bûi Bpàak clubs, with their wild and unique sex shows. He Americanized the name, just calling them Lips, and within a few months opened new ones in Pattaya and Kho Chang, and a second one in Phuket. He was way too successful. The business in other clubs in each town took a dramatic nosedive. The hardest hit were all owned by the same group of investors, a shady bunch with their fingers in smuggling, as well as distributing and selling throughout the region, methamphetamines from Burma.

When they got wind of Dok's plan to open an even more extravagant Lips club right across the street from their place in Bangkok, they decided to drop in on him. Underwhelmed by Dok's arrogance, they decided to drop him from the top of a building. So they did. Based on extremely shoddy police work and an incoherent note attached to the lapel of his tailored silk suit, the Bangkok press tagged it an inexplicable suicide by one of Thailand's leading citizens.

For the Djin Djin girls, busting the entire sex slave operation was a mixed blessing. When the forced emigration was finally halted, there were over 320 in the U. S. distributed among 4 major metropolitan areas. Some were working the streets but most were comfortably set-up in nice apartment buildings, which housed mostly sex industry service workers. While they had relatively little personal freedom, within the confines of these upscale brothels, they lived well.

With the massive sweep by the INS, indeed they were rescued from their sex industry enslavement. But now they were out of a job and the good life in America was at an end. The great majority of them were deported and repatriated, hence forced to confront the great unknown of what might await them in their home countries. There certainly was no guarantee that they would not get caught up in another cycle of forced labor under conditions considerably worse than they had in the U.S.

Repatriation itself was a nightmare. Though the girls could at least identify their country of origin, many named villages which did not appear on the most detailed current maps. Even their own governments were at a loss for determining what remote settlement they were from. So they were sent back and dumped in the laps of their countries of origin but without any specific place to return to, bereft of the comfort and what meager support their original families might be able to provide.

A few of the Djin Djin girls managed to elude the swarms of INS officers that rolled through the red light buildings, and are still at large. Of course, trying to work and live as an undocumented alien is a minefield in itself. They effectively could provide no history. 'Djin Djin Girl' or 'sex provider' was not the kind of thing to put on a job application under *Previous Employment.*

Five of the Djin Djin girls were beneficiaries of a bizarre bit of media grandstanding by a prominent member of Congress. The tragic loss of life from the accident at sea and the busting of the Asian sex slave ring, at least for a while put the plight of the Djin Djin girls front and center on all of the news media platforms. This particular congressman decided to take under his protective wing five of the Djin Djins that were apprehended in his San Francisco Bay Area district. In the wave of public sympathy for the sweet young victims, he sponsored and managed to get Congressional approval for a special bill which granted amnesty to the girls and conferred them Green Card status. His act of concern and magnanimity made him a darling of the major media channels, resulting in appearances on both the Jay Leno and David Letterman shows.

What was not public knowledge and incomprehensibly never came to the fore, was that what motivated his actions on their behalf, which certainly went far above and beyond the call of duty as a public servant, were certain of his activities as a private citizen. He had been divorced for several years and four of the Djin Djin girls had given him much comfort on repeated occasions. The congressional act paid them a generous tip for their amorous attention and bought their silence on his promiscuity and partiality to Asian prostitutes.

One of the girls who benefited from the amnesty bill was Kimnai. She had been sent to Miami shortly after John Harrison had burned down the warehouse where the New York Djin Djin girls were staying, then out to San Francisco to work in one of the beautiful San Mateo condominiums. She had been there for almost two months when the INS came in. With her new Green Card and the publicity surrounding her "rescue", she was overwhelmed with offers of foster homes. Once the family was approved by social services, she moved into her new home in Fremont, California. She is attending high school there and is an honor student. She emails Lenny regularly, though he is not very dependable about replying. He does call her at least once a month. She also keeps in regular contact with the other four Djin Djin she worked with in San Mateo.

Realistically, the whole Djin Djin enterprise was on a short fuse anyway. If any honest and thorough law enforcement agency had done more than a cursory background check, none of the girls would pass. They were all completely undocumented, though they carried some superficially passable forged IDs. It was sheer dumb luck and some greased palms which had kept the INS unaware of the status of the girls. Thus, it was just a matter of time before some Dudley Do-Right blew the lid on the whole thing. Moreover, the health issues were another time bomb ticking. While being processed for deportation, medical exams were performed and more than 20% of the Djin Djin girls tested positive for HIV. Afraid to attract any attention, none of them had taken advantage of the free STD clinics available to sex workers in the cities where they lived and worked. Tragically, sending them back to their third-world native countries was tantamount to signing a death certificate, health services being what they were back home. Unfortunately, drippy-eye concern quickly turns to cold paranoia as soon as HIV enters the picture. As saddened and horrified as Americans had been over the plight of the young girls, if they were carrying 'the disease', then the prevailing sentiment instantly became, the quicker we get them out of here, the better.

The Others ...

Ying Mae and Dawa: Ying Mae actually had a valid passport, but unfortunately had no visa. She was deported and returned to Taiwan. She managed to find the ex-serviceman she had been with years before. They got together briefly but the magic of their previous hot romance was gone. They parted friends, promising to always keep in touch, which they don't. She is still single and works at a semi-conductor assembly factory outside of Changhua.

Dawa also faced deportation, a fate she could not suffer. As she saw things, America was her home now, and she would do whatever she needed to do to stay. At her physical examination, the final stage before being shipped back, she asked to use the restroom. The immigration officer guarding the girls was frontloading amorous attention on an attractive nurse. Dawa took advantage of his amatory distraction and slipped out of the government facility unnoticed. She disappeared and her whereabouts are still unknown.

Captain Fiori: The mayor's office issued a statement denouncing any activity which might be construed as abuse of the power of law enforcement. *"Any law enforcement officer using his official position within the community to benefit himself personally or enrich his family and friends, will be identified, taken before the disciplinary board, and punished to the severest extent possible under existing regulations."* So it read.

After a year of interviews, investigations, public allegations, radio talk show brawls, and witch hunt rhetoric from public officials of every rank and ilk, two patrol officers were each given a month leave without pay. Captain Fiori was promoted to Deputy Chief of the Organized Crime Control Bureau headquartered in Manhattan. The file on alleged recent incidents of police corruption at the Brooklyn precinct was closed.

Shawna and Lilly: Both Shawna and Lilly were "retired" from the streets by the developments surrounding the break up of the Chicago-run trade. Streetwalking wasn't what it had been before the age of internet-based sex, so it was just a matter of time before they had to move on. Move on they did.

Lilly, with her acute sense of organization, contacted the funding agencies for the STD Prevention Center, who clearly were unhappy with the prior performance of that office. The plain Janes had been fired and the office temporarily closed, until Lilly presented her ideas. They liked what they heard, turned the money spigots back on, and she re-opened the office under the name Good Neighbor Community Services, providing not only STD counseling and HIV/AIDS testing, but drug user intervention and rehabilitation programs, abused women's counseling, and a safe-house battered women's shelter. She also regularly conducted a host of roundtables, workshops, and support groups addressing various needs in the community.

Shawna, looking frantically for some way to repair her desperate financial situation, had taken up buying New York lottery tickets. On her fourth try, she landed 5 of the 6 numbers plus the bonus number, and won $187,803. She gave her good buddy Lilly $5,000 and made a nice contribution to Good Neighbor itself, then set herself up in a tiny storefront as a Shaklee distributor, right there where she used to walk the streets and peddle her big butt. She called it

Shawna's Shaklee Shack. She only opened her doors 30 or so hours a week, depending on how badly she wanted to get out of bed in the morning. But when it was open, the place was always packed, the conversations loud, and there would be Shawna, offering her outrageous advice and opinions on everything under the sun. People always left with their bags brimming full of eco-friendly cleaning products and their bellies hurting from laughing so hard.

Markham and Keary remained friends but went very different ways. Markham had been secretly working in his spare time on building a computer game. He had put hundreds of hours into a simulation type of program called *Sim Sex*, similar in principle to the revolutionary city-building computer game developed by the California software company MAXIS. But instead of building an urban community, with *Sim Sex* you built a person. As the outside of the box said when it appeared in specialty stores and on the internet, "Create The Perfect Lover". It was especially popular among 12 to 15 year old boys, though they had to resort to extraordinary measures to get it, since it had a big Parental Advisory sticker, and 50 to 70 year old men. Markham made a fortune and bought a luxurious condo on the Upper East Side before the year was out.

Keary gradually reduced his attendance at support groups as he found himself increasingly smitten with one particular girl. This was Penny, the young lady who he had hired to work as a data entry clerk. The one with Tourette's. After a brief but intense courtship, you could say it was all over but for the shouting. They were married and moved into an apartment the size of an appliance box in the West Village off Bleecker Street. Penny started participating in a number of volunteer drug trial programs conducted all over the city, but mostly at NYU, to determine the effectiveness of a new generation of pharmaceuticals addressing Tourette's and related neurological diseases. Keary supported them as a go-go dancer in a Soho gay bar five nights a week. The other two he gradually perfected his stand-up comedian act on open mic nights at area comedy clubs. Penny attended every performance, cheering him on, shouting vulgarities, and laughing uproariously at jokes she had heard a hundred times.

Billy Gresham and Peter Mangione: The ACLU took a special interest in the case of the two Guardian Angels who had been busted for allegedly running a drug ring from their Brooklyn headquarters. The Guardian Angels had been traditionally beyond reproach, and as an "alternative" vehicle for providing community policing services, which stood apart from the sometimes corrupt establishment policing institutions, they aligned themselves philosophically with the charter of the ACLU itself. Bail was raised and a crack team of attorneys assembled to handle the case. Ultimately, the court declared a mistrial on the basis of overwhelming evidence of gross improprieties by the team which raided their office, and legal technicalities surrounding their arrest and incarceration. Charges were dropped. Billy is attending law school at Columbia University, and Peter works as a community outreach counselor for the City of New York.

Coltern, Sutter and Rabinski: Coltern retired and is raising huacaya alpacas at his ranch outside of Great Falls, Montana. He goes salmon fishing as often as he can in the local rivers and streams. Sutter and Rabinski are still working at their respective FBI regional headquarters. Both were given citations for their outstanding work on the Djin Djin case. Sutter framed his and put it on his office wall. Rabinski left his on his desk and spilled coffee on it a week after receiving it.

Yoshikaze: While in custody, as part of his own plea-bargaining, Lenny brought it to the attention of authorities that Yoshikaze not only admitted to but took great pride in having murdered Franklin and Martin. Forensic testing of the weapon found on Yoshikaze at the time of his arrest also confirmed that this was the weapon used to kill the Bishop. Yoshikaze was his own worst enemy at his trial, openly defiant and manifestly without remorse, so leniency of any sort was out of the question. He began serving several consecutive sentences at Joliet State Prison, in Illinois. After the first three years of his twenty-seven year incarceration there, most of it in solitary confinement, Yoshikaze was assigned to work in the commissary. As a permanent contributor to the dietary regimen of the men at this progressive institution, he offered his own unique touch to the menu. Joliet is now the only prison in America known to serve once a week at supper on Sunday — though it is by any measure very rudimentary — a meal of sushi rolls and miso soup.

Tony: Tony's was considered a neighborhood landmark and loyalties among its regulars ran long and deep. Money, of course, has a way of eradicating tradition and reshaping the rituals of common men. Tony was made an offer which he could not refuse, by development investors who bought up all of the property on the block where his tavern was situated. Their plan was to create there a sprawling condominium complex called Whispering Paradise. He took the cash and opened an ultra-chic imbibery on the Upper East Side of Manhattan called *Anthony's MO!*, a popular place-to-be-seen which serves DayGlo designer Martinis and has a ultraviolet-lit Oxygen Bar with a Clockwork Orange theme.

The Master: After Dok jumped ship, the essential organizational structure which made the Siddartha schools so profitable, effectively disintegrated. The Master thought it a disgrace and un-Buddha-like to waste the wisdom embodied in his finely-wrought philosophy of masochistic self-denial and the gutting of the ego. So he set up a special spiritual retreat in Chang Mai, catering mainly to truth seekers from extremely upscale urban areas in the U.S. and Europe — those with enormous amounts of disposable income being the only ones who would be able to afford the obscenely high cost of spending two weeks cleaning the ancient stone floors of the monastery, then sitting prone at the Master's feet for exhausting lectures on the value of worthlessness. The enterprise has proved so successful, he recently franchised it. New spiritual retreats called The Master's Conquest Camp for Spiritual Surrender and Ego Annihilation, are planned or have already opened in Ibiza, Spain; Ojai, California; Sedona, Arizona; and Traverse City, Michigan.

More Books by John Rachel

If you were dazzled by what you just read, please check out these other fine novels by this author and political blogger.

"The Man Who Loved Too Much"
Trilogy

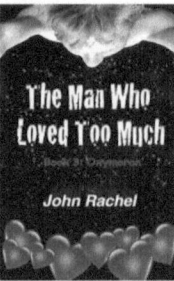

Billy Green is bright, enigmatic, and lost. He spent his first 28 years trying to figure out who he is and where he fits in. His life has been a wild, unpredictable quest to attach himself to some reality he can grasp and live with. He grew up in an abysmal suburb of Detroit, escaped to university life at Cornell, got married and divorced before being thrown headlong and entirely unprepared into the insanity and social chaos of New York City.

Book 1: Archipelago
Amazon (Kindle): amzn.to/1tyIRiw
Amazon (Print): amzn.to/1z8F8aD
Barnes & Noble: bit.ly/ZDnQVO
Apple iBook: bit.ly/1ycltFD
Smashwords: bit.ly/1w62HOX

Book 2: Entendre
Amazon (Kindle): amzn.to/18x1ZnS
Amazon (Print): amzn.to/1xfmjp3
Barnes & Noble: bit.ly/18OGY85
Apple iBook: apple.co/1bkFQe7
Smashwords: bit.ly/1AMUCPz

Book 3: Oxymoron
Amazon (Kindle): amzn.to/1LJnMc
Amazon (Print): amzn.to/1NZPU9Y
Barnes & Noble: bit.ly/1fvzxXD
Apple iBook: apple.co/1DfoG9g
Smashwords: bit.ly/1LJnRgJ

"An Unlikely Truth"

In this political drama, a bright, young, idealistic, Green Party candidate in his bid for the congressional seat of a conservative district in Ohio, teams with a beautiful, fiery African-American intern to combat the slick deceptions and ruthless tactics of a sweet-talking right wing incumbent.

Amazon (Kindle): amzn.to/1jetpiY
Amazon (Print): amzn.to/1lddvsp
Barnes & Noble: bit.ly/1l5FmuG
Apple iBook: bit.ly/1gT2O7w
Smashwords: bit.ly/1fIU3Mq

"Blinders Keepers"

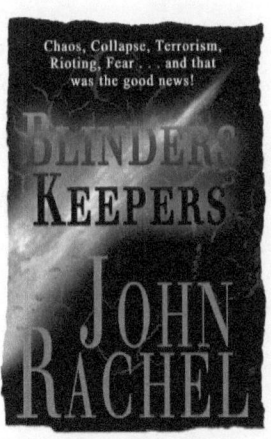

In this dark comedy, a young man who escapes his hopelessly hayseed home town in Missouri is mistakenly labeled a terrorist and must survive a manhunt by government security agencies, while the President of an America in chaos and collapse perpetrates an end-of-the-world hoax, attempting to reclaim control and get himself re-elected.

Amazon (Kindle): amzn.to/122cnyF
Barnes & Noble: bit.ly/17MtgjE
Apple iBook: bit.ly/11WqJiv
Smashwords: bit.ly/190zmgs
Kobo: bit.ly/18wHki2

"11 - 11 - 11"

Noah was turning 23 and desperate to get out of town. Pulnick, Missouri had always been bland and soporific, but now it was now being invaded by white supremacist meth heads, plagued by an unprecedented crime wave, exploited by spiritualists and local politicos, and driven to hysteria by paranoid rumors that the world would end November 11th.

Amazon (Kindle): amzn.to/1sEWaf0
Barnes & Noble: bit.ly/1nlgS2Z
Apple iBook: bit.ly/1z8TCKS
Smashwords: bit.ly/1paiJ6j
Kobo: bit.ly/T7181J

"12 - 12 - 12"

Welcome to the parallel universe of 12-12-12. This not what actually happens during 2012. But what unfolds is not more implausible. Nor is it less implausible. It is dark satire, a portrayal of reality with healthy doses of surreality and comedy, spawned by the tragic absurdity of our times. One reviewer calls it "laugh-out-loud brain food for hungry minds."

Amazon (Kindle): amzn.to/1DaFrDL
Barnes & Noble: bit.ly/1w5Yw5D
Apple iBook: bit.ly/1sJasMO
Smashwords: bit.ly/1o9GaSg
Kobo: lnk.ms/c1CWm

"Candidate Contracts: Taking Back Our Democracy"

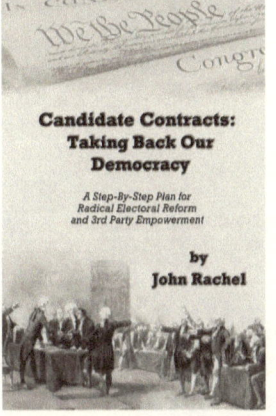

Prepare to understand contemporary politics as never before! Prepare to see the future of American democracy! This manifesto offers a detailed, step-by-step plan for cleaning up the corruption in Washington DC. This is electoral reform so radical that in one master stroke, it puts America on the path to a healthy economy and directly addresses its #1 and #2 challenges: the suicidal march to war and the destructive impact of a historically high level of wealth inequality.

Amazon (Kindle): amzn.to/1QJRiNZ
Amazon (Print): amzn.to/1Cuq0du
Barnes & Noble: bit.ly/1GpTTLq
Apple iBook: apple.co/1BXnPcy
Smashwords: bit.ly/1B4DQCp
Kobo: bit.ly/1QETE64

"Fighting for the Democracy We Deserve"

This is a manual for constructive voting in the 2016 election. It presents a concrete plan for wresting control of the country and our democracy back from the rich and powerful, and restoring the constitutional mandate of government of the people, by the people, and for the people. It's not just more whining. It's a real plan!

Amazon (Kindle): amzn.to/1VMf2Ft
Amazon (Print): amzn.to/1L9SdIC
Direct from printer: bit.ly/1i7ISFM
Amazon CA: amzn.to/1in513n
Amazon GB: amzn.to/1KfjtQO
Amazon JP: amzn.to/1OMslBG

<u>Coming Soon</u>

[2016 and beyond]

"Sex, Lies and Coffee Beans"

"Love Connection"

"The Last Giraffe"

"Happy Happy Dreaming Girl"

"The Naked American"

"St. Jerome's Home For The Sexually Insane"

• •

Author John Rachel

About The Author

John Rachel has a B.A. in Philosophy, has traveled extensively, been a songwriter and music producer, and is a bipolar humanist. He has spent his life trying to resolve the intrinsic clash between the metaphysical purity of Buddhism and the overwhelming appeal of narcissism.

Since 2008, when he first embarked on his career as a novelist, he has had eight fiction and two non-fiction books published. These range from three satires and a coming-of-age trilogy, to a political drama and now a crime thriller. The two non-fiction works were also political, his attempt to address the crisis of democracy and pandemic corruption in the governing institutions of America.

Never knowing when enough is enough, the hyperthyroid Rachel continues to be very busy. He has three more novels in the pipeline for publication late 2015 through 2016: *Sex, Lies and Coffee Beans*, a spoof on the self-help crazes of the 80s and 90s; *Love Connection*, a drug-trafficking thriller set in Japan; and finally *The Last Giraffe*, an anthropological drama involving both the worship and devouring of giraffes, which unfolds in 19th Century sub-Saharan Africa. Several major publishers have declared that they will do everything in their power to make sure these books never see the light of day.

Moreover, he recently increased his output of incendiary political blogs, sure to alienate the remaining few remnants of his meager literary following.

John Rachel's last permanent residence in America was Portland, Oregon where he had a state-of-the-art ProTools recording studio, music production house, a radio promotion and music publishing company. He still writes music and, much to the annoyance of his neighbors in the traditional rural Japanese town where he now lives, attempts to sing his original songs.

• • •

You can follow John Rachel's adventures
and developing world view at:
jdrachel.com

• • •

Since the open mind recognizes no borders, you are also
invited to join us in the ongoing dialogue about
literature and the writing arts at:
literaryvagabond.com

Legal Notices and Disclaimers